HOLIDAY COZY MYSTERY SERIES COLLECTION
BOOKS 1-3

TONYA KAPPES

D1715604

TONYA KAPPES
WEEKLY NEWSLETTER

Want a behind-the-scenes journey of me as a writer?
The ups and downs, new deals, book sales, giveaways and more? I share
it all!

As a special thank you for joining, you'll get an exclusive copy of my cross-over short story, *A CHARMING BLEND.* Go to Tonyakappes.com and click on subscribe in the upper right corner to join.

FOUR LEAF FELONY

A HOLIDAY COZY MYSTERY BOOK 1

"What's wrong?" the flight attendant asked me. She put one hand on me when she noticed my knees were giving out, and with her free hand, she pulled the flight attendant seat down, easing me into it.

"I…" I gasped for air. "I…"

"You're having a panic attack. It's okay," she assured me, reaching behind her to get one of those throw-up bags. She put it in my hands. "Just breathe slowly in and out into the bag."

"No." I shook my head, trying to get away from the bag she'd shoved into my face. "Body. Body," I gasped and pointed to the bathroom. "There's—" I rolled my eyes up and tried to take a deep breath. "There's a body."

I pointed and gave up, resting my head back against the airplane's wall.

"Someone was in there?" She made an *eeck* face and smiled. "They probably forgot to lock the door. It happens all the time."

I reached up, grabbed the front of her uniform jacket, and dragged her down face-to-face with me.

"Dead body. Blood." It was all I could get out.

CHAPTER ONE

"And my daughter." Pride spilled out of the woman. Her smile, her eyes, her entire face lit up as she showed me the photos on her phone. One after the other she scrolled.

"She has three little children. Let me tell you"—she put her hand on her chest—"I never thought the girl was going to give me any grandbabies." She tapped the phone with her finger.

I slowly sucked in a deep breath, reminding myself that this was just a temporary situation. After the airplane landed, I'd never have to see this woman again.

"Look here." She shoved the phone in my face. "This is Joey."

I could practically smell the cookie he was holding in his picture. It was so close.

"He's a handful. He loves his mom. This is little Chance. He's a handful, but he loves his mom too." She scrolled past a few more until she landed on little Chance.

She'd done this photo dump on strangers a time or two. She did it flawlessly.

"This is my little Lizzy." The woman giggled. "She's just a doll baby. She's the cutest. Just the cutest," she repeated as if I'd not heard her say it the first time. "She's the cutest."

She stared at me.

"Oh." I realized she wanted a response. "Yes. She is."

She bragged on her three grandchildren, which I was far removed from. I mean, honestly, I had no idea what I was going to do for the rest of this four-hour airplane ride.

I knew I shouldn't have made eye contact when I first got on the plane. It was the eye contact that opened the flood gates of chatty granny.

The only hope I had was the connecting flight. What were the chances she'd be on that one and be seated next to me?

"Excuse me for a second. I had a little too much Diet Coke," I told her and unbuckled the safety belt.

"Airplane bathroom are awful. If you were my daughter, I'd told you to go to the bathroom before we got on the airplane." She wagged a finger at me. "You hold on. It's no fun squatting on that little toilet when there's turbulence." Her eyes grew with fear as though she had first hand experience.

"Thanks." I stood up and took a big deep breath before I took my first steps of freedom away from my seatmate.

This entire plane ride was nothing like I had in my head when I woke up. Really was anything ever turn out the way we imagined them?

There were things I needed to do to prepare myself for the biggest interview of my life. I would've loved to hear about little Lizzy and her brothers on any given day, just not today.

Today was the day I'd been waiting on for—well, I couldn't even remember how long. That was long if I couldn't remember.

"Get yourself together, Violet," I told myself under the fake smile as I stepped over a child playing in the aisle when the child should've been in a family member's lap. I tossed my long blond hair, which was perfectly styled today, over my shoulder.

Carefully I stepped over her.

"I'm sorry," a woman mouthed. She must've been the little girl's mom, they had the same eyes.

"No problem." I waved it off and continued down the center of the airplane toward the bathroom.

All eyes were on me. I'd been a reporter in my hometown of Normal,

Kentucky for Channel Two news, where I also had my own show called "Good Day in the Park." I wrote a monthly column for my hometown newspaper, so I was used to the perfect smile.

I'd spent my career giving up any social life so I could get my one big break. This was it. Nothing was going to ruin it.

Just a few short days, you're gonna see me on TV, being a big-time reporter, I thought to myself when I noticed people glancing up at me.

Like my Aunt Lucinda told me, *Violet, honey, you've got to fake it until you make it.* That was exactly what I had done in Normal, and here I was—on my way to making it big!

The flight attendant was busy getting the little food cart ready to push down the aisle and stepped out of the way of the bathroom door when she noticed me going for the handle.

"Are you having a good flight?" she cordially asked. Her brown hair was parted to the side, pulled back into a low ponytail. The maroon uniform showed off a very appealing figure that showed she took care of herself. Something I could definitely understand.

It was one of the many things I needed to do to stay camera-ready at any moment.

"Yes. I am." I curled my fingers into the small opening of the handle and pulled the accordion bathroom door open. "Oh my gawd!"

My body shook. My breath heaved in and out at a rapid pace.

I slammed the bathroom door shut.

"What's wrong?" the flight attendant asked me. She put one hand on me when she noticed my knees were giving out, and with her free hand, she pulled the flight attendant seat down, easing me into it.

"I…" I gasped for air. "I…"

"You're having a panic attack. It's okay," she assured me, reaching behind her to get one of those throw-up bags. She put it in my hands. "Just breathe slowly in and out into the bag."

"No." I shook my head, trying to get away from the bag she'd shoved into my face. "Body. Body," I gasped and pointed to the bathroom. "There's—" I rolled my eyes up and tried to take a deep breath. "There's a body."

I pointed and gave up, resting my head back against the airplane's wall.

"Someone was in there?" She made an *eeck* face and smiled. "They probably forgot to lock the door. It happens all the time."

I reached up, grabbed the front of her uniform jacket, and dragged her down face-to-face with me.

"Dead body. Blood." It was all I could get out.

CHAPTER TWO

One Week Earlier
"One more week in this cold town is going to kill me," I told Gert Hobson, the owner of the only coffee shop in my small hometown of Normal, Kentucky.

Really, there weren't many shops and zero big-box stores. Some would say it was what made my hometown a tourist destination: the small shops and the locals, not to mention the Daniel Boone National Forest that curled up around the town like a hug from Mother Nature.

"The weather getting to you?" Gert asked. She flipped the switch on the coffee machine she used to make my special espresso combined with cocoa and ground chocolate and topped with steamed milk that delivered the best sweetness to my palate.

"No, though it has been unseasonably cold this winter." I leaned on the coffee shop's counter and drew my shoulders up to my ears when I twisted around and looked behind me at the line of customers in the cute coffee shop. "But I'm so tired of reporting on things like new trails discovered, all the reenactments, or how to be safe during the upcoming hunting season. I want to report on real things."

"What about 'Good Day in the Park'? Everyone loves it." Gert was trying to be nice. She always had that personality.

"You and the three others who watch it." I never told anyone in Normal how it was my segment and the station manager of Channel Two didn't give me my own cameraman. He'd told me it was my show and they didn't budget for any extra staff.

So to make me look better in front of everyone around here and get my own show, I paid for the cameraman out of my own pocket, making it look as though he was from the news station. He wasn't. I found him in the Help Wanted section for a videographer in the *Normal Gazette*, another place I did reporting just to make ends meet.

"I think you're selling yourself short." Gert frowned and handed me the coffee over the top of the glass display counter, where she kept the most delicious desserts. Some she made, and some were from the Cookie Crumble, the local bakery. "What do you want to eat? On the house."

"Nothing." I patted my stomach. "I've got to watch the calories for when I make it big."

I didn't dare think about the calorie content in the fancy coffee.

"Then your coffee is on the house." She looked past me to help the next customer in line.

I whipped around and knocked smack-dab into someone, spilling the hot drink down the camel-colored trench coat.

"Oh my gosh, I'm so sorry. I'm so sorry," I pleaded with the man and reached back around to get the towel Gert had extended over the counter. "You know what," I rambled and wiped the front of his coat down, seeing the stains of all of the delish contents not coming off. "I have a friend who owns a laundromat across the street. I can take your coat to her, and she'll have it all cleaned up in no time."

"Don't worry about it. It's fine." He smiled, and the creases around his eyes deepened. His brown hair was cut and blended better than Helen Pyle could do down at the Cute-icles Salon, Normal's only option to get a haircut. "I have another coat."

"I insist." I started to tug at the collar. "I'm not taking no for an answer. My mama taught me good manners, and it's just good manners for me to get your coat cleaned. What do you like to do? Hike? Kayak? Camp? Rock climb?"

"No. No. No." He shrugged off his coat. He was a well-to-do man with a blue button-down and the shiniest cufflinks I'd ever seen. "I'm passing through on my way to Tennessee to catch a flight back west."

"Flight?" I wondered, the journalist side of me. I was pleased as a peach with his coat in my possession.

"Yep. I was in Lexington doing some business, and my flight back to California got cancelled. They don't have any idea when the plane will leave. It could be a day or next week." He smiled. This time I noticed his dimples. "I'm a doer, which means I made other arrangements for a flight out of an airport in Tennessee. I was driving through your town and decided to grab me a coffee."

"Not wear one?" I joked.

"I don't think it looks good on me. Apparently you don't either, since you're so insistent on getting my coat cleaned. Which isn't necessary, seeing I've got to get going. I don't want to miss that flight." He tried to take his coat, but I held on to it. "Really. You don't need to clean it."

"You might'swell let her do it. Once Violet gets something in that noggin' of hers, she doesn't let go." Just hearing the voice of Dottie Swaggert before I saw her face made my stomach curl. "After all, she's failed at the other idea of getting out of this town. Can't you throw the gal a bone?"

"Dottie, go smoke a cigarette." I swiveled around and shot her a look before I turned back to him. He had a look on his face that said he was very entertained.

"A feisty go-get-it kinda gal." His lips drew up in a grin, and his head tilted with one big nod. "I like that in a woman. In fact, I came to Lexington to interview a woman who I thought had your gumption but disappointed since I didn't see that side of her. On television she comes off confident. In person, not so much."

"Television? Did you say television?" No wonder he was so fancy. He had to be a movie star. There were no shortage of them that came to Normal to get away. In fact, a lot of movie stars loved to escape to the mountains in Appalachia, where they tended to be left alone.

"I'm not big-time." He held his hands out.

"I'm a reporter, so it got my interest. In fact"—I reached around and brought Dottie back into the conversation—"Dottie can tell you how I'm a big reporter for Channel Two as well as host my own show here in Normal called 'Good Day in the Park.' Right, Dottie?" I nudged her maybe a little too hard in the ribs.

"Mmmhmmmm," she ho-hummed. I had to do a double take when I noticed she'd already slipped a cigarette in the corner of her lips. It bobbled up and down as she spoke. "Yep. She's been trying to make me watch all them health segments she likes to do, but I think I'm just fine."

The man's eyes shifted to me like he was waiting to see if I was going to banter with her.

"As you can see, we have colorful citizens here in Normal, but I'm not planning on being here too much longer. I've got so many interviews with bigger markets, so I'm sure my time in Normal is limited." I lied but hoped he'd see something in me. "I'm Violet Rhinehammer, by the way."

I stuck my hand out from underneath his coat, which was folded over my forearm.

"Richard Stone." He stuck out his hand. "Violet. I like that name. Rhinehammer might not be a good stage name, but if you're willing to give up the name, I'm willing to interview you on one condition."

"What's that?" I gulped, trying not to show too much excitement.

"You have to fly to California to interview in one week." He looked down at the coat. "You can bring the coat with you then."

"She'd love to." Dottie reached around me and grabbed the card he'd taken out of his pants pocket. "We've been trying to get rid of her for years."

CHAPTER THREE

The more I recalled the morning where I thought my life had changed, the excitement, the phone calls I made to everyone and their brother, letting them know I'd made it to the big time, all started to pound down on my head like a gong.

A big one.

Or maybe the sudden migraine had to do with the dead body sitting just about three feet from me behind the little airplane accordion door.

"How are you doing, darling?" the flight attendant asked me like we'd just gotten back from taking a walk in the park or something so casual.

"How do you think I'm doing?" The bag I had still pressed up to my mouth muted the sarcastic tone of my question back to her.

The phone on the wall beeped, and she picked it up and gave all sorts of *mmhhhms* and *yes, okay, fine* to whoever was on the other end of the line before she hung up.

I kept my eyes closed, head down, and slowly tried to breathe into the bag. The heavy footsteps coming toward the back of the airplane made me look up.

"Hi there." The man had bent down between my legs. He couldn't've been any older than me. "I'm Jim Dixon, the pilot, and I understand there's been an issue."

"An issue?" I looked up at the flight attendant. "A dead body is not an issue. It's a murder, and someone on this airplane did it."

"Violet, right?" He looked up at the flight attendant. She nodded to confirm. "I do understand we have a deceased passenger confirmed, but we have no way of knowing how our passenger died."

"Yes. Yes, we do. Stab to the neck." I hung my tongue out for good measure. "And there's a killer on this airplane. Oh gawd. What if I'm next?"

The sudden realization of mortality started to set in.

"Where's my phone? I have to call my mom. I have to tell her I'm okay." I started to get up, but the heavy hand of Jim Dixon on my shoulder pushed me back down.

"This is what we cannot have on here right now. We are thousands and thousands of feet up in the air." He talked to me like I was a kindergartener. "And if you or anyone else goes around yelling about what you had seen behind the door, then we will have an airplane full of panicking people. And we don't want that, do we?"

Slowly he shook his head, and I mimicked him.

"Can I ask you to sit here while I take a look for myself? Not that I don't believe you, but I've got to make the decision on whether or not we make an emergency landing. Do you think you can stay calm?" Jim's tone was somewhat soothing and a bit comforting.

I nodded to confirm I could stay calm. Just to make sure, I put my head back between my legs and kept the paper bag over my mouth in case I started to hyperventilate again.

He patted my leg and stood up. Remember the sound of long fingernails running down a chalkboard and how the sound made goose bumps curl up your body? The sound of the folded slats of the accordion door sliding together when Jim pushed it open gave me the exact same feeling and chills.

There was a huge pause and silence that made me look up.

"Everything is fine, everything is fine," the flight attendant assured me, batting her long eyelashes. There wasn't a smile on her face to go with her words.

My gaze shifted from her to Jim.

"Cherise, there is a dead body in the bathroom." He said it like he wasn't expecting it. "We are going to need to land the plane."

14

"I told you." I couldn't help but confirm to him that I was right. "There's a killer here," I said with a hushed whisper out of the side of my mouth.

"And that is why we don't need to alarm anyone. You leave this up to me. Understood, Violet?" His face was so stern, as if something bad was going to happen if I didn't listen to him.

"Yes. Fine." I went back to the bag and couldn't help but hear that door unfold back to close.

There were some murmured words between Cherise and Jim, but I didn't bother trying to listen to them. My mind was preoccupied with telling my stomach not to throw up since my heart had pumped all the blood to it because of the panic attack I was having. I knew if I stood up, my brain would be lacking oxygen because the heart was so selfish it took all the oxygen too.

Before too long, my organs and I were left in the back of the airplane with Cherise and the dead guy in the toilet.

Ding, ding. The chimes for the airplane's announcements were piped through the intercom system, followed up by the static noise of the cockpit before Jim's familiar voice came across.

"Ladies and gentlemen, this is Pilot Jim Dixon. I'm sorry to interrupt our flight. Unfortunately, we need to make a quick landing into the closest airfield in Holiday Junction." The rattle of chatter began to fill the inside of the airplane. "Cherise will be coming down the aisle to collect any garbage you may have. Please put up your tray tables and bring your chairs to an upright position. We will be landing shortly and be there for a small amount of time before we take off to our destination of sunny California."

"Trash? Trash? Trash?" Cherise's happy tone had a nervous click to it as she asked each passenger row by row. "I'm sorry. Do you think you can turn around and buckle up? We are descending." Her voice was becoming much harder with each passenger she had to tell to turn around.

People started twisting around, and chatter continued to fill the cabin of the airplane. All of a sudden, when I looked up, eyes were all on me.

"I think she's sick. That's why we are landing," I overheard someone say.

Cherise gave up and came back with an empty garbage sack.

"What about the family? What about his family? Somebody has to be on board." My mind was racing.

The phone buzzed again.

"Mmhmmm. Hold on." Cherise put the phone to her chest. "Do you think you could peek in there and see if you can find some sort of identification on him?"

"You want me"—I pointed to myself—"to go in there"—I moved my finger to point to the accordion door—"and rummage through his pockets to see if I can find any ID on the dead man?"

"Dead man?" I heard someone ask. "Did she say dead man?" The person in the row just in front of the bathroom turned just enough around the corner to look at me. "Did you say 'dead man'? Is there a dead man in there?"

"Everything is fine. Just fine." Cherise didn't sound so convincing. She used her finger to gesture for the passenger to turn around. "We will be landing soon. Please turn around."

"I overheard you telling the woman you were sitting with that you were some fancy reporter." Cherise had bent down and was whispering into my ear. "What more of a story do you need than this? So get in there and find out the information. Just think about it. You get the big scoop before the police even get it."

Boy oh boy. Cherise sure did know how to dangle a carrot in front of my nose.

CHAPTER FOUR

It was like a movie. The eerie music played in my head. Suddenly there was voiceover too.

Violet Rhinehammer hit the big time, and it was nothing like she expected. The small-town Kentucky girl had her hopes set on interviewing for a big television network. Little did she know, her quick-witted reporting while on an airplane when a passenger was murdered would not only show the world what a gift she was, but she'd get her own reporting talk show.

The idea of just how big this could be for my career washed over me as I gripped the handle of the accordion door to prepare myself to get in, get the wallet, and get out.

In one fluid motion, I ripped the door open. The man's eyes were open, staring at me, and the knife glistened.

"Nope. Can't do it." I shut the door and began to heave between words like a child with a bad case of the stomach flu. "No." My gag reflex had me sticking my tongue out. "Bag." I reached out for the paper sack. "Bag," I gagged out the word before I almost lost my cookies.

"Some reporter you are. What are you the reporter for, the first day of kindergarten?" Cherise tossed me the bag. "Girl. If you're going to make it big, you're going to have to get some tough skin. Those looks, fake lashes, and pearly-white smile aren't going to get you far."

"I'll show you," I muttered into the bag and kept my head down until the wheels of the airplane bounced on the pavement, signaling touchdown.

I kept my head forward when the overhead bells dinged to let us know the plane had come to a complete stop. The sound of people unclicking their seat belts echoed throughout the cabin, and people jumped up to get a good, long stretch. Little did they know why we were here. A few of them looked back at me as if it were my fault we landed in Holiday Junction.

I shoved my hair behind my head and straightened up my shoulders. *I am a reporter*, I reminded myself. *I am supposed to do hard things*. I continued to pump myself up. Besides, who was going to do it for me now that I was on my own adventure?

Granted, it was just an interview for the job, but I needed to start now even if no one was ever going to see my heroic act.

I collected myself, as my mama would tell me to, and stood back up, handing the bag to Cherise. Again, I reached out, gripped the handle, and ripped the door open. I kept my eyes on the man's pocket. There was a hint of a leather edge sticking out of it.

"Gloves. I need gloves." I put my hand out for Cherise. "Gloves, Cherise. We can't mess up any evidence."

A sly smile crossed her lips. Quickly, she turned on the plastic soles of her shoes, which I'd never be caught dead in, and whipped open a cabinet. She pulled a first aid kit out, opened it, and scoured through it until she found a pair of gloves.

There were some rumblings going on in the front of the airplane, and without paying any attention, I slipped my fingers through the holes of the gloves and sucked in a deep breath. With the vision of my gorgeous hometown with the backdrop of the Daniel Boone National Park in my mind to distract me from the actual scenery, I carefully reached between the man and the wall, where I grabbed the tip of the wallet.

"Got it!" I held it up like I'd won something where I got a trophy. "Got it."

"You did!" Cherise's excitement mirrored mine. Both of us squealed.

"Thank you, ladies." The larger-than-life deep voice came from behind us. "I'm

Chief Matthew Strickland with the Holiday Junction police department.

You can join the other passengers in the airport while we assess the situation. We will be taking statements inside."

He stepped aside, planted himself next to the aisle, and gestured for us to leave the airplane.

I gulped and did what he'd told us to do. A few more men in uniform made their way to the back of the airplane, stepping aside for me and Cherise to continue down the aisle.

"Did you get the information I asked for?" Jim Dixon stood in the doorway of the cockpit just like he would do at the end of any flight.

"Oh, yeah." I looked down, remembering I had the wallet of the dead man. "I'll take it back to Chief Strickland."

I moved my way around Cherise and made my way to the back of the plane, but not without first opening the wallet.

Inside there was a driver's license behind the clear plastic film. It showed a man with a big smile and black hair that could've been brushed before the photo, but that didn't matter now.

Jay Mann.

I snapped the wallet shut and held it out.

"I took the wallet out of his pocket." I handed Chief Strickland the leather wallet, which just so happened to be very high quality.

"You disturbed the body?" he asked.

"No. No." I shook my head. "I was very careful. Even wore gloves. See?" I lifted my gloved hands in the air, wiggling my fingers.

"Interesting." His eyes lowered, as did his voice. "I think I want to talk to you first."

"Great. My name is Violet Rhinehammer. I'm a reporter." I proudly stated my job. "I'm on here going to a big interview out west. Which makes me wonder, how long do you think you'll take to get the"—I clicked my tongue and nodded my head sideways toward the bathroom—"body out so we can get on our way?"

I made a little whistle with my mouth and used my finger to mimic an airplane taking off.

"Seeing how this is a crime scene, it looks like you'll be grounded here for a few days. You might want to give your possible new employer a little phone call letting him know you're to be a few days late." It was as if he was mocking me and taking pleasure in telling me that my big break was on the brink.

"Days?" I questioned. "I don't have days."

"Ms. Rhinehammer, please exit the airplane. I'll be with you shortly." He turned his back to me, leaving me feeling infuriated and, well, just about beside myself.

I stalked down the aisle and found myself standing on a small metal platform with about ten steps that took me down to the runway.

"Great." I stood there and looked around, knowing this was not how I pictured the end of this flight. I pulled my phone out of my pocket and thumbed through the call log to find the number of Richard Stone.

"Have you landed already?" Richard asked.

"You're not going to believe this." I proceeded to tell him as I took the steps one by one, careful to not get my heels caught.

"Violet." He sounded very serious. "This is going to be your interview. I'm asking you to go live right now. We can dial you into the station, and you can bring us an update. We will get a leg up on all the national networks with this breaking story."

"Breaking story?" I asked.

"Yes. Murder in the sky." He said it like it was some big headline. "This is going to get you on the map, and if it's big enough, you're automatically hired. Starting salary is two hundred thousand dollars."

"How do I get dialed in?" There was no doubt this was my big break. For a second, I felt like I should thank Jay Mann, but I didn't. Instead I said a little prayer for him and his family, wherever he was from.

CHAPTER FIVE

"Violet, can you have someone hold the phone while you do the broadcast? Do you have some earbuds you can put in?" Richard Stone kept me on the phone. "It's important you get this story, and now. There's word on the line that there's been a murder on board a domestic flight. You're there. You were on it."

"Cherise." I grabbed her as soon as she walked through the terminal doors from the runway. "I need you to hold the phone for me."

"Are you joking? I'm not your assistant. I'm going to give the officer my statement then go to the hotel, where I'm going to knock back a few." She waved her finger at me. "You should too. From what I was just told, we are going to be here a few days."

"Few days?" I bit my lip. It was even more crucial than before that I get the shot and seal the deal before Richard heard I might be stuck in Holiday Junction. "You have to do this. You owe me. I went in and got the wallet. I'm doing a live shot for my job, and I am the only one here to do a live, which means my footage will spread all over the world as the reporter who broke the story. I will tell them how I did all the work to find out who this man was and let them know how you refused to go in there. How safe will that make this airline seem? A flight attendant refused to help during an emergency."

"You wouldn't." She gasped.

"Try me." I wiggled my freshly plucked brows.

"Fine." She huffed and grabbed the phone from me.

"Thank you." I looked around for the best possible place to shoot the live and noticed a wall filled with four-leaf-clover cutouts next to the huge window where you could see the entire airplane, from which they'd yet to take out the body. "That's cute."

I'd almost forgotten we were coming up on St. Patrick's Day, but this place looked like it was the St. Patrick's Day headquarters.

"Over here," I told Cherise and had her follow me to the wall. Out of habit, thank goodness, I was able to put my earbuds into my ears and talk to Richard. "Richard, I'm ready."

Richard gave me all sorts of instructions on how to tap into the studio's network, which magically let me stream straight into the newsroom.

"And this is going to secure my spot on the news team?" I wanted to make sure.

"This is one heck of an interview that would be hard to beat." He made me feel so much better about my decision to pack my bags and follow my dream. "We are going live in three, two."

Before he said one, I handed the phone to Cherise.

"This is Violet Rhinehammer. International Correspondent." I smiled into the phone and did my best not to sound like a hick. I had been able to use my on-air personality voice, but when I was all aflutter, that southern twang just came out of me, and nothing was going to reel it in. "I'm coming to you live from—" I stopped talking because I'd forgotten where we had made the emergency landing.

"Holiday Junction." Cherise peeked over top my phone.

"Holiday Junction, where there's been an emergency landing. The information I'm about to tell you is not for younger ears, so now is the time for them to leave the room. This information has not been confirmed by law enforcement, but I can confirm that I've seen it with my own eyes, as I was a passenger on the airplane." I felt like my explanation took enough time for anyone with children watching to get their children out of earshot. "There has been a murder on the airplane. I can confirm this because I bravely went into the bathroom to retrieve the man's information, which I will not disclose at this time, due to the fact I'm not sure if his family has been notified."

"Violet, send me the information, but for now, sign off and tell the world you'll be back. Good job." Richard was in my earbud.

"Again, there has been an emergency landing here in Holiday Junction because I discovered a murdered body. This is an unfolding situation. This is Violet Rhinehammer. I'm reporting to you live at the scene because no other news channels can get through security to get this up-and-personal broadcast to you." The confidence was bubbling up in me as I found my footing with talking into my phone, and people started to gather around me.

They were watching me. They came one by one, standing in front of me as I found my strong voice.

"I will be broadcasting live footage and keeping you up to date." I reached out and grabbed the lady who had sat next to me on the airplane. "Can you tell me what you saw on the airplane?"

"What?" She looked at me. "Honey, I don't know if you are tick-tocking or whatever it is you young people do, but we are watching them bring out the body."

With big eyes, I looked back at Cherise. She was rolling her hand for me to keep talking after I'd realized the crowd wasn't watching me broadcast. They were watching out the window behind me.

Chief Strickland had one end of the black bag while another guy had the other end. They had to carry the body down the steel steps, and there was another person waiting for them at the bottom with a gurney.

"As you can see, they have now de-planed the body." I took the phone from Cherise and held it up to the window. I had pinched in a closer shot when I noticed Chief Strickland had taken a phone call, and for a few short seconds, he looked my way.

"Get off that phone!" he mouthed and pointed to me. "Hang up the phone!"

"You better do what he wants you to do, or he might take you to jail," the woman who sat next to me warned.

I turned the phone around to me and said, "This is Violet Rhinehammer. International reporter."

I clicked off just as several messages from friends back in my hometown of Normal, Kentucky came through by text.

"I see you're making quite a fuss." A man in a security uniform sidled up to me.

"Who wants to know?" I decided not to look at the texts from the people from home since they'd never really seemed to think I was going to make it big, and here I was on the national news.

"I'm Rhett Strickland, and I was told by that guy." He pointed past me out the window. I followed his finger and noticed Chief Strickland standing with his legs apart, his hands fisted on his hips, his eyes staring right at me.

"Chief what's-his-name?" I turned back around and rolled my eyes. "There was a murder, and there's a murderer in this room." I lifted my finger in the air. "I'm a big-time reporter, and it's my job to keep the public informed." I looked at his uniform a little more closely. "What are you, a mall cop?" I shook my phone to his badge. "And is your name really Rhett?"

"I loved that movie." His dimples deepened. At one time, those dimples would've made me wobbly in the knees.

Not today. Maybe just a little weak when I took in his dark hair, olive skin, a face that should be in a magazine, and a body to match. They sure didn't build them like that where I was from.

"And I am the airport security, but Chief 'what's-his-name' is my uncle, and you are right about a murderer being in this room." He snatched my phone out of my hand. "And if you keep broadcasting all sorts of things happening with your amazing reporter skills on this thing, you're giving them all the details so they aren't on their toes."

He slid my phone into his other hand when I lunged forward to get it back.

"You see, if the murderer doesn't know what's going on, they get a little fidgety and nervous. Kinda gives himself away." He made a good point.

"Himself? We think it's a man?" I picked on this one little detail.

"Just the semantics of the word. Himself or herself. Either way, it's not gender specific." He let out a long sigh. "Are you one of those reporters?"

"One of those?" I felt a smidgen offended. "I'm sorry if I've offended you" —I leaned in to look at his name again on the pin on his jacket—"Rhett Butler."

"Nope, not named after the movie character. It's a family name, and my last name is Strickland." The dimples faded. My phone beeped, and he looked at it. His dimples showed and deepened as he read my messages. "I'm guessing you don't look like this all the time?"

"Funny." I reached up and this time grabbed my phone.

"If we catch you doing another live broadcast or whatever it was you were doing to get on the national news, my uncle will lock you up for obstruction of justice." He gave me one last look before he snorted and walked away.

"At least I have my phone." I flipped a long strand of hair behind my shoulder. I decided to slide my phone open to read the texts.

"What is this?" I looked at the video text sent from Helen Pyle, my hairdresser from home.

Looks like you made it big-time, she texted along with a video.

I clicked the video. She'd sent me a link to my live broadcast.

Me.

The hair that I thought looked nice and neat, the makeup I'd carefully applied this morning before the flight, looked nothing like the image in my head of the person doing the reporting.

I gulped.

My hair was clumped in a few different places from my sweating, and my mascara had dripped down and dried on my face, making me look like an NFL football player. My fake lashes were half on.

"No," I gasped and frantically clicked over to social media.

Post after post was a photo of me standing in front of the four-leaf-clover wall and looking like the character the Joker.

Amateur reporter reports there's been a murder and looking for murderer. She looks like she killed someone. Honey, look in the mirror. You're giving yourself away.

I had become a meme.

CHAPTER SIX

"Oh, come on, don't be sore." Cherise had found it very amusing that I'd become a meme. "It's funny. Don't you have a sense of humor?"

"Not when it comes to my job. I am a professional and want to be taken very seriously." I was never so happy to give Rhett the Mall Cop my contact information so they would release us from the airport. "I just want to get to a hotel and get in bed. It's been a long day."

I gripped the hotel voucher they'd given the passengers.

We were standing outside the tiniest airport I'd ever seen. Literally you walked into the airport, and there was one person at a computer before Rhett let you through security into the one-room lounge before you exited the double slider doors to walk to the airplane.

I was guessing not too many people flew in or out of Holiday Junction.

We stepped outside, and there were mountains in the background on one side and flat land that led to the seaside area of Holiday Junction.

My phone vibrated, and I looked at it. My cheeks puffed up for a long exhausted sigh at seeing the battery level in the red.

"What now?" Cherise had stopped next to me, the pull-up handle on her luggage in her grip.

Somehow she'd been given access to take her things, but no one else was even allowed to think about asking for their belongings. Heck, she could've been the killer for all we knew. She was back there the entire time.

Hmmm, I thought to myself and wondered if my time here could be well spent doing my own investigation. Then I could do a huge segment on the national news where I'd be able to show those who mocked me on social media how I was a real investigative reporter.

"I should've put my phone charger in my purse, but I put it in my carry-on, which is on the airplane." I shoved my phone in her face. "I'm in the red. It won't make it until the morning."

"I don't have that type of phone, or I'd give you mine," she said with an empathetic smile on her face. "If it's any consolation, they are talking about leaving first thing in the morning."

"How am I going to know that if my phone is dead?" I asked and took a step back when a car came to an abrupt stop right in front of me, almost hitting me.

"I'm sure the hotel will have something for you."

The door of the car popped open. She hit the button on the handle of her luggage and pushed the handle down into the top before she picked it up and threw it in the back seat of the car.

"You got an Uber?" I asked and wondered how I was going to get to the hotel. "We can share. I can pay half."

"Uber?" She laughed. "You are so funny. I live here. Maybe you should be one of those comedic reporters on Saturday Night Live." She put her left foot in the car. "See you in the morning."

I leaned down to see who was in the car.

All I saw were big blue eyes staring at me and the back of Cherise's head because they were wrapped up in a big kiss.

"Ta-ta." Cherise's fingers drummed in the air before she tugged the door shut and the car zoomed off.

"Yeah. Ta-ta," I groaned, shaking my head as I watched the taillights fade off into the distance. "Now for a taxi."

"Taxi?" I looked up when I heard the voice next to me. I guessed I didn't realize how loudly I was talking to myself. "We don't have taxis in Holiday Junction. But we have scooters," Rhett continued.

He pointed to a row of battery-powered scooters.

"And you're lucky there's one over there, since I'm sure everyone is heading down to the Shamrock Parade." He seemed really happy about this parade. "It's the talk of the Village, and you certainly don't want to miss out while you're visiting."

"Is that right?" I asked, as thoughts of me on a scooter didn't seem so appealing. I almost corrected him to remind him I was not visiting, just passing through.

"I bet you can even get that fancy international news network to do a piece on Holiday Junction's St. Patrick's Day week of festivities while you're here." He shrugged. "Maybe you can even get a piece printed in the *Junction Journal.*"

"The *Junction Journal?*" I snickered. "No thanks."

He didn't need to know how I'd just left a small town, and from what I could tell by how people were talking, Holiday Junction was much smaller than Normal.

"I don't plan on being here long enough to write any sort of piece for the paper." My tone softened. There was no need to be nasty to Rhett. He was trying to be helpful.

"It'll take a while for my uncle to sort through the mess. With limited officers due to the holiday, they are pretty short-staffed." He didn't bring me any sort of good news.

As hard as I tried not to show any emotions, since I was on the verge of crying, my brows bumped together in a scowl.

"Is there a lot of crime in Holiday Junction to warrant officers working a small-town parade?" I needed to know what I was dealing with here before I called Richard Stone to see exactly where he stood on my little unexpected trip to Holiday Junction.

"We are a village," he corrected me.

I rolled my eyes. "Village. Town. Potato. Potaaato." I gestured both hands in the air like a scale.

"Crime?" he asked, displaying a wide grin. "You don't get it. Today is a holiday, and most officers take the day off to be with their family and friends."

He unbuttoned his security guard shirt one button at a time. My eyes shifted away from him and back several times as I tried to figure out what he was doing.

"And if you'll excuse me, that's where I'm headed." He unbuttoned the final button and slipped out of the shirt, exposing the green T-shirt underneath with a huge white four-leaf clover on it. "You should come out of the hotel for some fun festivities. You have nothing else to do until Uncle Matthew takes your statement."

"There's been a murder." Did I have to remind him? "What kind of town am I stuck in?"

"Village," he corrected me. Again.

"I see you don't like what I just said." He grimaced in a "who cares" way, flipping the shirt over his right shoulder, where he was visibly flexing his muscles for me to see. "Either way, scooter or feet." His lips formed a thin line, and his head gave a quick tilt to the side before he waved goodbye.

My eyes burned watching him cross the street to the parking lot that serviced the small airport. He jumped in his car, slid back the convertible top, and headed the way he'd gestured for me to get to town as if he didn't have a care in the world.

My shoulders slumped, and my walk was slow on my way over to the scooter.

"My oh my, I'm being tested." I looked up to the sky and wondered if this was one of those times the interim preacher at the Normal Baptist Church, the church I had attended in my hometown, had talked about. The preacher would preach about being tested on our way to our purpose. "I'm up for a challenge to prove I do deserve to go to California and be on television."

Just as I made it to the last scooter, someone rushed around me and grabbed it right out from underneath me.

"Hey! I was going to use that!" I yelled after the boy, but he took off and didn't turn around. His hat was turned around backward, and it, too, had a shamrock on it. "I see that hat! These people are nuts."

I glared at the kid, who still didn't turn around, and noticed Rhett had stopped his car and put it in reverse. I looked down at my phone so he wouldn't see me looking at him.

"Great," I moaned after I noticed my phone had completely died. This day was turning out to be nothing like I had planned it to be.

I put my fists on my hips and let go of a deep breath in exchange for a cry.

He brought the car to a complete halt.

"I saw what happened. You snooze, you lose." Rhett patted the passenger seat. "What about a ride? I'm heading that way."

"No. I'm good. I can walk." I didn't know him from Adam. "Besides, I don't want to be the next murder victim your uncle has to investigate."

"Trust me, you aren't my type, and I'm only being friendly. Suit yourself." He shoved the gear shift back in drive.

The hearse rolled up, making me take a step back, and the sound of some squeaky wheels caused me to look back over my shoulder to the entrance of the airport.

They were bringing out Jay's body. I shuddered.

Everything happened so fast. They opened the back door of the hearse and pushed the gurney into the hearse before it zoomed off.

"Wait!" I called after the hearse when I noticed something had fallen from the gurney. It was a black silk pocket square with green four-leaf clovers imprinted on it, along with the stitching of the letters J and M. "His handkerchief fell out!" I waved it in the air.

Rhett was still parked as if he were waiting for me to jump in.

"Fine." I tucked the silk square into my purse and opened the car door. "You take me to the hotel, and that's it."

I knew if I could just get to the hotel, I'd be able to find the morgue, where I would give them the square.

Rhett gave me a cocky wink and confident smile that told me I was in trouble.

CHAPTER SEVEN

T he wind whipped my long blond hair all around my face. Unsuccessfully, I tried to gather all of it up in my hand around my neck, but once I got a good handful started, the other side would fly up in the air.

Out of the corner of my eye I could see Rhett looking over every once in a while and smiling. I wasn't about to let him see how much his attitude infuriated me.

When I didn't see any sort of town, um, Village up ahead, my heart started to palpitate.

"Do you have a phone charger?" I asked Rhett.

"Help yourself." He lifted the console in between the seats with a free hand, and there was a cable hidden in there.

"I didn't think," I paused before I accidentally said town since he seemed very sensitive about it "Village was this far out. How much longer?" I asked, trying to keep a steady voice.

"It's been like three minutes." He said it just as we got to a sign that read "City Limits," right before a little bit bigger sign that read, "Holiday Junction: Celebrate Good Times."

"You like that." He'd noticed the grin on my face.

"It's cute. I guess it's interesting how you celebrate St. Patrick's Day. I'm not Catholic, so I don't know a whole lot about St. Patrick." I shrugged and noticed the row of houses on each side of the street.

There were lights dotted along the sidewalk, with four-leaf-clover flags waving along with the slight breeze. There were large trees giving shade to the many people who were all walking toward what I'd guessed was the downtown area.

"Catholic? What does religion have to do with how we celebrate?" he asked.

"I'm just saying how you seem to go all out for St. Patrick's Day, but I guess Chicago turns their river green." My face reddened from embarrassment. "I was just saying…" I felt like I needed to clarify and not sound so, well, dumb.

"Do you celebrate Christmas where you're from?" he asked and beeped his horn after he stopped in front of one of the houses.

"Oh, where I come from, Normal, Kentucky, we love Christmas." My heart tugged at the thought of me not being there this Christmas since I was going to be living in California. I threw the emotion out of my head.

"Is it your birthday?" he asked.

"No. It's Christmas." I pulled my head back, and my eyes narrowed.

"If it's not your birthday, why celebrate?" he asked and this time gave the horn two quick beeps.

"You've gotten your point across. I'm sorry I offended you about St. Patrick's Day." I rolled my eyes and put my head in my hand as my elbow rested on the door of the car, my hair gathered in my grip.

"St. Patrick's Day?" His head laid back on the headrest of the car seat, he cocked his head to the side and gave a relenting stare. "Holiday Junction celebrates every holiday. It kinda sucked growing up because it's such a cliché, but as I got older, I watched tourists such as yourself come and their eyes light up. Gave them something inside."

"I am not a tourist. I am a victim that wouldn't even have known Holiday Junction existed unless there was a murder on the airplane." I heaved in a deep breath and kept my mouth shut.

What was this guy thinking?

"Why are we here?" I asked when he beeped again.

"For her." He sent a nod past me, and I turned to my right to see this woman coming out of the house we were parked in front of, wearing a lime-green scoop-neck three-quarter-length-sleeved tea-length lace dress. She had black hair pulled back into a neat bun on top of her head and large black sunglasses to hide her eyes.

She was tall—or at least the black high heels she wore made her appear taller than she probably was—but she was thin and very striking.

"Get out and let her in," he instructed me.

"Girlfriend?" I asked as she approached the car.

"Hardly," he muttered. "Hey, Fern. This is…" He appeared to have lost my name.

"Violet Rhinehammer. International news correspondent in town for the big murder." I thought it would grab her attention, but it didn't seem to faze her.

Out of the corner of my eye, I noticed Rhett had opened his mouth to correct me, but he snapped it shut.

"It looks like you could use these more than me." She tugged off her glasses and handed them to me. "Where'd you pick her up, Rhett?"

"Pick me up?" I darted the question to him and then looked at her as she got into the car and literally sat on top of the convertible top in the middle.

"Airport. Tourist who needed a ride." He shot me a look as if to tell me not to say a word about the murder.

That got my attention. There was something he did want me to keep to myself.

"We can talk later, Fern." He put the car in drive and started back down the road.

"What's the speed limit?" I asked when I noticed a couple of kids on the street had passed us on the bikes. "And isn't it dangerous for you to be sitting up there? Where I come from, it's illegal not to sit on a seat with a seat belt on."

I looked up when I heard a marching band playing just as we drove underneath the ladders of two firetrucks, one on each side, the Irish flag hanging from the extended ladder on one of the trucks and the American flag hanging down from the other fire truck.

"Elbow. Wrist. Wave." Fern had an exhausted tone in her voice as she waved to the crowd gathered along the road. "Where's the candy?" she asked Rhett.

"Violet, can you grab that bag of candy underneath your seat?" he asked.

"I'm in some sort of twilight zone." I blinked a few times when I realized we were part of a parade. "I thought you offered to take me to the hotel." I reached underneath my seat and pulled out a large bag of lollipops.

"I did. I just didn't tell you that I had to drive Miss Holiday Junction in the St. Patrick's Day parade on our way. The hotel is on the route." Without him even looking my way, I could tell he was enjoying every single bit of discomfort he was putting me through, and he was doing it on purpose.

"Elbow, wrist, wave," Fern kept repeating behind her fake smile as she did the motions over and over. She'd take a handful of lollipops and whiz them past my head, cackling when she'd notice me duck a little. "Don't worry. You'll only get one upside the head if you try to hit on Rhett."

"Stop it, Fern." Rhett's body tensed, his knuckles white as he gripped the wheel. "I'm only doing this as a favor to my aunt."

"Mmhhmm. Just smile for the paper when we get up here." She tapped me on the shoulder. "Can I have my glasses back?"

I pulled them off of my face and handed them back to her, only to have her throw them on the floorboard, where I had to pick them up.

"Smile!" I heard someone yell when my head was between my legs. When I jerked up with the sunglasses in my hand, I realized Fern had thrown the glasses on the floor so whoever was taking a photo of her and Rhett didn't get me in the picture.

I cocked a brow and glanced back at her. She wore what we called in Kentucky a shit-eatin' grin. Forgive my language, but that's what it was.

Little did she know just who was in the car with her.

My name was Violet Rhinehammer, and I was going to show Holiday Junction just who had landed in their town, um Village.

A name they'd never forget.

CHAPTER EIGHT

There was literally nothing I could do.

Literally.

Rhett knew it too. Underneath his mirrored sunglasses, I knew he was side glancing my way, because every time I impatiently drummed my fingers on the door, he'd smirk.

Adding to it, the toe of Miss Fancy Pants's heeled shoe kept digging into the back of my arm. When I'd glance back, she'd murmur an apology under her smile.

"Why couldn't we have that official?" I pointed to the convertible in front of us, where there was a dog hanging out the window.

"That's the most important official in Holiday Junction. I'm second." Fern's toe dug into my arm.

Instead of giving her the satisfaction of me showing any sort of grimace, I slowly scooted closer to the car door. It would be obvious if she toed me again that it was deliberate.

"Who is he?" I wanted to know who had the cute dog. That's the kind of person I wanted to hang out with while I was in this crazy Village.

When we rounded the corner, I got a good look at the cute dog. Fern threw out two handfuls of candy, one for each side.

The smile grew on my face when the little black ears popped out of the window. The children along the parade route went crazy, and when the dog turned its little black head, I noticed the white upside-down wishbone markings that started between the pup's eyes and along each side of its nose.

"Boston terrier?" I questioned with glee. "I have to know who that is in front of us."

"Miss Paisley. She's the Village mayor, and she's a—" Fern started to tell me, but Rhett interrupted her.

"We will introduce you when we get to your destination, which is where the parade route ends." Rhett's words made Fern chuckle.

"What? Is Miss Paisley not a good mayor?" I couldn't help but notice there was some sort of secret between them.

"Everyone loves Miss Paisley. In fact, she's never ever had an opponent during the elections," Rhett said, getting my curiosity up.

"It sounds like Miss Paisley is someone I need to interview while I'm here." I wasn't going to tell them, but I was going to get an interview with the mayor and let her know just how messed up this entire investigation had been going.

I was sure Miss Paisley had no idea the officials had been granted the day off when they should've been called back in because there was a dead body.

I'd spent the rest of the three-mile-per-hour drive down what appeared to be the main street of Holiday Junction thinking about what I was going to say to Mayor Paisley.

The houses had gotten much bigger and stood tall, brick mansions with elaborate fences around them, and I'd guessed they all had nice front yards due to how far the houses were set back.

Holiday Junction was definitely a place that had money, unlike my hometown. The houses melted into the center of Village, where various small shops were next to each other and looked to be interesting. For a second I made a plan to visit a couple of them, but I realized quickly I wasn't going to be here long and put the little shopping adventure out of my head.

The parade route seemed to have stopped at the end of the heart of the Village, and Rhett pulled the car over.

"Move it." Fern had already tried to climb over me to get out.

Pftt, pftt. I spit her tulle out of my mouth and tried to get it out of my face so I could jump out and see the mayor.

"I'm trying," I told her and opened the door to get out. "But you aren't giving me any time."

"I don't have time. This is a major deal, and I've got to go sign some autographs." She adjusted her dress once she got her footing on the sidewalk. When she moved away, the mayor's car was empty.

"Great." I groaned and wondered just how I was going to get in front of the mayor.

The parade continued past us. I could tell by the lineup the mayor was the head of the parade, followed up by Fern, so Fern was well beloved in Holiday Junction.

I stood on the sidewalk, waiting for Rhett to tell me how to get to the hotel.

"Neat, huh." He walked around the convertible and watched the amazing floats pass by. He pointed to the men and women walking in front of the bagpipe band. "That's the Holiday Junction parade committee."

"Y'all have your own parade committee?" I asked and snorted then saw a rooster trotting in front of them. "Someone lost their rooster."

"That's Dave." Rhett smiled. "He's head of the parade security."

"You're joking, right?" It was hard for me to keep my jaw in place as it dropped in disbelief.

"Nope. Dave keeps everyone in line."

The rooster did seem to know what it was doing with its head held high as the committee walked behind him.

"The parade ends with a full day of shamrock fun. Tomorrow is the greening of the Village fountain, which is out in our big park. There's even a small lake there where you can take a pedal boat out." He was talking over the bagpipes as they passed. It was hard to hear him, so we stood there for a minute as the young Celtic dancers did their dance.

"Wow. Those are gorgeous dresses." It was hard to not compliment the dancers' outfits. "I love the huge four-leaf clover on the front."

"Each dress is custom printed, cut, and sewn just for the dancers. That's her over there." He pointed across the street to one of the older dancers. "Leni. She's our local tailor, so she takes her work seriously for the festivals."

"Festivals?" I asked, noticing the woman he'd pointed to was having a heated discussion with another dancer before she gave her a little shove.

"This is just St. Patrick's Day. We have festivals for all the holidays." He nudged me. "I told you that you were going to like it here."

"Fat chance," I told him and stood there watching the large float pass by.

There was no denying the work the organizers of each float had put into their float. All of them had either a skirt of green material wrapped around the outer portion or some sort of crepe paper. One of them was built in the shape of an old Viking ship with cutouts of leprechaun faces, horseshoes, and the Irish flag along the sides of it.

"There's a lot of floats." When I looked down the street, there wasn't a visible end to the parade in sight.

"Yes. Each shop has their own float." He pointed to the next float, where men in kilts and leprechaun hats were singing. "That's the local band, which does perform at the Jubilee Inn." He pointed behind us.

The building was five stories tall with several small balconies across each floor. Some had people standing on the balconies, watching the parade.

"I have a room there?" I asked, digging into my purse for the voucher.

"Yep. I'm not sure how they pulled it off because most of the time the rooms are booked during the holidays, but maybe they had a room for one." He shrugged. "Let's get you inside."

I wasn't sure what it was before it was an inn, but the Jubilee Inn was very cute. The inside was more of an open-type setting, with a lounging area you had to walk through to make it to the back wall. There, a woman was waiting behind a counter.

"Hey there, Rhett." She greeted him by name, which was very comforting to me because where I was from, everyone knew everyone by name.

"This is Violet Rhinehammer." Rhett introduced me to Kristine Whitlock. We shook hands. "She's a big-time reporter. And she's going to be staying here while the"—he leaned over the desk—"crime scene is cleared, and, well, she wants to interview Miss Paisley. I told Ms. Rhinehammer you could facilitate that for us since, well, this is Miss Paisley's residence."

"Mayor Paisley?" An odd look glazed over Kristine's face.

Kristine appeared to be in her sixties with her salt-and-pepper hair. She had a few wrinkles on her forehead and long smile lines that stayed etched on her face after she stopped smiling.

"Yes, ma'am. The one and only mayor. You see, Ms. Rhinehammer here has a problem with the officers taking off today for the parade."

I interrupted him.

"I feel like it needs to be brought to the mayor's attention how no one seemed to worry about Jay Mann's murder. And trust me, it was a murder. I saw him with my own two eyes." I closed my eyes as a shiver rolled up my spine from the memory.

"I see." Kristine finally saw how important it was to me, even though Rhett had seemed to be poking fun at me. "Yes. I think I can arrange it."

"Say around 7 p.m.?" I wanted to make sure I had time to prepare, and that meant getting all the information I could about Holiday Junction's police department as well as finding out anything I could on Jay.

"That's the mayor's dinnertime." Kristine's brows furrowed. "And she does love her dinner."

"I think it's perfect. Where I come from, Normal, Kentucky—" The way she looked at me was the look I always received when I told people I was from Kentucky. They either wanted to know if we all drank bourbon, just how fast were the horses, or if we wore shoes.

Kristine seemed to be thinking the latter as I watched her eyes swoop down to my feet.

"We love to have little chitchats, and eating food is a great time to incorporate those conversations." I watched as Kristine and Rhett both shrugged to each other at my suggestion.

"I guess, but you better be prepared, because she's vivacious when it comes to her food," Kristine said.

"And the well-being of the Village," Rhett followed up.

"Good. Then I have no reason not to think that Mayor Paisley and I will see eye to eye." I took the room key off the counter. "See, I've been here under a couple of hours, and I am already going to be making lemonade out of lemons." I turned but quickly turned back. The two of them jumped to attention as if I'd walked back into a private conversation.

"Hmmm," I sighed so they knew I knew that they were being secretive. I let it go. "Do you happen to have a phone charger I can buy or borrow?"

"We have those in the rooms for our guests. If you need to purchase one, you can take a right out of the inn, and just a couple of blocks next to Brewing Beans is the Jovial General Store."

"Brewing Beans? Is that a place to get coffee?" I asked. "I love a good cup of coffee."

"Yes, and it's good, too, but I'm sure the line is long today because of all the festivities. But it's worth the wait." Kristine's face told me it was the place to go.

"Thank you." I smiled on my way up to my room because seeing the sunny side of things always put a little giddyup in my steps.

CHAPTER NINE

Immediately I put my phone on the charger to get it good and juiced up so I could get in touch with Richard and schedule another live for the station. It was a surefire way for me to slip right on into the open broadcaster position I was destined for.

It felt so good knowing exactly what my life was going to look like. It was a sad and unfortunate event about poor Jay Mann, and, well, if it weren't for his untimely death, I mightn't've gotten the job. But I was sure it was in the bag now.

"There." I had found the phone charger on the bedside table, just like Kristine had mentioned, and I sat down just to take a load off my feet.

They were killing me, but there was little time to really stop and rest. I couldn't change my shoes because they were on the airplane and Chief Strickland hadn't released anyone's luggage.

"Something told me to wear sensible shoes," I said to myself. I took off the pumps I wore because I hadn't wanted Richard Stone, or whoever was picking me up at the airport to take me to the interview, to see me in tennis shoes.

I rubbed my feet and closed my eyes to think about the beach a few blocks from here and how nice it would feel to put my toes in the sand. Heck, it would be nice to bury my head there too.

I looked at my phone after it beeped a few text messages, one after the other. I wasn't sure if I wanted to look at them or not. I couldn't bear to know who in Normal saw how disheveled I looked in the national headlines.

I was a glutton for punishment, so I went against my better judgement and reached for the phone.

"It won't hurt to scroll through." I scooted down the edge of the bed to get closer to the bedside table so the charger wouldn't get pulled out of my phone.

I snorted a laugh when I noticed the texts were from people I tried to stay away from. Unfortunately, it was those people that would probably help me out the most.

Then I came up to a text message from Maybelline West. She had moved to my hometown without a penny to her name, and she'd made a big life for herself.

Sorta the same situation I was going to be in. Sorta. Only her past was that she had to move because she was broke. Still, we both moved some-where where we knew no one. Though I wasn't to my final destination yet, she just might be someone to help me out of this little pickle because she did know a few things about snooping around to get some answers.

I hit the message and didn't read it. I clicked on her name and hit the call button.

"Hello?" I could tell by the way Mae answered the phone that she was a little taken aback by my call.

"Hi, Mae." I cleared my throat. "I-I-I," I stammered.

"You're in a little situation, aren't you?" she asked. "You need some help? I'm here to help."

"I know that you and I did some snooping around a few times during my time at the *Normal Gazette* and Channel Two." I didn't have to remind her how we'd gotten keys to the city and all that.

Both of us were good at what we did. There could've been a little healthy competition between the two of us, but it was all in fun.

"Violet, you don't need to say anything to me. We are friends, no matter how much we disagreed in the past, and there's nothing I'd love to see more than for you to succeed in whatever that may be. How can I help you?"

"I'm stuck here in St. Patrick's Day hell, literally. The entire Village is crazy for this holiday, and everywhere I turn, there's green, green, and greener." I smiled when I heard Mae snickering on the other end of the phone as I told my crazy story, including how I'd gotten stuck in the middle of the parade with Miss Holiday Junction sticking the heel of her shoe in my side.

"Rhett, huh?" There was a tickle of tease in Mae's voice.

"He's a nice guy, and in a different life, maybe we'd date. But he is the security guard at the airport." I proceeded to tell her how his uncle was the police chief and how the other officers were off for the holiday. "As much as I hate to admit it, this could actually seal the deal for the job if I could solve it while the airplane is grounded."

"It's part of a small Village." Mae reminded me of just how backwards Normal could be sometimes too. "You just have to take matters into your own hands."

"How do I do that?" I asked her.

"First off, you need to find out everything you can about the victim. Where they are from. If they are married. Stores he liked to frequent. Family member, anything." I tried to write everything she was saying but Mae West talked so fast. "Once you get that information, find their phone numbers, emails anything to get in touch with them. Then you ask around as you call the stores, get food, call his local newspaper, or the paper boy, about the victim and what type of person he was. Then you just might have to ask some basic questions, like did he have any enemies or make someone mad. Make a list."

I reached into my purse and took out the notepad to write down all the things Mae was saying, even though I knew most of this stuff as a journalist. It was good to hear it again because being in the thick of a murder and finding the body put me in a much different headspace than doing a story where I was far removed from it.

"If you can get your hands on a police scanner, that'd be great too." Mae started to jog my memory on all the things I knew to do, and it took me right back to college, to my Journalism 101 class. "You know all this stuff. I think you are just nervous and grabbing at straws to get you to the job interview. If you take a moment to put down some thoughts on paper, one thing at a time, and really keep your ears open, you'll get some clues that'll help you solve the murder."

"It's funny how when I lived in Normal, you were doing this to solve the murder while I was doing this to chase the story. It's much different solving than gathering facts to type up." I laughed, realizing just how much I'd judged Mae for getting up in everyone's business.

"At the end of the day, I think both of us were trying to do better for our community. While you're in Holiday Junction, you're going to have to think of it as your community for right now. You'll get the story. I don't know if you'll be able to solve the murder, but I do know you are smart. Any clues you do gather will help the police so they don't have to chase after the clues, which will get them closer to solving the murder and you closer to your dream job."

"Thank you, Mae." My heart tugged as I thought about how she and I could've joined forces much more while I lived in Normal to solve all the crimes together. But it hadn't been the right timing for either of us. "This will make me a better journalist for sure."

"You're already a great one." Mae gave me the vote of confidence I needed to get out there and get my ear to the ground. "Call me if you need to bounce any ideas or anything you hear off me."

"Will do." We said our goodbyes.

While I let my phone charge up even more, I went into the bathroom and wiped off the makeup from underneath my eyes, ran my fingers through my hair, and retrieved the lipstick from my purse. I was at least a little more presentable than before and not so scary. Granted, if Holiday Junction had been celebrating Halloween, I would've fit right in as a zombie news reporter.

I grabbed my notebook and my phone, threw both in my bag, and set out into the streets and Shamrock Festival, where I was determined to get some clues.

"Violet!" I heard Rhett's familiar voice calling to me.

I ignored him by pretending I couldn't hear over the crowd. I slowly turned my head in the opposite direction on purpose.

"Violet Rhinehammer! Violet!" His voice got so loud on the last call of my name. I shifted my body so my back was to him.

"Give her a little nip!" I heard Rhett call out to the barista as he made his way down the counter.

"No, you will not!" I jerked around.

"Ha! I knew you could hear me. Were you ignoring me on purpose, Ms. Rhinehammer?" Rhett sidled up next to me.

"Don't you dare put anything but black coffee in that cup," I warned the barista.

"They don't have liquor here." Rhett leaned his hip on the counter. He smelled of beer. "I knew it would get your uptight attention." He laughed when I picked up the coffee. He threw down a few dollars. "On me."

"I can pay my own way, thank you." I dug down into my purse.

"No. Keep your money. It's the least I can do to tell you how sorry I am for Fern. She can be a little over the top sometimes. No one in the Village has come close to giving her any competition until you." Rhett caught me off guard.

"Excuse me?" I asked before I could get my money out. The barista took Rhett's, and he took me by the elbow to lead me out into the street.

He dropped his hand and lifted his chin up to the sky. He sucked in a deep breath and let out a long sigh. He pointed left.

"This way to the Shamrock Festival Stein Competition." Vigorously, he rubbed his hands together. "You can be my partner."

"Shamrock Festival Stein Competition?" I felt an overwhelming sensation of intuition telling me *no way, no how, hell no* was I going to do any sort of competition.

"Everyone keeps asking me who the new girl is and why was she in my car with Fern. Fern doesn't like it one bit, and, well, she's not only Miss Holiday Junction. She's also in the five-time Shamrock Festival Stein Competition champ group." He looked down at me and grinned. "You're stuck here for at least a couple of days. Enjoy the Shamrock Festival. You might end up liking it and come back next year."

"This time next year I'll be doing a huge interview like—" I searched my brain. "You name the movie star, and I'll prove to you that I'll be doing that this time next year."

I loved a good challenge.

"Then you will look back fondly on your time here and maybe one day fly through to where you can say that you were the talent we needed on my team to bring down the five-time champs in the Shamrock Festival Stein Competition." He smirked. "Your name will be engraved on the big stein forever."

"Oh, I do like that." My shoulders lowered. "Fine. What do I do?"

"Come on." Rhett grabbed my hand and wove us in and out of the crowd in the street and down a little farther, where they'd marked off twenty feet.

"Isn't this competition more for a German festival?" I asked when I noticed there were four teams with a set of five in the group.

They stood in front of a table with five steins filled to the brim with golden, bubbly beer.

"Maybe." His right shoulder lifted, as did his lip as though he didn't have a care in the world. "But it's a competition we do here for the Shamrock Festival, and we drink on this day. Now Mother's Day is around the corner, and there's zero drinking on that day." He lifted his hand in a gesture of zero.

Fern tossed her hair, catching my peripheral vision. I was sure she'd done it on purpose, because when I looked her way, her face wore a vengeful scowl before she leaned into the ear of a burly man wearing plaid, who had shifted his gaze from the ground over to me.

He smirked.

She sashayed her way over to my new group.

"I see you've been recruited. Didn't he tell you how they've never won?" She cackled. "Or are you just the new tourist flavor of the week?" She tapped her temples. "I don't recall him ever bragging about a girl from Kentucky."

"I'm a woman, and I'm not a tourist, nor do I have any interest in Rhett Strickland." I took a big swig of my hot coffee.

Just the sight of her looking at my hot coffee made my body temperature rise, and I had a picture of me being the one on this team to clinch the win, holding up that big—and what looked to be plastic—stein trophy with my name on it up in the air as she ran off crying.

"And we are going to win." I dropped my coffee in the trash can as if I were doing that whole drop-the-mic impression.

"I'd be worried if I were you." She winked and went back to join her group. They all turned and laughed before they huddled together.

"Everyone, this is Violet Rhinehammer, and she's going to be our fifth." Rhett's announcement to the group sure didn't sit well. They talked among themselves as if I weren't there.

"Really, Rhett?" The other woman besides me on the team peered over top of her eyeglasses. "She was just drinking coffee."

"At least let us know she does drink beer." The skinniest man in the group eyed me up and down.

"Or is even legal to drink." The other, heavyset guy put in his comment.

"Come on, guys. Give her a chance." Rhett put his arm around my shoulders. "Right, Violet?" He gave a hard nod and looked at me with a smile. It faded. "You do drink, right?"

"Yeah, sure." I lied because I just wanted to prove Fern and now them wrong about me. "Let's do this!"

"That's what I'm talking about." Rhett put his hand in the middle of our little circle. "On the count of three, we do 'shamrock.'"

All of our hands were one on top of the other.

"One"—our hands started to bounce to Rhett's count—"two, three!" We flung our hands high above our heads. "Shamrock!" we all yelled.

For someone who had no idea what this competition was about and also who rarely drank, I did really well on my first go at it. Let me be clear that I had no idea of the rules, and if I'd known that I had to run the distance to the other table at the far end of the course with the full stein of beer with little to none sloshing out, only to down the entire thing before I picked up another stein, only to go back to where I'd started, I'd not have said yes to Rhett.

Whichever team had just one member standing was the winner, and when it got down to me and Fern, my ignorance of not only this competition but of drinking was what carried me that far.

While my teammates were taking their turn, I'd decided to focus on Fern's team and take my mind off the fact I was about to drink a beer.

Bleh.

"Hurry up and go take off that dress. If you spill beer on it, no more fancy stuff for you," the man in Fern's group told the woman I'd recognized from the parade.

Not the woman who made the dresses, but the woman who had bumped into or stepped on the other. The one who got shoved.

"Don't tell me what I can and can't do." She got right back into his face. "I might be your wife, but I'm my own person, and you can't make me do anything."

"It's my money, and you spend every dime!" He got up in her face with his chest popped out.

"Your turn!" Fern had noticed the argument between the man and wife. She put her hand on the man.

He gave one more glare to his wife before he grabbed a beer stein off the tray and headed to the other side of the maze, where their other teammates were cheering him on.

"What?" Fern snarled.

"You're gonna get fat." I knew that'd get her attention.

"I can exercise." She grabbed the stein before I could even get mine, and she darted off.

After I'd gone twice around the maze, I ignored how Holiday Junction was spinning around me and held onto the image of me holding that plastic trophy above my head as my team chanted my name.

"Mmmmhhhh awwww." Fern wiped her mouth with her forearm after she'd downed the next stein on the third round.

"All of those calories. I don't care," I lied, trying to gulp back the beer. "And where I'm from—" I started to say.

"We know. You're from Kentucky." She belched the last bit as we stumbled along the course to make it to the finish line, where we would have one last beer.

"Yeah, and we drink real moonshine. Not that fake stuff. The real deal. So this beer is nothing to me." I went to grab the last stein and down it, but as luck would have it, Fern threw her hands up in the air.

"We have a new champion!" I heard the voice scream out before Rhett and the members of our team grabbed me up and threw me in the air.

"I told you I was somebody." My words slurred, and I pumped my fists in the air.

It was a moment I was sure I'd never forget if I could only remember all of it, but all I heard after Rhett took the trophy was how I was going to be late for my dinner with the mayor.

"But I didn't even get to investigate the police force," I said as I stumbled along the street on the way back to Junction Inn. The crowd of onlookers at the competition had joined us on our victory walk, clapping the entire time.

I pulled the black silk square from my pocket and whirled it in the air.

"And I didn't get to take this to the morgue!" My head was flung back like I had no muscles. "Rhett, what am I going to do?"

"You're going to go to bed, and the mayor will have to wait until the morning." It was the last thing I remembered.

CHAPTER TEN

The knock at the door of my room brought me to life. I sat on the bed, wondering how on earth I'd gotten there, then I remembered.

"Rhett," I seethed. I tumbled out of bed and tried to get my footing before I went to the door and swung it open. "Rhett, you did this."

"Good morning." Kristine Whitlock stood on the other side with a tray. The little black-and-white Boston terrier was at her side.

"I thought you were Rhett." I opened the door wide for her to enter. "I was going to give him a piece of my mind." I bent down and patted the dog.

Her lips twitched as though she was trying to contain the smile growing.

"I thought you could use this." She put the tray on the small table next to the double doors that led out to the balcony that jutted out over the main street.

There was a covered plate along with a small bottle of headache medication.

"I also thought you might need to take a couple of these. If you don't have a headache now, you will." She picked up the bottle and shook it. "You've made quite the impression around here. I don't ever recall another tourist becoming so well-known in just a few hours. Everyone is talking about Jay Mann being found." She pulled the blinds on the double door open.

The sun popped out to show the glorious weather for today.

"I'm not a tourist." I stood up and walked over to the king-sized four-poster bed with a canopy. It had a thin ceiling curtain that was white and sheer and fell around the bed, making it look like a little princess bed.

I loved it.

"The police let out his name?" Now I knew everyone all over the world would know the story before I could get a jump on it.

"Yes. He will be missed." Kristine put her hands to her heart.

"Wait. You knew him?" I questioned and grabbed my notebook off the small desk next to the double doors where I could do some work if I needed to over the next few hours. I hoped that was all the time the police needed before they let us leave.

"Jay was a very prominent citizen here, and I bet Melissa is beside herself. She and Jay have a granddaughter who needs a kidney transplant. Something about a rare condition. From what I understand, Jay and Melissa have been traveling back and forth to their daughter's home. That's why he was on the airplane, coming home."

"Where's the daughter live?" I asked and wondered if I could make it there to talk to her.

"An airplane ride away." She had no idea. "Jay was coming back home for the festival since he was being honored as a past Hibernians Grand Marshal today. Something they do every year during the Shamrock Festival."

She lifted the lid off of the plate. The smell of the eggs, bacon, and toast fluttered throughout the room.

"Anyways, the Manns drive two hours to Banchester, where they catch an airplane to go to their daughter. From what I understand, he was on his way back when he was killed."

"His wife was not with him?" I asked.

"No, but I also heard she, Sandra, and the granddaughter are on their way back now in light of what happened." Kristine's lips twitched back and forth. "I can't remember the name of their grandchild for the life of me. I know it too. Kristine talked about it so much at the Ladies of the Hibernian Society."

I recognized the name Banchester since it was the only stop on my flight where I had to disembark and grab another airplane to my final destination.

TONYA KAPPES

"Hibernian Society?" I questioned.

"Oh yeah. It's a big deal in Holiday. Really it's more for our Irish citizens, but I'm not Irish, and they needed members. Jay and Melissa, or maybe just Melissa, have some Irish descent in their family, so they were big contributors to the society."

"I wonder if he was murdered by someone in the society?" My little journalist mind came to life, forgetting all about the hangover.

Give me a good lead, or in this case possible lead, for a great story, and all the adrenaline made all the aches and pains go away. My blood was pumping.

"I don't think so." Kristine shook her head.

"Cute pup." I changed the subject because I could tell by the way she was acting that she didn't even think it possible.

As a journalist, I knew anything was possible, even the unthinkable.

"I saw him in the parade with the mayor." I referred to the dog and walked over to pick up the piece of toast. I needed carbs to soak up the beer still left in my system.

"Her. She's a her," Kristine corrected me.

"I should've known because you are so cute." I talked baby talk to the pup. "What's your name?" I bent down and looked at her little pink collar with the metal tag. "Paisley. Just like your mayor. How cute."

"This is Miss Paisley," Kristine said.

"I see that." I scratched her head before I took the mug of coffee from the tray. "Must be a popular name because of the mayor."

I snickered before I took a sip of coffee.

"No. This is Mayor Paisley." She referred to the dog.

I spit my coffee out of my mouth, showering Kristine's shirt.

"I'm so sorry." I put the mug down and tried to help wipe her down. "I am not generally like this, but I thought you said this dog was the mayor."

"She is." Kristine ran her hands down her shirt. "She has been our elected mayor for seven years now."

"You know what?" I shook my head and walked over to my phone. "I'm thinking there's a rental car place here, and I can just drive across the country to California."

"You're not crazy. She's our mayor."

"How is that possible?" This was almost as intriguing as why someone would kill Jay Mann.

"The Village has never had a human mayor. Each election cycle, people from around the world cast their votes to elect a canine one. It's mostly just fun and a distraction from the tension of human politics, but each voter pays one dollar per vote, and proceeds go to the Holiday Historical Society. This year, they raised nearly twenty-three thousand dollars."

"What?" Now this might be a story that'd go viral over the AP.

Kristine laughed.

"Okay, I have to know what Mayor Paisley's duties are."

"They include sitting on the front porch of the inn, taking pictures with visitors, and chewing on bones, as well as wearing her cute little outfits." Kristine ran her hand down Mayor Paisley. "She's a doll, and she's all mine."

Suddenly I felt so dumb as I recalled how I'd acted yesterday, demanding to see the mayor. Little did I realize how Rhett had played me like a fiddle and I fell for it.

"Anyways, there's been another murder." Kristine's eyes shifted to my bedside table, where I'd put the silk pocket scarf that'd fallen off of Jay's body.

"Another one?" *Was this one related to Jay's?* How odd was this. My mind was racing so much that I hadn't noticed Kristine had moved over to the table, where she picked up the pocket scarf.

"Where did you get this?" she asked in a demanding voice. "Answer me now, or I'm calling Chief Strickland."

"It fell off of Jay Mann's body when the coroner took him out of the airport. I'm going to go to the morgue today and return it."

"Are you sure?" Kristine dropped it back on the side table. "Because Rosey Hume was found this morning in the Holiday Park fountain with the exact same pocket square stuffed in her mouth and what they think was a knife wound."

CHAPTER ELEVEN

I couldn't get Kristine and Mayor Paisley out of my room fast enough. Another person with the same pocket square was found dead, and both lived here in Holiday Junction. This story was greater than we'd initially imagined.

Holiday Junction was the big clue to me due to the fact that two of its citizens were murdered. There was no way that the two deaths weren't related in some fashion, and the killer on the airplane had to have been from Holiday Junction.

Was the killer right under my nose? Had I passed the killer on the street yesterday?

Had Jay Mann and Rosey Hume known each other and known something that made someone want to silence them forever?

I quickly got cleaned up and took the headache medication just in case, before I threw on some sunglasses to cover my puffy eyes and bolted out the door.

"Richard, it's Violet." I spoke in a serious tone to his voicemail. "I know you want me to report on the murder, but you aren't going to believe this. There are two murders, and I think we've got a real story here. I'm still not sure when the local yahoo police is going to let us take off, but in the meantime, there's no reason I can't snoop around."

I pinched a grin when passing another guest at the inn as I took the steps to the lobby.

"Call me back." I clicked the phone off and dropped my phone back in my purse.

"Where you off to?" Kristine called from behind the counter.

"Fountain?" I questioned, throwing my finger up in the air and pointing right and then left, giving her the answer to her question while asking for directions.

"Right. You can't miss it. Just keep walking and you'll run right smack dab into it," she said, her voice growing in volume as I pushed open the doors of the Jubilee Inn and walked right into a photo shoot with Mayor Paisley and a line of tourists.

Everyone looked like they'd walked through green slime from their head-to-toe attire. Even Mayor Paisley had on a shamrock dress.

Kristine was right. The fountain and the park was at the very end of Main Street. It was as far as you could go.

From a distance I noticed there was police tape around the large four-tiered concrete fountain. The closer I got, the faster I walked and maneuvered my way through the crowd.

When I got a good luck at the fountain I figured it to be about twelve feet wide and about a two-feet-deep pool where there were four ceramic swans with water flowing out of their mouths. There was a top on the fountain that was a large ceramic watering can ever so slightly tipped over, with water pouring out of it as well.

As I got even closer, I noticed there were four large sidewalks going away from the fountain. When I got to the sign I noticed it where each sidewalk would lead.

The south would take me to the seaside, the north would take me back toward the mountains, the east towards Village, and the west to the countryside. Too bad there wasn't going to be enough time to explore them all or even go to the beach, but where I was going, I would live by the beach.

The park was very large and grassy. Just like Rhett had mentioned, there was a small lake type body of water with pedal boats all tied up to a wooden dock.

There were benches along the sidewalks for people to sit, but other than that, it didn't have anything but grass. There was a large white structure with marble pillars and marble blocks that appeared to be seating in the grassy area in front. The structure looked like it was some sort of stage that was home to the Village Players, a local theater group.

After looking around to get a good sense of where I was, I turned around and recognized Chief Strickland and the man who had put Jay in the hearse where near the fountain. I headed that way.

"I can't believe it. Poor Rosey." There was some murmuring filtering through the few people I wiggled my way past so I could get up to the front. All of them wore green suits with white sashes with the words "Hibernian Society" glittering in gold.

"Why on earth was she trying to turn the fountain green when she knew it was part of the ceremony?"

"Rosey?" I gasped, putting my hand over my mouth. "That's awful."

"Two Hibernians in twenty-four hours." The woman tsked. "Do you think we are in danger? Are they plucking us off one at a time?"

"Rosey and Jay were Hibernians?" I wanted to be sure I heard everything correctly so when I reported it back to Richard, I had all the facts.

"Are you that reporter from the airport?" Another lady in the group noticed me. "You are, but you don't have all that crazy makeup on your face."

"It had been a long day and—" I found myself explaining my disheveled appearance from yesterday. "Yes." I decided not to even worry about it. What mattered was right now and these facts I was collecting. "Do you think you're in danger?"

"The members of the Hibernians never get along with each other. How could they? They don't even like each other." She rolled her eyes. "If Jay Mann wasn't dead, I'd have pegged him to have killed Rosey. They fought at the last meeting about who was going to turn the fountain green, and, well, as you can see, she was going to do it, but someone stopped her."

"What is the protocol for turning the fountain green?" It was something I could've easily looked up on my phone, but hearing from someone who'd seen it firsthand was much better for the reporting piece.

I took my notepad out of my purse and started to write down word for word what she was telling me.

"The Hibernians pick a child from the community to come to the ceremony, which better still be happening today." She shifted her weight and looked at her friend. They both nodded. "Just like Rosey to make it all about her."

There was no love lost between Rosey and this group of citizens.

"That doesn't matter now." The woman turned back to finish telling me about the fountain. "The child will pick up that small green watering can you see over there." She pointed, and my eyes followed but fell on Chief Strickland.

He was staring back at me. I acted like I didn't see him by looking back at my notebook. The woman continued.

"After some words are read, the chosen child will pick up the can and pour in the dye. Which is environmentally friendly. You can write that down." Her lips pressed together, and her eyes grew. Her expression told me she wanted the little fact on paper.

I scribbled it down, satisfying her so she would continue.

"It only takes a few seconds for the dye to turn all the water green. It lasts about three days, long enough until the end of the festival." She threw her hand in the air. "Hey there!" She hurried off with the other ladies following her.

"Can I get your name?" I called after her, but she didn't hear me. Instead of chasing her down, I decided I needed to go see exactly what Chief Strickland was thinking.

"I see you've made some friends with some of the locals." He didn't move his head as his eyes shifted to the right, looking in the direction of the woman who'd just given me the lowdown on the fountain. His eyes moved in a line to look at me. "I'm sure they have already figured out who the killer is since they know all the gossip."

"Matthew, there's bloodstains on the edge of the fountain, so she was killed here. Then a body must have been dragged into the water. I'd say we're looking for a knife with a long, thin blade."

"Can I get your name?" I asked the man, with my pen at the ready.

"Excuse us." Matthew stepped in between me and the coroner.

"I can find out his name. And you should just tell me. Besides, I have some information that might interest you and him." I opened my purse and took out the pocket square.

Both men's jaws dropped.

"Curtis Robinson." He stuck out his hand. "Where did you get that?"

"I was standing outside the airport when you pushed the gurney to the hearse, and this dropped off of Jay Mann's body." Leaning over to see around them, I saw the tips of Rosey Hume's shoes sticking up out of the water in the middle of the fountain. Everything else but the tip of her nose was submerged, and where her mouth was located, there was a piece of cloth floating in place.

"Ms. Rhinehammer was the passenger who found Jay on the airplane." Chief Strickland introduced us in his way. "I looked you up. From what I gathered from Sheriff Hemmer."

"You called Sheriff Hemmer?" I put my journalist poker face on, which I felt was pretty good when I couldn't help but wonder what on earth Al Hemmer had told him. "And?"

"He said you were a true journalist and you had a knack for using your skills to aid in a few of his cases in Normal, Kentucky." Chief Strickland stared at me.

"Ahem." I cleared my throat and tugged on the hem of my shirt. "He's right. I didn't leave those skills back in Normal. I'm willing to offer my services to you, Matthew."

He jerked his head as if I had the gall to call him by his name. His eyes narrowed.

"I can call you Matthew, right? I mean if we are going to be working together." I ignored Curtis when I saw him smirking. "It seems to me that these two crimes are related. The victims are both from Holiday Junction, both were in the Hibernian Society. It seems like there's a killer among us."

"Just how do you explain Jay being murdered on an airplane?" he questioned with a little bit of a grin as if he were testing me in hopes I'd fail.

"Obviously someone wanted him dead, and they had to be on the airplane. So do you have the passenger list?" I asked.

The sound of someone crying made me look. There was a woman near the edge of the park, talking with a Holiday Junction officer. He appeared to be questioning her. She had a dog on a leash.

"We do have the passenger list, and I've split it up among my officers to make sure we get all of their statements, taking their personal information, and letting them leave. We can't keep them here forever." Matthew's wide stance, hand on his utility belt, and stiff posture gave me the vibe he wasn't quite sure of me yet.

"Great! Then I'm sure you can get all this figured out on your own, because I've got to get to California. I'm already late for a big interview, and, well, I'm not qualified to do any sort of police work." I couldn't wait to get back to the Jubilee Inn so I could check out and get back to the airport. "If you'll excuse me."

"Hold up!" Matthew stopped me. "We are only on the B's, and you are an R for Rhinehammer, so we won't be getting to your part of the alphabet for, I'd say, forty-eight hours."

"Are you holding me against my will?" I hated always having my name be at practically the end of the alphabet. Even in school it sucked.

"I'm sorry, Ms. Rhinehammer. You were so eager to give your two cents and running around trying to get some sort of footage. I called that fancy station out in California, and they told me you didn't have a job but that interview. And, well, I guess I could hold you longer and make you even later." He had something up his sleeve.

"You can't do that." I jerked back and noticed a few more people being interviewed by the officers.

"If Sheriff Hemmer didn't give you such a glowing recommendation on how great you are at snooping, then I might've let you leave, but the fact you found the victim and you have the pocket square leaves me to think you might've taken the pocket square when you two could've argued on the airplane."

"Did someone say I was arguing with someone on the airplane?" My jaw dropped at the lie.

"I don't know. I've not gotten everyone's statement. You aren't cleared to leave, so why not just help out with that special nosy technique you have?" He had me. He knew it, and I knew it.

"My two cents is that they had a possible affair. His wife killed him and then her." I started to throw out ideas.

"Melissa is out of town and should be in before the Greening of the Fountain to accept Jay's award." He let me know she had an alibi.

"What about Rosey's husband? He heard about the affair. Let's face it. The top reasons someone is murdered is love, greed, and/or money." I shrugged.

"I would love to interview Rosey's husband, but we've already talked to him." His head tilted to the right, his ear nearly touching his shoulder as he crossed his arms.

"I'm going to need the passenger list." I knew all my excuses could have a comeback, and there was no way I was going to get to my already-day-late interview for another forty-eight hours. I might'swell make good use of my time.

"No problem." He whistled really loudly, catching the attention of someone I couldn't see due to the bright sunshine.

As the figure came into focus, I knew it was Rhett.

"Rhett is going to take you down to the station this afternoon, and you can look over some files. I normally wouldn't do this, but when Sheriff Hemmer gave you a glowing recommendation, I decided to use you while you are here." I heard him, but all I could think about was Al Hemmer and how I couldn't wait to give him a piece of my mind.

"Why is she still dressed in her green parade dress?" Curtis interrupted us and made a really good observation. Someone from the coroner's office had wheeled the cart to the fountain and had gotten in to retrieve the body.

"She'd been in the parade, so maybe she still had the dress on."

"The pocket square?" Curtis questioned. "It's the same as the one Violet claims fell off Jay, and I didn't see it on Jay's body when I took him off the airplane."

"Maybe it was in his pocket, and jiggling him down those airplane steps then wheeling him could've possibly wiggled it out of the pocket of his pants? Or maybe when I went in to get his wallet because the pilot asked me to—" I gulped, knowing Jim Dixon was adamant about me getting Jay's identification. He was definitely someone I needed to see.

"What?" Matthew had seen the light bulb in my head click on.

"Jim Dixon. Have you talked to the pilot?" I questioned.

"We let him go because he had to work, but we do have his contact information."

My jaw tensed after I heard this little bit of news.

"I'm going to need that info." There was nothing I could do about Jim now, so I focused on what I could. "That's how I got the square, but I can snoop around to see if anyone has seen these. Who found her?" I asked and slipped the pocket square back into my purse, since I knew they wouldn't use Jay's because I'd put my fingerprints all over it.

"Her." Matthew gave a slight head nod over to the woman still crying.

"And you honestly want me to see what I can find out?" I asked to make sure he wasn't going to cuff me then and there for some unknown reason. "No strings attached. No jail."

"Should I take you to jail?" He got awfully suspicious.

"No," I blurted. "I think it's odd you'd ask for my help."

"According to Sheriff Hemmer, I should use you while you're here if you're still going to insist on doing the story anyways." He made a great point.

"I get to see all the files?" I pointed to Curtis. "Even his files?"

Curtis shuffled his shoes and looked down at the ground.

"Yes. All the files." He made Curtis sigh and me smile.

"And I get to do the lead story with all the information?" I wanted to make sure I got something bigger than just having facts. I wanted the entire story.

"Yes. But I'm asking you to not write all the information until we get someone in custody. We won't talk to any other press." Matthew was being way too nice, but it was fine.

"Good." I turned back and stopped while I watched Curtis go back over to the fountain, where they were retrieving the body. It seemed they'd finished combing it for clues.

My jaw dropped when I recognized the woman.

"What?" Matthew had noticed my change in body language.

"I saw her in the parade yesterday." I gulped and recalled her as the woman who'd not only been shoved by the lady they said made those green dresses, but also as the same lady who'd been on Fern's team.

But who more importantly had argued with her husband.

61

"You're going to realize ninety percent of the residents were in the parade." He didn't seem that interested in my observation, so I decided I'd just keep my little bit of information to myself and see where it took me before I pointed fingers at her husband.

I glanced back at the woman who'd found Rosey Hume.

"What's her name?" I asked.

"Layla Camsen. Rhett, you want to go with her?" By having Rhett go with me, I knew it was a sign Matthew didn't fully trust me.

That was fine. I'd use the time with Rhett to quiz him on Layla.

"What does Layla do?" I asked Rhett as we took the long way around the fountain to give me time to get a little background information on Layla.

"She owns Holiday Junction Travel Agency. She and her husband, Joaquin. They are longtime residents and pretty well-liked people." He told me enough for me to come up with a couple of questions.

"Hi, Layla, I'm Violet Rhinehammer." I put my hands in my pockets when I noticed she'd given Rhett a glance as if she wanted to see if I was okay to talk to.

He gave a nod and slight smile.

"I know who you are. It's all over the paper this morning." First time I'd heard that, but I guessed when you get a big story out into the world like Jay's murder on the airplane, before Matthew had shut me down, the word still got out.

Even in Holiday Junction.

"I'm not here as a reporter." So that wasn't entirely true since I'd turn her statement into a piece after we got the killer. "I'm here on behalf of Chief Matthew."

"You think you were in the paper as a reporter?" she asked. "You were in the paper for knocking Fern off from the championship in the Shamrock Festival Stein Competition yesterday."

My eyes blinked a few times as the news settled into my brain before I lowered them.

I gulped, smiled, and laughed.

"How fun." I wrinkled my nose. "Anyways, I know you told the officers about finding Rosey. Can you tell me one more time so I can record it?"

"This is Monty, my dog. He loves to go on his walks here in the park. I knew it was going to be busy this morning, so we came a little earlier because he likes to run off his leash." Her eyes grew when she abruptly stopped talking.

"What?" I asked.

"Well, I guess it doesn't matter anymore, but Rosey was a stickler about leash laws here in Holiday Junction, and she'd tell on you in a minute if you did something wrong. But Monty has a hard time going number two on a leash. Right, Monty?" She looked down at her dog. His tongue was hanging out and his tail wagging, dragging on the grass.

I wrote down word for word what she was saying and found it very interesting that Rosey was what Layla called a stickler.

I wanted to get any and all complaints from the police department. What if she told on someone one too many times?

"What can you tell me about Rosey Hume?" I asked.

"Besides that, she was a very nice person. Though she did like to argue." Layla scoffed. "I bet she's arguing with someone up there." She lifted her brows to the heavens.

Rhett and I looked at each other and smiled, trying not to laugh.

"I understand you don't want to speak ill of the dead, and we aren't asking you to, but we just want the facts. So you are saying you were here earlier than normal. Like what time?" I asked.

"I don't know the time, but I do know it was still dark. So around six thirtyish." She shrugged. "The reason I know is because I heard this squeaking noise like wheels or something. It got Monty's attention, and I got a little scared. It sounded so eerie."

"Where did the sound come from?" I asked.

"Over there." Layla pointed to the woods a little distance from the fountain.

"You were in the woods?" I asked.

"Monty smelled something, so I let him lead me." She jerked her head up to look at me. "Oh my dear, do you think Monty was tracking the killer?" She bent down. "Good boy, Monty. You are so good."

"We don't know that, but maybe." I liked the idea.

"No. We can't say for sure." Rhett put a stop to Layla and me praising Monty. "Don't write that down."

"Fine." My brows furrowed, and I went back to the questions. "You heard a squeak noise, and then you did what?"

"I got out of the woods so we could go home. Monty does like to take a drink out of the fountain, which Rosey would die if she knew it."

"What else can you tell me about her?" I asked.

"Rosey is the secretary of the Hibernians and a long-standing member of the committee, as well as her husband, Zack." Now this was something I could hang my hat on.

"We were told she and her husband did have an argument yesterday at the Shamrock Festival Stein Competition." Again, I saw to it that I spun the words around just a little. "Did you happen to know anything about that?"

"No. I was busy at the booth. My husband and I own the travel agency here. Though I don't put it past them to argue. I heard you found Jay Mann, and if he hadn't been at the airport when he was killed, I'd say it was either Rosey or Zack who killed him."

My ears perked up, and I didn't dare look at Rhett. He was fidgeting.

"What do you mean?" I asked and stopped writing to look at her.

"Zack didn't like Rosey being the secretary because she had to work with Jay some. Zack is jealous of Jay. Zack was always saying how Rosey tried to keep up with the same lifestyle as the Manns but they didn't have the Mann money." She laughed. "No one has the Mann money."

She shrugged.

"That said, Zack tried to get Rosey to leave the committee, but there was no way she was going to do that. What on earth would Rosey do with her time? That's when she'd file all those reports on people. She'd hear some gossip then put herself in a situation to see if the gossip was real. If say, for instance, someone said my dear sweet Monty was off his leash, she'd stalk me until she saw him off his leash. Then she'd go run and file a report." Her body stiffened, and she curled the loose end of the leash around her hand to make it taut. "Not that she was doing that today. I didn't see her until Monty made it to the fountain for a drink."

"Was Monty off his leash?" I asked.

Layla looked left and then right before she looked back at me. She sucked both sides of her cheeks in like she was contemplating telling me the truth.

64

"No. In fact"—she rolled her eyes upward—"he'd jumped in the fountain, and I found him licking her face. Her dead face." She tugged the leash closer to her body before she leaned in and whispered, "Rosey Hume would die if she knew that Monty had licked her dead body, and she'd die if she knew that's the last thing people would remember if it got out. I'm begging you not to write that."

Rhett's lips pulled in tight.

"It'll be our little secret." I winked but still made the note.

"Good. Now I know this may seem unkind, but I hope the murder won't affect any of our other events. We have such a lot planned." She nodded.

"We are still doing the fountain," Rhett confirmed.

"I'm guessing it's Melissa Mann coming to do it, because she called me yesterday to get her on a plane back to Holiday Junction, since I'm her travel agent and all." Layla could prove to be really helpful when it came to who was on the plane with me and Jay Mann.

"About that." I flipped the notepad to a different page. "Can you tell me if you know offhand who from Holiday Junction was on the airplane with me? I'm also looking into Jay's murder."

"There's been so many people trying to get here for the Shamrock Festival, I can't remember who was on what flights, but if you stop by my office, I can take a look for you. Rhett knows where it is. He can show you. Right, Rhett?"

"Yes, ma'am." The polite side of him came out, taking me a bit off guard.

"Oh, and you need to look at Zack. If anyone could connect these two murders, he'd be it. He made all kinds of threats to people during Hibernian meetings. I know this is the busiest time of the year for them, but he's got a very short fuse, and when it gets lit, Layla was the only one who could put it out. And let's just say when the fuse was lit because of her, there was no hope for her until he calmed down." The more Layla talked, the more I was interested in learning about Zack Hume.

"Thank you. We might be stopping by your office," I told her before Rhett and I walked away. "Now. Where do I get a copy of that paper?" I asked Rhett.

CHAPTER TWELVE

"It's a small dying paper. Who cares?" Rhett tried to talk me out of going to get a copy of the paper.

"I care." I stalked out of the park and onto the sidewalk, heading back to the main street. "It might be a dying paper, but it still has a presence. It can take one article being picked up by the Associated Press to bring life back into a dying newspaper, and I don't want to be that one article."

I'd already dodged one bullet from the live broadcast from the airport where all of my makeup had run down my face and my hair was a mess, since the circumstances of finding a dead body and putting it aside to go live did save me some face.

Though I'd become an immediate meme afterwards, I was now being seen as a journalist who put aside her emotions to bring the story to the national news, and my live had been seen over two million times. That was a number I was sure was going to give Richard Stone the confidence he needed to hire me without me actually going to the rescheduled interview.

"Which way to the newspaper office?" I asked.

"Office?" he asked back.

"Yeah. Office." I pulled my phone out to see if Richard Stone had texted me back since I'd sent him ten text messages to confirm a reschedule.

Nothing.

"It's a decent-sized walk that way." Rhett pointed down the street.

"Past the Jubilee Inn?" I was trying to get a feel for how long it would take since I knew it took ten minutes to walk to the park from the inn.

Time was of the essence when it came to breaking news. A good reporter knew how to use her time efficiently, and while I had to be here, I could work on perfecting my skills so I would be in high performance mode when I got to my first day on the new job.

"Yes." He walked in that direction.

"Are you going with me?" I asked.

"I don't have anything else to do but go to the fun festival things. I'll tag along." He patted his stomach. "Have you eaten?"

"Kristine brought me some breakfast, but I only had time to eat the toast." I didn't want to tell him that I felt a little hungover.

"What else can you do to celebrate St. Patrick's Day around here?" I shouldn't've asked.

"Well, yesterday was the beginning of the fun. Violet Rhinehammer, you might be mad about your little layover here, but it's probably the best time to visit. Well, not unless you're here for Fourth of July. That's a much better celebration, if you ask me." He yammered on about the festival while I wanted to let him know that I'd be far away from here by July fourth.

"Over there behind Sharmel's Hardware in the parking lot are the amusement rides. They are open this week from five to ten p.m., but if you purchase an armband for seventeen dollars, you get unlimited rides all week."

"Oh goody," I said with a little snark.

"Even if you don't like amusement park rides, the money goes to the Mother's Day festival. This year they are calling it Tea Time." He put his finger up to his mouth. "That's a well-kept secret, so don't tell anyone, or the Daisy Ladies will have a fit."

"We can't upset the Daisy Ladies, now can we?" I didn't know who the Daisy Ladies were, but I didn't plan on giving their little Mother's Day festival another thought.

Ever.

"Then we have the beer garden along with many arts and crafts vendors, not to mention the delicious food." He was trying too hard to convince me how great the Shamrock Festival was and how lucky I was to be here.

"I've had enough of beer for a year. Possibly two." My stomach did somersaults at the mere mention of beer.

"I know beer's not your thing. What about music?" He walked sideways next to me as we passed festival goers.

"I do love music." I did, and taking in some live music did have some appeal to me.

"Then you don't want to miss the Emerald Stage today. The Mad Fiddlers are amazing. I'm hungry. Do you want a donut?" He indicated taking a pit stop at a food vendor stand.

"No. I'll wait here." I stayed on the sidewalk and let him fight the crowd to get a donut. Must be some good donuts, but I was really watching what went into my mouth. The beers were calories I sure didn't need, and it would take a day or so to get the inflammation I was feeling in my fingers to go down so I wouldn't look like a sausage on camera when Richard gave me my segment.

The thought of getting my own segment because of my amazing investigation work here in Holiday Junction excited me to no end.

"Excuse me." I apologized and took a couple of steps back when I realized I was in the way of people walking.

"Emily's Treasures." I read the sign after I'd turned around to face a display window.

Though it was a little gaudy, it was still cute with the shamrock lights all around the window and four-leaf clovers hanging down from the ceiling.

There was a similar dress to the one Rosey Hume was found dead in on display, as well as a man's outfit. The green coat had four-leaf clovers and a pocket square that looked exactly like the ones on Jay Mann's and Rosey Hume's dead bodies.

I hurried through the door, where a couple of musical chimes that sounded an awful lot like an Irish jig rang out.

"We can customize it for every holiday here in Holiday Junction." The woman must've seen my expression. "Welcome to Emily's Treasures. I'm Emily. What can I help you find? You must be a size six."

68

"Hi, Emily. Actually I'm a size four." Maybe a size four on a good day, but she wasn't ever going to see me again.

"Really? Hhhmm." Her head tilted. The wiggly four-leaf clovers on the wires of the headband in her hair went along with the green plaid shirt, khaki pants, and duck boots. "I'm usually spot-on. Must be the pint of beer I had last night."

By the way she said beer, I knew she recognized me.

"I was hoping you could give me some information on a pocket square." I opened my purse as I walked to the middle of the small boutique so I could pull out the square to show her what I was talking about.

There was a look of shock on her face.

"I wasn't expecting you to come in here for that." A brow rose with interest. "I thought you were going to come in here and ask me some questions for your investigative reporting."

She picked up something off the counter and tossed it in the small trash can next to the counter.

"Was that today's paper?" I had a very keen interest in seeing it.

"There's nothing in it. It's practically shut down for business. What is it you'd like to know?" She tried her best to get my attention away from going straight to the trash can.

"I'd still like to take a look." I shrugged, reaching down to pick it up before she gave it a good shove with her shoe.

"I don't want you to look at it." Her gaze shifted over my head. I swirled around to look, and Rhett was standing at the door, doing the whole finger-across-the-neck thing.

"He doesn't want me to look at it." I hurried over to the trash can now on its side with all the contents out around it. "I just want to look at the paper."

I carefully shoved the pocket square back in my purse and flicked the creased-in-half newspaper open.

That's when I came face-to-face with the photo of myself that was not the greatest, nor was the headline. It was from the beer contest. I had my mouth wide open, about to chug the beer. My eyes looked as if I were possessed, and my hair stuck out like my finger was jammed in a light socket. Not my finest moment.

Snooping Tourist: Holiday Junction beware!

"For the love of God, who wrote this?" I demanded an answer by just reading the headline alone.

"Now calm down, Violet. This is just the *Junction Journal*, and I told you it's on its last legs." Rhett's words brushed right on past me.

"Meddling? Dottie Swaggert called me a meddler?" I aimed my stare at Rhett. "She's one to talk!" I realized I was screaming when a customer came out of the dressing room and bolted out the door.

"I'm going to have to ask you to leave. You're scaring my clients." The woman shot darts out of her eyes at me. Not literally, but you get the picture.

"I'm sorry. But whoever wrote this piece went all the way back to my hometown to get statements from people who weren't always a fan of me." I said it in such a way that Rhett would know the people in the piece weren't always on the up-and-up. "In fact, this Dottie and her group of friends, they call themselves the Laundry Club Ladies. Really? Who on earth hangs out in a laundromat because they want to?"

"It was good to see you, Emily." Rhett had grabbed me by the arm and tried to lead me out, but I stuck in my heels, jerked my arm away, and took a deep breath.

"I'm sorry I scared off a customer." I was keenly aware of the other eyes upon me that belonged to a few people sort of hiding behind a clothing rack. "This is not a portrayal of who I am. I'm a little on edge, finding a dead body and all."

Rhett and Emily traded looks.

"I'm fine," I assured both of them. "I will read the rest of this later." I wagged the piece of garbage in the air and put it in my purse in exchange for the pocket square. "If I was so awful as that terrible article claims, then why would Chief Strickland have me looking into his case?"

"To get you out of his hair?" Emily muttered and busied herself with the piece of clothing the customer I'd scared off had left behind. "This was a two-hundred-dollar piece. That would've paid for Katie's piano lessons."

I looked at Rhett.

"Her daughter." He explained who Katie was.

"Again, I apologize." I walked back over to the counter and looked at the clothing. The sleeveless V-neck dress looked like a leprechaun had thrown up on it. It was this awful green plaid with four-leaf clovers sewn down the sides.

I set the pocket square on the counter and held my hand out.

"I'd love to try it on."

"It's a size six, and you told me you were a four." Emily was holding her ground.

"I'll take my chances." I gestured for her to give it to me. "Now while I try this on, why don't you tell me about Jay Mann coming in here and buying one of the pocket squares from you."

I headed back to the dressing room and kept the door cracked so I could hear what she had to say and prayed Rhett was listening.

"He didn't buy them from me." Emily didn't appear to want to give up any information.

"Really? What about Rosey Hume?" I asked with my mouth up to the crack in the door and started to undress.

"She didn't either." Emily wasn't any help.

I looked in the mirror and wanted to gag. I'd never be caught in something like this, much less something like this that was going to cost me two hundred dollars. But I knew if I didn't, Emily would stay tight-lipped.

There was some whispering between Rhett and her that I caught on my way out of the dressing room.

"I'm sorry, I didn't hear what you two were discussing." I made it clear I wasn't dumb and knew they were talking about me. "Now—" I opened my purse and took out two hundred dollars, knowing money was going to be tight until I got to California and Richard put me on payroll.

Maybe he could give me a starting bonus since I was proving myself to be really valuable.

I set the money on the counter. Emily eyeballed it and then me.

"I knew you were a size six." She gave me a sly smile. "Anyways, I do keep a record of who buys what. These are made locally, and neither of them bought one. But I do recall someone placing an online order from Jay's company. They bought two."

Now we were getting somewhere.

"His company?" I looked over my left shoulder at Rhett.

"I'll tell you about it on the way to the *Junction Journal*," he said, making eye contact again with Emily.

"You said these are made locally." I put the fabric square back in my purse. "Who makes them?"

"Leni McKenna."

"I know that name." I looked at Rhett again.

"The dancer from yesterday. The one who made the shamrock dresses."

"The one I saw push Rosey Hume after they had some words?" I questioned, knowing things really had gotten interesting.

CHAPTER THIRTEEN

"I'm guessing you know this Leni McKenna," I assumed after Rhett and I left Emily's Treasures.

The stares I got as we walked down the street in the direction of where Rhett said the office for the *Junction Journal* was located made me a little self-conscious.

"Yep. I do." He stopped at another vendor along the way down to the offices of the *Junction Journal*. "We will take two." He pulled some cash out of the front pocket of his jeans.

"I'm not hungry," I told him and tried to figure out the timing of all this and how it was going.

While he waited for whatever he was getting to eat, I got my phone out of my purse and checked to see if Richard Stone had called or texted.

He hadn't.

I dialed him.

"Hi, Richard. It's Violet. There's been two murders involving two people from Holiday Junction. I really think this story is getting much bigger than just Jay Mann murdered on an airplane." I pulled the phone from my mouth when I noticed Cherise, the flight attendant, standing near one of the band stages. "I have some interesting details that look like they're tied to the case. In fact, the main officer here, I guess he'd be the chief, has asked me to look into some details. He had checked out my past, and I have glowing reviews from Sheriff Hemmer in Normal."

I was really talking myself up. I had no clue what Al Hemmer had even told Matthew, but how I was asked to assist in solving the murders here had to be a good sign.

"I'm sure you're so busy getting my salary and bonus structure aligned" —I threw in the bonus thing because I needed it after all the work I was doing, and this dress I was wearing for the good of the investigation— "that you're not able to take my call when I do call. I have my phone on me now, and it's fully charged. Let me know what direction you want me to take on this murder investigation, since it looks like I'm stuck here another day."

I had made it across the street and over to where Cherise was standing out of her uniform. She looked way better than the day I'd seen her. She had a huge smile on her face, and her hair that had been up in a bun was now flowing down her back. The uniform did nothing for her long legs that went for miles in her red capri pants and thin arms that poked out of the sleeves of her snug white sweater.

"Oh my. Look at you, Violet." Cherise turned with a beer in her hand. "You have drunk the Shamrock Festival juice."

She looked me up and down with her assessing eyes.

"You wouldn't even believe it if I told you." I sucked in a deep breath. "Do you have any idea when they are going to let us leave?"

"No clue about your flight, but I'm on a flight tomorrow heading east." She smiled and pointed to the man next to her. "This is Patrick. I think you met him when he picked me up at the airport."

The eyes. I recognized the eyes. They'd locked lips before he zoomed off.

"No, I didn't. Hi, Patrick. I'm Violet." I took a side step to let Rhett in when he walked up.

"Yeah. Yeah. I remember you." He lifted his chin and put his arm around Cherise. The look he gave Rhett didn't go unnoticed.

"Hey, Patrick. Cherise," Rhett greeted them. "Here you go." He held out a brown paper napkin with a slice of baguette. "Irish soda bread. You're going to love it."

"On your hips," Cherise noted with raised brows.

"Are you ready? We need to get to the paper." Rhett nudged me and moved back in with the crowd.

"Nice to meet you." I gave them a wave before I turned to scan over top the crowd's heads to see where Rhett had gone.

"Welcome to Emerald Stage the Mad Fiddlers!" the announcer screamed over the microphone before electric fiddles took over.

"Hey!" I tried to yell at Rhett, but the Mad Fiddlers had started to sing, and, well, the crowd was going crazy.

Rhett had gotten back on the sidewalk, which was a lot less crowded and rowdy. I wasn't sure if selling beer all day was a great idea, but then again, I had no idea what Holiday Junction was like. All I knew was there were two murders that appeared to be tied and the Village newspaper was single-handedly ruining my career.

"Hey." I put my hand on Rhett's arm after I'd finally caught up to him. "Isn't this the band you wanted me to hear?"

"It's too crowded. Besides"—he put the end of the Irish soda bread in his mouth and bit off a piece—"we need to get to the *Junction Journal* before they close."

"Do you forget who you're dealing with?" I asked. "I'm an investigative reporter."

"I thought you were a journalist, Violet. Which is it? Investigative reporter or journalist?" He stopped with a look on his face that was so sore and mean.

"I see." It occurred to me that his personality had changed as soon as he found me with Patrick and Cherise. "What was the deal with you, Patrick, and Cherise?"

"There is no deal. Those two drive me nuts." Rhett held something close to his chest.

"How do you know them?" I asked.

"We live here. We grew up together." He took one more bite before he started to walk again. "Aren't you going to eat your bread?"

The Jubilee Inn was across the street, so I kinda knew where I was but still didn't know where the office for the *Junction Journal* was.

"I'm not much on carbs." I had to dig deeper. I knew he was holding something back.

"Trust me. You're going to love it." He took another bite along with making bigger strides in his gait.

It took two of my steps to keep up with his one, and before I could look up, we were rounding the corner away from the shops and going to where the big houses were located.

"You three didn't seem to get along very well. And it has to be something if you suddenly changed your mind about this awesome band you insisted I check out."

He abruptly stopped in front of a gate with a large brick wall on each side.

"There was too big of a crowd. We can listen to Patrick any ole day. He's my brother." He pointed to the red-brick home off in the distance behind the gate. "That's where the *Junction Journal* offices are."

"And they are going under?" I questioned.

"You could say that." He tapped a code into the silver box, and the gates opened.

"Here's a thought." I followed him inside. "They should sell this land to keep the *Junction Journal* afloat."

"I don't think it's about money. I think it's about age." He didn't make any sense. The *New York Times* started way back in the mid eighteen-hundreds.

"Too bad the thing wasn't dead before I got here," I said.

He stopped abruptly again and looked at me.

"What? It wasn't a flattering photo, nor was the article nice." I shrugged then muttered, "They deserve to not be printed."

Rhett continued to walk up the long brick sidewalk. The tall trees stood along each side with their fresh new spring leaves. I was a sucker for nature. I grew up in the Daniel Boone National Forest, where the seasons made the most beautiful landscape. Not a single photographer could come close to getting a picture to capture its true beauty.

This place would also give photographers a run for their money with the manicured lawn and the perfectly trimmed shrubs. I tried not to fall over my own feet when I twisted around to look back at that brick wall on this side of the street, which was lined with gorgeous hedges.

"Do you get all four seasons here in Holiday Junction?" I knew I'd made him upset about nosing into his relationship with Patrick and Cherise as well as the paper, or maybe he was just sensitive to the fact it was his home.

I knew better, and, well, as they say at home, it's easier to get something with honey. So I decided right then and there to put my nice foot forward. It shouldn't be too hard since I wasn't staying here much longer.

It was for the good of the story. Right?

"I swear I've died, because I know that's not you walking up on my front porch, Rhett Strickland." The older woman was sitting in one of the egg chairs hanging down from the large front porch of the offices of the *Junction Journal*.

"You've not died. I've brought a friend." He motioned for the old woman not to get up and hurried over to give her a kiss.

Unusual greeting for even a southerner like me.

"Nah. I'm getting up to greet any friend of yours." She wasn't feeble at all. She popped right up out of the egg chair and adjusted the brown shawl draped over her shoulders. Her hair was all silver and cut into a bob, neatly styled.

The outfit she had on was more of a lounging outfit, a cream matching top and bottom. She had on a pair of jeweled sandals that I felt it was too cold for, but then again, what did I know? I'd just spent a fortune on the silly dress I was wearing.

She gave me an odd look then took the glasses dangling from the chain around her neck. Putting them on, a smile grew on her face.

"You look nothing like the photo printed in today's *Junction Journal*." She grinned and slid her eyes to Rhett.

"That's why we are here. I'm demanding a retraction from the editor in chief." I crossed my arms and did a little stomp with my foot. "I mean you no disrespect, ma'am, but I certainly will not let a newspaper, if you call it that, such as the *Junction Journal* try to ruin my career. You have no idea where I'm going and how much this little murdery situation you have in your town." I stopped with my fists to my side. "Village," I corrected myself, "has cost me."

"You've got some spunk. We need spunk around here." She sighed and paid what I'd just said no attention whatsoever.

"I'm sorry?" I questioned.

"Honey, don't be sorry for that spunky go-getter attitude. I had one of those myself back when I was your age." She made no sense.

Then it dawned on me. She had dementia.

"Yes. Well, if you'll excuse us, we have some business with the paper." I tugged on Rhett's arm on my way to the door so I could march right on in and get them to retract that story.

When I entered the office building, I figured I'd be hearing someone, anyone, on a phone, computer keys clacking, maybe a printer or two. A newsroom at the least.

"Hi there!" This woman greeted me from a room to the right. She was lounging on a couch. "You must be from the Hibernians. Let me get you a donation. I sure hated to hear about Jay and Rosey." She got up and put her feet in a pair of slippers. She wore a bright-green dress, no doubt matching the festive occasion, and had silver hair.

It made me wish that I would look as pretty as she did when I was her age.

"I'm here to see the editor in chief about the *Junction Journal* and a retraction for the awful story written about me in this morning's paper." I looked around at the decorated crown molding, chandeliers, and the fancy furniture.

The credenza was filled with picture frames, and one face in particular I recognized.

Rhett Strickland.

CHAPTER FOURTEEN

"You brought me to your family's home?" I questioned Rhett through my gritted teeth with a smile hiding those. "I thought we were going to go to the offices of *Junction Journal?*"

"We did." He shrugged and looked at the two women standing in front of us in the fancy family room that looked more like a museum than a home.

I might be from a small Kentucky town, but I knew what high-end décor, custom window treatments, and expensive area rugs looked like from the magazines I'd thumb through when I stood in line at the grocery store.

"Did I blink?" I was curious as to how I missed the offices of the newspaper.

"You just met her." He pointed to the older woman. "That's my aunt Marge and my aunt Louise. They both run the *Junction Journal* right here from their home."

"With the internet these days, it's so easy to grab what we need and zip it on over to the printing press, where we've got Clara and Garnett Ness not only printing off *Junction Journal*, but their boy delivers it for us." Aunt Marge was the one I'd met outside. "That's how I know who you are, Violet Rhinehammer."

"Violet Rhinehammer?" Aunt Louise took an interest and walked over to join us. "I see." She drew a curious look from Rhett to me. She wagged a finger between us. "You two know each other enough to be gallivanting around town?"

"We aren't gallivanting." I didn't like the way she said it because it insinuated something more was taking place.

"Oh, you're definitely gallivanting, because I heard from Kristine from the Jubilee Inn, and she did tell me about you two then. Of course, I had to see who was at the Shamrock Festival Stein Competition so I could get those in the paper." Aunt Louise drummed her fingers together.

"Why on earth would you print something as awful as saying I was drunk and then go as far as saying that I wasn't a good reporter?" I was on the verge of crying.

"I didn't say that." Louise drew back and looked at Marge. "Did we say that?"

"No way. I edited the piece several times after you wrote it, and we sure did not print that." Marge shook her head. "I think we might've said something about the drinking, and we might've…" She hesitated and waved her hand. "Don't you pay no attention to the *Junction Journal*. Just like you mentioned underneath your breath, we seem to be on our last legs."

For an older woman, she sure did have good hearing.

"Why is that?" I looked around and pointed to a fancy painting on the wall. "I am sure you could auction that off and get a pretty enough penny to sustain the paper."

"Why do you care?" Marge asked.

"Aunts," Rhett interrupted.

"No, Rhett." Marge put a stiff finger up to him, and he retreated. "Let her answer." She followed up with a stern look.

"You said it. The internet has everything, but the newspaper is dying, and there's something about a small newspaper where you can see the obituaries, like Jay and now Rosey." I could see the emotions in both of their faces shift when I mentioned Rosey.

It appeared they'd not yet been privy to the information.

"Along with photos of weddings, birth announcements, and such keepsakes people love to cut out, put in albums." I knew these were very old-fashioned and not keeping up with the times. I didn't keep any of those, and I was still in my twenties, but my family did.

Heck, there were groups of my friends who spent a mint on scrap-booking materials and even hosted these crazy parties.

"Are you telling me that you have decided to stop the paper because you're tired of it?" I wanted to show them I was going to question them. "I'm sure the community has pushed back on this decision."

"They don't know. We were going to tell them at the next city council meeting." Louise held her phone in her hand and was scrolling on the screen. She didn't seem to care as much for the discussion as Marge did. "They don't fund it. So it's our decision."

"Who started the *Junction Journal*? How did you get it? Is there history there?" I asked.

"It was started by Rhett's great relatives. All of them. We've kept it in the family, but now the younger Stricklands like Rhett and Matthew, to name a couple, don't want to take over the paper. They want to do other things. Noble things like keep the Village in order. Which brings me back to what you said about Rosey. Rosey Hume?" Marge looked at Louise.

"I can't seem to find anything." Louise continued to tap at the phone.

"She was found in the park fountain with a silk pocket scarf stuffed in her mouth like the one Jay Mann had. I can see you perk up. Is your heart beating fast? The thought of you not on the big story? Big news?" I began to spout off exactly how it felt when a news story broke and you were about to write about it.

"When did this happen, and why don't we know about it?" Marge asked Louise.

"Matthew did call, but I was on the phone with Kristine," Louise said with a poker face. She looked like she was trying to remain calm.

"What time was that?" I asked.

"It was around seven a.m. Why?" Louise questioned.

"Because the murder was probably right before that, and she didn't come to my room until eight a.m. That's when she told me about Rosey, so she probably didn't know when she was on the phone with you. Which brings me back to my point." I gestured to her cell phone in her hand. "It's not on there yet, but it will be soon. You still don't have the story."

"We won't even get printed out until tomorrow since it's print." Marge lifted her hands. "Hence why we don't want to keep this thing running. If you've not noticed"—her eyes assessed me—"we are a little older than you."

"Little?" Rhett teased.

Marge smiled at him. By the way they acted toward one another, I could see there was a bond there.

"Why don't you keep the paper open and have it online?" I shrugged.

"I suggested that a year ago and even built them a site." Rhett had a know-it-all look on his face. "I love you, aunts."

"If the site is there, you can do a big print once a week, and then when stuff happens, like it did with Rosey, you can get it up and even do some marketing techniques to get the AP to pick it up." It was a no-brainer.

"You mean like you did with your video from the airport?" Marge took more of an interest in my suggestion than Louise did.

"Yes. But I was actually doing it for my job, not just some willy-nilly live from my phone." I needed to make it clear to them who they were talking to. "I'm on my way to my job, and this is just a pit stop until Matthew lets me leave."

"He told me yesterday they were starting to let people leave." By the way Louise eyeballed me, I could tell she was very leery.

"He said they were going by alphabet, and by my initials, you can see where I've always fallen—at the bottom." That did garner a couple of snorts from them, letting me know I had penetrated some part of their human side. Not the stiff newspaper side that takes years to develop.

"Uncle Matthew has Violet on the case as well. Just as a liaison type," Rhett told them. "Just while she's here. You know, since she's got the skills to find things out."

"Is that right?" Marge walked next to me and slipped her hand in the crook of my elbow. "Then I have a proposition for you."

"Aunt Marge, you can't possibly." Rhett tried to intervene again without success. "Fine. I'll stay out of it."

"What if you do a little write-up about yourself, and that's how we will fix our little article about you." Marge was sweet-talking me. The whole honey thing that I was supposed to be doing to them, they were doing to me.

But I was all ears. I did love a good sweet-talking.

"Then you write up a little article about what you saw on the airplane with Jay Mann. Interview a couple of passengers before Matthew lets them leave."

"I can interview Cherise. She was with me the entire time." The mere mention of the woman made her jaw drop. "Or not."

"You can interview whomever you want. You were on the plane, and they were too." Louise had bought into whatever Marge was selling me.

I listened with caution.

"Then you make a little write-up about your thoughts as an outsider during the Shamrock Festival."

"I don't think you want me to do that because I think it's all wrong how the police officers stayed off duty during the parade while a murder had been committed. Technically it wasn't committed here, but the plane landed here." I was making sense of it in my head.

"Are you sure it wasn't committed here?" Marge asked. "Louise, get the file."

"But..." Louise hesitated.

"We can trust her." Marge had more secrets and moves up her sleeve than I'd figured. "After you look over the file, then we want you to post to the online website Rhett built for us. He can give you the login." She shot him a look.

"Put your articles on there. We will call it a guest reporting appearance until you get the green light from Matthew to leave." Louise was all too happy to add more instructions for me.

These Strickland propositions were starting to make me think something fishy was going on. I didn't know what, but there was something.

It tickled my fancy, and, well, what was one more thing to take on while I was held captive in this kookie town?

There were two things I had to agree with—use their home as my office and come for the family supper tonight.

CHAPTER FIFTEEN

There was a stack of papers in the file Marge and Louise Strickland had given me. It was something I wasn't going to be able to get through while I was there. It was going to take some time, and, well, I still had my own little investigation going, which left me zero time if I was going to go see Leni McKenna, the tailor who made the dress Rosey had on and the pocket squares found on the two victims.

I had agreed to Marge and Louise's terms only because they seemed to think the murders were related, like me, plus they had a pulse on this town. They were in the know and part of one of the largest families in Holiday Junction.

"Now what?" Rhett asked me.

"Don't you have a job to do?" I asked him in hopes he'd let me work alone.

"I'm offended, Violet Rhinehammer. I've practically given you a job to do while you are here. Do you really think Uncle Matthew would let any old person, much less an outsider, snoop around without some coaxing? Do you really think he's good at looking people up on the internet and getting phone numbers to check people out?" He told me without really telling me that it was him that got Matthew in touch with Al Hemmer. "Besides, the airport is still closed down until Matthew opens it."

"What about the other passengers cleared to leave?" I asked.

"They are being bused to Banchester. That's really where most of the flights leave in and out from."

"Yeah, that's where I was making a connection." I recalled how I'd gotten on the airport website to see if I had to hustle from one terminal to the other. It was only a tad bit bigger than Holiday Junction. "You only work at the airport security?"

"Is that a problem?" he questioned. "Does that make me less-than in your eyes?"

"Don't take it so personal." I followed him down the front steps of his aunts' home and back down the way we came, through the gates that put us back on the street. "I'm used to working alone, that's all. Not having a shadow."

"That's what Matthew wants. But if it makes you feel better, after we go see Leni, I do have to be somewhere." He didn't offer where, and I didn't ask, thinking the time away from him could be when I'd look over the file from his aunts, which I'd stuffed in my purse.

"Where is Leni's shop?" I wondered before we turned down a little side street with smaller houses with nice-size yards.

Unlike the outside of the aunts' house, these houses had all the décor for the festival. They had stringy lights in the shape of shamrocks, and some had green streamers hanging down off their house. Their front shrubs were decorated like you'd do a Christmas tree, and some even had their windows painted green.

"The Lucky Leprechaun showed up here." He grinned and pointed to a life-sized Leprechaun with a big joker-type smile on its face at the top of the street. "Every year the Lucky Leprechaun shows up in a neighborhood. That's the Lucky Leprechaun. We don't know who does it, but it happens at Easter, Thanksgiving, Christmas, any holiday with a mascot. If the mascot of that holiday shows up in your neighborhood, the residents have to host some sort of community party in celebration."

"And you want me to write an article on this?" I asked. "Or is Leni's shop in her house too?"

"No. I live down here, and we are going to get my car." He shook his head. "Violet Rhinehammer, you are so uptight. Did you know that?"

I didn't say a word, even though I wanted to. I decided to keep my mouth shut. I waited outside of his house and wondered how much money a security guard at the Holiday Junction airport made, because it looked really nice from the outside. He had minimal decorations on the front, and by minimal, I mean he had a green rug in front of his door and two green pillows on the porch swing. Other than that, he didn't have any more Shamrock Festival decorations.

He didn't invite me in, and I didn't just walk in like we did back home. It didn't stop me from glancing into the windows, and I noticed he had leather furniture and nice pieces of other things. He didn't have much on the walls as in decorations, and he didn't seem to have any knickknack-type things sitting around there.

Pretty minimalist.

When the car horn honked, I jumped around.

"I don't know why I'd be surprised you were a peeping Tom," he called from the convertible, which made me think of Fern. "You could've come in."

"I'm not a peeping Tom," I said when I got into the car and slammed the door. "It's rude not to be invited, so you should've invited me." After I belted up, I dug through my purse to get the pocket square.

"Fine. You can come in later." He put the car in drive, and my mind hung on his word "later."

Little did he know there wasn't going to be a later. I wasn't even planning on getting through the second article the aunts wanted me to write. Instead, I was going to get these murders solved and get out of this village for good.

"What can you tell me about Leni?" I wanted to be as prepared as possible so I didn't spend a lot of time trying to figure her out myself. I took the pocket square out.

"What's there to know? She's a seamstress, everyone goes to her, and she does some pieces that are sold locally." He nodded to the pocket square. "Like those."

"What about the community? Does she participate? Hang out with people? Have any enemies?" I threw out the typical journalist questions.

"Leni? Heck no. I mean, I guess she could rub anyone the wrong way, like all of us can." I wasn't sure, but I thought his comment was directed toward me.

The wind whipped into the car as the car sped towards the airport.

I could see the airport in the distance and wished I was in one of the sitting airplanes, ready to take off. The images only made me want to get this thing solved so I could get myself out of here, not rely on the police department or Rhett.

"I do appreciate you taking me around," I thanked him. "I'm sure you don't want to be by my side since Matthew thinks I need a babysitter."

"I'm good. I've enjoyed getting to know you." He kept his eyes on the road.

"Your aunts seem to be fun." It was actually very endearing to see how they interacted with him.

"They are a lot of fun. Don't expect that from my parents." He spoke a little louder as the wind continued to pick up.

"Your parents?" I asked, not ever intending to meet them.

"Yeah. They'll be at the aunts' for supper tonight." He refreshed my memory.

"Oh. That." My voice faded off, and I turned to take in the scenery of the mountains as well as the flat land where there was some cattle grazing. I wasn't even sure if he'd heard me.

The sun pelting down into the car actually felt good on my face. I leaned my head back against the headrest and closed my eyes.

"We're here, Violet." Rhett's voice brought me out of my nap. "Wake up, Sleeping Beauty."

I opened my eyes and literally had to stop to think about where I was and who I was with.

"You took a nice little nap." He'd already turned off the car, and we were parked in front of a small brick cottage-style house with moss growing down the front of it.

There were a couple of homemade benches with flowerpots lined up on top filled with gorgeous greenery and pops of colored petals.

The cottage was nestled in a wooded area, off the beaten path, from what I could tell, since I'd been asleep the entire time.

"What do I owe the pleasure?" A woman with super-curly brown hair who I recognized as the woman in the parade popped out the door. She had her hand over her eyes to shield the sun to look at us. "I heard the gravel spitting up, and here you are. Do I owe—" she started to say.

"I'm here for my friend Violet Rhinehammer." He interrupted her before she could go on with what she was trying to say. "She's got a couple of questions about your silk pocket squares."

We got out of the car. I walked over and showed her the shamrock one.

"Your place is adorable." It had so much charm to it. The roof was tin and green, making it blend nicely with the background.

"It's been a saving grace for me to have my space and not in my home." She pinched a grin. "Don't get me wrong. I love Vern, but once he hit retirement, and, well, since the holidays are far between, he gets a little bored. He wants to travel here and there and everywhere." She looked down at the pocket square. "I loved making those. Who are you giving it to?"

"Giving it to?" I asked.

"Mmhmmm." She gave a few quick nods. "I'm guessing you bought it from Emily's Treasures. That's the only place I wholesale for during any holiday event. I don't make much off her, but the customers do like my quality of work, and they take my business card. They always call for more but different patterns." She waved us to follow her inside. "That's where I make up the money I lose when I mark items down for Emily."

"I was hoping you'd be able to tell us if you knew who purchased them from Jay Mann's office. She said they were anonymously ordered and sent to Jay Mann's office. That's why I wondered if anyone from his office bought them. Or just the small community say something to you?"

"My, that's a lot to take in. I have no idea who bought them." She shook her head.

The inside of the one-room cottage was literally filled with hooks on the wall with spools and spools of yarn and threads. She had one sewing machine in the middle, where there was a piece of cloth in position under the threading needle. It had to be the fabric she'd been working on when we got there.

Leni went back to the sewing machine, where she began to sew on whatever was stuck up under the needle. She glided the fabric through with ease as the machine put in stitch after stitch.

"Are you a member of the Hibernian Society?" I knew she was because she was in the parade.

"Me and most people in the Holiday Junction." She made it sound like a very dumb question. "Until someone gets mad and quits."

"Did you go to the last meeting?" I asked. "I understand the two victims had gotten into an argument. And I was wondering what that was about."

"Two victims." She stopped the machine and put her hands in her lap, looking up at me. "They are our friends. If you're going to be here, you need to know that no matter what kind of scuffles or arguments we get into, at the end of the day, we are friends. We've been living here a very long time. They have names. Jay and Rosey."

"I'm sorry. I didn't mean to upset you." I could tell she was visibly shaken by my comments. "If you can believe it, I'm from a town smaller than Holiday Junction."

This was when I knew I had to show my personal side instead of the journalist side. Like Mae had said, be part of the community while I was here, not as if I just wanted to take something from them.

"I have no idea what they were discussing. I'm not sure what you heard, but it wasn't an argument. They were talking in the corner, and from what it looked like, it did seem to be something of importance, but I wasn't sure what. I didn't ask. It was over before the meeting got started and nothing mentioned after that."

There was a bark outside of the shop. I glanced out and noticed it was Layla Camsen again and her dog.

"Layla never shuts that dog up." Leni went back to the sewing machine. "I drown the thing out by working. It's hard since she lives on the property next door."

"Next door?" I looked at Rhett. "I thought she took the dog..." I started to tell Layla's story from this morning because I was confused about the walking path she took with her dog.

"The park is right through the woods in the back of Layla's house. Holiday Junction might look really big, but it's not. Every wooded area connects to somewhere in the Village, and the seaside is that way."

"My goodness. I'm going to need a map," I joked. I turned back to Leni. "Did you happen to hear anything unusual this morning?"

Layla stopped sewing for a brief moment. She gave a slow nod.

"I did hear this strange squeaking noise coming from the woods, but I never looked out. I was too busy trying to get ready for Mother's Day. I get a lot of requests for aprons." She pointed to a table next to the sewing machine with some finished aprons she'd made.

"You're the second person to mention the squeak."

"I was thinking it was Layla's gardener. He's always crossing the property line and planting new rose bushes for Layla since she's the president of the Ladies of Mother Earth, our local gardening club. She believes she has to have the best roses and keep her appearance up for her presidency." Leni gave me someone else to look at. "Everyone told Layla she needed to purchase a new pushcart for her gardener since she insists he work for the Ladies of Mother Earth. If you ask me, she's using the funds for her own garden and not to keep Holiday Junction gorgeous."

"Do you have his name?" I asked.

"Reed Schwindt. He pretty much keeps to himself," she said.

I wrote it down in the notebook.

"Is there any way he'd have a motive to kill Jay Mann or Rosey Hume?" I asked.

She shifted her eyes to look at Rhett then back to me. She seemed to be surprised by my question.

"Reed?" She scoffed. "Are you kidding me? Have you seen him? He's creepy and has all of those knives. Plus he was fired by Jay Mann a couple of weeks ago." Her brows lifted. "I told your uncle that he needed to look at Reed."

I knew the next person I needed to see was Reed Schwindt.

"If you remember anything else, please call me. I'm staying at the Jubilee Inn until Chief Strickland clears the airplane for takeoff." I thanked her once again before Rhett and I left.

"Here you go, Rhett." She handed him a piece of paper. "You have to get the leaky—" she started to say before he interrupted her.

"I've got it." He flashed his smile, winked, and showed me to the door as he slipped the piece of paper in his pocket.

I stood outside of the door and quickly jotted down a few notes so I wouldn't forget.

"Let's go. I've got to get to the fountain." Rhett stood next to the car and opened the door.

I hurried over and got in. I had my notebook in my lap as I went over what Leni had said.

"Now what are you thinking?" Rhett asked and pulled out of the drive.

"I'm thinking I want to talk to Layla's gardener. And if Layla heard the sound, wouldn't she recognize it?" I asked. "Or was she trying to cover up it was him but also tell us it was him?"

"Loyalties do lie deep here in Holiday Junction." Rhett told me something that I was figuring out on my own and certainly something I needed to dig in deeper on.

"What did Leni mean when she asked if you were there for something?" I didn't let the little interruption in the beginning of our visit go untouched. There was something odd that Rhett didn't want me to know. It was the second time today he'd ended some conversations that pertained to him.

"I have no idea." He shrugged, keeping his eye on the road.

"What was on the piece of paper?" I questioned.

"Let's get you back to the Jubilee Inn so you can rest up for tonight's supper at the aunts'." He flipped on the radio and turned up the music, his way of telling me he didn't want to talk.

CHAPTER SIXTEEN

I didn't head into the Jubilee Inn. I knew it was getting close to the Greening of the Fountain ceremony, and I didn't want to miss it. Not only for the fact that I'd never seen anything like this and while I was here I might'swell go, but the bigger factor was I knew from years of investigative reporting—to be honest and clear, I'd never really done a lot of it, but from what I had done—it was possible the killer could return to the scene of the crime.

It was sort of a sick way for them to see how things played out.

And by the looks of the crowd, everyone was as curious as me. I walked around with my phone on video so I could take screenshots of what I needed for my big article for the aunts for the *Junction Journal*.

I made my way to the front of the fountain and slowly turned around in a circle to take in the masses of people that'd come out to see the annual festivity. Leni along with Layla was in a huddle with a couple of people on one side of the fountain. On the opposite side was Rhett, Chief Strickland, Fern, and the two aunts.

I shifted my focus to the far side of the fountain, where I recognized Kristine, Cherise, and Patrick. I found it very interesting Cherise and Patrick weren't next to Rhett.

There appeared to be a heavier police presence than there was earlier, and all of the police seemed to be alert. When I heard the Irish band playing, I looked up and saw Fern leading the small parade down the large sidewalk. They appeared to be going to the fountain.

She had on another fancy green dress with a huge sash stating her title. A few times she bent down to greet little girls in awe of her as well as blow a few kisses in the air to men whistling at her.

Our eyes locked when she passed, and she smirked before she continued to lead the band, the group of men who all wore Hibernian sashes, and a couple of women and a little girl, who I assumed were Jay Mann's family.

Melissa Mann's eyes were dark underneath, and the red line on the bottom lid showed she'd been crying, though she was trying to put on a brave face. Their daughter didn't seem to be able to have that in her as the tears continued to flow in silence. The granddaughter kept hold of her mother's hand. From what I understood, she was ill, and from her thin, skeletal body, I could tell what I'd heard was true.

My emotions were already on high alert, forcing me to look down when they passed by me. The rush of sadness formed like a hard ball in my throat. I gulped several times to dampen the feelings before the tears started to burn in my eyes.

It was a heartbreaking scene on such a wonderful day for the community.

Following the Manns, I noticed another man with a bouquet of daisies dyed green. He, too, looked as if he'd been crying, and I wondered if it was Rosey's husband.

He kept his eyes on the fountain and didn't look around, so I wasn't forced to look away when he passed. There was one last man in a kilt holding a baton, signaling the end of the small parade to the ceremony.

I took out my notebook and jotted down the emotions, not only what I was feeling but my observation of the family. It was going to be rare material for my article and something I wanted to put into my broadcast I was sending Richard Stone.

While the people partaking in the ceremony got settled and the microphone got set up, the crowd gathered around the fountain. I took a few snapshots that might or might not go into the article, but they would give me the scene to help me describe it.

"Welcome to the Greening of the Fountain!" The crowd roared to life as the man spoke into the microphone. "We would like to welcome Mayor Paisley"—he gestured to the side, where I hadn't noticed Kristine and Paisley had taken a spot—"as well as our city council members."

While he rattled off the city council members' names, I weaved myself in and out of the crowd so I could get as close as possible to the front to get a few snapshots. Mayor Paisley was dressed in a little dress made with a four-leaf clover pattern. It was the cutest thing, and a photo of her was a must.

"As you know, we have lost two of our Hibernian Society members, and their families are here today in recognition and support." The man gestured to the group behind him. "Zack Hume, the husband of Rosey Hume, our society secretary, will now lay flowers in the fountain in her memory."

A silence fell over the crowd. There were a few sniffles echoing around me. Everyone's eyes focused on the ground, and I took a few photos of Zack Hume walking up to the fountain and placing the flowers in the fountain.

He took a step back into the parade group.

There were a few more moments of silence before the man stepped back up to the microphone.

"As you know, Jay Mann was the master of ceremonies today. I'm honored to be able to step into Jay's shoes. I know they are going to be hard to fill, and I will try my best." Immediately Jay Mann's family stepped up to join the man, along with another man dressed in a kilt with a society sash on. He held out a book of sorts, as though they were going to do a swearing-in ceremony.

"Please repeat after me," the man with the book said. "I, state your name."

"I, Vern McKenna." His words popped my eyes open.

Vern McKenna as in Leni's husband? I wondered, scanning the crowd to see if she was there.

Deep in the crowd I saw her standing with a huge smile on her face.

Out of the corner of my eye, there was a movement. I looked back and noticed Zack Hume had left the ceremony, walking down the sidewalk that led to the seaside.

The swearing-in ceremony was giving Vern the presidential seat of the society.

"As your newly elected president, I'd like to have a moment of silence for

Jay Mann." Vern had taken the ceremony over and led the group in a little prayer before he introduced Melissa, Sandra, and Dana Mann.

None of them spoke but only gave a slight wave with a solemn expression on their faces. My heart dropped looking at them, and I captured the moment on video.

"Since it's my privilege to do the honors of greening the fountain, this year I'd like to hand the duties over to Jay's legacy, his granddaughter, Dana Mann." By the way the Mann family was taken by surprise, Vern had not informed them of his plan.

The crowd erupted, but the little girl didn't understand. Sandra bent down and whispered into her daughter's ear as she pointed to the small green water pitcher. The little girl's eyes grew, her head bobbled, and her body began to bounce in excitement.

The society members gathered around the fountain as Sandra and Melissa stood on each side of little Dana, both holding her hands as they led her up to the edge of the fountain. The bagpipes rang out while the little girl dropped her family's grip and took the water can from Vern.

He bent over and said a few words to the little girl. Dana nodded in agreement before Vern straightened up and gave her the go-ahead.

Melissa and Sandra, though they still looked grief stricken, had some pride glowing on their faces as they watched Jay's granddaughter fulfill something so special to Holiday Junction.

My phone captured the moment, and in no time, all the water was green.

"Excuse me. Excuse me." I made my way past the crowd and scanned the sidewalk, going toward the seaside. I was looking for Zack Hume, but he was gone.

I found myself continuing toward the seaside and looked back at the crowd at the fountain, where the bagpipes had started to play. It looked as though Melissa Mann was going to speak, and though I wanted to hear what she had to say, I wanted my own interview.

I wasn't sure how to get it, so I took off to the next best interview. I was in search of Zack Hume.

CHAPTER SEVENTEEN

The sun had begun to set when I popped over the hill away from the fountain. I knew I was on limited time to find Zack because I had to be at a dinner with the aunts.

The sidewalk led to a quiet stretch of beach, where the water on the horizon shimmered with a vibrant white glow.

I looked back at my surroundings and noticed the illumination on the sandy cliffs. Just over that was the small Village.

"Wow." I stood at the base of the cliffs and noticed the rocky reef gradually exposed by the retreating tide.

Soon darkness would begin to fall since we still hadn't had daylight savings time. Seagulls and sandpipers brought me back to my main purpose. Find Zack.

Too bad I wouldn't be here long enough to soak in the last glimmers of daylight, I thought to myself as I took in the beautiful hillside views and the sound of the ocean as it met the shore.

I headed down the sidewalk along the street, where there were a few shops, before I slipped into a small bar called Happy Birthday Bar.

The name made me smile as it, too, went along with what seemed to be the theme around here.

The bar looked as if it were an old gas station. The large garage-style doors were pushed up and let the breeze off the sea float in and the music on the jukebox flow out.

There was the sound of laughter and chatter from people oblivious to what was going on over the hill behind them, or they just didn't care.

"Hey, you!" A familiar voice I recognized, Cherise, called out to me when I stepped through the garage door.

I looked up, scanning the tops of heads to find her. She was sitting at the far end of the bar, waving me over.

Along the way, I stopped to look at the photos on the wall. They were of patrons of the bar, who wore the paper cone birthday hats, with a shot glass with a lit candle inside lifted up next to the smiling faces.

"Fancy seeing you here." I sat down on the empty stool next to her and plopped my purse on top of the counter. "I thought you'd be at the big fountain ceremony."

"Nope. My people are right here." She picked up the shot glass and pushed it around in the air before she flung the liquid into her mouth. "Happy birthday!"

"Happy birthday!" the patrons of the bar shouted back.

"It's your birthday?" I asked.

"No." She cackled. "But someone has a birthday today, so we celebrate here. Do you want it to be your birthday? You get a birthday hat, song, and a photo for the wall."

"No. I'm good. Not much of a drinker," I told her.

"Oh, I beg to differ. You beat Fern in the beer competition," she reminded me.

"That was a rare occasion," I confessed.

"So you were trying to impress the most eligible bachelor in Holiday Junction, Rhett Strickland?" She had a little slur to her speech, making me wonder how long she'd been at the Happy Birthday Bar.

"Most eligible bachelor? What makes an airport security guard with a rooster as his boss so eligible?" I asked.

She flung her head forward, and her eyes shot up, looking at me from underneath her brows.

With the shot glass still in her hand, she pointed her finger at me. "Are you telling me that you being the big-time investigative reporter you are had no idea Rhett Strickland is the richest man in the Village? He owns a lot of property."

"Are you sure we are talking about the same Rhett Strickland?" I questioned.

"What can I get you?" the bartender yelled over the music at me. I waved him off.

"Oh yeah. Me and Rhett go way back, until I cheated on him with his brother Patrick, who doesn't have a pot to piss in." She laughed out loud before she chased that shot with a swig of green beer.

"You what?" I put my hand in the air and waved to the bartender, pointing at the green beer Cherise had and indicating to get me one.

"Thatagirl." Her words slurred together.

"When in Rome." I shrugged, knowing I needed to pump her for more information, and from what I'd seen here in Holiday Junction, being part of the group was how I was going to get information I needed.

"Oh yeah, he owns most of the rental property. Like all of it." She held up her beer stein for me to clink for a cheers after the bartender slid mine down the bar, spilling most of it on its journey.

"Does he own Leni's sewing shop out near the countryside?" I asked.

"Mmmhhhmm," she ho-hummed.

"And you said you cheated on him with his brother?" I had to hit each bullet point one at a time as I pieced together my interactions I'd had with Rhett.

No wonder Leni had given him that piece of paper. I wondered why he didn't tell me who he was and found it interesting.

"Yep. Patrick is the black sheep of the family. He was exiled away from them a long time ago and didn't get a dime when none of them died. He does talk to the aunts but not Matthew." She rolled her eyes. "Patrick is my soul mate." She tapped her chest.

"He talks to Rhett though, right?" I asked because Rhett had told me what a great band Patrick's band was and how I had to go to the concert during the festival before we saw Cherise there.

"Yep. They are really tight. Don't let anyone fool you." She giggled. "I work a lot, so it's easy for the brothers to get along."

98

"Are you telling me Rhett still has a thing for you, and that's why he didn't want to stay around to listen to Patrick's band?" I asked.

"Look at you all inquiring-minds-want-to-know. You have a thing for him, don't you?" She smirked.

"No. Not a thing. I'm out of here on your first flight out, remember?" I knew she wouldn't remember any of this conversation.

"I remember. I also know the look of a Rhett Strickland lovesick woman, and my dear, I hate to tell you, but you've got that look." She got so close to my face our noses almost touched. "The look on Fern's face. That's the look on your face, so when you beat Fern in the beer competition, it was like you beat her in the Rhett competition, which is way more important to her. Wait until you meet the aunts. You think Fern is rough—they are brutal."

"I have met them, and let's say that they gave me some information to help me get out of here before my birthday, which is a few months away." I added the last part so she didn't signal to the bar that it was my birthday.

I opened my purse and pulled out the file Louise and Marge had given me along with the *Junction Journal*.

"Oh goodness, they've got that old rag still out. They need to drag that thing out into their mansion's backyard and shoot it. Put it out of its misery." She made me smile.

"I'm not saying you're wrong, but I do know I made an agreement with them for this file." I wagged it at her.

"Let's look." She grabbed it. "Shall we?" And she opened it. "Looks like they are doing their own little investigation. Here is the flight list."

"I asked Chief Strickland for that." I looked at the list along with Cherise.

"He is going to give it to his sister and wife before you," she said and drank the last of her beer.

"Sister and wife?" I wasn't sure I was following her.

"His wife is Aunt Marge." She put an emphasis on the name. "She's the worse one of the two aunts. Very judgy."

It was another thing Rhett Strickland hadn't told me. He wasn't obligated to tell me anything, but you'd think he'd introduce her by telling me she was Chief Strickland's wife.

No wonder they needed me to investigate. It would be a conflict of interest if she stuck her nose into the information. I'd been had by the aunts, and I felt the sting.

"You know, I shouldn't be telling you this, and maybe it's the liquid courage, but I should be fired for what happened to Jay Mann." She downed the beer.

Cherise and the bartender must've had some sort of agreement, because he continued to give her a new green beer after she'd finished the last.

"Why?" I looked down the passenger list and noticed Jay's name wasn't on it.

"I didn't clear the airplane before taking off. Something Jim Dixon checks off his list. As the head flight attendant, I'm supposed to go through the cabin every morning, every night, and between flights to make sure everyone was gone. I didn't do that, so I'm not even sure how long Jay's body had been there. But if you go back to the flight documents, I verbally told Jim I did these activities. So here I sit drowning my sorrows as I try to figure out how I tell the NTSB my story now that I heard they've been called in." Her words left me with my jaw dropped wide open.

She had referred to the National Transportation Safety Board, which would look at the flight now that there was a death. But if the death was nicely packaged up and solved, they would take that and close the case.

"If the NTSB gets here before the murder is solved, it could be weeks before I can leave." Worry lines increased on my forehead as my heartbeat quickened. "I've got to find Zack Hume and get an interview with Melissa Mann. I need to find out why Jay was on the plane and not on the list."

"Who knows." She shrugged. "Zack. He's right over there." She snorted a burp, and my eyes followed her finger over to the corner of the bar, way far away from the doors, to a silhouette in the corner. "I can get you an interview with Melissa. Sandra and I were best friends growing up. She moved, but we still keep in touch. She's in here, you know. Sad."

"Just how can you get me an interview?" I asked.

"I'll call," she said.

"You won't even remember this conversation," I told her.

"Yes, I will." She crisscrossed her fingers on her chest. "I feel bad for the Manns. They were so happy to tell their story about how they met when Melissa worked at the city clerk in the driver's license department as a teenager. Jay came in at sixteen to get his license, and that's how they met. Cute, right?"

"Wow, they've been together a long time." I knew this was a great love story to add to the article. Give Jay a little personal touch with family and love, which led to love of Holiday Junction and serving on the Hibernian board.

"Sandra was the cake, and Dana was the icing on their love story." Cherise sighed. "Something all of us want."

Cherise's mood had turned south, and I didn't want to be part of it. I needed to keep my head on straight, and that meant I had to talk to Zack.

"If you'll excuse me, I am going to go talk to Zack. Don't forget to get me that interview with Melissa Mann." I gathered the contents of the file and picked up the nearly full beer so I wouldn't look so out of place and headed over to Zack's table in the dark corner.

"I'm not interested." He greeted me with cold eyes.

"I'm not either." I sat down. "I'm with the *Junction Journal* and the *National News*."

He looked up at me.

"You're that reporter." He recognized me and shook his finger my way. "Aren't you? I can't tell much without all the black on your face."

"Not my finest moment finding a dead body, but hey, you can tell I had some emotions, which is why I came here to see you." I set the beer and the file on top of the table. "I'm looking into Jay Mann's case and now your wife's. I would appreciate anything you could tell me so we can bring her killer to justice."

His finger circled the rim of the beer mug, and his chin moved back and forth as though he was thinking about what I was saying.

"What do you want to know? She was a good wife. She was loyal even when it was hard for her to be." He sounded a little bitter. I sat and listened, careful not to interrupt him so he wouldn't stop talking. "She was proud to be in the women's part of the Hibernians as well as Jay Mann's loyal secretary..." His words fell off.

"Do you think she was murdered because she knew something about Jay Mann?" I asked.

"Seems like it, but I don't know why. I'm just blessed she gave me the last fifteen years. I chased her fifteen years before that." He smiled at the fond memory.

"I'm sorry. I really am. But do you know anyone who might've had motive?" I asked.

"No one. Rosey didn't see eye to eye with Layla Camsen, but I don't think it was enough for Layla to kill her." He reminded me of Layla's gardener.

"Again, I'm sorry for your loss." I gathered my things and walked back over to Cherise. "Do you know where I can find Reed Schwindt?"

"The Village maintenance man?" She leaned back with a curious snarl curled on her nose. "The odd-job guy?"

"That's him," I confirmed. "What do you know about him?"

"He did a lot of odd jobs for the Hibernian members at their homes." Her brows shot up. "But that's not a reason to kill somebody. About a week ago I was in here and he came in asking if there were any jobs that needed doing around the bar because he'd gotten fired from the society."

"Really?" I found that to be interesting. "He also did some work for the airport too."

"Yep. He is creepy with the old wooden cart he pushes around, and all those knives he sharpens gives me the heebie-jeebies." She shook.

"Do you know where I can find him?" I knew what Cherise told me gave him motive to have killed anyone who fired him, because it impacted his livelihood. Plus there were several accounts of hearing his squeaky cart.

"He's probably down at the jiggle joint about this time." She looked at her bare wrist as if there were a watch there.

"Where's the jiggle joint?" I asked.

She laughed. "About two blocks thataway."

CHAPTER EIGHTEEN

"Jiggle joint," I repeated to myself over and over as I approached the two-block mark where Cherise had told me I could find Reed, the maintenance man.

He'd been fired recently by a few of the Hibernian members as their handyman, and one of them was Jay Mann, the first victim. His murder seemed to be related to the second victim's murder.

It was also brought to my attention how he pushed a cart around the Village and kept knives, and I'm not talking dull knives either. From what I'd heard, he'd kept them nice and sharp.

"High-end gentleman's club?" I read a sign that pointed down an alley-way. My jaw dropped. "Jiggle joint." I shook my head at how naive I was for not realizing Cherise was talking about some sort of strip club.

I'd never in my life been to one of these, and I sure didn't know what to expect.

"It's for the good of your career, Violet," I told myself. "Buck up, girl. California is probably worse than this."

I didn't know anything about California other than they seemed to have a lot of big cities, forward-moving fashion trends, and really rich people. I'd seen photos all the time in the gossip papers with all the celebrities in their fancy homes and even the club with the bunny suits, so what was the big deal? I might'swell get my feet wet now so when I did have to do some big investigative work, I'd be prepared.

Yep. That's what I told myself right before I opened the door.

The stench of hot stuffy air and stagnant beer mixed with cheap cologne, hairspray, and smoke hit me as soon as I swung the door open. I sucked in a deep breath and held it once I walked in.

There was no way I could last in here more than two minutes. Okay, ten tops.

The strobe lights flickered to the beat of the overly loud music. There were shadowy silhouettes of a few patrons sitting around the stage at small round tables, watching the moon-shaped stage where there were two poles floor to ceiling.

Apparently that's where the talent performed. It must've been between acts because the stage was empty and the waitstaff was walking around with trays, taking orders.

"Honey, we aren't hiring," the bartender yelled at me.

"I'm not looking for a job," I told him and pulled out one of my old business cards from my purse. "I'm looking for Reed Schwindt."

"What? He stiff you on a job?" The bartender wiped down the counter, making me a clean spot to put my bag.

"No." I handed him the card.

He tilted it to the side for what little bit of light was in the place to hit it so he could read it.

A huge grin crossed his lips.

"You're that reporter. Honey, I sure didn't recognize you, but if you want a job, you got it. People are talking all about you, and, well, they'd pay to come see you." He slid my card next to the vodka bottle. "Can I get you a drink? On the house."

"No, thank you. I don't drink." I leaned in closer so I could talk to him without screaming over the MC, who was introducing the next talent.

"You don't?" He reached underneath the bar and pulled out the *Junction Journal*. "According to the journal, you sure did drink Fern under the table."

"That was a rare occasion." I glared at him and tried to take the paper, but he obviously anticipated my move, grabbing it before I could.

"What do you want then?" He leaned over, and his breath smelled of beer. "With Reed?"

"I am doing an investigation piece for the *Junction Journal*." I could see the hesitation on his face. "I know. Why would I help a paper who clearly railroaded me?" I nodded to the paper in his hands. "Anyways, I am working with them while I'm here. A reporter such as myself can't stop the tickle of the investigation just because I'm stuck here. I decided to take them up on their offer for me to join them."

"Is that right?" The right side of his lip curled. "I'll be right back."

He moved down the bar, leaving me alone with a couple of patrons at the bar, huddled over their drinks with their eyes on me.

"Good show tonight," I told them, lifting my chin to the stage and looking over my shoulder to see exactly what was going on. I didn't care for what I saw, so I turned back to the bar.

"Say, aren't you that reporter?" one of the men asked.

"Violet Rhinehammer." I took the opportunity to introduce myself since I could see the bartender using his cell phone. No doubt checking out my story. "I'm doing an exposé on the murders here in Holiday Junction, and I'd love for you to give me a statement concerning the two victims, Jay Mann and Rosey Hume. And if you know of anyone who had motive to kill them?"

"Nah." The one man slowly shook his head and looked at the other guy.

"Nope. I bet Jay did something to someone, and since Rosey was his secretary, she knew some secrets that someone didn't want out. Like you southerners say, sweep it under the rug." He eased the beer mug up to his lips and took a sip.

"How did you know I'm southern?" I asked.

"Honey, you're a stranger around here. Holiday Junction might be a little bit bigger city than where you're from, but the gossip isn't different. My wife told me all about you before you left the airport that day with Rhett Strickland."

My gut stung with a little bit of shock when I realized that everyone in Holiday Junction knew every single thing about me.

"Speaking of the Stricklands. I'm working for the *Junction Journal* while I'm here, so I'm using my keen investigating skills to find the killer." I said it with pride and confidence. "I'm actually here looking for Reed."

"He was here and fixed the sign, but he's gone now."

"What's your name?" I asked, taking my notepad out of my purse.

"The Easter Bunny." He elbowed his friend.

"Let me guess," I said to the other one. "You're Santa Claus."

"Me?" He snickered and swiveled his back to me. "Can't you see my wings? I'm the tooth fairy."

Both men got a big kick out of making fun of me.

"Owen. Shawn." The bartender had rejoined us. "Are you giving our new reporter a hard time?"

"I was just about to ask her what she wanted in her Easter basket." The man who claimed he was the Easter bunny had a huge grin on his face.

"Owen, that's not nice. Apologize to the lady." The bartender gave him a stern look then shifted his eyes to the beer.

"Fine. I'm sorry. Welcome to Holiday Junction," he said before he muttered under his breath, "I'm only sorry because Darren won't give me another beer."

"Darren?" My ears had perked, as had my brows. I looked at the bartender. "Well, Darren, did the sisters of the *Junction Journal* confirm my identity?"

"They sure did. Darren Strickland. Nephew to the family. You've created quite the stir in our happy clan." Now that I took a good look at him, there was a slight resemblance to Rhett. "I understand my cousin, Rhett, has been awfully kind to you."

"I think he wants the killer to be found just as much as I do. Which brings me to why I'm here." I flipped the page in the notebook in hopes of getting some real information about Reed.

"She's asking for Reed," Shawn said and stood up, dropping a couple of bucks on the counter.

"It's my understanding he'd be here." I wrote down the names of Owen, Shawn, and cousin Darren, just so it would look like I was really writing something down.

"You think Reed had something to do with the murders?" Darren asked, put a stein under the spout of a beer tap, and pulled it to fill it up. He placed it on a tray and filled up two more so the waitstaff could come get the order.

"From what I hear, he was fired recently and has a motive. Not only that, but he also has a lot of knives, and both victims were killed with a knife." I flipped the empty notebook pages back and forth like I was reading from them.

I was really playing the part, and I could tell he was trying to see what I had written down.

"A couple of eyewitnesses recalled hearing squeaky wheels coming from the fountain about the time of Rosey Hume's murder. I'd like to talk to him about that. Do you know where I can find him?" I put my pen to the notebook.

"You tell me where I can find some of that invisible ink." Darren knew I didn't have anything written down. "And I'll give you all the information I know."

"Fine." I shoved the notebook back in my purse, giving up the professional act. "You seem like a hardworking, decent guy. I'm only trying to help out your uncle, Chief Strickland. He asked me to help, and you know what? I have nothing to do, so I'm just trying to keep busy until I can leave."

"Honesty. I like that in a person." He paused as though he was thinking about what to say to me.

"Thank you." I smiled, giving him a minute to get his thoughts together. "I do appreciate any help you can offer me. I know in a place like this you hear a lot. Especially from men who have loose lips after drinking. I'm sure your uncle has already asked you if you heard anything."

"No. He only goes by the book, and he'd never even think about using common sense to get some clues." His demeanor softened. "Reed didn't do it. I would bet my jiggle joint on it."

His grin was infectious and made me grin.

"That's what Cherise called it, right?" he asked, even though I didn't have to answer because he knew. "What about Vern McKenna? He and Reed are pretty tight, and from what I understand, they've been seen together at all hours of the day and night. But I know Reed. There's no way he did it. Plus Vern has access to Reed's cart, and yeah, it does squeak. Reed told me once after I asked if I could grease up the wheels how he liked them squeaking so people could hear him coming. Now, if he were going to kill someone, he's smart enough to leave that cart behind. Have you checked out Vern's secret shed in the woods behind Leni's sewing shop?"

"Nope. I didn't even know about it."

"Rhett didn't tell you?" He scoffed.

"No. He didn't." I wondered why he didn't tell me or even point it out when we were at the shop. "He doesn't tell me a lot of things."

"I bet he left out the part where he applied to the Hibernian Society and they denied him." That was some news to chew on.

"Let me guess, Jay Mann was the president?" I knew the answer since Jay had been the president for a long time.

"Bingo." He gave me the handgun movement with his hand, indicating I was right on target. "And Jay Mann refused to let Sandra go out with him. He's not a fan of Jay Mann's."

I wasn't sure, but I really did feel like Darren was selling me the possibility Rhett Strickland should be looked at as a suspect.

"Vern and Rhett are tight." He crossed his fingers. "Like father-and-son tight."

"And Vern was just named Hibernian president." My thought shifted back to how happy Leni was to see Rhett and then the list of items she needed done for the shop.

"Vern is also his godfather. See the connection with Reed?" he asked.

The ringing phone took his attention from our conversation.

I flipped the notepad and started to scribble down the entwined relationships between Vern, Reed, and Rhett. Rhett had been burned in the past by Jay Mann because Jay wouldn't let Sandra go out with Rhett. Then Rhett's father had died, which I had no idea how, but it didn't matter. Vern was Rhett's godfather and wanted to see Rhett succeed.

But according to Cherise, Rhett had so much money he didn't know what to do with it. Money didn't give someone busy time, which was why Rhett wanted to be in the Hibernians, but Jay shot it down. Not only that, with Jay out of the way, Vern would be appointed as president, where he could approve Rhett for membership.

And if Vern and Reed were as tight as Darren claimed, it would be easy for Vern to have access to the cart so people would hear it. The nosy people who would recognize the sound would hear it.

This would be premeditated murder.

My mind was going faster than my hand could write.

Vern would also know that Reed was fired from doing work around Jay Mann's house, and I couldn't help but wonder if Rosey did know too much, making her the last victim so Vern could go through with his plan for his godson?

I tapped the head of the pen on the notebook and knew it was time I find that shed of Vern McKenna's.

After flipping the notebook shut, I threw it and the ink pen down into my bag.

If I timed it right, I could take the path along the wooded area back and check out the shed before I headed back in time for supper at the aunts'.

There I knew I could confront Rhett in front of his uncle and get him arrested right then and there.

"Violet!" I heard Darren call my name just as I reached for the door handle. I turned around. He had the phone cradled between his shoulder and ear. "Chief Strickland is my dad."

CHAPTER NINETEEN

There seemed to be a lot more depth to the Strickland family than I knew or even cared to know about. If I were living here, I might've tried to dig deeper into why these men all seemed to have some sort of family issues. There was some deep sort of feeling there, but I had no time to figure any of that out.

If Darren was right and Vern was the suspect his father should look at, then I was going to go there right now and get the answers so I could be out of here on the first flight in the morning.

When I looked away from the seaside, the mountainous background surrounded Holiday Junction. If my memory was correct, the fountain was the opposite way from Leni's shop, and the wooded country area would be toward the right.

Just past the seaside shops, which were your typical little hobby shops for tourists, was where the land gave way to sandy streets with small cottage houses.

I decided to walk down one going away from the sea and toward the mountains. Though I was in a little bit of a hurry since I was already going to be late for dinner, I still took in the scenery and noticed all the cute clapboard houses that lined each side of the street.

The sound of gentle waves lapping against the beach was behind me.

Each cottage home was painted a different vibrant color. Many had boats or motorized water vehicles parked under a car porch, along with a segment of chain-link fence to divide the properties.

With each step, I thought of how nice it must be to live in Holiday Junction with what seemed like the perfect setting to live, where you could pop over the hill and get a healthy dose of sun, sand, and seaside bliss.

My arrival as I passed along the houses was met with some barks and some stares from the homeowners, but mostly with a wave and friendly smile.

Holiday Junction was honestly pure charm. Too bad the murders were looming over such a festive time here.

At the end of the sandy street was a rickety bridge built out of boards. Clearly the salty conditions had taken a toll on it, as seen from the rusty nails popping up. I took one last look back and knew time was slipping past as the sun was starting to kiss the edge of the ocean.

I hurried down the sandy path and noticed each step of the way, the walkway started to turn into more grass and clay, taking me deeper and deeper into the woods.

I jerked my head when I heard a bark. I stopped to listen. It was definitely Monty, Layla Camsen's dog, which told me I was near their home. That meant I was near Leni's sewing shop. The building and land Rhett Strickland owned.

I whistled out to keep Monty barking. He would lead me right to the area I needed to be in order to find the shed. Darren said it was located on Rhett's property that Leni rented, and it did make sense because she was married to Vern.

Just like I knew he would, Monty continued to bark as I headed his way through the thick of the woods along the beaten path. I wasn't sure if it was a path made by woodland animals, but from the continued marks that resembled the marks of wheels, I could only come to the conclusion this was the path Reed took while pushing his cart.

The path reminded me of my home in Normal, Kentucky, which was located in the Daniel Boone National Forest. We had thousands of trails just like this, and it was kind of nice to feel safe for a moment.

The snap of a dried branch brought me out of my thoughts. I looked ahead and saw a small shed-like building with a tall, lanky man with thin-ning hair walking out of the shed. When he turned around, I recognized him as Vern McKenna from the Greening of the Fountain ceremony.

I jumped behind a large oak, placing my back against it in hopes Vern had not heard me. His footsteps were going away from me, which calmed my breathing a little more, and when I heard a car door slam, I knew I was in the clear for the moment.

When I leaned around the tree, the shed was on a beeline in front of me, and Monty was barking to the left of me.

"Good boy, Monty," I whispered for him to hear me when I hurried down the path to the shed. "You did a good job."

Monty's ears perked up, and he moved on to smelling something.

I opened the door to the shed and was met with the odor of paint. The opened spray cans littered the ground. As the last bit of sunlight filtered through the door, my eyes scanned up past the paint, and there was a large piece of wood cut out in the form of an Easter basket filled with lilies.

Suddenly a shadow draped the inside. I jumped around.

"What are you doing here? Who are you?" Vern stood at the door of the shed. "You." He wagged a finger. "You're that reporter."

"And I'm here to get answers about the real truth behind Jay Mann and Rosey Hume and your hand in their deaths." I took a step back when he stalked inside.

His hands were covered in paint. He drew a handkerchief from his back pocket and began to wipe them.

"What kind of investigative reporter are you?" He shook his head. "I have no reason or motive to have killed either of them."

"Then you can answer a few questions for me." Nervously I fiddled with my purse and dug down to get my notepad and pen. "I understand you were seen with the two of them. I also know you are Rhett Strickland's godfather, who would do anything for him, which is pretty convenient seeing how Rhett was denied membership to the Hibernian Society under Jay's presidency."

"You honestly think Rhett cares enough about the society to become a member that we'd have to kill someone to make it happen?" Vern continued to shake his head like a disappointed father. "I don't think so."

"How do you explain being with Rosey and Jay at night?" I asked.

"Because I am the Merry Maker, and Jay was going to take over for me."

My face scrunched up. "The Merry Maker?"

"Lucky Leprechaun, Father Time, Mother's Day Basket." He pointed to the large wooden basket.

"You are the secret person who puts out the big figures and picks the neighborhood." I remembered Rhett telling me about it.

"Yes. I'm getting older, and I simply can't continue to carry these around and at night. I've gotten Reed to help me out a lot, but Jay is—was much younger than me. He was going to take over, like I said. A few days ago, he told me he wasn't going to be able to commit to it because Dana was sick and he wasn't sure he'd even be here during all the holidays. Rosey said that she would do it and get her husband to help her."

"So you were showing them the ropes?" I asked.

"Yes. I didn't feel comfortable with it being just me and Rosey. I asked Reed to come, but he wasn't able to because he was doing some work for the police department that night." Vern walked past me, picked up a bottle of white spray paint off the floor, and painted another lily.

"That's why the police department hasn't arrested Reed, because he has an alibi." I wondered why Chief Strickland hadn't told me this little bit of information.

"Unfortunately, I'm going to have to go to the police now that you are here. They must think I killed Jay and Rosey." He threw the spray can down. "I guess I don't have to finish this because everyone will know I'm the guy." He laughed. "Leave it to me to break this hundred-year-old tradition for Holiday Junction. Leni is going to kill me."

I looked back at the big basket for Mother's Day and sighed.

"Chief Strickland hasn't mentioned to me that you're a suspect. I've been gathering leads and, well, the squeaky wheel of Reed's cart led me to information about you. Now you're telling me Reed was at the police station working, so that eliminates him as well." I flipped through my notes. "Darren sure did have my wheels turning."

"Darren Strickland?" Vern laughed. "My first words of advice are not to trust anything that comes out of Darren Strickland's mouth."

"Funny. He said the same thing about you." Not really in those words, but as he talked about Rhett, I could tell Darren didn't trust Rhett or Vern.

Again, something ran deep between Rhett and Darren, but I didn't care. I was too busy trying to get myself out of here. Not solve some family tiff.

"Speaking of the Stricklands." I shoved the notebook back in my purse, feeling a little defeated. "I've got to go. I was invited to supper by the aunts."

"Interesting. I've known them all my life—as you know, I'm Rhett's godfather—and I've never been invited for dinner." He made it sound like I was special. "You must be special."

I cackled out loud. "You've got to be kidding me. They don't want me around. Have you ever heard keep our friends close but keep enemies closer?" There was an eerie pause between us.

"What are you thinking?" Vern asked.

"I'm thinking I'm on to something the Stricklands don't want me to know." I gripped the straps of my purse, knowing the aunts had given me the file, and wondered if it was just a wild-goose chase they were sending me on.

"It wouldn't be the first reporter the aunts got rid of." His words sent chills down my back.

CHAPTER TWENTY

It was all set in my head when I left Vern at the shed to finish up the upcoming Merry Maker's secret job that I was going to head straight over to the Strickland mansion and confront the aunts about what they were hiding.

The one thing I knew was that none of the young men in the family got along at all. Patrick and Rhett were at odds due to Cherise, or so it seemed. Darren and Rhett, well, heck, I had no idea why they didn't get along. The two instances had one person in common.

Rhett Strickland.

Though Vern said that he didn't kill Jay and Rosey, he sure didn't exonerate Rhett Strickland himself. Even Cherise had said it—Rhett was the most eligible bachelor. Rhett sure was keeping tabs on me.

Who did he think he was? I was smarter than that. I was Violet Rhinehammer, *National News* correspondent, and the little attention he was giving me wasn't going to get me off track. If anything, it put me on high alert. Which also begged the question of whether Chief Strickland was on the up-and-up.

It wasn't common but also not unheard of for people in authority to do things to cover up something for a family member. Sending a fine investigative reporter like myself on a wild-goose chase would be a way to keep me busy running around Holiday Junction, knowing I was going to hit a dead end.

Then the aunts gave me this useless file?

My phone rang. I continued to walk and pulled my phone out from my bag.

"Hello?" I didn't recognize the number.

"Is this Violet Rhinehammer, *the* big-time investigative reporter?" Cherise cackled from the other end of the phone in her drunken-stupor voice, emphasizing a couple of words to mock me.

"Funny, Cherise." I stopped so I could concentrate now more than ever. "Did you get me that interview?"

I still wanted to talk to Melissa Mann and get her take on who she thought would want her husband dead.

"Sure did. Right now." Cherise rattled off the address. "They are at home now. Sandra said they were going to be busy the next few days getting the funeral arrangements ready for her dad, but you can go there now."

"Now?" My ear and shoulder hugged the phone while I took out my notepad to scribble down the Manns' address.

"Now or never." Cherise hiccupped. "And this will make you happy."

"What's that?" I asked.

"The NTSB cleared us for takeoff tomorrow night, so it seems like you're out of here." She hiccupped again. "That means I've got to call Patrick to come get me so I can get to bed."

"Really?" My heart raced, and for a second I thought about not going to see the Manns or going to the Strickland supper, but the little investigative reporter told me I had to find out what I could so I could report back to Richard Stone, who had yet to call me back from all of my voicemails I'd left him.

I wasn't too worried about him not getting in touch with me. He knew I was stuck here and working hard. He had to have been doing some investigating on his end too.

"That's great news, Cherise. Thank you!" I looked at the notebook where I'd written down the address. "I'll see you on the airplane tomorrow!"

She mumbled a few things before the phone went silent.

Quickly I pulled up the map app on my phone and plugged in the

Manns' address. The Stricklands were going to have to wait. Their little wild-goose chase they'd sent me on was going to be a joke on them. I was going to find something out. Something of importance, and I was sure Melissa or Sandra Mann would be able to give me some names.

"Richard, thank goodness I got in touch with you." I couldn't believe Richard answered my call on my walk over to the Manns' house, which according to the map was about a mile away.

At first glance I groaned at the walk, but now that he had answered, I picked up the pace and got a new breath of life.

"Good news. The NTSB has cleared our flight to leave tomorrow, so I should be in your office as soon as I get off the airplane." I would find out later if he was going to be sending a car for me, which was the least of my worries. "I've got some very interesting information."

I told him all about the Stricklands and the *Junction Journal* as well as all the leads that'd turned up empty or just didn't end in enough evidence to peg someone as a killer.

"Right now Jay Mann's widow and daughter are expecting me. I'm on my way there now to interview them, but honestly, I want to know who they think killed Jay. What do you think?" I asked.

"I think you need to stop the investigation on who killed Jay Mann and get the down low on the Strickland family. There's a lot of history there." Richard knocked me for a loop. "From the information we've uncovered, the founding fathers of Holiday Junction were Stricklands. The brothers had actually dueled each other to be the first mayor, and they both ended up dead."

"No wonder the mayor is a dog," I muttered and looked down at my phone when it beeped for me to take a right down the next street. "But I don't care about the Stricklands. I wanted to do the piece on the murders and continue my coverage for when I get there."

"I'm sorry, Violet, but as the editor in chief of the paper, I need to see all of your skills, and one of those is taking orders. If you can't pass that part of the interview, then you can just board the airplane back to Kentucky." His words stung, but I knew it was tough love to let me know that I'd made it to the big time.

"Besides, I've got our best investigative reporter headed to Holiday Junction tonight to start our live broadcasts with a real cameraman and crew."

"Great! I'm really excited to have the opportunity to get in front of the camera. When do they get here?" I asked.

"I don't think you understand, Violet. You're not going to be broadcasting anything. You can give our team all of your information, and we will see you for your interview tomorrow." He finished up with "Thanks, Violet, for your work" before he hung up.

My blood was boiling. It took everything in my body to resist calling up my parents, tucking tail, and doing exactly what Richard Stone said—hightail it back to Kentucky.

Then I couldn't help but wonder if he was pulling my leg. Was he really trying to see what I was made of? A team player?

"Yeah. A team player." I nodded and stopped right in front of the house that my map had pinpointed to be the Mann house.

The idea of Richard Stone testing me really got me excited. I was up for the challenge, and with Sandra's and Melissa Mann's thoughts on who they thought did this horrific act, I knew I would find the killer. Not only that, but I was so geared up to prove the Stricklands and the aunts wrong about me that nothing at this point was going to stop me. Not even the deep excitement about me boarding a plane to my dreams tomorrow.

The Mann home was exactly how I thought it was going to be ever since I saw his fancy silk square. It was the typical two-story brick home that looked modest on the outside and like it was built on a couple of acres. The houses in their neighborhood weren't too close together but not too far apart.

"You must be the reporter." A woman who looked to be my age opened the door after I'd rung the doorbell.

"Yes. Violet Rhinehammer." I handed her one of my old Channel Two business cards because it was all I had to prove my job. "I'm sorry to hear about your dad."

"Thank you." She looked at my business card. She waved me to follow her.

The inside had many pieces of expensive furniture that screamed they had money.

"I'm Sandra."

"Is your mom going to be okay?" I asked Sandra and followed her into their family room, where she gestured for me to sit on the couch.

"I'm not sure. I definitely won't go back home until she is. My husband and I will make it work. I'm so glad Mom got to spend some time with Dad at my house. I'm grateful Dad forgot his wallet at my house the night he flew out, because Mom said he embraced her and told her how happy he was with our family and life."

My heart ached for their loss. That the love was strong between them was apparent from how they spoke of each other.

"Are you two talking about me?" Melissa walked in on my and Sandra's conversation. "I'm going to be fine. It'll take time, but I hope with all the attention you are giving his murder, they will find the person who did this."

"I'm not sure if you heard, but there's been a second victim. Rosey Hume," I said.

"No! Not Rosey!" She buried her head in her hands. Sandra rushed over to her mom's side. "Who is doing this? Why?"

"I'm hoping you can shed some light on some questions that hopefully the killer will see in my piece." I left out the part that I was going to write it up in the *Junction Journal* as my part to keep good on my word to the aunts.

"Nana!" Jay and Melissa's granddaughter rushed into the room. "Mommy said I have to take off my dress."

"We don't want to ruin it." Sandra came back into the room.

"She won't. I'll buy a new one, two, or three for my little Dana." Melissa bent down and hugged her granddaughter. She slid her hand down the back of the little girl's hair.

"Careful or you'll pull out my tube." The little girl pulled out of the big hug.

"We can't have that now, can we?" Melissa reached for the little girl's hand. "I love you."

"I love you." Dana turned around and looked up at her mom. "See. Nana said she'd buy me another one."

Sandra looked at her mom and shook her head.

"Why weren't you like this when I was a kid?" she teased her mom and picked Dana up.

"I think parents are like that with their grandchildren." I smiled. "Can I get a photo of you two before I leave? For the article?"

"Of course." Sandra snugged Dana a little closer. "Smile."

I used my phone to snap a photo before they left the room.

"I thought it would be nice for you to see Jay for what he loved, not how you found him." Her eyes softened. "I can see you're shocked I know that you were the one who found him."

"I didn't know you knew." I occupied myself with taking my notebook out of my bag so I didn't have to look into her sad eyes.

"I have a question for you." She touched me.

I stopped busying myself and looked at her.

"Did you see his eyes?"

That struck me as an odd question.

"No. His chin was tucked, and when I noticed the blood, I immediately turned to Cherise. You do know Cherise?"

"Of course. She has been here several times when she and Sandra were children. I've talked to her since Sandra, Dana, and I flew home early. Like you, she said that when she looked into the airplane bathroom, she didn't look at his face."

Cherise told her that she looked at him? She might've for a minute, but she didn't get his ID like they'd told me to do. There was no need to even bring that up.

"He has the kindest eyes." Melissa motioned for me to follow her out through the sliding glass doors that led to the backyard of the house. On the way, she grabbed a set of keys off a set of hooks close to the door. "When we first met, it was his eyes that made me fall head over heels in love."

"From what I gather, you two have been together for a very long time." I tried to walk behind her and write down things as she talked.

"We have. I think I chased him all over this Village." She stopped and let me catch up with her. "That's his man-cave out there." She laughed. "He could stay out there for hours. I had no idea what he was doing."

There was a small house-type shed in the back corner of their property that backed up to the woods.

Melissa fumbled with the keys in the lock. After trying a couple different ones, she got one to work and unlocked the shed door.

"As you can see, I hardly ever came in here, much less had the opportunity to unlock it." She felt around for the light switch, illuminating the inside, which I'd have called more of a workshop. "What happened to Rosey?"

"The same thing that happened to your husband, not really the same thing, but they were both, um." I bit my lip.

"Go on. I can take it," she sniffled.

"Both stabbed and they both had the same pocket square on them." It was starting to sound like I was the magnet for these murders. "I was looking for your gardener, Reed, because a few people have mentioned he pushed around a squeaky cart."

"What does that have to do with anything?" She blinked as if she were trying to put two and two together.

"People have heard squeaky wheels at Rosey Hume's crime scene. Plus he does the landscape for the airport." I knew I was laying out the motive for her. "And I understand Jay had recently fired him from doing your landscape. I was by the seaside and heard he walked through the woods."

There was no need for me to tell her it was a jiggle joint and how Jay had gone there a lot.

"You mean the people at the strip club told you?" She rolled her eyes. "Those guys." She tsked. "They honestly had no idea we wives knew they were there. I guess it was nice when Jay went there because I received the benefits afterwards, if you know what I mean."

I skimmed over her observation because it kind of made me feel a little icky.

"Are you saying Reed killed my husband?" she asked.

"I'm not sure, but it does look like it was his knife. I'm not sure who killed him. I can't help but wonder if he was about to attack someone and they turned his knife on him, but I'm sure Chief Strickland will get it all worked out." I flipped the notepaper to a clean sheet. I didn't tell her the police claimed Reed had an alibi. "Why don't you tell me about these articles?"

I wanted to give her some time to think about what I'd just said, so I changed the subject to let her talk about something that was in her memory. It was a little technique we liked to use to get to know a victim's family so they'd open up about their loved ones, and it was truly magical how they would see the reporter as a friend and just open up.

There were a lot of framed photos and articles on the wall in the shed.

"He loved to cut articles out of the *Junction Journal* about the Hibernians. He was the youngest to be elected president of our chapter." She pointed to the frame with the photo of a young Jay with Melissa by his side.

"As you go down the wall, you can see the story of his life. These might be good to just hang up in the funeral home as his eulogy." She looked as proud as I would expect him to look if he was here to show me himself.

"Is that Sandra?" I pointed to the one with them holding a baby. Both of them were dressed up.

"Yes. That's when we brought her home from the hospital," she said, her voice breaking.

"You look great for just having a baby." I didn't mean for it to sound like it came out. "I'm sorry. I don't have children."

"I do look good there." It was her way of giving me a pass. "We adopted Sandra twenty-eight years ago."

I knew Sandra was my age.

Melissa looked at the photo of them holding the little baby.

"Adoption is a wonderful thing, but as you know, my granddaughter needs a kidney transplant. And, well, now I wish we'd known who the mother was so we could get the donation. Downside of adoption. Jay and I thought we were doing a great thing, but the heartache with my granddaughter is almost too much to bear. Now I have to go through it alone." She looked away and down at the floor.

"What do you do now?" I wondered about the granddaughter but was careful considering the sensitive subject matter. "For your granddaughter?"

"We wait. That's all we can do. Just wait for a donor. You can see she has chronic kidney disease, and, well, she's a trooper." She tapped the photo. "Jay and I both hoped we could be donors, but neither of us could."

"What about Sandra and Dana's dad?" I asked.

"They aren't compatible either." She frowned. "DNA is a funny thing."

Melissa ran her finger over her husband's face before she broke down in tears, bringing her fingers to her wedding band before clutching them to her chest.

"I'm so sorry." I reached out and ran my hand over her arm. "I know I don't know you, but I'm sorry you have to go through this. It seems like one tragedy after another for you. It's a lot to take in."

"If it weren't for baby Dana, I'm not sure I could survive. At least I live another day to pray she'll get a donor and live a full life." She let go of a long sigh and wiped away the tears from her face. "Goodness. I need something to drink. Can I get you something to drink?" Melissa asked. "You can take some photos while I go grab us something refreshing."

"Sure. I'll have whatever you're having." I knew she needed a moment to herself so she could gather her thoughts for the interview.

I took some snapshots of the photos. It appeared to be Jay's trophy wall, the things he was most proud of. All of his life was there in frames. I could see him aging through the progression of the photos.

"Mom! Mom!" Sandra rushed into the shed. "Where's my mom?" she asked me after she looked around and saw me standing there alone.

"She went inside to get a drink." I noticed Sandra was excited. "Are you okay?"

"More than okay. Rosey Hume is a match for Dana!" she screamed out with a look of disbelief. "I had no idea she was a donor until the doctor just called and said we have to get to the hospital now. It's what we've been waiting for. Who knew? The donor was under our noses this entire time! I've got to find my mom!"

Sandra slammed the shed door behind her, making one of the photo frames fall off the wall, scattering the glass all over the floor.

I bent down to pick up the pieces and noticed a piece of paper had also fallen out with the photo. The photo was the one where Jay and Melissa were holding Sandra on the day she was born.

I unfolded the piece of paper and read the caption, "I know you'll be taken better care of by your daddy. I will always love you. Rosey."

"Rosey?" I reread the caption again. I glanced back at the photos along the wall. Jay's wall. Jay's photos. "Sandra is Rosey and Jay's daughter?"

The ice rattling in the glass of tea caught my attention. I looked up. Melissa was standing in the door with two glasses of tea.

"I'm sorry I didn't hear you come in." I gulped and stood up, looking the killer in the eyes.

"I was coming here to let you know I need to cut this interview short, but it looks like I'm going to have some business to attend to with you before I can go." She glided her foot across the floor and used the heel of her shoe to shut the door.

"So you took two lives for one," I said and pretended to write something down on the notepad in hopes my hunch was right. If it was, this would be the biggest story of my life.

"Excuse me, you've got it wrong. Three." She reached up to another photo, the photo where Jay had been anointed as the president, and took the frame off the wall. "Jay, Rosey, and you."

The sound of tape ripping crippled my instinct to run out of the shed as fast as I could, then she exposed a knife.

"You can just let me go now that Chief Strickland believes Reed murdered Jay and Rosey for firing him. Let me get on my airplane to California. I'll never think of this again. It's up to you." I tried to make a good compelling argument for her to let me go. "No one will ever know you are trying to frame Reed for the murders."

"I really wish I could do it, and when I checked you out, you didn't seem so smart." She snickered. A far cry from the tearstained face she'd had a short time ago. "Guess I was wrong."

"If you're going to kill me, let me take a stab at what happened." I was doing anything I could to buy me some time to try to think up some grand scheme for how to get around her without getting a knife stuck in my side.

"You don't have to guess. I'm more than happy to confess. Get it off my chest. Let you take it to the grave." She had this gross jovial laugh that caused her shoulders to shake to life. "It goes way back to when Rosey had her claws, her filthy, wrong-side-of-the-tracks claws into Jay. That's when she tried to take him away from me by seducing him. I can't have children, so she got pregnant on purpose, but I wasn't going to let him go."

"You're saying he had no hand in the affair?" I blurted out when my fear turned to anger when I realized Melissa had given him a pass all these years. "And you did the right thing by adopting Sandra?"

"Sandra was our daughter. Mine and Jay's." She held the knife down, scraping the fancy green dress against her leg with the sharp end. "Rosey was just the vessel for her to come to me."

"Why did you kill them?" I asked and kept my peripheral vision on the knife she was still dragging along the side of her leg. A red streak was forming on the fabric, which told me she had no idea she'd cut herself.

"All these years I ignored Rosey. No one knew she was the vessel carrying my daughter. When we found out she'd seduced Jay and became planted"—her choice of words let me know I was dealing with a wacko and I had to tread this situation lightly—"she had nothing. Jay wasn't going to leave me for her, so we told her we'd take care of the baby by adopting the baby and wouldn't ruin her name here in Holiday Junction. The only reason she was around was the deal we'd made. Of course Jay was able to stay friends with her, and I'm not so sure she wasn't blackmailing him, because recently I found them sneaking around at night."

I found it so interesting how delusional Melissa was about the affair. In her mind she felt like it was all Rosey's fault and somehow Rosey was carrying the baby for Melissa.

"Sneaking around? At night?" My jaw dropped. "You don't know."

"Don't know what?" She glared.

"Jay and Rosey helped Vern put out the Lucky Leprechaun." I hated to tell her the big secret identity, but she needed to be set straight. My words took the color right out of her face. "Rosey and her husband were happy. Jay loved you and your family."

"It doesn't matter. I knew she was the one who could help Dana since none of us were a match. I also knew she was an organ donor because she'd always picked the option on her license when we were younger and I had a job at the clerk's license office. Jay knew it too. He even asked her at the last meeting if she'd consider getting tested, and she refused. She was born with one kidney, so I took it. Jay told me not to do something crazy, and I knew I had to save Dana with or without him."

"But how did you kill Jay?" I had to know.

"Jay never kept track of his schedule. I told him his flight was that night, and I had a ticket as well, but I'm sure you followed up on how I didn't take the flight. I got on the flight, and like always, he goes to the bathroom before they close the door. It's a thing with him. I followed him into the bathroom, and that's when I killed him."

Two and two weren't adding up for me.

"How did you get a knife on board the airplane?" I knew if I could get out of here, this article would definitely be the final fork I needed in order to secure my job with Richard Stone.

"Easy. The same plane goes back and forth to our daughter's. You've seen how things work around here. I simply took Jim Dixon a homemade pie for being such a great pilot and walked into our airport, where Rhett Strickland let me walk right on in." She was so cunning. "Jim took the pie and walked into the cockpit while I sashayed my way down the aisle of the empty airplane, where I slipped this little knife in the paper towel holder in the bathroom. That way when I got on the flight that night with Jay, the knife was already on board."

"Mom!" The door swung open with force, hitting Melissa in the back. She was flung forward, dropping the knife so she could use her hands to catch herself.

The knife skidded across the shed floor.

Melissa and I scrambled, knocking each other out of the way to get the knife.

"Stand back!" I screamed at Melissa, waving the knife in front of me. "Sandra," I tried to talk to her calmly.

"Don't listen to her, Sandra. This woman is crazy. You are my daughter. Not Rosey's. Do you understand me?" Melissa pleaded with Sandra.

Sandra looked at me and back to Melissa. She looked at the photo and the piece of paper on the ground. She picked it up.

"Don't believe their lies! I am protecting you! You are mine! All mine!" Melissa sounded like a mad woman who'd do anything to keep her life going as it was.

"Mommy, did you tell Nana I'm going to live?" Dana stood at the door with the cute little dress on and a little suitcase in her grasp.

"Your real Nana saved your life." Sandra picked up Dana, put her on her hip, and headed up to the house. I was sure they were going straight to the hospital.

Melissa curled up into a ball. Sandra's words killed her more than me holding her at knifepoint, which made it easy for me to call Chief Strickland to come pick up the real killer.

CHAPTER TWENTY-ONE

"Why don't you let me give you a ride over to the Lucky Leprechaun?" Matthew Strickland had offered to give me a ride to the Jubilee Inn after I'd given him my statement about what had happened.

They'd taken Melissa into custody and given Sandra and Dana a police escort to the hospital, where Sandra's birth mother had given the ultimate gift. Life to Dana by being the organ donor.

By the torn look on Sandra's face, I knew there was going to be a lot of healing going on in that family. I was almost happy she didn't live here in Holiday Junction, where I was sure everyone and everything would remind her of what had happened.

It was best she took Dana back after the surgery and lived a full life with her husband there.

"Nah. I better get back to the inn so I can get a good night's sleep since I'll be heading off to California in the morning." It was nice to offer, and I appreciated it, but I didn't need to go and see Rhett, nor did I care to find out what their big family secrets were all about.

There was no doubt the luck of the Irish was with me when I was in Jay Mann's shed. Plus I wanted to look my best when I showed up at Richard's office, where my dream job would be offered to me.

"Oh, come on. Everyone will want to congratulate you on finding the real killer." He glanced over at me from the driver's side. "You did some real good work for an amateur."

"I'll have you know that I'm a real investigative reporter," I snapped back and knew I still had something to prove before I left. "Fine. Take me to the Lucky Leprechaun party."

"You've got it." He sped up a little. "I hear you met my sister and wife."

"Yeah. I didn't appreciate the wild-goose chase they tried to send me on." I took the file out of my purse and laid it on the seat between us. "You can give them back their file."

"I don't think they were sending you on a goose chase. I think they were seeing if you were good enough to do the job." He gave a sideways glance to the file. "I wondered where my file went."

"Your file?" I asked.

"Oh yeah. My wife likes to butt into things. She thinks because I'm the chief, she can come down to the station and just take whatever she wants. Granted"—he turned on what I recognized as the main street—"we've not had a lot of big crimes. But when we do, she likes to have all the insider information because she likes to think she's got a leg up on people. Between me and you, the stuff I don't want out in the public is stored where she can't get to it."

"Are you telling me that you deliberately set stuff out so she will inadvertently tell the public so it'll lead to some gossip which might give you some clues?" I liked his devious little scheme.

"You are a good investigative reporter." He didn't admit to what I'd uncovered, but he didn't deny it either. "Here you go." He stopped at the top of the street where the huge painted leprechaun stood.

Images of Vern, Jay, and Rosey sneaking around in the dark to get the darn thing up put a smile on my face.

"Aren't you coming?" I asked and opened the car door.

"I've got to get my report finished and send Melissa Mann to the state penitentiary to be held. We don't have a big department, and I'd have—" he started to say when I interrupted.

"You'd have to have officers leave the Lucky Leprechaun party." I laughed and got out of the car.

"You're a quick learner. You might just make a good editor at the *Junction Journal* after all." He took off before I could ask him what on earth he was talking about.

"We've been waiting for you." Marge Strickland and her sister Louise were standing on the curb. "There was a young man that came to our house. He said he was with that fancy news station you were interviewing with. He also told us that you weren't doing the investigation. In fact, he said you weren't even hired."

"That's right." Louise nodded. "We did a little digging, and we talked to a Richard Stone. He said that you weren't there on time for the interview, so he hired someone else. But we didn't tell that reporter nothing. Kicked him."

"We had to call Dave to come and peck him to death off our property." Marge tucked her arm into the crook of my arm. "I can see by the look on your face that you're upset. But we have got a good offer for you."

"Rhett said he'd get the online paper and equipment needed for the modern-day online newspaper. We also talked to Garnett and Clara Ness over at the printing press, and they are willing to give us a good deal on a one-day-a-week paper where we'd post things like the obituary and social functions." Louise continued to tell me their plans while Marge walked me down the street.

I listened to them and took in all the vendor booths that hadn't been there when Rhett and I had stopped by his house. There were food vendors touting all sorts of green foods or foods they'd turned green for the occasion, as well as a few local vendors selling things locally made. Leni was one of them.

Vern stood next to his wife and looked at me with a smile when I passed by with the aunts. He lifted his finger up and pointed to the Lucky Leprechaun, then slid it up to his mouth.

His secret was safe with me. Besides, who was I to take away how happy he made the citizens of Holiday Junction as the Merry Maker?

The Lucky Leprechaun had really planned a great party to end the Shamrock Festival.

"Are you going to come work for us or not? We need a real investigative reporter." Marge tugged my arm closer to her body. "Heck, we just need a reporter."

"Wait." I stopped. "Are you trying to tell me that I don't have a job with Richard Stone's network?"

Both of them shook their heads.

"Excuse me." I pulled my arm away from Marge. "I need to make a phone call."

I hurried down the street to the only house I knew, Rhett's. I slipped around the corner of his house to be alone so I could call Richard and out of earshot of the party and the Mad Fiddlers.

"Richard, it's Violet Rhinehammer, international reporter." I stated my truth with a stern voice. "It's my understanding you've sent a colleague of mine to do the reporting for the murder that I happened to solve tonight."

I was going to give him the opportunity to take back what he'd told the aunts about my employment status before I told him exactly where to go.

"I'm afraid the position you've applied for has been filled" was all he had to say.

"You never even gave me a chance." I made sure my tone didn't sound desperate. Then I took a downward spiral. "I packed up my life to come for that interview. I left my home. An amazing job. Friends. Family." I rattled off the list of creature comforts that made me who I was.

"I'm sorry, Ms. Rhinehammer. I'm more than happy to keep your application on file, and when a new reporter position posts, I'll let you know." Richard Stone hung up the phone, closing my dream down.

"I'll fix him." I pulled the phone from my ear and hit the contact button to find Mae West's number.

"Violet!" She greeted me in her oh-so-happy way.

I snarled.

"We are so excited to have found out that you solved the murder. The Laundry Club Ladies, including Dottie Swaggert, were rooting for you. I bet you're so excited! When do you leave for California? When are we going to see you on the big television?"

"About that." I sucked in a deep breath. I jerked around when I heard a branch snap behind me.

Rhett was walking around the back of his house. He looked as surprised to see me as I was him.

"Oh, and before I forget," Mae continued, "they filled your position at the

Normal Gazette. A big pain in the you-know-what."

My heart dropped. I had been about to tell her I would be on the next airplane back to Normal.

"Since you know about the case being solved, I better let you go. They are having a St. Patrick's Day party, and I don't want to miss it." Mae and I said goodbye, and I turned to Rhett.

"I hear the aunts made you an offer." He didn't have to tell me how he'd heard about my big dream job going up in smoke.

I didn't know him well, but by the way he was acting I could tell he knew and was trying not to show it.

There might have been some underlying issues with Rhett and his family, but underneath it all, I could tell he had a heart. And I didn't really care about their family history. It wasn't my business. Yet.

"Mayor Paisley and I would like to take this time to welcome our new citizen and new reporter at the *Junction Journal*. Give a warm Holiday Junction welcome to Violet Rhinehammer!" Kristine had taken the stage alongside of Mayor Paisley and the aunts. All of them were looking toward Rhett's house.

I smiled and lifted my hand up in the air, wondering what on earth I had just done.

The claps and roars erupted.

"The aunts don't like to take no for an answer." Rhett joined in on the celebration.

I tried not to make eye contact with too many people because I wasn't even sure if I was going to stay here.

As I made my way through the crowd, it was kind of hard not to notice Darren and Rhett Strickland flashing their cute dimples at me, clapping as both of their smiles grew.

The news I would be reporting on for the *Junction Journal* might not be that interesting, but it felt like my personal life was going to be quite the opposite. I was up for a good challenge. Besides, I had no other offer on the table.

Celebrate Mother's Day with Violet Rhinehammer as she joins Holiday Junction as a citizen. And when her mama shows up, southern twang and all, let's just say Mother's Day in Holiday Junction will never be the same.

MOTHER'S DAY MURDER

A HOLIDAY COZY MYSTERY BOOK 2

"Mama." I had hit the green button.

"Violet, I need your help." Her voice was cold and exact. "I'm in a bit of a pickle."

"What's going on, Mama?" I tried to ask in an unalarmed voice. My insides went from one excitement to a whole different kind of excitement.

"I need you to come to the Lustig Spring as fast as you can." Her tone had become chilly. Then she said something I never imagined. "Sally Westin is dead."

CHAPTER ONE

"Hey! Don't I know you?" It was the first thing I heard before I'd been able to take a sip of the steamy hot cup of coffee I'd gotten from the Brewing Beans, the local coffee shop in Holiday Junction.

I'd not even gotten the toe of my shoe on the first step of the trolley before I heard the familiar voice.

"You!" The trolley driver shook her finger at me.

"Yes. I'm the new reporter for the." I started to rattle off my new job at the Journal Junction the local newspaper.

"No. No. No." The visor she wore on her head had blinking lights on it.

Of course it did. Everything in Holiday Junction was lit up, glittered, sparkled or shined. And if it didn't, the residents of the small town made sure it did somehow.

"It's me." She took her hands off the trolley wheel. "Goldie Bennett!"

My eyes narrowed as I looked at her trying to recall any sort of memory of her but I was pulling a blank.

"You know Joey, Chance and Lizzy's grandmother," she said it like I should know these people. "Duh," her mouth was open. "From the airplane. We were seatmates."

"Oh." The horrible memory popped into my head. "Yes. I'm sorry." I held up my cup of Joe. "It's still a little early."

"It's ten o'clock a.m.." she told me like she didn't believe my excuse. "Different strokes for different folks," she muttered and put her hand back on the handle before she said, "Are you riding or not?"

"Yes." I took the last step up into the trolley, barely making it inside before she whipped the door shut nearly catching my heel, which would've hurt if it did get caught since I was wearing flip flops.

I eased down, careful not to spill my coffee, and put my briefcase in my lap.

"Well aren't you going to ask about Joey, Chance, and Lizzy?" Goldie asked out of the side of her mouth as the trolley rattled down the Main Street before it hung a left down Peppermint Court, a row of really cute cottage style houses that not only had the feeling of living in the city but also a nice view of the dunes and sliver of the seaside.

"How are your grandchildren?" I was having déjà vu all over again from the first time I'd met Goldie. My hands started to tremble thinking about it.

No. She wasn't terrible to sit by now that I knew what had come after. Of course I was in a different mindset when I stepped on the airplane that morning. I thought I was headed to my dream job in California as a big-time new reporter for a national news station. Little did I know when I sat down next to Goldie, I would excuse myself to get away from looking at photos of her grandchildren to go to the bathroom. I had to be in the zone for the shot at the big time but when I found a dead body in the airplane's bathroom, my life took a turn that I never saw coming.

Just like this morning. I never in a million years thought I'd see Goldie again. At least she didn't ask me about the body or worse, seen all the social media memes that'd been created of me after I'd gotten the brilliant, not so brilliant, idea to go live to show off my reporting skills since I was the only reporter in the locked down airport.

Reporter 101 tip, if you do go live on the spot make sure your eye make-up hasn't bled down your face creating a stream of black tears. Not a look viewers want to see.

"You know, we are in full swing of tee-ball. Lizzy. Whooo-wee that Lizzy. She can rock a pink tu-tu better than any of them dancers down at the Groove and Go." She whipped the trolley down a back alley before she took a right back on Main Street so we could head the opposite direction.

"Elvin isn't happy with her going down there because he said Tricia Lustig don't need all the money," she tsked. "You know they've got that Lustig Spring everyone goes on and on about."

"Lustig Spring?" I wondered.

The trolley came to an abrupt stop. Goldie leaned to the right and grabbed the handle, pulling the trolley door open.

"Your stop." Her chin swung over her right shoulder and she looked at me.

"Already?" I looked up and saw we were already at the office of the *Junction Journal*. I stood up about to take those steps off the trolley. "I didn't know I told you where to stop."

"Now, now, Violet." She tsked again, only a little louder this time. "Everyone knows who you are in Holiday Junction. They can't say that they really know you like I do."

I stood on the side of the road staring back at her wondering exactly what that meant.

She slammed the trolley door shut and took off heading to the next stop.

CHAPTER TWO

After I stepped off the trolley and watched as it pulled away, I shook my head along with any notion what Goldie had just insinuated about my reputation in this town so I could do the job I'd stayed in Holiday Junction for, a reporter at the Journal Junction.

In truth, there were two elder sisters, Marge and Louise, who owned the *Junction Journal* and from what I'd learned over the past couple of months since making Holiday Junction my home, they wanted to get rid of the paper and no one in their family wanted the dying rag.

Me. I was a journalist. It was in my veins and though my true longing was to be a big-time television reporter, I knew I could be satisfied with owning and operating my own newspaper.

For the time being.

Things in the industry changed so much and so fast, there was no better way to learn than to jump feet first. That's just what I did. When the sisters had offered me a job, since I'd found myself without one due to a dead body or two, I honestly didn't have a better offer.

I'd told myself then I'd look around and take my time while I stayed in Holiday Junction instead of tucking my tail and admitting failure by going back home to Kentucky. It'd been two months and here I stood outside of the practically dilapidated seaside house I'd talked Rhett Strickland into letting the *Junction Journal* lease since the office was in his aunts' family home.

It was a hard sell for the aunts to buy my reasoning to move the paper but when I told them how much it would make for an easier transition when they did go to sell *Junction Journal* and the fact I'd be working all hours of the night since I had nothing better to do, I didn't want to keep them up at night. Plus I wasn't comfortable coming and going from someone's actual home when I did go to work.

Rhett was an altogether different sell. He didn't want to rent the place, he said he'd loan it for free because it did need a lot of work and he could do most of it even though he was coming up on his busy season at the Holiday Junction Airport where he worked as the one and only security guard to the one room building airport.

By busy season, I meant the flurry of holidays around the summertime. Mother's Day, Father's Day, Fourth of July were just a few to name and the major ones I'd seen on the town council's docket for upcoming issues where I needed to report on them.

That also meant I wasn't able to go home for Mother's Day which left Millie Kay Rhinehammer, my mama, in a bit of a tizzy, as we'd say in the south.

"Toto, we ain't in the south." I shoved the key into the lock of the front door of the house and did my best impression of Dorothy from the Wizard of Oz. "Nope. We are in the middle of nowhere USA."

I stepped inside of the house, with my hand on the door handle I paused to look out over the seaside laying out in front of me.

The water shimmered with each slow passing wave and glistened with little twinkles of light as the sun hit it perfectly.

I giggled at just how different my life was now that I'd moved away from home where I was surrounded by mountains. Holiday Junction was like no other town I'd ever seen or known of in the states.

There were literally four types of different terrains in the small town. There was the seaside, the mountain side, the countryside and the town. It was definitely a place that filled my creative well which actually was what gave me peace during this transition in my life.

The seaside gave way to the small beach area and a long concrete sidewalk big enough for the street carts and vendors that had been erected since the temperatures had gotten warmer. There were also shops where tourists loved to visit.

My phone chirped deep in my journalist bag.

"Time to work." I shut the door and headed inside to the one and only room that was actually completed with a desk and view of the seaside. I'd found myself many times over the last month staring out, coming up with all sorts of ideas for the *Junction Journal* and how I could save it.

Time would tell.

I put the bag on top of the old desk the sisters had let Rhett bring over for me to work and opened the zipper where I kept my phone tucked in one of the inside pockets.

"Hhmm." My brows knotted. "What does Vern McKenna want?" I questioned since I had no business with him other than him being the Merry Maker, which no one knew about.

The Merry Maker was a unique undercover job in Holiday Junction. I shouldn't've even know he was the Merry Maker and I'd like to think it was my journalistic instincts that'd uncovered this little secret but it wasn't. He'd ended up telling me due to the fact I had done my own investigation into a murder a couple of months ago and pointed to him as a possible suspect.

Boy was I wrong.

Vern had an alibi, being the secret Merry Maker.

Holiday Junction loved holidays. The town went all out for every single one with a full parade, beauty queen and festival. It was the Merry Maker's job to secretly name where the big festival finale would take place.

There was a large sign for each holiday, and wherever it was posted was where the big festival ending took place. For instance, the first holiday I had the pleasure of spending in Holiday Junction was St. Patrick's Day.

A huge wooden leprechaun showed up at the end of Rhett Strickland's street one day. No one knew how the Merry Maker did it, but somehow the Merry Maker—Vern in this case—would come up with the location and put up the leprechaun without anyone in the community noticing. Or they just acted like they didn't notice.

Once the sign for the particular holiday was put up, the townsfolk in that particular area had to come up with the final send-off of the holiday.

With Mother's Day approaching, I wondered if Vern was calling to ask me how I was going to cover the Merry Maker, or if I was going to spill the beans that he was the Merry Maker.

My lips were sealed. I wasn't telling a soul Vern was the one who had the ability to sprinkle the joy around for the holidays.

Instead of checking the text, I would wait until after I got some research done about the Lustig Spring that Goldie had mentioned. It got my attention.

There were many things to explore in Holiday Junction, and I knew I'd not even scratched the surface of things to do. But the Lustig Spring and the reason for Goldie's husband not wanting little Lizzy to take dance lessons from Tricia Lustig at the Groove and Go really had sparked my interest, and my gut told me to investigate.

I put the phone down and got out my laptop and paper and pen before I sat down.

The first thing Rhett did was install internet for me since we'd just recently taken the paper online, where residents could get the daily news. Things important to them were like the daily lunch specials at the local diner, today's fresh coffee selections at Brewing Beans, any birth announcements, death notices, and photo opportunities with Mayor Paisley, who just so happened to be a Boston Terrier dog.

She was the most sought-after celebrity here in Holiday Junction. Since I currently resided in the Jubilee Inn, where Mayor Paisley kept office, I was blessed with the opportunity to know her full schedule.

"Today Mayor Paisley will be sitting for photos at noon before her one p.m. nap." I tapped on my computer to update the online "today" section before I moved to the "sponsored by" part of the update. "Be sure to head over to Emily's Treasures. Tell Emily you saw this in today's paper." The cell phone rang, taking my attention for a moment. I continued to finish so I wouldn't lose my train of thought. "You will receive ten percent off your full purchase."

The phone rang again.

"Good morning, Vern," I answered without looking. "I'm sorry I haven't called you back. I was a little late getting to the office. What did you need to see me about?"

"Vern?" Mama's voice questioned.

My stomach dropped. I'd been so careful screening my calls from her over the last couple of days, I hadn't even thought of looking down at my phone to see who was calling.

"And why is he texting you?" There was concern in her voice. "I told your daddy there was going to be some pervert out there trying to hit on you and you needed to come home where you have family and friends who love you. Look out for you when some man tries to hit on you. Texting you at all hours of the night and day."

Mama always assumed the worst when it came to me and taking care of myself.

"Mama, I wish you'd go see Betts Hager. She'd love to have you on the Bible Thumper—um, the prayer team." Mama had nothing to do now that I was gone. I was their only child, and she'd made it her job to tell everyone back in our hometown where I was going to be and what channel I was on and made sure everyone tuned into my local broadcast.

Now that I didn't live there for her to keep those tabs on me, she'd spent the better part of her waking day calling me, texting me, and emailing me when she couldn't reach me the first two ways.

"I don't want to be in no prayer meeting. I've got my own prayers to worry about rather than mix it up with other people's problems." Mama sounded out of breath. "Are you sure you won't be coming home for Mother's Day?"

"Mama, you know I love you so much. I miss you and I wish we were together, but I simply can't be home. I'm under a huge deadline." I typed "Lustig Spring" into the Google search engine and was surprised at all the hits it got. "I promise I will get back before summer ends."

There were some birds chirping in the background, and I wondered if she was on a hike in the Daniel Boone National Forest, where my hometown was located. My stomach clenched again hearing the familiar sounds of home.

"Summer ends?" Mama cried out. "That's just not soon enough, Violet Rhinehammer. I'm your only mama, and one day you will regret this."

"Now, now." I hated when she used her southern mama guilt on me. "You are the one who taught me to follow my dream."

"I didn't mean for you to follow it out of town," she cried out.

I pushed myself back in the chair and got up. All the information I was about to dive into about the Lustig Spring made me excited. I knew there was a story there I wanted to visit, which was going to require all of my time.

This meant I needed to get off the phone with Mama.

"And you also taught me to be the independent woman with my own job, career, and future." I walked to the back of the office, which used to be a kitchen, and looked out over the landscape where the mountains stood tall in the distance.

There was a knock at the door of the office.

I jerked back to look over my shoulder, wishing I'd had a glass door to see who was on the other side.

"Mama, I've got to go. I promise I'll call you back." I clicked off as Mama was saying something. I walked back to the front door. "I sure hope it's not Marge or Louise," I said under my breath since I'd yet to have anything prepared for them this morning. "You've got this," I told myself with confidence, knowing it was something my mama would've told me.

I rolled back my shoulders and smiled before I flung the door open.

"Remember how you just said I taught you to be independent?" Mama stood on the other side, the sound of waves lapping behind her. "I'm taking my own advice. Your daddy and I are getting divorced."

I didn't know what I was shocked about most. Mama standing right there in front of me or her news about my parents' future.

CHAPTER THREE

"You're what?" I completely overexaggerated my question after I'd hurried Mama into the office, not even giving two cares in the world on how she'd gotten Rhett Strickland, of all people, to give her a ride.

That would be addressed for another time.

"Have you lost your mind?" Of course she had. "Mama, are you sick? Ill? Been diagnosed with dementia? Early onset of Alzheimer's?"

Mama made herself right at home in my office chair. She elegantly, as she always had, eased down into the chair and crossed her ankles with her hands folded in her lap. She looked the southern lady part as she did not fit in with the citizens here in her monogrammed three-quarter-length sweater, shoulder-length blond hair with a hint of gray around the scalp, and her makeup as perfect as if she'd just left the makeup counter at a high-end department store.

Not a hair out of place, and none of her pink lipstick had bled into the tiny wrinkles around her mouth.

I leaned in a little closer to her face.

"Did you get Botox or filler?" I jerked back. She simply stared at me. No expression whatsoever. "You're having a midlife crisis in your sixties!" I pointed to her before my hand found its way over my mouth as I tried to take back some of the accusations I'd thrown at her.

Something I'd never done before.

Total disrespect.

"Violet," Rhett choked out. "I think it's time for some food. Why don't you take your mom to one of the food trucks in Holiday Park? All the Mother's Day activities are starting today, and I think she'd love to go."

"That sounds lovely." Mama perked up. "I am a little hungry. I tried not to eat too much at the airport after I'd gotten an Uber ride all the way from Normal to Lexington." Mama spoke directly to Rhett. "It's about a two-hour drive, and sometimes I get a little nausea on all the back roads."

I tugged my shirt down at the hem and sucked in a deep breath.

"Can I talk to you privately?" I told Rhett—not asked him, told him—with a gesture of my head toward the back of the office.

"Don't be long. We don't want my sugar to drop," Mama called out when I turned and walked down the office hallway to where the kitchen once was located. "Did I tell you that I'm prediabetic? That's what the doctor said."

I could feel the tension rising up in me with each step before I turned to face Rhett, fully expecting to be out of Mama's capacity to hear us.

"How on earth did you find her?" The muscles spasmed furiously in my jaw as I tried to whisper.

"It's your mom," Rhett said like I didn't know. He smiled, deepening his dimples I had to work hard at not noticing. His dark hair against his olive complexion didn't help matters. "She was so excited when she got off the airplane and asked me, the security guard, which way to the Jubilee Inn."

"Let me guess, you rescued her like you did me the day I stepped off the airplane." Not that the airport was big. In fact, it was one room, and when you departed from the airplane, you had to walk down a set of rickety steel steps.

I could only imagine Mama's horror when she saw the steps and the airport.

"Wow." Rhett's nose curled just enough for me to see he wasn't happy with my reaction. He ran his hand through his hair. His short sleeve rose slightly toward his armpit, and his bicep formed. "I guess when she told me who she was and if I knew her daughter, I thought you'd be happy to see her. From the way she talked about surprising you, you'd think she was expecting a daughter who was happy and loved her."

"Lower your voice." I batted the air. "She's got supersonic hearing." I gnawed on my bottom lip, my forehead wrinkled, reminding me of Mama's recent work on her face. "And she looks so much younger than she really is. Plus she informs me she's divorcing my dad."

"She did leave that little detail out." He gave a wry smile. "But she told me all about you growing up in Kentucky and how you were destined to become a star."

Mama must've told him some doozy of tales, and from the amused look on his face, I did not want to know.

"Listen, she only wants to spend Mother's Day with you. That's why she's here." Rhett reminded me of the holiday.

"I told her I was working and couldn't come home. She should've known I was busy." I was making excuses for myself to feel better about shoving her off. "I sent her a card and had ordered flowers to be delivered."

"She delivered herself. Why don't you just take her to the park and talk to her?" He shook his head. "What on earth is possibly keeping you here this morning? From what my aunts tell me, you're doing a great job, and the online edition is already prepared for weeks in advance."

"There are several sponsors, and I did just update the 'Happening around Holiday' section." I felt I was missing something to put into the paper, but my mind was so jumbled I couldn't remember.

"See, you can go and enjoy her. It'll give you some headspace to think about what her visit looks like, get some insight on what she's thinking with your dad, and maybe get a game plan." He crossed his arms over his chest. "In the meantime, I'll go get her checked in with Kristine at the Jubilee Inn."

"You make it sound all so great, but trust me, it's not great. Mama has a way of making people uncomfortable." I put it mildly. "Have you ever heard of the southern 'bless your heart'?"

His head tilted in confusion.

"In the south we say 'bless your heart,' only it really isn't blessing your heart. It's a bit sarcastic." I tried my best to explain, but there was still a deep look of confusion on Rhett's face. "Oh look there, it's not a compliment in most cases. It's what one says when they are referring to someone pitiful."

"Oh."

Mama had a way of doing the whole "bless your heart" to where people had no idea what hit them.

"The best way to respond to Mama when she blesses your heart is to give a sympathetic nod. It stops her dead in her tracks." Here I was, trying to explain to Rhett how to treat Mama as if Mama was going to stay in Holiday Junction and have interaction with him on a regular basis.

Then it hit me.

"You're right." I reached out and grabbed his bicep. I gulped when both of us realized I'd been so bold to give him physical contact after we'd kinda shared some moments when I'd decided to stay.

I'd done a really good job distancing myself from him and finding alternative places to be when his family would invite me to gatherings. He knew it and I knew it, but it was unspoken.

From what I'd been told, Rhett Strickland was the most sought-out bachelor in Holiday Junction, and from my experience in the past, those were the men you stayed far away from.

"I can entertain Mama for the day and get her back on a flight tomorrow." Slowly I removed my hand, pretty darned pleased with my plan that wasn't a real plan until I got that flight booked.

"No flights out until Monday." He made air dots with his finger. "Like a week from today. Monday is today."

My shoulders slumped, my head dropped, and my long hair fell forward.

"Yeah. I forgot the airport only flies out on Mondays." That was something I actually appreciated about the small town. The slow lifestyle and not all the tourists coming and going like they did in my hometown.

Of course there were tourists here, but they were low-key. Something Mama was not.

"I guess I could take her to see the Lustig Spring. I have been researching it." Now I had to plan a full week's worth of activities, and Mama would be expecting such grand events. "I guess I could take her to Emily's Treasures."

"What about all the weeklong festivities? The parade, the cooking classes this week, the movie night." Rhett rattled off all the activities I'd been talking about in the paper. "She looks like she'd just love to spend time with her daughter."

"I guess you're right. I have been trying so hard to keep the *Junction*

Journal relevant and if you've not noticed, I love a little order in my life and not surprises." A weak smile formed and when he noticed, his smile grew huge.

"That's the girl." He gave me the good ole halfhearted and loose fist nudge on my arm. "Does she chug beer like her daughter?" He winked, sending a little tickle to my insides.

"No. Don't remind me and don't tell her," I warned, poking him in the chest. "The last thing she needs to know is how I got snookered on my first night here."

"Snookered?" He snorted. "You were drunk."

"Not my finest hour." I did like the fact I'd beaten Fern Banks, the local beauty queen in the St. Patrick's Day stein competition. "Did I mention I'm competitive?"

"I know you." He stood a little too close and looked down at me with serious eyes. "Why don't I take you and your mom out to dinner tonight?" His soft-spoken voice was like a sweet musical tone that vibrated every nerve in my body.

"We'd love to!" Mama had her very stylish fanny pack buckled around her waist and a white visor now on her head. "I can't get all that sun on my face." She gave the bill a small tug but not enough to mess up her hair. "I'm ready to go to Holiday Park like he suggested."

"I told you she had supersonic hearing." I shook my head and walked over to give her a hug.

"On the way over you can tell me all about you getting snookered," she whispered in my ear.

"It was nothing, Mama," I told her after we'd left the office and decided to stroll along the beach and take the path that led up to Holiday Park. "I was trying to fit in and get all those murders solved quickly, remember, so I could get to my interview in California."

It was really simple. I'd found a dead body on an airplane, and I had the interview of a lifetime with a big-time news station in California. The pilot had to make an emergency landing, which put me smack-dab into Holiday Junction. The NTSB wasn't going to let us leave until they felt confident. The dead body turned out to be a murder, and only when everyone on the airplane had been absolved of the crime were we going to leave Holiday Junction.

Just like a good investigative reporter, and due to the fact I was on a mission to land my dream job, I did my own investigation, and that meant hobnobbing with the locals. That included the beer drinking competition. Fern wasn't that nice of a person to begin with, so I did go to the extremes to win. It took me days to recover, and I'd not had another drop of alcohol since.

Today could possibly end that streak.

"We don't need to talk about that." I had to change the subject to her big news about her divorce from my dad. "Not that I want to believe what you said, but are you really divorcing Daddy?"

"Is it really that terribly shocking, Violet?" Mama had taken me by the elbow as we slowly walked down the sidewalk. The waves lapped up on the beach, making the young children playing in their wake run giggling up to their parents, who were enjoying watching their children play.

I remembered doing that when I was a little girl and my parents took me to Florida every year for a summer vacation.

"Your father and I haven't been married in the sense of how a marriage should be in a very long time." She told me something I had no idea about. "I can tell by how you tensed up you don't want to know the details, and well, there's nothing to tell. After you left for college, we just drifted apart. From all the marriage counseling sessions we had, we found out it was normal for some marriages."

"Why didn't you try a hobby together?" I asked. My heart had lodged in my throat, and no amount of swallowing was making it go back behind my ribs where it belonged.

"We did, honey. We tried everything. We took dance lessons, cooking classes, even joined a couples book club, but we realized we just didn't have anything in common. Not that I'm looking for someone in my life to give me a boost of excitement, but I realized I don't have many years left on this earth. Forty if I'm lucky."

I snorted.

"What?" she asked.

"Forty more years, you'd be one hundred." Did I really have to do the math for her?

"Which means that I've got to get crackin' if I want to have the best time for the rest of my life." Mama had become someone I didn't know.

It made me wonder, had I really ever known Mama? I mean, she did raise me, and she was Mama.

Mama.

I looked at Mama while we walked. Her lips were flapping, but the thoughts in my head were louder than her speaking to me. All I saw when I watched her was her mouth moving. It hit me. Mama was a person just like me. She wasn't just Mama, the woman who brought me into this world and many times told me I wasn't too big for a whoopin' when I got sassy. But outside of those traits, she was a person who had feelings, cares, needs.

Just like me.

"Mama." I led her down the sidewalk past all the vendors and slightly tugged her away from gawking at one of the shops in particular. "I'm so glad you're here."

"That's nice, honey." She patted my hand that had found its way into the crook of her elbow as I gently guided her more toward the sandy side of the sidewalk and not the street, where the place of business she was rubbernecking to see was a jiggle joint.

"I have never really looked at you as someone other than my mama." I was really trying to accept her feelings and wanted her to know, but she clearly was not paying me a bit of attention. "Mama!" I stopped and stomped. "Are you listening to me? I'm trying to tell you something."

"Oh dear, I'm sorry." She turned. Her eyes pinched, but there were no signs of wrinkles. "What is it?"

"Now that I have your attention, I was just saying how I've never really looked at you as a person. Just like me." I smiled at her, and my heart lifted with the knowing that a piece of home, a slice of comfort, was right here in front of me. I filled up with gratitude and felt sorry for Mama. "I have never even thought about how you and Daddy keep your relationship going. I know for me, I want passion, love, surprises." As I heard myself say those things, I realized my daddy was none of those.

He was routine, liked good ole beef and potatoes, and rarely liked to leave his couch. Mama was none of those things. If I dug deep enough, I did recall Mama was the one, not Daddy, who had told me to get out of Normal and get a career, have my own money, and enjoy life.

"I'm sorry I never paid attention to what was really going on in your heart and life." I sensed a connection between us. "I guess I have you to thank for me leaving town to follow my dream, and I hope I can help you get through and support you for whatever you need."

"Good." Her voice was flat and unaffected by the speech I'd just given her. "Let's go get a drink."

She grabbed my hand and dragged me across the street and right into the jiggle joint before I could even protest.

CHAPTER FOUR

"We will have two vodka and sodas with a twist of lime!" Mama held up two fingers after she'd tapped on the bar to get Darren's attention.

"Wow, this is a surprise. Who is our new friend?" One of two regulars was saddled up to the bar on their usual stool.

"I'm Millie Kay Rhinehammer, and let me introduce you to my eligible and highly intelligent daughter." She pointed over her shoulder at me. "She's an investigator like the kind you hear on those mystery podcasts that are so popular."

"Mama, they know me," I whispered, but she kept talking. "And since when have you listened to podcasts? And crime ones at that?"

Apparently I didn't know my mama as well as I thought I did.

"Like I was saying before my daughter forgot her southern manners." Mama gave me a hard look. The kind she used to give me when we were in church and I was talking when I shouldn't've been. Or when she thought I shouldn't've been.

"Violet is a very serious investigative reporter, and she's about to make it big-time." Mama was talking to Owen and Shawn, two men I'd met my first week in Holiday Junction. "Look at that face. And she's got the most sweet, southern accent." Mama pointed to me. "Go on, honey, do that reporter talk you do."

"Mama, I know them." I finally got her eyes on me.

"Oh. Then introduce me." She put her hand out like she was the queen and they were supposed to kiss it.

"Mama, meet the Easter Bunny and the Tooth Fairy." I knew that would make Owen and Shawn laugh.

"These drinks are on me," Owen told Darren while Shawn pulled up a stool, nestling between him and Owen so that Mama could sit.

"Honestly?" Mama put her hand up to her chest. "Which one is the Tooth Fairy? Because I think you get a raw end of the stick. And what on earth do you do with all of those teeth?"

Mama entertained these men more than the women rolling around on the dingy stage were doing.

"You've got a pretty funny mom," Darren leaned over and said. He gave me a slight nod to move away from the three of them as if he wanted to tell me something.

I stepped aside and waited for him to give Mama her vodka and soda. He slid mine to me.

Darren Strickland. Boy oh boy, was he a looker. The only problem with him was the bar he ran. It was a case of me, like I'd done with Mama, not getting to know him as a person and just what he did.

Run a strip joint.

I guessed all towns had them, but ooh. Yuck.

Over the past couple of months, I'd been here, but only for the bar portion, since it was the only bar in town. Sometimes I did take a little nip of the juice when I would leave work on my walk back to town, using the path leading from the seaside and then going down Main Street, where the Jubilee Inn was located.

Back to Darren. He was Rhett Strickland's cousin and the bar owner. From what I'd heard around town, Darren was single and poor. Today his choice of clothing was a wrinkled button-up shirt with rolled-up sleeves. His hair was a little too long in the back, making it flip up in a curl from underneath his turned-around baseball cap. His dark eyes were deep and hid underneath his thick brows.

"Violet, you never even mentioned this place on the phone," Mama called from the other side of the bar. She picked up her drink and led the cheers between her, Shawn, and Owen.

"It looks like your mom got the fun gene of the family." Darren's brown eyes twinkled in amusement.

"I had no idea she was coming to town." I couldn't help the feeling of the news hitting me again like a sack of potatoes, knocking me in the gut. "The first thing she told me is that she's divorcing my dad."

"Yeah. We are going to need to make this a double." Darren went to grab my glass.

"No." I put my hand on his to stop him from taking it. I saw a heart-rending tenderness in his gaze that made me pause.

"Yeah. Sure." He pulled his hand out from underneath mine. "You go take care of your mom."

"What did you want to tell me?" I asked since he'd yet to say why he'd asked me to come to this side of the bar.

"Nothing." He waved me off. "We can talk after your mom leaves. You enjoy her. Actually, the two of you should take that cooking class being offered for Mother's Day at Freedom Diner."

"Freedom Diner," I said and nodded my head. "Isn't that the diner owned by the Lustig family?"

"Yeah, why?" He reached behind him, took the bar towel, and wiped down the counter as he listened to me.

"I'd heard something about their family spring." Signing up for the class could do two things. Pacify Mama by spending some time with her as a Mother's Day treat, and allow me to get some information from the family and possibly an interview.

"People have been coming to the Lustig Spring for decades. People believe the untreated water is healthy and even a healing tonic." Darren was making me want to research the spring even more.

"Healing tonic?" That sounded a little woo-woo, but I was down with hearing more about it.

"The Lustigs live forever. They all grew up drinking from the spring, and when people realized they were outliving practically everyone in Holiday Junction, they took notice." He shrugged. "They had a hard time keeping people off the land after a few had snuck in and filled up jugs. After they drank, the word got out that they had more energy and felt better than they had in years."

"They don't put anything in it? Fluoride? Nothing?" I asked.

"Nope. Colorless and wet like all water." He grinned. "Rich in minerals."

"You drink it?" I wondered and leaned up on my forearms to look behind the bar to see if there were any sort of jugs filled with water.

"On occasion." He smiled. "When I go to eat at the diner. Supposedly that's all they serve there for water. And if you ask anyone who works there, Nate Lustig, the owner of the farm, is really grumpy about people coming to the spring now."

"Why?" I wanted to know all the juicy details.

"Look at you being all reporter-y for my aunts." He grinned. "According to your mom, this is just a pit stop for you."

"What?" I pulled back.

"I've got double hearing. It's a gift and a curse." He threw his head back and laughed when he noticed my confusion. "I can be talking to you and hear what you're saying while on alert for when someone calls out for a drink, or hear a conversation on this side." He pointed to his right ear, which was closest to Mama and her new friends.

"She told Owen how she was here to get you set on the right path and not settle like she did." He put his hands flat on the bar and leaned about an inch away from me. "So are you trying to mess with my mom and aunt?"

The question lingered, as did his stare.

"My aunt I don't care so much about it, but my mom, that's a different story." He left me gasping inside for air after he pushed himself away from me.

"No. Ahem," I cleared my throat to get back into my head, shocked by my response to Darren not only taking up for his mother but how he had invaded my personal space.

Calling it invaded made me feel better.

"No." I shook my head and picked up the drink, taking a large sip. "My mama doesn't know anything. I told you she just showed up out of nowhere." I took one last drink before I left the drink sitting there. "You said Nate Lustig." I walked back to Mama. "Does he own the diner?"

I needed clarification.

"He does. And he's giving the cooking class." Darren slid a few beer steins off the shelf behind the bar, grabbed a tray, and started to fill each one as the beer poured from a spicket of many.

The waitress drummed her fingers, waiting.

"Cooking class?" Mama's ears had perked up. "Did you say there's a cooking class? Violet could learn to cook."

"She doesn't cook?" Darren asked.

I was getting a sense he was thoroughly enjoying all the tidbits Mama was giving them about me. Ones I'd hoped to have left behind when I left my hometown.

"Oh yeah. Burns water." Mama got up off the stool between Owen and Shawn.

"Don't burn the Lustig Spring if you do decide to put an article in the *Junction Journal* about it. People around here won't let you leave town alive." Darren had some pretty serious parting words that would come back to haunt me later.

Water. Who knew?

CHAPTER FIVE

"Why did we leave?" Mama asked. I had to drag Mama out of the jiggle joint. "I was having fun with the Easter Bunny and Tooth Fairy," she teased, a side of her I'd never seen.

"Because if you want to do the cooking class for Mother's Day before you go back home" —which reminded me to make sure she had a seat on the airplane out of here at the end of the week—"then we have to sign up. All sign-up for all the activities are in Holiday Park."

"The Strickland boys sure do have good looks, but I really like Rhett." Mama wasn't so subtle in her matchmaking skills. "I hear he's available."

"You heard from him he's available?" I asked, knowing she'd already pried into his life.

"Yes. And did you know he owns a lot of property in Holiday Junction? Property is where the money is. I'm telling you. I tried to tell your father to get one of the campgrounds years ago, and look at Mae West and that group of yahoo women she hangs around with. They are swimming in a gold mine in that nasty Happy Trails Campground lake water." Mama rambled on and on about the success stories at home before she came to the realization of me being here in a similar small town. "But you don't need a man. We have to get you to California so the world can watch my baby on the news. The next Barbara Walters. You know Diane Sawyer is from Kentucky. She's pretty big."

We took the beaten path up from the seaside going toward the park. My mind was lost in doing an article on the Lustig Spring. I had grand ideas of finding people who had gotten water from there and who claimed to be healed from those minerals Darren had mentioned. I also found it interesting how Nate Lustig didn't want people on the property. That would make for an interesting story. Or at least a way to get him to talk to me.

I could tell him I'd heard about the spring and how he didn't want all the traffic on his property, and that's why I would be honored to do an article in the *Junction Journal* to inform the public. Plus I'd get my own sample of water to not only taste but get tested for all the claims, since it didn't sound like people had actually tested the water.

Before too long of a walk, the path opened up to a large grassy area called Holiday Park. It was a magnificent ending to Main Street. Main Street actually stopped at the beginning of the park where there was a parking lot.

The park was filled with large trees and had a few places for gatherings. One of those was the amphitheater where the local group I'd gotten to know pretty well, the Leading Ladies, were practicing for their Mother's Day play.

The Leading Ladies were actually leading ladies of Holiday Junction and married to a lot of the prominent men. Louise and Marge were both leading ladies, and they seemed to be in charge of the entire town. At least their personalities were.

From where I was standing, at the edge of the path and the park, I could see both of them on stage. Mama would get a kick out of meeting them, and it would be a great time to tell them Mama was in town but not to worry, as I was still working.

There was a nice-sized lake in the park where people were paddling around in those cute paddleboats. The boats were different sizes. Some held two people while others held four, where they sat back to back, but the most popular paddleboats were the ones shaped like a swan.

"We have to!" Mama bounced with glee and made a beeline for them.

"Wait, Mama. We have to sign up for the class or it'll get filled." I felt like I was chasing around a two-year-old in a candy factory.

"Yes. Then the paddleboats," she insisted before she heard the music playing and jerked toward it. "Is that a cake walk? And a band?"

"It looks like it." I hadn't seen a cake walk since I was in elementary school.

"We have to do that now." Mama literally was like a squirrel running around the park, going from activity to activity not knowing which one to do first.

When we finally made it over to the folding chairs positioned in a circle, Mama eyeballed all the cakes coming up for the cake walk competition. They were setting up for another game, and Mama had already signed herself up.

"Do you want to play?" she asked in her excited voice, the kind she used to have when the Piggly Wiggly had a sale on Coca-Cola when I was growing up.

"No. I'm good. You do it." I tried not to eat too many sweets since I was in the public eye and wanted to be ready just in case the big news stations happened to call me back in for an interview.

I hadn't given up on my dream and saw Holiday Junction as a detour. I was content, and for now that was good enough for me, even though I questioned it when I looked at Mama.

She'd been the epitome of content when I was younger, and look where that got us. Here. In line to participate in a cake walk.

A cake walk game was pretty simple. As music plays, the participants walk around the perimeter of the chair circle. When the music stops, everyone must immediately sit in a chair. The one person left standing without a chair is out of the running to win the cake. With each round a chair was removed, and the music continued until only one person was left. That person was the winner of the cake, which made for a pretty sweet deal considering Mama was competing to win a raspberry bundt cake from Freedom Diner, making the whole notion of me investigating this magical spring a must.

Patrick O'Malley and the Mad Fiddlers, a local band, started off the next round of cake walkers. Mama was walking so slow around the chairs, and when the band stopped, she plopped down in a chair, making her eligible to participate in the next round.

"Wooohooo!" Mama pumped her fist in the air when she and one other woman were the last two competitors. It was between Mama and this woman. Boy, did Mama have a serious game face on.

It was then and there I'd realized my competitive nature had come from my mama. For all these years, I'd thought I'd gotten that trait from my father.

Patrick and the band started up, and they played for a really long time before they abruptly stopped. Mama and the other woman were both on the side of the chair when they both went to fall their fanny in the seat. Only Mama gave the woman a nice push with her tushy, sending the woman flat on the ground.

"Ouch." The lady grabbed her ankle and groaned in pain. "What is wrong with you?"

"You're just mad because I won fair and square." Mama sat in the chair, refusing to get up until the cake walk volunteers put the cake in her hands.

They didn't bother with Mama. They hurried to the other lady's side to help her up, and when they did, they realized she couldn't stand alone.

"I think it's broken." The woman winced in pain.

There were a few calls made on some walkie-talkies, asking for medics.

"Mama, get up and apologize," I insisted through my gritted teeth. My face was red, which wasn't a good look against my blond hair and flush. I was so embarrassed.

"I'm not doing no such thing. I won fair and square. I want my bundt cake." I'd never seen this selfish side of Mama, and I was appalled.

About that time, there was the sound of a cluck, making Mama jump to her feet.

"What is that?" Mama snarled toward Dave, the rooster.

"He's in charge of security around here, and apparently someone's called security on you." I made a joke about it, but when I saw Chief Matthew Strickland following closely behind, I realized someone really had called the law on Mama.

"Ma'am." Chief Strickland greeted Mama with a firm nod underneath his white chief cap. "I understand you pushed Sally Westin to the ground, and she would like to file assault charges."

"That's ridiculous. We were playing a game, and she's the one who tried to push me out of the way just so she could win that cake." Mama pointed to Sally while the medics were looking at Sally's ankle.

I noticed a slight smile on Sally's face, like she was playing some sort of pitiful-me card.

"Nope. That's a lie." Someone from the crowd came over with their phone. "I was streaming it live on social media, and I have the footage right here."

Chief Strickland, Mama and I watched the replay, and as clear as day, Mama had used her booty to bump poor Sally to the ground. But Sally didn't land on her ankle. She landed on her booty, making the ankle claim a farse.

"What can we do to make it better?" I asked Chief, and he looked at me before he walked over to Sally.

Mama huffed and puffed, shifting from side to side, looking up at the sky then the ground before she crossed her arms.

"What's going on?" Marge Strickland, the chief's wife and Darren's mom, not to mention my boss, had seen the commotion from the amphitheater and had quickly come over.

"That woman claimed I shoved her out of the chair to win the raspberry bundt cake, but I didn't. I won fair and square," Mama proclaimed. "Fair and square!" she hollered for good measure.

"Did you say raspberry bundt cake?" Marge questioned Mama.

"She'll take the cake and not press charges." Chief Strickland held the cake, Mama salivating as she looked at it. "Deal? Or charges?"

"Deal," Mama muttered.

"I wouldn't've taken the deal." Marge sighed. "That cake was made by Nate Lustig. He only makes one a year with his special spring water. Now that he fired Sally Westin from the diner, she can't get her hands on anything Lustig Spring-related, and well, let's just say it's made her a little crazy."

"I'm Marge Strickland. I think our very own reporter, Violet Rhinehammer, needs to interview you for this crazy cake walk mishap." Marge's brows rose high on her forehead, something Mama's forehead was unable to do at this moment.

"Millie Kay Rhinehammer." Mama did that limp handshake thing with her hand again. "Violet's mama."

CHAPTER SIX

To say Mama made a big splash for her first public appearance in Holiday Junction was an understatement.

It was almost too much to bear with Mama's little surprise visit, then the news of the divorce, her competitive nature around the cake walk, plus the claim by Sally Westin about Mama assaulting. I knew I had to get her to the inn and let her rest so I could get back to work.

"I can't believe you made me give that woman my cake." Mama was still protesting on our way back to the Jubilee Inn.

"It was the right thing to do. You don't want to have an assault charge put against you. That'd make you have to stay in town for court appearances, and I'm sure you've got things to get back to at home." I wanted to make it sound terrible so she wouldn't want to stay. I also wanted to make sure she didn't upset anyone else.

"It was a game." Mama stood in front of one of the small shops on the sidewalk, taking a look at the display window.

Every shop had some sort of Mother's Day theme. It was adorable on a good day, but today was proving to be a tad bit challenging.

"Why does everyone forget games have a winner and a loser? I can't stand this whole 'everyone should get a participation trophy.'" Mama was old-school southern.

"Today's world doesn't operate that way." I tugged her to come on. "Besides, it was just a cake, and after I take you back to the inn, I'll be sure to stop by the Freedom Diner to sign us up for the cooking class. Then you can make your own cake plus pick Nate Lustig's brain and use that southern charm to get his secret raspberry bundt recipe."

Mama looked off into the distance. I could tell she was noodling the idea and noticed her face soften more and more with each step, liking the plan.

"Do you have to go to work?" Mama asked with a guilty tone after she'd considered the idea of us doing the cooking class. "I just got here, and we've not seen each other in a few months. Marge seems like a family woman. She'd understand."

"Marge is a family woman when it comes to her family." I motioned for Mama to cross the street once we were across from the Jubilee Inn. "She's also a businesswoman, and I had talked them into keeping *Junction Journal* going since they were going to stop producing it. There's a lot of time and money involved in my keeping it going, so I have to go to work. At least for a few hours."

"Fine." She sighed, and her shoulders fell. "What's going on at the inn? Another Mother's Day celebration?"

I drew my eyes to the crowd. There was a line going along the front of the inn and around the corner. I'd seen this before.

"Mayor Paisley is out for a photo opportunity for the Mother's Day cele-bration." I could see people out with their phones to record the event with the mayor.

"My goodness. They must love the mayor." Mama's head bobbled as she tried to see around the heads of the crowd to get a look at Mayor Paisley. "I think you need to write to your hometown mayor so she can get an idea how to woo the citizens of Normal like this."

"I don't think that'll happen. Mayor Paisley has no political views, loves everyone, and happily gives her attention to them." Once we were across the street and standing near the front of the line so we could get inside of the inn, I pointed to Mayor Paisley.

"The innkeeper is the mayor?" Mama asked when she noticed Kristine Whitlock, the owner of the Jubilee Inn, sitting next to Mayor Paisley.

"No. Mayor Paisley is sitting next to her in the pink floral dress." I made sure to watch Mama's expression as she took in the Boston Terrier dog.

It was hard not to smile when I watched Mama's face contort from confusion to glee.

"You're pulling my leg." Mama laughed.

"No. Mayor Paisley is a dog." While Mama and I watched tourists walk up one by one to greet Kristine and Mayor Paisley, I told her how the town was run by a town council and how they elected Paisley and the other animal candidates to help raise money for the holiday festivals the town put on for each holiday.

"She's got the cutest face," Mama said, referring to Paisley's little black pointy ears and her white upside-down wishbone markings that started between the pup's eyes and along each side of her nose. "I've got to get a photo myself."

"I've got connections." I stopped Mama from going to the back of the line. "We can get our own personal meeting with the mayor, and you can voice your concerns about how the games work."

Mama laughed, knowing I was teasing her.

Mama and I weaved through the crowd to get inside of the inn. It was a small, basic place to stay and the only place I'd stayed since I'd gotten here. Eventually I'd get a more permanent place, and in my mind, I was testing out the waters here in Holiday Junction to see if I was really going to stay here, make a career for myself or not. These were some big life decisions I had to make, and for now those decisions were going to have to be put on hold.

Mama was going to take up any capacity on my head and make my living arrangements and the decision to stay in Holiday Junction go to the back burner of my thoughts.

"You live here?" Mama looked around the small room with a look of disapproval.

"I do for now. I've not had time with work to look for a place to live. It's on my list, but for now I'm here and focusing on my career." I handed her the room key. "You make yourself at home, and I'm going to head back to my office. If you need something, just call my cell."

"You never answer me." The dig was said under her breath.

"Mama, I'll answer you." I had to say it and reinforce I would so she wouldn't show up at the front door of the office like she'd done before.

"Fine." She sat down on the bed and looked down at her feet with her pouty face. One I wasn't falling for. "I'll just sit here all by myself."

"Sounds good. Take a nap. We will get supper later." I kissed her forehead and headed out the door.

My main focus was to get me and her signed up for the Freedom Diner Mother's Day cooking class and do some research on the Lustig Spring. If I could get some of that completed today, it would be a good workday.

"Violet," Kristine called my name when she saw me maneuvering around the crowd.

I looped around a few clusters of tourists and made my way to where she was standing. Hubert, her husband, was taking his turn sitting with Mayor Paisley.

"Good afternoon," I greeted her. "It's a gorgeous day, and this crowd is amazing."

"Everyone loves Mother's Day." Her voice carried above the laughter and chatter of the crowd. "I met your mother. I had no idea she was coming into town. If I'd known, I'd have saved her a room."

"You're booked?" I quietly snorted in the back of my throat. Of course they were. My luck. No place for Mama here meant no place for Mama but with me.

"I am. I hate that." There was a look of empathy in her eyes. "But I'm more than happy to give her the first room available after Mother's Day."

"Oh, she won't be here after that. In fact, I've got to make sure she's booked on the first flight out next week." I ran my hand down my long blond hair as a sudden gust of wind swept past.

I looked up to see what the weather was doing in case it was about to rain, though I knew the forecast didn't call for it. It was sunny and bright, making it strange there was a breeze.

Chill bumps made waves along my arms, sending me a shiver shake.

"Are you okay?" Kristine asked.

"Yes. I'm fine." I crossed my arms and shifted my weight to my right hip. My head tilted. "Do you happen to know anything about the Lustig Spring?"

"Sure. Everyone does." Kristine had been a great resource for me. She was able to help me get information for the paper and research as someone who grew and stayed in Holiday Junction. "Why?"

"I was on the trolley with Goldie this morning, and she mentioned the spring in a passing conversation." I left out the fact Goldie's husband Elvin didn't like little Izzy taking lessons at the Groove and Go due to the fact he didn't want to give the Lustig family any more money because it didn't matter. "I was in the process of researching the spring when Rhett showed up at the office with Mama."

The look Kristine gave me was probably due to the tone of my voice.

"I love Mama, don't get me wrong." I uncurled my arms and placed both hands on my heart. "But she can be much, and well," my brows pinched, "Mama has informed me she is divorcing my dad."

That garnered a gasp from Kristine and an immediate "I'm sorry."

"I'm not entirely convinced that's happening, but Mama showed up here without me knowing." I didn't let Kristine know I'd also planned on calling my dad about it. I had to hear from him before I truly believed they were headed for a divorce. "Mama kinda got into a little scuffle with Sally Westin. Now I have to know all about the spring, because not to waste your time on all the details Marge mentioned after Mama agreed to give Sally the raspberry bundt cake made by Nate Lustig, I found it interesting that was all it took for Sally to not put an assault charge against Mama."

"Did Marge tell you Nate fired Sally?" Kristine asked.

"Yes, but she didn't tell me why. Do you know?"

"I certainly do. I heard Sally was going to the diner after hours and stealing jugs of the water Nate filled from their Lustig Spring," Kristine told me. "About two months ago."

"She was fired for stealing?" I made sure I understood what she was telling me.

"Pretty much." Both of us turned around after we'd heard a honk from a car.

It was Rhett Strickland. He gave a slight wave before he waved me over.

"We can talk later. I'll be sure your Mama is okay." Kristine was great about being a good host, and I'd found she was true to her word.

"Hey," Rhett called to me out of the rolled-down driver's side window.

"I'm sorry about dropping off your mom. She didn't say you weren't expecting her."

"It's fine. I guess I'm glad it was you and not someone I didn't know." I was appreciative of his kindness. "I've got her at the inn while I head back to the office."

"Jump in. I'll take you." He leaned way over and opened the door from the inside.

"Are you sure?" Too late to even ask the question since I'd already gotten in and was in the process of clipping in my seat belt.

He didn't even bother answering.

"What are you working on at the paper? I'm sure my aunts will let you take a few days to be with your mom." He drove down Main Street carefully since tourists were jaywalking, and he took the roundabout at the end next to Holiday Park so he could drive back up Main and out to the seaside.

"It's fine. I'm not sure how long she'll be here. But I'm working on the Lustig Spring. Especially now that Mama has insulted a former employee." The story I told him, about the cake walk incident between Sally and Mama, made him laugh.

"You southern women sure do stand up to your reputation." I wasn't sure what he meant by the statement or even if it was a compliment or put-down, but I didn't want to know. "There is such a history about the spring that when the property finally got inherited to Nate, he had so many tourists and locals showing up at all hours of the night. Not only did they park all over his property, making it hard for his family to function in day-to-day life, but people started having fights. My uncle was called out there a lot. Even a gun was pulled out once."

"No wonder he doesn't allow people there." I didn't blame Nate after hearing Rhett tell the history of why Nate didn't allow anyone to use the spring.

"Sally's sister has an autoimmune disease, and she swears the spring has virtually healed her." Rhett made me want to know more about the disease Sally's sister had.

This could make a huge story the national press would love to pick up. A big article going viral was just the thing I needed to reboot my career, but was it the right thing to do for Nate Lustig?

This was one of those moral questions I'd have to consider as a journalist. Of course my ego said to run with it and get all the exposure I could, but the compassion and love I felt for Holiday Junction held me back from making any sort of decision about what I'd do after I had collected all the information.

"That's why she wanted the cake." I stared out the window and noticed we weren't headed in the direction of the seaside. Granted, I'd not lived here long enough to learn shortcuts, and hadn't even driven anywhere since I didn't even have a car. "You are taking me to the office, right?"

"I thought I'd run you out to the spring so you can see it for yourself." He took his eyes off the road for a split second to look at me as if he were trying to make sure I was good with the idea.

"Yeah, if you think we can get in to see it." I was all about getting up close and personal to the actual spring. "I was going to try to sweet-talk Nate Lustig into getting in to see it, but if you can get us there, that'd be great."

"I think I can." He had a faint smile on his lips.

There was so much more to Rhett than I knew. From what I gathered and encountered with his entire family, they all seemed to be well-respected, stand-up folks. There were some rifts in the family, but with as big a family as the Strickland gang, it wasn't unusual to have those types of relationships.

No doubt in my mind, the arguments were like the waves, in and out, up and down.

A few miles out of town in the countryside, Rhett pulled off onto a dirt road. There were several cars lined up with people standing outside with various sizes of jugs and containers in their hands as if they were waiting to be let inside.

The car drove over a cattle guard. At the second cattle guard, there was a gate with a speaker.

Rhett reached out the window and pushed the small black button.

"Can I help you?" a woman's voice came through, crackly from the speaker.

"Palmer, it's Rhett" was all he had to say before the gate started to open. He drove forward and waited for the gate to fully open before he drove through it.

I shifted around in the seat to look back and watch the gate close, with people standing a few feet away from it shouting and lifting their containers up in the air over their heads. The emotions on their faces ranged from hope to anger.

"Palmer is my godmother," Rhett let me know.

"Palmer is a Lustig?" I asked.

"Yep. She's married to Nate. She and my mom were friends. They are like a second family to me." We weren't able to explore that any more since we'd pulled up to a two-story clapboard country house with chipped-up paint.

An older woman with her salt-and-pepper hair pulled up in the back, with several stray pieces falling around her face, framing it, stood out in the yard, waving her arms wildly over her head. There was a huge smile on her face.

She had on an apron tied around her waist and was wiping her hands off on it like she'd just washed them. Her eyes shifted to the passenger seat, and when she noticed me, the smile faded and her eyes appeared more alert.

Maybe it was just me thinking she was taking me in, judging me, and wondering who this woman in her godson's passenger seat was when it clearly wasn't Fern Banks, the local beauty queen who had claimed Rhett as her own.

"I admit I was surprised to hear your voice over the speaker." Palmer greeted Rhett by hugging him.

Once the embrace was over, she patted him on the back a few times.

"Who's your friend?" She tilted her head and looked at me from across the hood of the car as I made my way around.

"This is Violet Rhinehammer." He used his full upturned hand to gesture to me.

"It's nice to meet you, Mrs. Lustig." I outstretched my hand.

"Such formalities." She graciously took it. "Southern girl?"

"Yes, ma'am." I nodded with the southern pride on my face.

"Don't 'ma'am' me or 'Mrs. Lustig' me. I'm not that old," she joked. "Can I get you something to drink?"

"No, ma'am." I gulped. "No thank you, Palmer." I was going to go right on into why we were here. I'd never been great at beating around the bush, and with Mama in town, there was limited time to do any work, which meant I needed to use what little time I had wisely.

"Violet has recently moved here and is working for my aunts at the *Junction Journal*," Rhett said.

Her head slightly fell back and her mouth opened a little as the light bulb went off in her head. "I like what you've been doing with the online edition. I subscribed because of you." Those were words I'd not figured she was thinking and certainly not the ones I thought would come out of her mouth.

My history of finding a local murderer when I got into town was what most people here remembered after they recalled my name. The fact Palmer didn't mention that little fact told me I was getting a little better of a reputation.

"I'm guessing you're wanting to get some information on the spring." She was direct and to the point.

"Yes." I decided Palmer was a no-sugar-added type of woman and that being a straight shooter was the best approach with her.

She looked at Rhett as if he were the deciding factor. He gave several bobbed nods and smiled.

"The reason my interest is piqued is my mama is in town, and we were at the Mother's Day cake walk when she was called for assault after she'd bumped Sally Westin for the final chair to win one of your husband's raspberry bundts. My mama loves a good raspberry bundt." I could see that cake now in my mind, and it made my mouth water.

"Sally Westin is a troublemaker." Palmer shook her head disapprovingly.

"She did drop any sort of claim of assault only if Mama gave her the bundt cake." My words kept Palmer's eye focused on me as her chin lifted into the air. A brow arched. "When I questioned the reasons why she wanted it so bad, I was informed about the spring."

There was no way I was going to tell Palmer how Marge had divulged the information, since a good journalist never gave up their source. It was a trust issue between the source and the journalist. The trusted source. It was also how I would establish a good relationship with people so they'd know they could trust me.

There was a gaze from Palmer to Rhett that passed between them.

"You can trust Violet." He must've noticed Palmer needed a reassurance to continue. "She checks out."

"What would you like to know?" Palmer turned her back to walk toward the long front porch of the home.

"I would like to do some sort of article about the spring." I followed closely behind her and didn't take a seat in one of the many rocking chairs until she gestured for me to sit. "I understand you don't want people here, and from what I'd seen when we pulled in, people don't listen. I'd love to do something to reinforce your family wishes, along with the research along the way from testing the water, cooking with the water, and drinking the water to show people who insist the spring has these healing properties that they aren't scientifically backed."

"This could take months." Palmer's toe pressed into the old wooden planks on the front porch pushed the rocker back and forth in a slow motion.

"Yes. I know. But I have a lot of great resources over the years from various other articles I've researched that I feel can possibly help speed up the process." By articles I meant dead bodies from when I did investigative reporting back home, but it was best to leave such a tidbit out.

"What kind of access will you need from me if I were to agree and get Nate on board?" Her voice was steady. There was no indication in the inflection of her tone whether she was leaning toward a yes or a no.

"I would need to get some water from the spring. Enough to have to drink, cook, possibly wash my face, even bathe in it." That would be a lot of water to bathe in it, so I changed my mind. "Really a foot soak, not a full bath."

"A foot soak?" she asked

"There's such things as magnesium foot soaks that have healing properties from transdermal, which if your body is deficient in a mineral, the fastest way for your body to get the vitamins it requires for full function is through the skin." I explained to her how transdermal therapy worked. "In this case, people are drinking a lot of it because they feel like they are getting some sort of healing. I'd love to send samples off to a friend I've known over the years with a lab so we can truly test the property of the

174

water, which could simply mean the spring is sitting on a magnesium-type basin, which would really explain a lot of how good it makes people feel."

There was a pause, and when she didn't answer with an agreement for not only the article but the research I'd need to do, I jumped back in.

"If my hunch is right and that's the case, then we can tell people they need to take magnesium supplements instead of driving all over the country to get to your Lustig Spring." I looked between Rhett and Palmer to see if I could read the situation. "It's a case of informing the public, and with the right research and article, I think we can do that."

"Let me talk to Nate, and I'll let you know." There was no way I was going to get her on board without her husband.

"Thank you. I appreciate it." I knew I had to keep digging, and just because she'd not agreed to what I was going to do, it didn't mean I was going to stop.

I was a journalist, and a good journalist knows when there's a great story to research. I knew in my bones this was one of those, and I wasn't going to back down.

Even if Nate didn't agree.

CHAPTER SEVEN

"What did that mean?" I asked Rhett once we got into the car.

"What?" He played the confused angle well.

"You know what. The whole checks out." I shifted in the seat of the car. "You checked me out."

"Me and the aunts." He turned the radio on. "Do you honestly think we could take a risk from an outsider to come in and work for us? Them?"

"I thought my word and actions would be good enough, but I guess I'm wrong." I shifted to look out the passenger window as we headed back toward the main area of Holiday Junction.

"We've been burnt by reporters who have come into town to report on a few of our holiday celebrations and their intentions didn't do us any good. They simply would call us clichés and all the insults that go along with how we live here. The aunts would rather keep our town quiet and away from tourists, so when you came into town, did that crazy live viral video, they looked you up."

"I'm glad I passed." I couldn't disagree with what they'd done. If it was me in their shoes, I'd have done the same thing.

"With flying colors." He smiled to himself, but I noticed. "What about a bite to eat?"

"I don't think I can do that. I'd like to get back and get a jump on the research." I was about to tell Rhett how I still planned on doing the article and research with or without the consent of the Lustig family.

"There's no greater research than having food made from the water at the Freedom Diner." His suggestion showed I didn't have to tell him I was going to continue the research on my own.

He was already on board.

"You think I have a good case for doing the article?" For some reason I wanted his support and felt it was necessary to have. It felt good having someone on my side.

"I think it'll solve a lot of unanswered questions. But you have to realize people around here don't care so much about the scientific part. All Nate and Palmer see are people milling around their land, being nosy and just in the way. If they knew the spring water does contain some sort of mineral that truly is natural and helps the body, even aids in illnesses, I think they'd be more open to doing something to let people have access to the spring."

I took in everything Rhett was saying and realized I'd not even said a word as he drove us to the diner.

Like the rest of the shops and stores in town, the diner was a dingy white clapboard house with a covered front. A banner of stringed-together triangles with the American flag hung down along the front, and a small blue sign with "Freedom Diner" written on it in plain letters hung out from an iron arm.

A Coca-Cola machine as well as a bagged ice machine sat underneath the covered porch to the left of the door. To the right of the diner door were two chairs that didn't match. One was a steel-framed, straight-back chair with a padded leather cushion with a big crack down the middle while the other was a folded chair with braided seat used as a picnic chair. Many of the webbed braids were frayed and looked a little dry-rotted.

The inside of the diner was like every other diner I'd been in, even in my hometown. It was the typical diner seating with acrylic-top tables, padded chairs, and a bar with stools lining it. I couldn't see back in the kitchen, but when Rhett and I sat down at the counter, I noticed the multiple large jugs of water behind the counter.

I also noticed the few glass cake stands along the counter filled with plates of slices of delicious pies and cakes that tickled my taste buds.

My phone chirped, taking me out of my observations, though I'd stored all the details in the back of my mind. They would come in handy for the article.

I looked at the phone and noticed it was a text from Vern McKenna, a local man I knew as the Merry Maker, a secret identity kept from everyone in Holiday Junction but me and Reed Schwindt, the local handyman.

"Everything okay?" Rhett asked. "You look confused."

"I'm fine. Just a text from someone I wasn't expecting to get one from." I didn't tell Rhett since I wasn't sure if Vern wanted something specific to his job as the town Merry Maker or something else. "Excuse me for a minute."

Rhett's eyes narrowed. He looked at my hand where my attention had gone and gave a slight nod.

I got up and walked out the diner, hitting Vern's number as I passed a few customers on the way in.

"Violet, how are you?" Vern asked as soon as the phone connected.

"I'm good. Are you okay?" I asked. "If you're calling about the Mother's Day Merry Maker, I'd love to know where you're posting the—" The sentence dangled.

"It's a cutout of a wood basket filled with painted flowers. It's been used for a few years now, and it's still in pretty good shape. That's why I'm calling." He had my attention. "I wanted to pass the baton down to you."

"Baton?" I wasn't sure what he meant.

"You're younger, and you seem to really enjoy doing the articles on the Merry Maker. So why not let you take over? There's no work you have to do. All the signs are in the shed, and you know where that is. Reed is more than happy to help get them where they need to be and set up. You just have to be the one to decide where the festival party ends. That's all." He made it sound so easy.

"That's all?" I snorted and pushed a strand of my hair behind my ear as I paced back and forth in front of the Freedom Diner, glancing in every few steps to see if Rhett was paying attention to me.

He was.

"I can't have that kind of responsibility. This town revolves around the holidays, and I might screw that up after all of these years. I barely have my own life in check at this moment. I can't wreck an entire town." I couldn't imagine taking on such a task. "Besides, I'm not even sure how long I'm passing through Holiday Junction," I whispered when I noticed a few of the Leading Ladies eyeballing me when they skirted around me to get to the diner door.

"Passing through?" Vern asked. "From what I heard from Leni, she said she'd heard you've pretty much taken over the *Junction Journal*, got a fancy new office, and are doing all sorts of online things. If you weren't planning on staying, why would you put so much time and effort into a dying paper when you could be putting effort into getting out of here?"

That was a question I'd asked myself. One I wasn't prepared to answer or be asked by anyone else.

"I don't know, Vern." I bypassed his question with my answer to him wanting me to take over as the all-secretive Merry Maker.

"That's something you've got to find out in your soul before you continue to make commitments to people."

"No, I mean I don't know if I want to be the Merry Maker, not about I don't know why I'm not spending my time looking for a way out of Holiday Junction." All this back and forth was making me anxious. His question was something I didn't want to answer, but I started talking when I knew I needed to keep my mouth shut. It was like Vern had turned on a faucet and there was no emergency off button.

"I guess I like it here. Yes, I did move the *Junction Journal* office from the Stricklands' family home off the far end of Main Street only because I thought it was weird to be listening to Chief Strickland and Marge discuss family things. And it really is just good for the business." I rambled on why I'd gotten the journal moved to the cottage on the seaside. "For business it just looks better. I mean when someone wants to fill out an ad or just have a conversation for a feature. Then there's the entire thing about if the right job comes open and I apply. I mean, why would I go back home when ideally the job I want is national news and a little closer geographically than home?"

"Listen." Vern stopped the chatter for me since I couldn't seem to get a good grasp on it. "I think you've got a lot of time to figure those things out. You're young. People in Holiday Junction really like what you're doing with the paper, and you can write your own articles about the Merry Maker. I think it would be a great fit for even the little time you're here. I really think." He was really selling me on it.

"No. You're right. The readers might love a new segment in the paper from the Merry Maker." It really did light a little fire in my gut, and that's how I always knew when a good story was crossing in front of me. "What is the right way to go about it?"

"Be at the shed tonight at midnight. Wear black. All black." He clicked off the phone before I could even ask a question.

And just like that, I'd agreed to be Holiday Junction's next Merry Maker.

CHAPTER EIGHT

Rhett was talking with Nate Lustig when I came back in from my phone call with Vern.

"You must be the young lady Palmer was talking about." He smiled and took the coffeepot from the holder then leaned over the counter to fill up the mug Rhett had gotten for me while I was outside. "She mentioned something about you doing an article on the spring, and well, I just don't want you to do that."

His brows hooded over his eyes, his lips curled in, and he gave one hard nod before he moved down the counter to fill up the other empty mugs.

"I guess that's that." I sat on the stool with my back straight, hands between my thighs and eyes looking at Rhett. "I'm going to do my own investigation, I guess, without him."

"You can't be serious," Rhett said with a disapproving look on his face. "You are. You are going to do an article without the owner's permission?"

"I am a journalist. That's what I'm paid to do, and when I feel like there's a story, I follow the leads." I tipped my head back when I noticed the look he was giving me. "I see. That's not how things work at the *Junction Journal*."

"I think we all like to live around here in peace, and if you start digging around things—" He abruptly stopped talking and pulled out a few dollars from his pocket. He tossed them on the counter and got up from the stool.

Apparently we weren't going to eat here any longer.

The young waitress behind the counter shuffled over and slid Rhett's money back to him.

"I can pay for my half cup of coffee." I wasn't about to let Rhett pay for it since he had what appeared to be either a disapproving or concerned look on his face. It was hard to distinguish the two.

"Don't worry about a cup of coffee, Rhett." "Patty" was embroidered on the pocket of the Freedom Diner shirt. "He'll come around." She tried to make me feel better. "You wouldn't believe how many people come in here and beg him for some water or even just a few minutes to talk about the spring. Plus, with Palmer kinda in charge, he wants everyone to think it's out of his hands."

"Like a good excuse not to let me." I laid a five-dollar bill on the counter. "Keep it. Thanks for the information."

"Yeah. Let me know if you need anything else." She took the money and put it in her apron pocket along with the rest of the tip money sticking out.

"You didn't need to pay." Rhett turned to leave.

"I'm sorry you feel I shouldn't be investigating." I talked to the back of Rhett's head as he led the charge out of the diner. "I feel like there must be a story there he's covering up, and from what the waitress says, Nate is able to use Palmer and her not wanting to let people in as his excuse, when in reality, he's the one not wanting people to come."

"And what is so wrong with him not wanting to have people on his property at all hours of the night?" Rhett jerked around once we were outside standing on the sidewalk. "I guess you'd get sick of it. Why can't you leave well enough alone?"

"It's not my job to leave well enough alone. I'm an—" I was about to rattle off my job title as investigative reporter, only Rhett put his hand up to stop me.

"You are a *citizen* of Holiday Junction. You are a member of our community, and no good comes from trying to dig out secrets that never need to see the light of day." The serious tone of his voice struck me.

There was definitely something here, but for now I would do what Rhett asked and not snoop yet.

"Fine. I'll just do Mother's Day and focus on getting the paper really up and running online." Rhett's face softened, and his lips curled in a slight smile. "Now I have to go back in there and sign up for the cooking class."

"I signed you and your mom up when you took the phone call." He pulled his car keys from his pocket.

"That was very kind of you. What day?" I asked. "And time? Mama will want to know all the particulars."

"Tonight at seven. It was the only slot they had left, and that's why I signed you up."

"Well, it does give us something to do." I also had to keep in mind to meet Vern at midnight wearing all black. I wasn't even sure if I had anything black to wear.

A stop at Emily's Treasures just might be where I needed to go next.

"The office?" Rhett opened the passenger door for me.

"No. I want you to take me back to the Jubilee Inn. Since I don't have a big story to investigate"—*yet*, I wanted to say—"I will take Mama shopping and back to Holiday Park for a little more fun. Plus maybe make a few calls to the airport to make sure she's on a flight back to Kentucky."

CHAPTER NINE

"Mayor Paisley taking her afternoon nap?" I glanced behind the counter at the Jubilee Inn when I noticed the Boston Terrier sleeping in the dog bed next to Kristine's chair.

"It's hard being the mayor and a celebrity." Kristine made both of us laugh.

"I hope Mama is taking a nap too." I started up the steps.

"Millie is not here," Kristine called after me. "She asked if there was a car rental company around here, and I sent her over at Harold Harvest's car lot. But before she left she also asked me about Holiday Junction Travel Agency. I gave her Joaquin's name."

"Oh good. That means Mama is thinking about her return trip home." I smiled.

"Um. I think she wanted to talk to Joaquin since he does the real estate around here. He only uses Layla's office to do the paperwork since most of his time is spent going around Holiday Junction."

"Why would Mama want to talk to Joaquin?" I asked.

"I'm not sure." Kristine didn't sound so convincing and I would've probed her more, but the phone saved her from talking to me. I wasn't sure if she was really involved with the customer on the phone as she busied herself with the computer while she talked, or if she was doing it to make her appear to be busy so she didn't have to talk to me.

I slipped a wave to let her know I was leaving and heading right across the street to the travel agency just to see what Mama was up to. It wasn't like it was too far. Just a hop and a skip away, but I didn't have to go too far to find Mama.

"Violet!" Mama called from behind me.

I whirled around, and she was sticking her head from around the door of Emily's Treasures, waving me in.

"I was just coming to find you." I gave her a hug after I'd gotten inside. "Hi Emily." I waved to the owner, who had her latest spring clothing pieces in just in time for Mother's Day. "I see you've met my mama."

There were several hangers banging together from the layers of clothes draped over her forearm.

"Most of these are for you. You've got to look nice when it comes to the job." Mama peeled the first item off the top and held it up to my chin before she snarled and stuck it back on the closest rack. "No." She repeated the process two more times before she said, "Perfect. Go try this on."

"Mama, I have clothes." I did keep an eye out for a black something-or-other for my secret meeting with Vern as she shoved me back toward the dressing room. I plucked a pair of black joggers and matching black short-sleeved shirt on my way past the rack.

"You do not. I looked through your clothes at the inn, and let me tell you, you don't have anything that screams newspaper editor in chief."

"Whoa," I turned around shy of the dressing room and waited in line with Mama right next to me like she did when I was ten at the local mall. "That's not my title. I really just do small things, like behind-the-scenes things to get the online paper up and running."

Mama pinched a grin when a customer vacated a dressing room, making it around her to make sure she nabbed it.

"Not for long, dear." Mama's forcing the dressing room door to shut made me take two steps back into the dressing room. "After you do the big story on the Lustig Spring, you might be the most sought-after reporter this side of the Mississippi. We live on the other side of the Mississippi," she told the lady waiting for a dressing room behind us and shut the door, leaving her on the other side of the dressing room.

"This doesn't look like me." I held the lime-green sweater up to my face and didn't bother trying it on since I knew I'd never wear it or anything in the color family.

"I don't think you know what looks like you, picking out something all black. That's morbid." Mama was just like most southern women. She loved all things floral, fluorescent, or that looked like wallpaper. "Not to mention a jogging outfit."

"It's all about comfort right now." I opened the door and handed the sweater to the young girl Emily hired to work the dressing rooms to handle such items needing to be put back on the rack. "When I go on camera or need to do an interview where I need a photo, I promise you I'll—" I was about to tell her, but she'd gotten a call and walked clear out the door.

Emily stood behind the small debit register when I walked up to the counter. I gave a last look over my shoulder to see what Mama was doing outside, and she was still talking on the phone. A huge smile on her face.

"I guess you met my mama." I handed Emily the hangers.

"She's so sweet." Emily's first interaction with me months ago wouldn't have been described as sweet. She'd practically kicked me out for being too loud. "She loves Holiday Junction. She said you were writing up a big article about the Lustig Spring. I can't wait to see what you dig up. People have been up in arms about the spring for years since Palmer told Nate to end all the traffic."

I smiled but found it interesting how Palmer had told me the exact opposite. I tucked it away as simple hearsay.

"You know Nate's family didn't like him marrying Palmer. Said she was a gold digger, and from the meeting she's been having over at the library with those fancy people from that cosmetic company, I hear she's going to make a mint off of it." Emily was full of information that changed the entire trajectory of this story.

"Yeah. I'm guessing she's going to turn the water into—" I snapped my fingers and looked in the air, acting as if I couldn't remember.

"Ask Joaquin about it." Emily nodded toward the front of the shop. I turned around and saw Joaquin talking to Mama. "Apparently if Nate puts the land in Palmer's name, then she can turn around and sell it, making a huge profit on packaging the spring water for health alternatives. Not makeup."

Now that was a story. A very interesting one.

"Which would make this sleepy little town a lot louder." Emily cocked a brow and handed me the bag with my black outfit in it. "But just like Millie Kay was saying, it might not be a bad thing since we could use a steady tourist season around here instead of just during the holidays. I told Millie Kay we could use a lot more citizens with her point of view in Holiday Junction."

I took the bag with one hand and tapped my fingertip on the counter with the free hand.

"Don't be going and giving her any ideas." My eyes darted about as my mind tried to process all the information Emily had given me and how Mama had some sort of opinion.

"Thank you, Emily," I called out with my bag lifted in the air as my hand waved goodbye.

I looked at Mama having her big conversation outside on the sidewalk, looking more comfortable talking to the locals than I ever did, even now. She looked like she was settling in. A little too much.

CHAPTER TEN

"There she is now." Joaquin Camsen greeted me with a huge smile. "I was just telling Millie Kay about the new two-family that hit the market this morning."

"Isn't that great?" Mama rocked back on the heels of her tennis shoes. "I was hoping for a single-family to pop up this week, but a two-family is pure perfection." She beamed, slipping her soft hand into the crook of Joaquin's elbow.

"I'm glad you're here to go see it." He patted Mama's hand and looked down at her. "Shall we?"

"We shall," Mama's voice grew an octave as Joaquin led her to the parked golf cart.

"And I've got you a surprise when we get there."

"I can hardly wait," Mama squealed. She got into the passenger side. "Well? Violet? Come on?"

"I guess I'm a little confused as to why we are going to see a home, much less a two-family."

The golf cart had a back seat facing backward, and apparently it was the only place for me to sit.

"Hold on, ladies." Joaquin jumped in and clicked the gear into drive as he pushed the pedal down then whipped the cart around in the middle of the street, headed away from Holiday Park.

Barely missing the person on the moped, Joaquin jerked the wheel left, putting us on Heart Way. I gripped the metal structure for dear life because Joaquin wasn't paying too much attention to where he was going, and all his focus was on Mama. He laughed at the story she was telling, and I had no idea what it was since I was trying to recall the chin tuck and roll we had learned when I'd taken bicycle lessons as a child. It was how they taught us to contort our bodies if we were to wreck, and right then my only concern was to survive this golf cart ride.

"Hold on!" Joaquin yelled out of the side of his mouth. "These roundabouts might get ya," he joked. I swore the golf cart went up on two wheels before he exited the roundabout onto Reindeer Road.

He pulled into the first driveway, which led up to a light-blue house with what looked to be a yellow carriage-style house behind it. A cute wooden picket fence ran along the front and what I could see of the sides of the house. There was a blue golf cart parked snugged up to the garage.

"Here we are." Joaquin jumped out of the golf cart and ran straight around to help Mama out. "Millie Kay, what do you think?"

Joaquin put his thumbs in the elastic of his polyester pants and dug his body weight in the heels of his white shiny patent-leather shoes. His light-blue and too-tight button-up was literally unbuttoned more than one button. The sun hit his gold chain perfectly, making the Jesus piece, the cross, twinkle among his tufts of chest hair.

"She's a beaut, this one." He nodded, his lips duck billed. "Won't be on the market long." He took his thumbs out of the elastic waistband and pointed to the blue golf cart. "That is for you. Harold over at the car lot told me you were looking for some wheels, and the locals all drive golf carts."

"She's not a local, and I'm not able to afford this house." I didn't even bother getting out of the golf cart. I reached around to the passenger seat and gave it a hard pat. "Come on, Mama. Let's go."

"You might not be able to afford it, but I can." She didn't look at me. She grinned and looked up at Joaquin. "Look at this view." She pointed to the mountains in the background before she got to the line of trees planted along the backyard that covered up any sort of road or downtown views.

"I'm not going to take your money." I did get out on that one, but she was right about the gorgeous view. It would be nice to sit here and look at the sun come up over the mountains every morning. "This is why I don't live at home anymore, Mama. I want to make it on my own, and I'm doing fine."

"There's no way I'm going to let any daughter of mine live in a motel, much less one room, and it's not good for your figure to eat out all the time. You need a good place to put your panties." It was Mama's way of saying I needed a place of my own for my things. "Not where some maid rummages through your things."

"And it's got the cottage out back for your mama." Joaquin was right about one thing. When Mama did come to visit, I didn't want her right up under my nose.

"And I just so happen to know the owner, and he's giving us a deal," Mama said just as Rhett Strickland pulled up and parked behind both golf carts. "There he is now."

"He has the keys for us. Special showing just for you, Millie Kay." Joaquin tapped Mama's nose.

"Ladies, Joaquin," Rhett greeted us. "What do you think, Millie Kay?"

"I think I'm going to take the big house and let Violet live in the cottage out back. My rocking chair will go perfect." Mama stopped herself. "Heck. I'm going to get all new furniture."

"What?" I blinked, confused.

"I've made the decision," Mama said. "I'm staying in Holiday Junction."

"You're what?" I asked through a gritted toothy smile as my-oh-crap-no meter went to high alert. "Mama, you can't do that. I'm not sure how long I'll be here."

"You aren't?" Rhett's brow winkled with a contemptuous thought. "What about the *Junction Journal*?"

"Rhett, please." I put a hand out. "Mama."

"Why don't we go in and take a look around," Joaquin suggested, a little nervous tic in his tone.

"Mr. Camsen," I moved my hand his way now.

"Joaquin. Please." He put his hand on his shirt before he took a few steps forward. "Shall we?'

"No. We need to go," I insisted. My brows had managed to draw all the way up to my hairline. "Now."

190

"I can't wait to see it." Mama moved past me.

"Rhett?" I managed to say his name under my stiff lip.

"I'm just the seller. Anything you've got to discuss is between you two," he said smoothly with little to no expression on his face.

"Don't you dare step foot in that house, Mama," I told her, but do you think she listened? Heck no.

She walked in the front door like she owned the place, but not first without pushing the doorbell.

"Nice and loud." She twisted around at the threshold and wiggled her nose to Rhett. "Just how I like it, right, honey?" she asked me. "Come on. Be a good girl and get in here!"

My shoulders slumped. The sheer realization of how Mama always vexed people was evident. She had Rhett and Joaquin eating out of the palm of her southern hand. And at that point I knew Holiday Junction had not only gained one Rhinehammer in the local phone book, but two.

CHAPTER ELEVEN

"I'm going to have to get used to these pedals." Mama herkie-jerked the golf cart all the way through town, nearly scaring the skin right off my bones. "What are the laws concerning a golf cart? Can you park anywhere? What about drive on a sidewalk?"

"Mama, I know you are serious about divorcing Daddy, but you're making an awfully lot of big decisions on top of that huge lifestyle change. I'm not sure you should be doing that right now." I sighed and again found myself holding on for dear life as she tried to maneuver the golf cart on the road, barely missing cars, other golf carts, and tourists on scooters.

"Violet, I know what I'm doing. I might be older, but I'm not senile." Mama wasn't old. In fact, she was only fifty-one.

She and my daddy got married right out of high school. A couple of years later they had me, and only me, so I was used to the three of us.

"How does Daddy feel about all of this?" I asked since I'd yet to hear from him.

"He is right as rain." Mama tugged her mouth in a thin line as if she were really trying to keep her loose lips from flapping.

Of course, Mama wasn't going to say anything negative against Daddy. How could she? He was nothing but short of amazing. And probably why I'd never been able to find a good man. I'd compared everyone to my daddy and how amazing he was as a dad and husband, making it hard for any man to stand up to his standards.

"Oh, Mama." I groaned. "Can you imagine Daddy dating Betts Hager or even Dottie Swaggert?" Both women were single and from our hometown.

Betts was a catch while Dottie was a thorn in Mama's side, so I gave the best of both types of women Daddy could be dating.

"Then they'd be lucky to get him." Mama sure sounded confident and in complete assurance she'd made up her mind.

There was one thing about Mama—when she made up her mind, it was done. Nothing anyone could do or say would make her change her mind, not even me.

"Are you sure you want to uproot yourself? I mean, you've lived in Normal all your life." I made it sound like Normal was this amazing place to live, but when you got down to the root of the town, it was filled with tourists and gossip, no different than how Holiday Junction was turning out to be.

"I am sure. Just like you, I want to make a fresh start where no one knows me." Once she got back on Main Street, she drove straight to the Freedom Diner. "Hi, Emily!" Mama waved and called out when we passed Emily walking down Main with a cup of coffee in her hand. "Hello, Layla! Just bought a house from Joaquin! Monty sure is a good dog." Mama pointed out Monty, the Camsens' dog Layla was walking.

So much for not knowing anyone. Mama waved and smiled at everyone walking around. Some people I didn't even know.

"I've been thinking about this spring." Mama pulled up in front of Freedom Diner. There was a sign posted that said, "closed for Mother's Day cooking class." "And I think we need to get our hands on the stuff. I can be the test model for your research."

"Go on. I'm listening." Mama sure did know how to pique my interest. I was falling for her trickery.

"Well, from what Emily mentioned about Palmer contacting those big cosmetic companies, that could be a good piece as to why Nate has put his foot down on anyone coming there. The money." Mama did the "make it rain" money gesture with her hands. "Since you obviously are going to take weeks to write the piece since no one is being cooperative and I know you and how you take a while to research, me and you need to get our hands on some of that water. I'll drink it, bathe in it, and wash my face in it, and we will take lots of photos along the way. If by the end of your deadline we can see some visible changes, we can go to Palmer and Nate to show them just how it works."

"Then they will let me do the story because they will be able to bring the product to market with all the research and proven changes by you being the perfect age test market." It was the best idea Mama had ever given me for a story. "That will gain me huge exposure."

"Wait." Mama hesitated, blinking with bafflement. "Are you still planning on looking for a real job?'

"Real job?" I snorted.

"You know, like out in California? I know I was telling you when I got here how I think you need to set your horizons a little bit bigger than Holiday Junction, but now the town has grown on me, and I think it would be good for you." Now Mama had changed her tune.

Typical Mama. When it's good for her, it's good for everyone.

"Like you said, this story could take months to unfold, so we will cross that bridge when we get to it." My shoulders lifted to my ears as I expelled a big sigh. "Let's go cook."

Mama and I got out of the golf cart and walked up to the diner door. There was another sign next to the closed sign telling the participants who signed up to come around to the side entrance.

Mama and I made our way around quickly since we were a little late. Chatter filtered through the screen door. When I went to reach for the handle, I noticed a small wooden sign above the door that read The Incubator.

"The Incubator?" I put my hand on the back of my head. I looked around to make sure we were at the right side entrance.

"Come on in!" Nate's familiar voice welcomed us. "Yes, you, Violet." He must've noticed me looking in.

I grabbed the handle and squeezed to open the door.

"The sign threw me off." I held the door behind me for Mama.

"What's 'the incubator' mean?" Mama asked and reached out to take one of the two aprons he was holding out for us to put on.

"This is my passion." One corner of his mouth twisted upwards. "I love to help locals, and when I opened the Incubator, it became a labor of love."

The Incubator was much different than what I expected the kitchen area of the Freedom Diner to look like. It was a fairly large open space with a stainless-steel table running the full length of the room. Along the wall was more of the same but with a few sink areas. The opposite wall had rows upon rows of metal shelving with various dry ingredients, bowls, mixing equipment, and really anything you could possibly need to cook, bake, or run a restaurant.

"The Incubator is a nonprofit organization that provides a hand up and a push forward for food entrepreneurs in our area. I wanted to create a shared kitchen space to support foodpreneurs with an affordable, comprehensive approach. To learn, and it's not just for Holiday Junction residents. I get students from all over. In fact, the Cupids Cupcakes really doesn't bake the goodies inhouse. Devine bakes them fresh nightly here in the Incubator kitchen, where she leases a workspace." He had really come up with a great idea here.

"Fascinating." Mama was smitten with the concept.

"But you two aren't here for that. You're here to take a cooking class for Mother's Day." He used his finger to gesture for Mama to twirl around so he could tie her apron. I rolled my eyes. Mama had a way with men. Even though Nate seemed to be happily married to Palmer, her charm lay on him like a blanket. "I think I'll put you two up here."

He patted one of the few open spots left on the long steel table.

"If you need anything, Patty will be more than happy to help you." Nate pointed out a young lady behind our spot with a Freedom Diner short-sleeved uniform top and a pair of tan shorts to match.

"Hi again," I greeted her as Mama and I took our spots behind the long steel table. "I saw you earlier when Rhett and I popped in."

"Yes." Patty clasped her hands in front of her. "I thought I recognized you." She went over the different items on the steel table that we were going to use for the class.

There were various size clear bowls, measuring spoons, and baking sheets in front of us along with a knife, cutting board, two medium saucepans, coffee cup, and a crepe pan.

"Today we are going to make one of my very favorite desserts. It will warm your palate with sweet and savory as well as go perfectly with a Mother's Day brunch you and your mother will never forget."

"My mouth is watering!" Mama shouted in glee. "Thank you." Mama looked at Patty when Patty set a flute of champagne in front of us.

"Shhh. Mama." I gave her the side-eye and popped one of the fancy crackers and cheese from our personal charcuterie board Patty had also placed between us.

"It's fine. Millie Kay is very excited, and that's what I want all of our friends here to be." Nate rubbed his hands vigorously as he took his place next to the facing small butcher block island on wheels, where it appeared he was going to be working.

"Flour, salt, pepper, oranges, vanilla extract, milk, eggs," Mama continued to rattle off the clear dishes with ingredients in them that weren't labeled. "Butter. Oh, ricotta cheese, sugar. Mmmm cinnamon." She hummed with delight. "Raisins and raspberries?" She looked at Nate. "Now the roma tomatoes, red onion, mozzarella, and lemons have me stumped, but if I had to guess, this is the savory part of our sweet."

"I see you know your way around the kitchen." Nate appeared to be entertained by Mama. "And yes. The crepes are sweet and savory."

The class was exactly what I had thought it was going to be like but with the extra added touch of the champagne and tasty snacks. While we listened to Nate tell us more about him and how he had come to own the Freedom Diner as well as his vision of the Incubator, Patty handed us a small boutique of fresh flowers with a note attached from Flowerworks, the local florist with fireworks. Only instead of flames shooting out of the firework, it was flowers.

"Cute." I tapped the card and knew I had to make a stop in there to get some freshly cut arrangements for the office.

Mama's brows rose as she lifted the champagne to her lips and took a sip. She was really enjoying the class, and I was glad.

Nate held up the ingredient we were to put into the bowl, and we did it. It was pretty much hand-holding the entire time. There was a gray-headed lady at the far end who made a few comments under her breath, and a couple of times I noticed she'd been filling up her water bottle with the jugs of water Nate had for refreshments. When I wondered if it was from the spring. I did pour Mama and me a red cup full, but it didn't taste any different to me.

We ended up making a sweet cheese crepe and a savory caprese crepe to go along with a coffee station from Brewing Beans.

While Mama was doctoring up with coffee she went in for the stab of information since Nate seemed to be enjoying her.

"I heard about this spring water of yours. The Lustig Spring," Mama reminded him as though he didn't know his name. "I'd love to get a sample while I'm here. Is there any way I can stop by and fill up a jug or two?"

"That would be up to my wife. She has been very upset lately with people coming on our property. If they'd just stayed at the spring and not wandered into our living area, I'm sure Palmer would've been much better, but she's tired of the invasion."

"Liar!" a woman at the far end of the table screamed and ran over to the refreshments, snatching one of Nate's jugs off the floor as she darted past Nate and Mama. "You are a liar!"

Mama reached out like a ninja to grab the woman, but got a full head of hair, only the woman kept running. A gray wig was in Mama's grip.

"You!" Sally Westin stopped, slowly turned, and reached out, getting a fistful of gray wig. She jerked. Mama didn't let go.

Mama jerked. Sally jerked.

"Ladies!" Nate put his hand on Mama. "Sally is not worth it. Let her take the jug. Next time I'll have to make sure my staff vets the Incubator guests better."

I hated to break it to Nate, but Mama was fiercely competitive, and he wasn't going to win this one. Not now. Not that Mama had already had to give up the raspberry Bundt cake to her during the cake walk.

"I swear I'll file another charge against you, and no amount of cake, pie, or crepes will get you off this time," Sally snarled at Mama. "Go back to the hole you crawled out of."

I gulped and closed my eyes, knowing there was a good ole hissy fit boiling up in Mama.

"You might've been able to get away with that type of behavior before I came to town, but now that I've bought a house and am making Holiday

Junction my home, I'm going to make it my citizen's duty to teach you some good southern manners." Mama didn't let go of the wig.

"Is that a threat?"

Mama pulled the wig a little closer to her body, bringing Sally with it.

"It sure is." Mama let go of the wig, sending Sally stumbling backward, barely able to keep herself on her feet but just enough to scramble out the door.

There was definitely a story here. Maybe it wasn't the spring. Maybe it was Sally and her need.

"Patty." I turned to talk to the waitress. Her eyes were huge, and her hand was over her mouth from the shock of the argument between Mama and Sally. "Do you remember this morning when you told me you'd be more than happy to answer any questions?"

"I do," she said.

"When can I take you up on that offer?" I asked.

"I'm off tomorrow." She shrugged. "I'm open all day."

"Great!" I quickly went through my to-do list, which at this point was pretty much open. I'd just have to get Mama to do something while I met with Patty. "What if I meet you at Flowerworks and we walk along the beach, grab something from one of the stands, and head back to my office where we can chat and eat?"

"That sounds like a lot of fun," she said, and we finished making the arrangements while Nate got everyone else in the cooking class settled down from the little hiccup he referred to as Sally.

"I'm sorry about Sally." Nate looked pretty fed up with her as he talked to Mama. I was busy trying to measure out the ingredients perfectly and wished I was as willy-nilly as Mama had been. She just shoved her hand in all the ingredients and tossed in a pinch here and there. "She really needs to go away. Far away."

CHAPTER TWELVE

Mama and I had overstayed our welcome at the Incubator. We were the last ones to leave. It ended up Mama had the touch to make the thin crepes turn out perfectly, and after several tries from the people in the class, Mama joined Nate and Patty to help everyone with their final creations.

There was an undeniable chemistry between Mama and Nate, not a romantic one but one of professional interest. It was nice to see Mama doing something she was passionate about. Of course she always provided a fabulous supper for me and Daddy, but I never realized until tonight just how much love and care she put into each one of those meals.

"I'm exhausted." Mama rubbed the back of her neck once we got inside of the golf cart. "Those beds at the Jubilee Inn do nothing for my sciatica."

"When we get back, I'll take my work downstairs so you can take a nice long bath." I held on for dear life as Mama did a U-turn and pushed the pedal of the golf cart as far as it would go. "I will even have Kristine send up a nice bedtime tea."

"That sounds so good." Mama liked the idea, and I did too.

Me telling her I was going downstairs to do some work was truthful, even though I was going to have to go downstairs to leave the inn so I could meet Vern in the shed to discuss his problem with being the Merry Maker and him trying to pawn the secret job off on me.

"Do you really want to move here?" I took the moment of silence and Mama's tired state to see if I could get some straight answers out of her and not some positive mumbo jumbo, because sometimes I felt my mother did say those things to make me feel better.

"I do. I am going to put a counteroffer in on the house on Heart Way. Even if you don't want to live with me." That was something I didn't expect her to say. "I want you to, but I also know you have a life. That's why I thought the little cottage out back would be nice for you to rent."

"Rent," I repeated. "That sounds good."

Renting from Mama made me feel so much better than living off Mama.

"With the rent comes a nightly supper though." Of course Mama had stipulations. "Unless you end up having something better to do, like a date. Not work. Work cannot be an excuse."

"Mama," I said sarcastically. "You can't be serious."

"Serious as dog dirt." She nodded and whipped the golf cart to the left in a parking spot in front of the Jubilee Inn. "I want us to have supper together, and you can invite your boyfriend."

"Boyfriend?" I questioned.

"Rhett, of course." She shoved the small lever of the gear shifter into park before she took the little key out.

"Rhett is not my boyfriend." I had to stop any notion she had of it.

"From what I overheard at the Incubator, he is smitten with you, and he's the most eligible bachelor in Holiday Junction. Naturally you are the most eligible bachelorette in Holiday Junction." She put her two pointer fingers together. "What a perfect combination."

"I don't have time for a boyfriend. We did try to have a date or two, but they've never been able to happen, so you can put any type of notions about me having Rhett over for supper with you out of your head." I assured her nothing was happening between me and him.

"If you say so, dear." She and I walked into the Jubilee Inn.

"How was the cooking class?" Kristine bent down in the foyer, clipping a leash on Mayor Paisley's collar.

"It was splendid." Mama's face lit up. "I was able to help and not just participate." Mama frowned. "I should've brought you a crepe back. That's not very kind of me. I'm so sorry."

"Don't you be sorry. This is your Mother's Day, and you need to enjoy it while you are here." Kristine knew all too well I was trying to get Mama on the next flight back to Kentucky.

"You didn't hear?" Mama looked between me and Kristine. "I'm staying. I'm going to be the newest resident of Holiday Junction."

Kristine looked at me with an element of surprise.

"Yes." I lifted my chin. "Mama has had a long day, so I told her she should take a nice long bath and have a good cup of your special tea so she can get in bed and enjoy some much needed sleep."

"I'll get that tea for you right after I take Paisley for her bedtime walk," Kristine said and left with Mayor Paisley.

I was confident Mama was all settled since she'd gotten a nice long bath and Kristine had brought up the tea, which sent Mama into a nice deep sleep. Her snoring told me the bed wasn't the issue for her sciatica.

I grabbed my work crossbody bag and hung it across me as I got ready to head downstairs. I quietly closed the door behind me. I stood on the other side of the door with my ear up to it and felt pretty confident Mama was out when I heard her snoring through the door.

As I made my way down the steps to the lobby of the inn, I tried to think up some good excuses as to why I was going out so late. Not that it was anyone's business, but Kristine or even Hubert was sure to ask me.

There was a framed note on the front desk of the inn, which Kristine and Hubert put out when they retired for the evening with all of the emergency numbers the guests might need for the night. So I knew they'd also gone to bed for the night, making my little secret getaway something only I would know about.

I dropped my bag next to the counter, a little hidden from sight, and headed out.

The carriage lights twinkled in the darkness where night had fallen over Holiday Junction. It was a time that reminded me of home. It was, in fact, the only thing that reminded me of home because the two places were so different when it came to daylight. But for now I took comfort in thinking about home while I walked down Main Street toward Holiday Park.

My route to Vern's secret shed out in the woods would be to take the trail leading from Holiday Park to the seaside, where I'd pick another trail up from a small neighborhood street that just so happened led to the wooded area where Vern wanted me to meet him.

All the shops along the way were long closed for the night, and even the ducks on the lake in Holiday Park had tucked their heads in their wings for the night. However, the sounds of life from the creatures in the woods and along the seaside indicated they were as awake as I was.

The chirp of grasshoppers singing their lovely nighttime songs created a little beat as I took the path down to the seaside, where I was greeted by several skittering crabs on the beach. I stopped briefly at the water's edge just as the wave broke and stood there taking in the movement of the ocean as the moonbeams flitted across, putting a spotlight on the vast body of water.

The sound of boisterous laughter from a few too many alcoholic beverages spilled out of the jiggle joint and into the street. I couldn't help but smile remembering Mama's experience in there as even more darkness fell upon me, making me leave the peacefulness of the ocean as I made my way up the sandy dune to the sidewalk, past the jiggle joint and down the neighborhood street.

The echo of gentle waves lapping against the beach was behind me as the night breeze swept along my ankles. The little neighborhood didn't have any lights, leaving each cottage home all the same dark color outlined by the moonlight. It was memory that recalled how each house was painted a different vibrant color and how most of them had boats or motorized water vehicles parked under a car porch, along with a segment of chain-link fence to divide the properties.

Tonight even those residents and their dogs were fast asleep like the rest of Holiday Junction. All but me and Vern.

I took my phone out of my pocket when I got to the edge of the trail and hit the flashlight feature. There was no way I wanted to step on any sort of creature I wasn't familiar with from the area—again, something new I was going to have to learn. Not like home. I knew all the animals and their habits in and around the Daniel Boone National Forest back home.

A feeling of excitement mixed with fright was a little unsettling as I put one foot in front of the other, but I also felt a sense of pride because of how I was actually putting myself out there and exploring an entire new life I still wasn't sure how to live.

My mind circled back to Mama and how she must be feeling with her new life change. Quickly my mind shifted to Vern as a small light fluttered through the shadow of the large trees in the woods as the moon peeked through. It was the shed.

Lightly I knocked on the door, and Vern opened it immediately. Without a word, he held the door open for me to come in, where I was greeted with the odor of paint. A familiar smell.

The shed wasn't any tidier than the first time I'd stepped foot in there. The opened spray cans littered the ground. The past large wooden structures for the Merry Maker that were made here were propped up against the wall, with the gorgeous and brightly painted basket overflowing with a colorful assortment of flowers the very one to see.

"Amazing." I gasped at the beauty. I could only imagine how much more beautiful it would be in the daylight. "You are so gifted."

"It did turn out much better than I'd anticipated." A pleased look settled on his face. "Now for business."

The door opened, and in walked Reed Schwindt, the local handyman. From what I could gather he was kinda homeless, though I'd venture to say he wasn't and found shelter in this shed.

"Good evening, ma'am." Reed was much older than me but had a great deal of manners. It was apparent from how he addressed me and him taking off his hat.

He wore a pair of tan work pants with dirt stains on the knees, probably from hours of working in clients' gardens. He had on a white T-shirt with the neck pulled a little loose, and his baseball cap bill was torn around the edges. His round face was soiled with grease, and his brown hair was nice and short, the tidiest thing on the man.

"Violet." I offered him a warm smile. "Definitely not 'ma'am.'"

"Sorry, um, Violet." By the tone and hesitation, he wasn't sure how to take me.

"Let me first start off by asking why on earth do you think I can do this? And how on earth do you think I can do this?"

"You wouldn't be the Merry Maker alone. Trust me. It's hard, and when I took it over, I knew I wanted to remake the signs the Merry Maker puts out during the holiday signaling where the final party would be for a great send-off until the next celebration. I'll keep doing that. I love building them and painting them. It gives me an outlet away from Layla." When he mentioned his wife, I was hoping he would follow it up with a "just joking," but he didn't. "You know Jay Mann was supposed to take over as the Merry Maker, and we all know what happened to him."

I'd found Jay Mann dead in the airplane bathroom on my way to my big interview in California, only to have the airplane make an emergency landing in Holiday Junction, only to never leave.

"You look like you're not going to do it," Reed said. I was definitely underestimating his ability to read me. "I can help. I'll go with you to put up the structure so you don't have to carry it. Or not.

"It's simple really. I'll give you a list of the holidays we like to celebrate outside of the large ones, and you get to make all the plans. I thought it would be fun for you to do an article in the *Junction Journal* like they used to when I was a kid." He piqued my journalistic interest.

"There were articles on it?" I asked.

"Oh yeah." He walked over to the bench where there was a small metal filing cabinet nestled underneath it. He pulled out the top drawer and extended it. He ran his finger along the top of the files, clicking each tab as it passed over them. "Here we go."

He pulled the file out and retrieved his glasses from his shirt pocket. He laid the file on the workbench, opened it, and took out a yellow page from an old newspaper.

"Here is an article." He handed it to me.

"Where Will The Merry Maker Strike Next?" read the masthead. I smiled as I read through the cute article about how the Merry Maker was like a ghost in the night. No one knew their identity, but everyone had their suspicions.

"No one would ever guess a newcomer like yourself as the Merry Maker." The wry smile on his face told me he was excited with the possibilities of the best-kept Merry Maker identity. "I even thought it would be fun for you to do secret identity interviews. Throw people off."

"I can see you're liking that idea." Reed once again read my body language.

"It's not bad. But what if I don't stay in Holiday Junction for long?" It was a real possibility I was going to leave at some point. "I guess I'm not sure how long I'm planning on staying."

"Then we have to get going." Reed must've been hard of hearing, or a piece of grass or dirt was stuck down in his ears.

"I don't know how long I'll be living here." I threw my mouth toward him.

"Why are you talking so loud?" Reed asked. "I'm not deaf."

"I'm sorry. I didn't think you heard me correctly when I told you my future plans are unknown." By the looks of things, I wasn't sure I was going to be able to wiggle myself out of this Merry Maker role.

By the time I was completely finished talking, I was named and dubbed the Merry Maker.

"How did this happen?" I spat when I headed back the way I'd come with the plywood basket in my grip. Too bad this one wasn't too heavy and I could claim I couldn't carry it, but Vern insisted the Merry Maker had to put the sign out tonight.

Tonight. My feet stomped one in front of the other in hopes my frustration would be beaten out of me.

The moon was going to light my way, and hopefully the walk would ward off some of the steam I could feel billowing up inside of me.

"Why didn't you just say no?" I questioned myself. "The idea of writing a piece in the paper does sound fun. And I might be able to stumble upon something fascinating."

Now I was trying to talk myself into the acceptance of what I'd done.

"So are you leaving soon?" Darren Strickland walked out from behind a tree and exposed himself on the trail in front of me.

"Oh my gosh, you scared me." I tried to regain my composure so my heart would stop pounding. "What?" My head registered some sort of question he'd asked, but instead of really hearing it, I had been trying to cover up the big sign by sticking it behind my body, which wasn't really working.

Darren danced back and forth on his feet to see what I was hiding.

"What did you say?" My moves mirrored him, trying to hide my new secret.

"I know you're the new Merry Maker. You don't have to hide the sign from me." He gestured behind me.

"Great. I stink at that too." I put the sign down on the path and wrung my hands since they were a little achy from gripping so hard.

"Back at the shed you told Vern and Reed you weren't sure how long you were staying?" He let me know he'd heard the entire conversation.

I curled my lips in and gave him a flat look in hopes he'd just go away.

"I saw you were walking alone when you passed my bar, and I don't like you being alone this time of the night." He was now my bodyguard? "I'm sorry. I can see you don't like that."

"Maybe you should've called out to me then instead of following me. If I wanted someone to know where I was going, I would've brought them along." I wasn't sure why he would wait even after he'd seen me go into the shed. "Why did you wait?"

I picked the sign up and started walking down the path.

"I got a little curious after I heard their proposal and hung around. That's all." He followed me. "I'm sorry if I've upset you. I'm a late-night guy, as you know from my business, and when I see a new person in town, I end up a little curious. That's all."

"I'm fine, so you can go home now." I picked up the pace and made it off of the trail and back on the sandy road of the neighborhood.

"Yeah, well, the gentleman in me won't let me do that until I know you are indoors and safe for the night." He was hot on my heels.

"Really. I'm fine." I held tight to the sign with one hand and stretched out the other hand as I kept walking.

He reached around me and took hold of the sign. I stopped, tugging it to me.

"I'm sure you're fine." His head tilted, and the moonlight hit his face perfectly, exposing the strong jawline and the little indention of his dimples. "Let me carry the sign."

I let go. His dimples deepened, infuriating me.

"We can either go find a spot to put the sign or I'm going to keep following you until you get back to the Jubilee Inn. Just ignore me." The faster I walked, the faster he walked. "Or we could sit by the lighthouse and enjoy a little midnight breeze."

"It's midnight?" I stopped and jerked around. "And I don't even know where to put the sign."

"You're right. It is midnight. That's why I don't want you walking around by yourself." Darren acted as though Holiday Junction was a high-crime town, which I'd never heard. "It makes me feel better. Sorry."

The lighthouse was just a little ways down the shoreline, and it was a place I did want to go, during daylight hours.

"The lighthouse is probably a better place to go during the day." I looked up at him, trying to avoid his dark and mysterious eyes. "How do I know I can trust you by being alone with you? My mama taught me not to talk to strangers."

"Really? I think we aren't strangers, and didn't you see how much your mama liked me today?" He grinned, reminding me of Mama's little adventure at the jiggle joint. "You're serious." He acted as though it wasn't possible. "If anything, I'm a true gentleman. I think Cherie even told you that."

Cherie. Cherie was the flight attendant local to the area. She knew the Strickland family well and dated Patrick Strickland, Rhett's brother.

"She did," I confessed. She raved about Darren.

"And." He pulled a set of keys out of his pocket. "I live in the lighthouse. I bought it about five years ago. Still a lot of work, but I'm chipping away at it." He jingled the keys in the air. "It's pretty cool up there at night."

He had my interest for sure, and how cool would it be to look over the ocean from way up there? My eyes scanned the tall red-and-white lighthouse in the distance.

"I can see you staring at the lighthouse." His tone was teasing. "We can have a beer while we sit up top and ponder where to put the Merry Maker sign." He did a little shimmy shake, moving the sign back and forth in front of him.

He did make it sound so much easier than me thinking about this new job of mine alone.

"Fine. One beer. One conversation about that." I pointed to the sign.

"Perfect." His voice was almost a whisper compared to the waves lapping up on the shore.

In silence, we walked along the sandy beach just where the surf hit, and after a few minutes of silence and halfway to the lighthouse, Darren stopped.

"What?" I looked at him. His eyes stared straight ahead.

"Shhh." He didn't look at me but gave a very subtle nod to look ahead.

If it weren't for the crystal-clear night, I'd not have been able to see the sand pushing up all over in front of us before a little baby turtle head popped through. One after the other dashed toward the sea to begin their lives.

It was unlike anything I'd ever seen.

"Amazing, right?" Darren's childlike smile mimicked how I was feeling inside.

"I… I…" Literally I was speechless. "I've never seen anything like it."

"I'm glad you got to experience it with me." Darren didn't say too much more. He gave me the space I needed to be with my thoughts and process the amazing new life for the baby turtles.

The closer we got to the lighthouse, the more I tried to talk myself out of why this was a bad idea, but my feet had another idea. They just kept moving me forward, even though I did look back a few times to the path leading up to Holiday Park.

I noticed people were gathered near the lighthouse. Their flashlights darted about. They were probably crab hunting like I used to do when my parents took me to the beach for vacation.

"They must be thirsty." Darren had noticed all the water bottles people were juggling in their hands. "You wouldn't believe how many people are on the beach at night."

I wondered if the beach was as safe as he was making it now sound. It seemed safe, even though he'd told me he didn't want me walking by myself in the dark. My suspicions were on high alert.

"You're really going to keep this Merry Maker thing a secret, right?" I asked before I stepped into the large wooden black door Darren held open. I was a little nervous.

"Yep." His head tilted, and his brows rose, as did the corners of his lips. "How about that beer?"

"Sure." I gave in and stepped inside. "Wow." I blinked a few times and looked around. "Something else I never expected to see tonight."

"It took me a while to fix it up, but I think it's turning out nicely." He moved about the open round room, leaving me at the door. "When I bought the lighthouse, the lead paint was peeling off the walls, mold was present, and it was covered in bird droppings."

He set the Merry Maker Mother's Day sign next to the door.

He opened the refrigerator door and took out two beer bottles. While he took off the caps, I walked around in the circular room. There were windows here and there looking out over the sea, and I could imagine just how gorgeous it was during the day, because the night was spectacular.

"Cleaning was perhaps the biggest project next to the light." He handed me a beer and walked over to the center of the room, where there was a set of circular steel steps. "The second floor I put up one long wall in the middle with a bathroom on each side." He stepped up on the first step. "Want to see?"

"Yeah." I was all in, but first I took one more long look around the ground floor and noticed it was more of a family room/dining room open area.

One half of the room was a built-in half-moon couch that begged to be laid on.

"The lighthouse was built in the 1800s." He spouted off facts, climbing the steps. "Actually, 1899 was the exact year. It's cool to say 1800s instead of 1900s."

"It's like a real-life kaleidoscope." I took my time walking up the steps so I could look out every single window along the way. "Do you keep the light on?" I asked as I watched the sea light up in the circular movement of the beacon.

"I have it set on a timer even though boats don't use it to navigate. It really is a tourist thing." He looked back at me. "You doing okay?"

"Yes. I'm great." I laughed and found myself smiling.

"You look great." He returned the smile before opening the door at the top and holding it open until I made my way to him.

"Oh my stars." I gasped when I stood up and realized we were at the very top observation deck. The actual beacon was located underneath us.

For miles the dark ocean lay in front, with only the moon and every so often the light to shine, exposing just how vast the sea was in front of us.

"Let's go sit over there." He gently guided me to a spot with a blanket already in place and two pillows.

"I see you bring all your lady friends here," I joked but found myself wanting to hear his response.

"Nope. I sleep up here." He couldn't have thrown me off more. My face must've showed it. "What? Just because I own the type of bar I do doesn't mean I'm some gigolo." He sat down on the blanket and let his legs dangle over the edge. "The bar is a business. A very good one, and if it means living like this, then I'll sling drinks all night long while my customers enjoy the show."

He used the word *show* very loosely.

"Careful." He held his hand out to help me sit down.

"I'm shocked." I took a drink of my beer and looked out. "I'm sorry. I wouldn't've ever thought you were—" I stopped, not able to find the right word.

"A businessman? Someone with brains?" He didn't get what I was thinking exactly right.

"So deep. Someone who really cared for his town." I just said something basic but with truth, only I wanted to tell him how he seemed to be this total package.

The gorgeous smile, those dimples, good business sense, and a great house, and I gulped back the thought of how he was making me feel.

"What about you? Why did you stay here?" He asked me a really great question.

"You know, it feels right. There's a lot to explore here and some stories that don't need to be swept under the rug." I noticed the huge grin on his face. "What?"

"You have these sayings that make me smile." He was referring to the southern sayings I'd grown up hearing and had become part of my everyday vernacular. "Like what things need to be brought to life by Violet Rhinehammer?"

"Like the fact Palmer Lustig wants to make the spring into some sort of national fountain-of-youth type product." I took a drink of the beer to wet my whistle. "I don't know all the particulars, but Emily told me about Palmer."

"You know how gossip around here goes. I bet that's not true." He made a point.

"Yes. I know gossip, and I know how after it starts it transforms into something altogether different than how it started. But Emily isn't the first person to mention this fountain of youth, which would explain why Palmer doesn't want people on the property." It was something to think about and something I was going to look into.

It would take some research to learn about the various companies Palmer had talked to or if anyone had seen her take meetings in and around town, but I had a way to find these things out. Time was all it was going to take, and in a town like Holiday Junction, I had a lot of time to kill.

"Embrace Holiday Junction and what it can give you. Like the turtles, the seaside here at Holiday Junction gave them a place to start. The land and people around allowed them the space to grow and mature into their next stage of life." Darren's leg dangled over the edge of the platform. His forearms rested on the cable wire attached to the perimeter so no one could fall over. Slowly he pulled the beer bottle through and took a drink.

There was more than looks and a good time to Darren. This was a side I really enjoyed.

"I know you don't want to take on the Merry Maker job, but I can help if you want." He slightly turned his head, and the way he looked at me sent a brief shiver through me.

I looked down at his lips as he talked but didn't hear anything but me trying to swallow back the uncharted territory fluttering deep inside of me.

There was a pull between us, and just as his lips were about to touch mine, my phone buzzed from my pocket. We jerked apart.

"Mama." I had hit the green button.

"Violet, I need your help." Her voice was cold and exact. "I'm in a bit of a pickle."

"What's going on, Mama?" I tried to ask in an unalarmed voice. My insides went from one excitement to a whole different kind of excitement.

"I need you to come to the Lustig Spring as fast as you can." Her tone had become chilly. Then she said something I never imagined. "Sally Westin is dead."

CHAPTER THIRTEEN

"Are you sure she said 'dead'?" Darren asked from the side of his mouth while I held on for dear life on the back of his moped.

"Yes. I know she said 'dead,'" I told him as the wind whipped around us. "Can't this thing go any faster?"

"It could, but you're squeezing me so tight I'm afraid you're going to cut off my breathing and I'll pass out, killing us. Plus it's hard to drive with one hand."

"If you would've left the Merry Maker sign at the lighthouse, you wouldn't've had to carry it," I told him.

"You wanted me to bring the sign, and I thought you were going to hold it while I drove. I had no idea you've never been on a moped before." He didn't sound too happy with me.

The dark road out to the Lustig Spring was very visible from the small headlight. I had no idea how far away we were.

"You can let loose a little. I do know where I am." His voice rose above the wind.

"I'm sorry." I mentally had to force myself to loosen my grip and let a little air move between his back and my chest as I pulled slightly back. My shoulders fell a little and I closed my eyes, praying and hoping Mama was wrong.

When we got to the entrance of Nate and Palmer's house, we noticed the front gate was closed. There wasn't a car.

"Do you think she snuck in?" Darren asked as if it weren't a possibility.

"I sure do," I said. "You don't know Mama."

Darren turned off the moped and used the heel of his shoe to put down the kickstand. He got off and helped me off.

"Do we need to call someone?" he asked, hanging his helmet on the handle. I followed, doing the same with mine on the opposite handle.

"Let's just make sure Mama is right." I didn't find it necessary to call any sort of authority since Mama did have history of being a smidgen dramatic. "Is there a way we can sneak in without triggering some sort of alarm?"

"Yep." Why had his response not surprised me?

"Take me to her."

Darren was turning out to be all sorts of surprising to me and definitely not what I'd pegged him to be. You know the "whole judging a book by the cover" thing totally applied with me in his case. He was thoughtful, making sure I was okay all night, and now every step of the way through the wooded untrailed area to find Mama. He was smart about business and the history of Holiday Junction, and he was business savvy.

Plus he was carting around that dumb Merry Maker Mother's Day sign.

Once we made it to the edge of the Lustig property where the woods ended, the moon was a spotlight on the spring and the large stone structure with the family name engraved. Mama was sitting on the ground surrounded by a few jugs, some filled with water and others still empty.

She wasn't alone.

Rhett Strickland was with her.

"What on earth is going on?" I asked, looking between the two.

"What's he doing here?" Mama looked to Darren Strickland.

"I was going to ask the same thing." Rhett's voice pierced the darkness.

"Does that matter?" I asked with urgency. "Where is Sally?"

Mama gestured in the direction behind the spring's stone. The sound of trickling water mixed in with the pulsing of my veins rang in my ears.

I used my cell phone's flashlight to guide my steps, and when I saw the body, I knew what we had to do.

"What are you doing?" Mama tried to jerk my phone out of my hand. "They will lock me up." Her words rushed out in a whisper.

"Why? Did you kill her?" I asked, not realizing Chief Strickland had answered.

"Who killed who?" Chief Matthew Strickland asked me back.

"Um. Chief, um, Matthew," I wasn't sure what to call him since I'd gotten to know his family pretty well. His wife was my boss, his nephew had been my guide, and well, his son—I had no idea what Darren was to me.

Yet.

"It's Violet Rhinehammer." At least I got that much out.

"Yes. I saw on my phone. Who's dead?" he asked again with authority.

"Sally Westin at the Lustig Spring."

There was a moment of silence before the line died.

"What?" Mama asked as I slowly put the phone down. Her eyes widened with alarm by her keen observation of my actions. "What, Violet?"

"He hung up." I shrugged and looked back at the cousins.

"That means he's on his way. It's how he springs into action," Darren said.

"What were you two doing?" I overheard Rhett ask Darren while I took the opportunity to give Sally Westin a once-over.

"Say, do you think you should be doing that?" Darren ignored anything Rhett was saying and walked over then quickly looked away once he saw Sally lying in the tall grassy area behind the spring stone.

"For someone who is spending time with my daughter after she snuck out of the Jubilee Inn, you seem to not know how she's seen a lot of dead bodies before." Mama's displeasure of me and all of my actions from tonight was in her sarcastic voice.

"You have?" Darren didn't seem to take much offense to her but more offense in the fact of me seeing bodies.

"Murdered people," Mama clarified. "You know, like in those crime podcasts."

"Murdered?" Darren asked like a parrot. His eyes narrowed as he tried to process what Mama was saying.

"Yes." I only wanted to talk to Darren since Mama was right. She'd put herself right on the pickle.

"I've seen my share of dead bodies. Jay Mann wasn't my first rodeo and apparently not my last." I shined the light closer to Sally's face.

Her eyes were still open, and there was something around her lips.

"She died of poisoning," I pointed out.

"How do you know?" Darren curled his head around me to get a look.

"Her pupils are large." I moved the light to her eyes. "There's a little bit of drool dried on her chin, which tells me she's been here at least a couple of hours." Then I moved the light to her chin. "But look around her lips. Do you see the red little bumps?"

"Yeah." Darren had gone from grossed out to really inquisitive.

"That's a sign of poisoning." I moved the light off of her and darted it around the tall grass. Nothing visible came into the light, and I didn't want to really look around since I didn't want to disturb any sort of evidence.

The sound of sirens echoed in the background.

"That's Dad. We better move back." Darren had an excellent idea. "We don't want him to think you were involved. Again."

His "again" statement garnered a questioning look from me.

"You were a topic of conversation many times at the bar." Darren smiled. "Now I can say none of the things we were thinking about you are true."

"Gee. Thanks." The two small lights off in the distance away from the sirens caught my eye, and when the golf cart came into view, I saw it was Nate and Palmer Lustig.

"What is going on here?" Nate pointed to me and Mama. "You and you?"

"Your dad called us and said Sally Westin was dead down here." Palmer had also gotten out of the golf cart and hurried over.

"Behind the stone." I gestured. "But you don't want to—" I sighed when I couldn't get it out fast enough and Palmer fainted after she'd seen Sally. I finished in a whisper, "Go back there and look."

Too late.

"What have I walked up on?" Chief Strickland was in a wrinkled sheriff's uniform. "Is she going to be okay, or do I need to call paramedics?"

"She's coming to, but she might need to be looked at," Nate said. He had one knee on the ground and the other propped up by his foot with Palmer resting in his arms.

She was groggily moving her head back and forth.

216

"I'm gonna need the EMTs to the Lustig Spring." The chief had called someone and walked behind the spring's stone where his big flashlight gave off way more light than my little phone flashlight. "I'm going to need you to get Curtis down here."

Curtis Robinson was the Holiday Junction coroner. I'd had the not-so-much pleasure of meeting him when the whole Jay Mann thing went down.

Rhett stood eerily quiet. A personality trait I'd never seen from him.

"What did you do?" Nate stood up, pointing his accusatory remark toward Mama. "Why would you kill her? I told you to let her be."

"Me? Are you talking to me?" Mama took a few steps back, her jaw tightened. "You can't possibly think I killed her."

"I recall, and I quote, 'You might've been able to get away with that type of behavior around here' and you followed up by saying you were going to teach her some southern manners." As Nate spouted out loud the teeny-tiny threat Mama had made to Sally at the cooking class, I squeezed my eyes closed, trying to ward off the brunt force the words would have in this situation.

"Did you say that?" Chief Strickland asked Mama directly.

"Yes, but I didn't—" Mama began to explain herself, only Nate cut her off by telling the rest of the conversation between Mama and Sally.

"I'm not done yet." Nate wagged his finger. "Sally asked you if you were threatening her."

"Oh Lordy!" Mama called out as if she were hearing a great sermon at church.

"You responded, it sure is." Nate stomped.

"Did you tell her 'it sure is'?" Chief Strickland asked, puffing his chest out and resting his hands on the too-loose utility belt he'd apparently thrown on after I'd waken him up.

"It's a 'bless your heart' kinda thing. You know." Mama's chest heaved up and down as audible exhales came out of her mouth. Then her lips pressed together as her head shook with anger. "It's a southern thing. And I would-n't've hurt her physically."

"People do things in a time of rage." Chief Strickland gave Mama a good long hard stare. "What's those?"

"Water containers," Mama said under her breath.

"You were stealing from us?" Palmer had finally come all the way to and stood up with the help of Rhett. "She was stealing from us."

"No different than her." Mama was making things worse as she continued to bring Sally back into the fold. "I mean, she had to have been here too. I didn't see her until I was, um—"

"Mama, don't say another word. I think we need to leave." I walked up and put my arms gently around her shoulders so I could guide her out of here before she was accused and cuffed.

"There's no way you're taking her from here just yet," Chief Strickland said before he answered his ringing phone. "Mmmhmmm," he hummed. "I'll let them know."

He hung up the phone and moved his attention away from Mama to Palmer and Nate.

"Curtis said he needs to get the hearse in the gate. Do you mind going to open it for him?" He didn't specifically talk to either Nate or Palmer exclusively.

"Do you need me here?" Palmer looked over at Sally's body before she started to hyperventilate all over again.

"No. You go on and open the gate. Nate can handle any questions I might have." He patted Palmer on the arm. "You take care of yourself. I'm sorry you had to see this."

Nate walked Palmer to the golf cart, and they exchanged a few words. I noticed Nate ran a loving hand down her face, assuring her things were going to be okay as he wiped a tear from her cheek. Palmer stood there nodding at him as she sucked in a few sniffles.

After he'd gotten her into the driver's seat and made sure she was out of the area, he turned back to Mama.

"I can't believe you've done this. I told you to let it go." Nate started in with his accusations.

"Listen," I stepped in between him and Mama with Chief Strickland on one side of me and Rhett on the other. Darren was still near the body. "Mama hasn't done anything. She took up for you at the Incubator, and that's it. You and I both know right is right and Sally was the one stealing from you."

"All of this will be determined by the timeline of Sally's death, cause of death, and alibis." Chief Strickland was getting a little ahead of himself.

"First off, we don't know where Sally went after the cooking class. I know where Mama was." I pointed to myself. "Secondly, we don't know if she was murdered, which means Mama is free to go."

"It doesn't mean I can't ask questions." Chief Strickland knew I was right about him not being able to keep Mama there unless he was charging her, which didn't seem like the case. "And if you're telling me Millie Kay was with you all night and you're her alibi, then we can let her go, but I'm going to need you two to come to the station bright and early tomorrow morning to give a statement."

"That's right. Me, Millie Kay and Violet were together all night," Darren lied. "Violet and Millie Kay came to the bar, and we got to talking about the *Junction Journal*. Violet said she was going to do a story on the Lustig Spring. After she told me how she'd been researching and Palmer had decided to pitch the spring to a large company to use for not only healing but to stay youthful, she was going to do an undercover story using her mama as the test. In order to do that, they needed some spring water."

"Yes." Mama agreed wholeheartedly. "I am going to eat food with it, drink it, bathe in it."

"Wait a second." Chief Strickland looked at Nate. "You mean to tell me you stopped people from coming to get water from the spring because you're going to bottle it up and sell it as some sort of fountain of youth?"

"I never said that. I've never heard of that." Nate's brows hooded over his eyes. "Palmer and I only want what's best for us. And right now Sally Westin lying murdered on our property next to the spring is not good for us."

"Now wait a minute," I spoke up. "We don't know if she was murdered."

"That's right. Sally was desperate to get her hands on your spring water, and you know it." Mama was giving it back to Nate.

"She did accuse you of assault earlier today," Chief Strickland said.

"But she dropped it if I would give her the raspberry Bundt cake which was made from the spring water," Mama pointed out. "And when she dressed up in that wig pretending to be a customer at the cooking class, she ran out stealing a few jugs of spring water."

"Is that so, Nate?" Chief Strickland asked.

"Yes, but I told Millie Kay to let her go after Millie jerked off the wig." Nate wasn't about to take any part of Mama's behavior for his own.

"This is going to have to get straightened out in the morning." Chief Strickland scratched his head.

"You've got to get her out of here before daylight, or it'll be around town my spring is killing people," Nate observed.

"You sure do seem to be making this about your business." Mama was right. "You fired Sally as a waitress, isn't that right?"

"Well, I—" Nate was trying to explain, but Mama pulled the "what's good for the goose is good for the gander" sayin' and interrupted him as he'd done her.

"I nothing." She stopped him. "Sally has been a thorn in your side, and it just so happened that your wife wants to turn this into some sort of fountain of youth like Chief Strickland said. But not with someone like Sally Westin acting all crazy and unpredictable like she'd done in the cooking class. She signed up under a fake name and wore a wig. You even said you need to keep an eye on who did sign up."

The hearse rattled up to the Lustig Spring, and Curtis got out with his black doctor bag.

Mama didn't pay him no attention. She just kept on giving a good reason why Chief Strickland should make Nate a suspect if Sally was murdered.

"Where were you tonight? This is your property. How do we know you didn't catch her on your property and kill her? You heard me and—" Mama hesitated. She didn't seem so sure she wanted to continue with Darren's lie about us being together. "Darren and Violet come up, making us a good target to take the heat for your crime."

Chief Strickland stood there letting Mama and Nate duke it out while Curtis walked behind the stone structure to get a good look at Sally.

"We don't even know if she was murdered," Rhett mentioned. "Sally Westin has been removed from here a million times." He pointed to Nate. "You've called Uncle Matthew at least once a week where she's trespassed."

"The fact remains she was poisoned this time." Nate pointed to Curtis for confirmation.

"Maybe not intentionally." Curtis popped up from behind the stone structure. He had put a headlamp on. The thing made a spotlight to where we were standing. "By the looks of her lips, color of her skin, and her pupils, Sally has died of poisoning. Of course I won't know what kind, but I can tell you she has a mouthful of water, which makes me think since she's so crazy about the spring, she might've been here filling up the bottles lying around her body and stopped to take a rest and refresh with a drink."

"Are you trying to tell me my spring is poison?" Nate looked as though he were seeking a plausible explanation.

"That's it!" Chief Strickland decided to put his foot down. "I'm in charge here, and as of right now, I'm looking at this as a homicide. Whether you did it—" He pointed to Mama. "Or you did it—" He pointed to Nate. "Or that did it," he finally gestured to the Lustig Spring, "this spring is closed. And I want to see you two—" At first he gestured to Mama and Nate. "Nope, you four, five first thing tomorrow morning."

"What's this?" Curtis's headlight flashed on the Merry Maker's Mother's Day basket sign.

"It looks like the Merry Maker was here." Rhett walked over. "It is the Merry Maker." He slid his chin to turn to his uncle. His eyes grew. "Sally Westin was the Merry Maker."

"And she wanted the spring water so much, she was going to make the final Mother's Day Festival happen right here." Darren was disguising the real truth, and I knew it was only to bide me some time to figure out exactly who had killed Sally Westin.

CHAPTER FOURTEEN

M ama and I had gotten a ride back to the Jubilee Inn from Curtis in his hearse. Not like it was our choice, but it was the only way she and I could ride together. Chief Strickland was going to remain at the scene with the deputies to collect evidence and clues in case Curtis had determined Sally's cause of death was murder. There was no way three of us were going to fit on Darren's moped.

Mama would've tried, but at this point it was best for me to keep my distance from Darren. He knew too much about me, and I knew too much about my feelings that seemed to be bubbling up about him. There was no way I was going to get into a relationship with Darren Strickland.

I could see the masthead headline now. *New* Junction Journal *Reporter and Holiday Junction citizen Violet Rhinehammer snags Chief Strickland's son in attempt to get her own mother off the suspect list for the killing of Sally Westin.*

It was how my mind worked. Plus I couldn't even begin to think how I was going to handle the fact the Merry Maker sign made it look like Sally was the Merry Maker.

Which made me restless and sleepless all night. Deep down I knew Mama didn't kill anyone, and I was going to prove it due to the fact Mama wouldn't have any way of having poison.

"We have to go to the sheriff's department," I told Mama after she'd gotten an early-morning shower and dolled up for the day.

"I told you I can't. We have to meet Rhett over at the house for the inspection this morning." Mama was looking at herself in the mirror and snapping on her clip-on earrings before she took the lipstick out of her purse and carefully rolled it up just enough to get the perfect width to use on her lips. "Matthew will just have to wait. I'm sure you can get your new boyfriend to help us out with his dad."

"Mama," I gasped. "Darren is not my new boyfriend."

"What were you doing with him so late? Why did you sneak out and go be with him if he's not?" She ran her hand down her white eyelet dress as she walked across the room to slip on her flats.

"Why did you take the moment I didn't have an eye on you to trespass to the Lustig Spring?" I sat on the edge of the couch and rubbed my neck since I'd gotten a crook in it from laying my head on the arm of the couch so Mama could sleep in the bed.

"Don't you make this about me, young lady." Her threatening tone as she used with me as a child came back in spades. "But if you need to know, I was going to make sure we did the research. When I got to thinking about how protective Palmer was about the spring, I knew if Nate didn't let me go after the jugs Sally had stolen, he wouldn't go after me if he found me on the property."

"Which brings up a good point about Palmer." Another thing I'd been thinking about all night was how Palmer could've killed Sally. "What if Palmer saw Sally at the spring? She could've poisoned Sally somehow."

"Why would she kill Sally?" Mama took another look in the mirror at herself before she stepped away with a satisfied look on her face.

"Sally has been stealing the spring water, and Palmer can't have that. She has this grand plan of producing it and marketing it as a fountain of youth, then Sally is going to have to purchase it. Like I said, Sally was a thorn in the Lustigs' side." If and when Sally's death was ruled a homicide, Palmer Lustig was the first person I was going to investigate.

"Oh well." Mama tapped her watch with her fingernail. "Run a brush through your hair. We've got to go meet the inspector. I'll be downstairs waiting for you." She opened the door but turned around to say, "We also need to figure out how to get your Merry Maker sign back."

I stood there tongue-tied.

"Honey, Mama knows everything. You are the Merry Maker, and Darren is your boyfriend. Your secrets are safe with me." She shut the door with confidence behind her. "He wouldn't've said we were all together if he didn't think of you as a girlfriend."

"You are the Merry Maker, and Darren is not my boyfriend," I mocked her with a snarled nose as my head jiggled like a bobblehead's on my shoulders. "I'm not his girlfriend."

I felt the eleven lines between my eyes deepen as I thought about Mama's reasoning for why Darren did say he was with me and Mama at the bar. Why would he do that? Lie to not only his dad, but his dad who was the chief.

"Your secrets are safe with me," I repeated in my best Mama-mimicking voice.

While I was in the bathroom getting my teeth brushed and quickly getting ready since Mama insisted on going with her to the house inspection, my phone rang.

"Good morning, Marge." I wondered if she was going to fire me for not being in the office over the past couple of days. "I already posted to the site this morning. All of today's Mother's Day festivities have been updated, and I'll get the death notices as soon as they come in."

"You already have a death notice. Sally Westin." She'd heard. Of course she'd heard. Her sister and my other boss, Louise, was married to Chief Strickland. "And she was the Merry Maker. It's all over town, and I overheard Matthew tell Louise your mother is his number one suspect."

"I was worried that was going to be the case." There was a sore already forming on the inside of my bottom lip where I'd gnawed the heck out of it from worry. "You know I don't think Mama did it, but she was there."

"This is the exact story we need for the *Junction Journal*." There was a strange excitement in her voice. "You get down there and get it written up. You have firsthand knowledge."

"I'm not going to write about my mama nor about the fact we happened upon it." Since she'd not mentioned anything about me and Darren, I was going to go with the idea me and Mama were at the bar and use his lies for my good.

"I see." There was a pause. I slipped on my shoes since I knew I had to get to the office. This little inspection thingy had to go fast. If it didn't and Marge made it to the office before me, I was afraid she'd post the story online. "You mean to tell me you're not going to put aside your personal feelings and be a journalist?"

"I didn't say that. I said that I'm not going to write anything that would implicate my mama when we already told the chief our alibi. I can write the facts and what we happened upon." I grabbed my bag and threw it across my body. "I've got a quick interview this morning about Sally Westin," I lied to buy myself time. "Then I'll be in the office to write up a piece, but I'm not going to write anything about Mama."

"I wasn't asking you to give up your mama. There's a bigger story than Sally Westin getting poisoned." I gulped when she said poisoned, as she confirmed everyone already knew pretty much everything. "It's the fact she was the Merry Maker. That's the big news. Now what happens? Who appoints the new Merry Maker? There's a list of questions Holiday Junction has never had to face in the over two hundred years of the Merry Maker."

"Two. Two." I shuddered. "Two hundred years?"

Vern left out the little detail that the Merry Maker role had been over two hundred years old.

"Oh yes. The Merry Maker is a very big role to have, and now that we know it was Sally, I'd love for you to get an interview with Raymond Westin," she said.

"Who is he?" I hadn't heard of him, but with that last name, I figured on him being related to Sally somehow.

"Sally's husband. He's the pharmacist at the drugstore in the hospital. You know where the hospital is, right? Cross the way from the police station, and according to what I overheard Matthew tell Louise, you are to go there this morning to give a statement." She reminded me how my to-do list was getting longer and longer by the minute. "I'll see you in the office this afternoon. Bye."

The line went dead right when I walked into the lobby of the inn. Mama was standing at the counter, talking to Kristine.

"I told Kristine me and you'd be checking out this afternoon if we could. I plan on not worrying about the inspection because Rhett said he'd fix whatever needed to be done, and I already wire transferred the money to him, so I'm not worried about that." Mama rambled on.

"I'll let you know about me." I grabbed Mama by the hand and dragged her out before Kristine could ask me anything. "You didn't tell her about Sally, did you?" I followed Mama to the golf cart.

"No. She already knew. And you're going to have to take the trolley." She pointed to the trolley barreling down Main Street with Goldie dinging the bell to signal the stop. "The cart is full. I had my things delivered today and told Rhett to put them in the cart."

I'd just noticed the luggage piled up in the golf cart with no room for me and barely enough room for Mama to sit in the driver's seat.

"Don't look so stunned, dear. I had to have my clothes sent to my new home. I spent a mint on getting them shipped here. Too bad I couldn't've flown them. Do you think we could form some sort of committee to get more flights in and out of Holiday Junction?" She fluttered from one topic to the other, leaving me dizzy-headed as she took off.

"You comin' or not?" Goldie hollered from the trolly stop. "I don't have all day!"

I sighed, looking around as I tried to decide whether or not to walk over to Heart Way and take my time so I could ponder everything changing around me and in my life, or just take the trolley, the fastest way.

"Groove and Go," I whispered, recalling Goldie had mentioned Elvin's dislike for little Lizzy taking dancing lessons from one of the Lustig family members. "Coming." I smiled and waved.

"Heard you found another dead body." This time I liked the fact Goldie didn't waste any time getting to the point. "I guess you'll be writing a piece on that in the paper. It was the first thing I looked up this morning after I got the call."

"And who called?" I asked.

"Just a few friends." She shrugged and waited for me to sit down before she pulled the door shut and started to drive the trolley toward the house.

"I'm going to Heart Way." I reached into my bag, took out a few of the trolley tokens I'd stocked up on, and slipped them into the metal container attached to her seat. "My mama is moving here and looking at a house on Heart."

"Not the big house?" she asked. I caught her eyes looking at me from the rearview mirror glued on the large windshield.

"No. Not the big house. Contrary to what you think, Mama didn't hurt a fly." How ridiculous for anyone to think that. "From what I know, the law states you're innocent until proven guilty."

"From what I know," Goldie bit back, "your mama and Sally Westin had two arguments in the span of a ten-hour day."

"I'm not going to confirm or deny, but I do have a question for you about little Lizzy's dance teacher." The subtle shift in Goldie's posture didn't go unnoticed. Her arms had stiffened a little, her back grew a little taller, and her chin lifted a smidgen. "Which Lustig was she?"

"Tricia Lustig. Why?" she asked.

I grabbed the handle next to my head so I wouldn't fall over when she turned near the corner of Heart Way, where the trolley stop I needed to get off was located.

"I was wondering if you thought she'd be open to answering a few questions for me?" I asked. "Maybe you could give me her phone number?"

"The only number I've got is the Groove and Go, but I'm sure you can stop down there. She's always there." The trolley came to a stop. Goldie slightly turned in her seat to face me. "You think she had something to do with Sally Westin? I mean, I know she was mad she didn't get the family spring and had to continue to keep the dance studio open to pay her bills, but a killer? Tricia?"

"I don't know. I know that I'm doing a story on the spring, and she might have a different perspective than Nate." I stood up. Before I got off the trolley, I asked. "How is Tricia related to Nate?"

"Siblings." She gave me some interesting information. "See you later!" She grabbed the string dangling from the bell, gave it two good shakes, and took off.

The trolley stop was actually between the small market and Groove and Go right before the roundabout that circled around to Heart Way. Neither I'd been to yet, but both interested me.

The Groove and Go had twinkling lights all around the front of the window with nothing else to shield from seeing inside the dance studio. There were wooden floors and a long mirrored wall with two wooden bars running the full length of wall. One was higher than the other, and I'd seen in shows before where dancers held on to those bars for support.

There were a few padded-type chairs along the back wall, but other than that, it was wide-open space.

"Can I help you?" A woman startled me from behind.

"I'm looking. That's all." I shrugged and noticed the woman was about five foot nine with strawberry-blond hair parted to the side and a little wavy. The ends grazed her shoulders. She had on a pair of flowing pants and matching cardigan with a pair of sandals.

The canvas bag dangling from her arms had a pair of pink toe ballet shoes in it, the ribbon sticking out just enough for me to recognize the item.

"Are you Tricia Lustig by any chance?" I asked.

"Who wants to know?" She stuck a key into the Groove and Go door and twisted the lock.

"Violet Rhinehammer from the *Junction Journal*." I decided to be honest with her even though what had happened had been at the Lustig Spring. "I understand Sally Westin was found poisoned at your family's spring, and I wanted to get your take on it since I heard Palmer, your sister in law, had recently decided to package the spring water into some sort of fountain of youth."

Her body moved ever so slightly, making the perfect ballerina, but to the trained investigative eye I had, I could see something I said was news to her.

"Did you not hear about Sally Westin?" I asked.

"Of course I heard about it. Like you said." She stood inside the open door of the dance studio. She didn't ask me to come inside.

Interesting.

"It's my family's spring. Nate called me immediately." She was lying. I knew it because her fingers were busy outlining the keys in her hand and the edges of her nose flared.

"Nate called you?" I knew that was part of the lie, because if he'd called her, he surely would've told her I had been there.

"Yes. Now if you'll excuse me, I have to get some things ready for the Mother's Day theater." She turned to go into the studio.

I started to follow her.

She whipped around.

"I'm sorry. We are closed." She had to forcibly shut the front door since it was on a slow-release hinge, twisting the lock just as the door shut in my face.

"Where were you last night?" I asked just to let her know I was on to her hiding something. "Mmhmmm. I'll find out," I whispered and sighed, watching her through the door as she slipped out of sight.

Putting Tricia Lustig and all the things Goldie had said about her in the back of my head, I took the short walk down Heart Way to get to the house, and in the distance I could see a couple of golf carts in the drive along with Rhett Strickland's car. It looked like they were outside waiting on someone—me.

I was certainly glad I'd decided to take the trolley instead of walking because Goldie just gave me not only another suspect but a reason why Tricia Lustig would kill Sally. It also gave me the opportunity to see Tricia and let her know I was on to her.

I took my phone out and hit the memo button so I could get my train of thoughts on the record and not forget.

"Tricia Lustig has a very good motive for wanting not only Freedom Diner to go out of business but also the spring be tainted by putting into the public fear that the spring has been poisoned." I laid out in detail how she was jealous, needed the spring money for herself, and was upset she didn't get even half of the spring, not to mention her own brother actually letting his wife, an outsider, take the reins. When Tricia found out about Palmer's decision to market it as a fountain of youth, it sent Tricia over the edge. In turn she killed Sally Westin since Sally had been fired by Nate as well as been caught on the property several times, not just last night.

"Good morning." Rhett's tone wasn't his usual, where he was happy to see me.

"Hey." I offered a smile knowing he was mad about Darren being there last night.

"Violet Rhinehammer, Garret Gerard." Rhett did the introduction. "He owns Gerard Home Inspection and will be performing Millie Kay's house inspection."

Garrett had a round face and light-brown hair with a comb-over. He had more facial hair than hair on top of his head. He had a friendly face with a nice smile, one I'd call an honest look.

"Do you have any questions before we begin?" Rhett asked me.

"Can I talk to you in private?" I needed to clear the air.

"Sure. You two can start the inspection without us. I've got somewhere to be soon anyways." Rhett looked at his watch. I knew by the way he was acting he was lying.

Boy, he and Darren had the same trait. They found it easy to lie. Must've been in the DNA.

Mama and Garrett walked up to the little blue house and headed around the side as if he were doing the outside inspection first. Rhett and I stood in the driveway.

"What's up?" he asked, looking down at me. He also got the good-looking DNA too.

"I wanted to clear the air about Darren and why we were together last night." I started to tell him how I was on a walk, leaving out the part about the Merry Maker. "I had to get away from Mama. I wasn't tired, and she was going to go to sleep."

"You don't owe me any explanation." He stopped me. "It's not like I'm your keeper." He snorted then grinned, showing of his dimples, yet another DNA family trait. "Wait. Do you think I've got some sort of feelings for you?"

"Well, no." I laughed off the notion as if it were ridiculous, though I totally thought there'd been something over the past few months brewing up even though we'd never fully explored anything. "You seem so stand-offish that I thought maybe you wanted to know."

"I don't. Darren can do what Darren wants to do, and you can too. You're both adults." His phone rang, and he rudely answered it. "Hey, Fern. I'm just leaving now. Grab your bathing suit. I've got the boat all gassed up for an entire day on the water."

Even though he turned as if he didn't want me to hear, his voice was so loud I heard every word.

"Sorry about that." He'd turned back to me, taking out his car keys. "Garrett will let me know if there's anything with the inspection, but I'm sure it's all good."

The sound of a car pulling down the road made us both look, and it was Chief Strickland's car.

"You're going on a date with Fern?" I asked in disbelief. I'd learned Fern Banks, the local beauty queen and busybody, had tried to get her claws into Rhett for years. I'd also heard from Rhett himself how he was never interested in her. "That's a turn of events."

He laughed. Hard.

"By the way you're acting, Violet, I'd think you were a little jealous." His face became still, his eyes bore into me.

"Don't be silly." I shrugged and turned my attention to Chief Strickland when he got out of the car. "Chief."

"I heard I'd find you here." He moseyed over. "It's true your mother is moving here, huh?"

"Looks like it. And since you and your family own about the entire town, it looks like Rhett is selling her this house," I said. "Mama and I were on our way down to give our statements after the inspection."

"I was on my way to the office, and I figured I'd just stop by here and let you know Sally Westin was poisoned." Now I knew her case had been turned into a homicide. "We are going to send off samples of the spring to these fancy labs to test the water. I'm trying to find out if your mama got any water that we don't know about. We sure don't want anyone else getting poisoned."

"So it's not a homicide case?" It very well could be some sort of natural poison, and in that case, we would be missing a big bullet.

"Since you and Millie Kay were at the jiggle joint with my son, I think you have an alibi." His judgement of our whereabouts was written all over his face. His phone rang. "Excuse me for a minute." He walked away to take the call.

"That was a relief." I sighed about the fact they were ruling Sally's death as an accidental poison.

"Yeah. Not sure Holiday Junction can withstand another murder," he joked, even though the little dig was at me.

"In that case, I better get some of these boxes in the house." I walked over to Mama's golf cart and grabbed a box, but not well enough. I dropped it, spilling the contents all over the driveaway.

Rhett and I took a break from talking as we busied ourselves with picking up the items. I didn't even notice Chief Strickland had walked over.

"What do we have here?" He picked up a baggie from one of the items that'd fallen out of Mama's box.

"That's mothballs. Mama insists on putting them in her clothes." There was a very curious look on his face. "Moths eat right through clothes. They leave little holes."

"And they leave people dead if they ingest them." He held it toward me with a cocked brow before shifting his focus to Mama and Garrett when they walked back around the house.

"Millie Kay Rhinehammer, I'm placing you under arrest for the murder of Sally Westin." Chief Strickland took his cuffs off his utility belt, bolting toward Mama. "Rhett, don't you touch another thing. Back up from that box."

"What?" Mama's shock and dismay waved over her facial expression as desperation came from her mouth. "I would never hurt a fly."

"Maybe not a fly, but what about a moth?" He made no sense until he said, "Curtis just called me. Sally's toxicology report came back. She has naphthalene in her system."

"I don't even know what that is." Mama said over her right shoulder, trying to see as he cuffed her.

"The ingredient in mothballs." There was the sound of the cuffs clicking around Mama's wrists.

"Violet!" Mama cried out. "You've got to help me! I don't look good in orange. Call Diffy! He'll help you. I've heard how this happens when someone plants things on people to make them look like a suspect."

"Diffy." I had to repeat it a few times to even try to remember the name. "What?" I asked her as my feet felt like they were cemented to the ground.

"This is just like the crime podcast. Call Diffy. He'll know what to do!" Mama had gone from crying to hyperventilating.

"So is she buying the house or not?" Garret Gerard so rudely asked.

"Of course we are." I hurried over to the sheriff's car. "What on earth are you doing, Chief? Come on," I begged.

"Don't you touch a thing. Not in the golf cart, not in those boxes, and not in that house until I can get someone here to process this scene. It's currently part of my crime scene, and I'm going to take your mom down to the station to book her. You can see her in about an hour." Chief Strickland got into the car, did a U-turn, and headed down Heart Way.

Mama's head was twisted around, and she kept screaming, her eyes filled with fright.

CHAPTER FIFTEEN

"Diffy Delk." I typed away on the computer at work to find out who this person was whose name Mama kept screaming out the cracked window of the chief's car. It was a terrible memory, her screeching.

I scanned down the computer screen, and when a smarmy-looking fellow popped up, I read the snippet of text before I clicked the link.

The sound of waves echoed through the open window, and when I looked out, I could see a boat taking off from one of the small docks I'd recognized as Rhett's. Mama's arrest didn't bother him any. When I noticed the large floppy straw hat attached to a woman in a hot-pink bikini, I rolled my eyes and went back to the computer.

"I'd rather talk to Diffy Delk than deal with Fern Banks." I sighed and looked at this lawyer's site.

I clicked around a bit before I settled on the "About" tab.

"I fought the law, and I won." I smiled when I read the motto on his website. There was a photo of him sitting behind a large brown desk, dressed in a brown suit with a burnt-yellow silk-type shirt with a tie to match. His receding hairline stopped with what appeared to be some sort of toupee. "Where on earth did Mama find this guy?"

He was located in an office near the police station, which would be good since I needed to get Mama out of jail. Plus I still had to go to the hospital near there to see if Raymond Westin was in, though I couldn't imagine he would be working after his wife was found dead last night.

"Hello, is Mr. Delk there?" I asked the person on the other end of the phone after I'd called the number.

"Who's calling?" The person on the other end of the line spoke through a nasally tone.

"My name is Violet Rhinehammer, and my mama is Millie Kay—" I was about to go into the entire spiel.

"Millie Kay!" The voice turned into a deep baritone. "I adore her. This is Diffy. You're her daughter. She told me all about you and how you always wanted to be a big-time news reporter only to land here."

"Yes." I had to stop myself from thinking Mama had been talking all about me, and it didn't sound like she was too proud. But that was Mama.

"Is something wrong? Did you get in some more trouble? You know you should've called me when you found Jay Mann and what's-her-name." His words were spoken together into one long breath. "But that's all water under the bridge, and if you need me, I can make sure the prosecutor will never say a word while you're on the stand about whatever it is you—" He took a breath. "Wait. Are you the one who found Sally Westin? You didn't knock her off, did you? I mean if you did, I can still prove you innocent, but the truth of the matter is that you've already been associated with two murders, and three is kinda pushing it. Hard to swallow, if you know what I mean."

"It's Mama. Mama's been arrested for Sally's murder, and she told me to call you." I moved my head from the computer screen to the window after I heard a car door shut. It was actually a truck.

"Millie Kay? There's no way that sweet woman killed Sally Westin." He snorted. "You're not joking."

"What gave it away? Me calling you to hire you?" I watched the woman from the truck unstrap the steel ladder from the rack in the bed and hoist it over her head. She turned and headed up to the house.

"No." My cheeks puffed out as a sigh escaped me. I wondered where on earth Mama had met this man. "In fact, when Chief Strickland was putting her in his car to take her to the station, she told me to call you."

"Got it. Be here in an hour, and bring twenty thousand dollars." His words made me momentarily rendered speechless. "If you don't have that much liquid cash, then bring two thousand for the bond bailsman."

"Thank you. At your office?" I asked to confirm.

"Yes. Don't forget the two thousand dollars." He hung up.

I pushed back from the desk and walked out the room to the front door. The woman had already situated the ladder up against the cottage and fully extended it to the top rung.

"Hey there." She greeted me with a smile. "I'm Ladawna. You must be Violet." She took a business card from the front pocket of her overalls.

"I am." I took the card and looked at it. "Ladawna's Home Repairs."

"I'm here to look at the roof for Rhett. Me or some of my workers will also be in and out doing all the repairs." Her hands gripped the outside of the ladder. One foot on the ground while the other was propped up on the bottom rung. "It's gonna be a hot day. I tell you, once Mother's Day comes and then goes, it's like Mother Nature gets mad since her day is over for a year, and she scorches us out of the water."

I gazed toward the sea as she mentioned water. The sound of Rhett's boat motor was getting farther and farther away.

"Thank you. Any word on the air-conditioner? Not that I'm hot now since there's a nice breeze off the ocean up here, but I bet it will get hotter." I hadn't complained and was grateful so far for the office, but I knew I was going to have to really be working overtime to pay back my savings since I was going to have to withdraw two thousand dollars for the bondsman.

"Eeeee." Lawanda's neck veins popped as she dragged her lips into a thin line. "That's probably going to be after we tear out all the walls."

"The walls?" This was the first time I'd heard this. How was I going to be able to work with no walls?

"Yep. That starts next week." She nodded and tucked the stray strand of her black curly hair back up in her baseball cap. "For now I've got to look at the roof for the new shingles."

"Okay. Let me know if you need anything. I'll be here for about a half hour." I had to add going to the bank to my long list of things to do.

I wished I was able to head on down to the station, but I knew I also had to work and get an article online so Marge and Louise wouldn't be over here hounding me.

It felt like I'd already had a full day, and it wasn't even ten o'clock a.m. yet.

Lawanda's footsteps were loud as she walked on the roof above my head, so when I called Vern I walked through the cottage house to the back where I could talk to him.

"I'm in a little bind," I told him after we'd greeted each other. "Did you hear about what happened to Sally Westin?"

"Hear about it? Are you kidding?" He scoffed and whispered, "Layla's phone has been blowing up with gossip. And the Merry Maker thing is good because now you can do it without anyone ever expecting it was you."

"The sign was left at the Lustig Spring, and how on earth is there going to be a Mother's Day final party there?" I asked.

"I don't know, but it's what the Merry Maker wanted." He acted as if Sally was the Merry Maker and she wanted it there.

"Oh." This crazy idea started to formulate in my head. "I've got to go."

I hurried back into the cottage as the idea of using what everyone thought was the Merry Maker's choice for the location of the final gathering for the Mother's Day celebration to my advantage, to get back to the spring.

Before I could post anything, I needed a timeline. I knew Sally had been fired about two months ago for stealing the water.

"Who on earth ever heard of someone getting fired over water?" The more I questioned this firing, the more questions that had to be answered came to me.

I grabbed the dry-erase marker from the pen holder sitting on top of the desk and walked over to the large whiteboard Marge had Rhett screw on the wall for various holidays we had to make sure were covered in the *Junction Journal*, which made zero sense. Holiday Junction celebrated every single holiday and it was practically thrown up all over town. You wouldn't be able to forget.

"They are going to have to write it again." I picked up the eraser and swiped the board clean. "I've got another murder to solve."

I wrote Sally's name in large letters at the top and listed possible suspects below, including Mama.

"Millie Kay Rhinehammer." It pained me to even write it. "Nate Lustig, Palmer Lustig, Tricia Lustig, and Elvin Bennett."

So Elvin was a long shot, but he didn't like the Lustigs, according to Goldie, and well, I needed someone else to point a finger to besides Mama.

Under each one of their names, I made little bullet-point reasons I felt they had motive to have killed Sally. Of course Mama's wasn't so much a motive as the fact she'd been seen arguing in public with Sally, which led into Mama threatening Sally. And I couldn't forget how the mothballs were found in Mama's things.

Underneath Nate Lustig, who I lumped with his wife Palmer, I wrote, "Fired Sally, Sally was a pain in their sides, she continually trespassed, she stole from them, she was going to ruin any sort of deal Palmer had with the health company." Then underneath Tricia I wrote how she was upset she didn't get part of the Lustig Spring and was jealous of Palmer, and how if Sally was murdered from an apparent poisoning, it would look like the spring was natural poison and no one would want to buy any fountain of youth from Palmer.

"This is good." I sat down and clicked on the computer keys, bringing the computer to life. "Natural springs in Holiday Junction," I googled, and to my delight, I found an interactive site for the area. I typed in Nate's address, and up popped the map and a clear blue trail where the spring meandered through their property and led exactly to the tap where everyone filled up their little jugs of Lustig Spring water and where Sally Westin met her demise.

There was a plus sign on the map to blow it up. I clicked it a few times and used my finger to follow along with the trail of the spring.

"Lustig Spring looks like it can be called Holiday Junction Spring." My eyes zeroed in on where the spring went onto the Lustig property, and it was just shy of the lighthouse.

Darren Strickland's lighthouse.

I pulled up the online newspaper site so I could plug in today's big story. "Merry Maker's Last Wish."

I looked at the masthead and smiled.

"Oh yes." I couldn't stop the grin from curling up on my lips as I continued to talk and type. "Sally Westin is believed to be the Merry Maker. The Merry Maker's Mother's Day sign was found at the Lustig Spring, where our Merry Maker had taken her final breath. It was her dying wish as the Merry Maker to end this year's Mother's Day celebration at the Lustig Spring."

I sat back and looked at the screen, wondering if I should or shouldn't report what I knew.

My shoulders drew up and back, my hands rested on the keyboard, and my fingers flew without letting myself think about what they were typing.

"Sally Westin had spent most of her life at the Freedom Diner. She'd dedicated her life to Nate and Palmer Lustig as a valued employee, until Nate fired Sally because Sally was taking some of the Lustigs' spring water to give to her ailing sister. In fact, Sally's sister was getting better, and when Sally would talk about the miracle spring water, it was then Palmer Lustig decided she would bottle the spring water. With a little investigation work, the staff at the *Junction Journal* has uncovered some information that would give the right for Sally Westin to possess all the spring water she wanted, along with the rest of the citizens of Holiday Junction, for that matter. Be sure to keep an eye out for tomorrow's online *Junction Journal* for up-to-the-minute updates, and stay tuned to the developing story on where this year's Mother's Day celebration will come to a close."

I reread the article a couple of times. I found an old photo of Sally Westin at the diner with Nate Lustig in the archives on the computer's hard drive to add to the article. She and Nate looked awfully happy.

CHAPTER SIXTEEN

Theshe sun might've been bright and shiny on my face, but there was darkness in my heart thinking about Mama in the jail. It hurt my heart, and I knew if Daddy were here, he'd know what to do.

I walked down the sidewalk near the seaside, and from the looks of the sidewalk chalkboard sign at the Freedom Diner, they were serving raspberry pie. The same Bundt cake Sally Westin had stolen from Mama during the cake walk. Getting a piece for her would be something she'd enjoy, so I headed that way and decided to call my dad to let him know what was going on and get some much-needed Rhinehammer support.

"Hi, Dad." Hearing his voice pinged even more sadness in me. "Mama's gotten herself into a pickle."

"A pickle?" He laughed. "When has she never been in a pickle, Violet? I told her not to bring our problems out there to you, but she insisted you wanted her there for Mother's Day." There was a pause. "What has she done and gotten herself into now?"

"She's been arrested." I couldn't bring myself to say the word "murder."

"Geez. Who did she southern this time?" By southern, I knew Daddy meant insulted enough to get some sort of assault charge against her.

"She didn't southern anyone. She poisoned them, or so the law here thinks she did." As I continued to tell him what had happened from beginning to end, I knew by the exhausted sighs coming from his end that it wasn't unbelievable to him.

"She's a piece of work, that mama of yours." Daddy started in on her. "For years we've kept the fact we've been having troubles from you, but Violet, I just can't take her behavior no more. Do you realize I was kicked out of the hunting club because of her? The Bible Thumpers wouldn't even let her in their group in fear she'd be making everything about her. Do you know how hard it is to live in a house where the ego of the other person leaves no room for my shoes?"

"Now Daddy—" I was about to take up for her.

"Don't you 'now Daddy' me nothing. That's exactly what Millie Kay would've said, but Violet, maybe sitting in jail will be good for her ego for a few days until they get the real killer behind bars." Daddy was unbelievable.

"You mean to tell me you are going to let her sit in there without any sort of nothing?" I had no clue what people even did in jail, but I knew it wasn't for Mama. "She'll go nuts."

"Then let her." Daddy was stern. Hard.

"Are you serious right now? We are thousands of miles away, and you're going to let the woman who birthed me, had supper on the table for you every single night, did your laundry without complaining about how stinky you are, not to mention kept a clean house." A speck of dust didn't live in our house for too long. "You are going to just let her rot, all because she has her own mind? Her own opinions, and a small town like Normal thinks that's a bad thing?"

"Violet, hold on a minute." Daddy tried to do what he called "talk sense into me," but I was going to talk some sense into him. "Your mama killed my dreams, Violet. Now it's my time."

"You and Mama taught me to be independent. An individual. My own thinker, and when I didn't fit in, you encouraged me to keep going. That's no different than how Mama acted. So if you want to use the good excuse that she was a stand-up citizen in Normal and she didn't play by anyone's book but her own, then you can just stay there and find someone at your age who will do all those things for you!" I hung up the phone and jerked open the door of the diner.

As I made my way to the counter, I couldn't help but notice everyone was on their phones. Not something unusual in today's world, but definitely strange when all of them were looking, scrolling, and even chatting.

"Looks like I need to be on my phone." I snickered when I sat down on one of the stools at the counter, and Patty, the young waitress, came over with her order pad in her hand. I looked at the glass-covered pie plate sitting on the counter next to me. It wasn't pie though, it was one of those raspberry Bundt cakes.

"It's your article they are all talking about." She tapped the counter with her fingernail.

"Really?" I slowly turned to look back behind me and over the diner.

"Yep. They are more concerned with the Merry Maker being Sally Westin than the fact she was killed by poison." She leaned her hip on the counter. "What can I get you?"

"I need a piece—no, make it two." I noted it was never good to eat alone. I had to take one for the team and eat with Mama. "Two pieces of raspberry Bundt cake." I pointed to the pie.

"It goes fast. I'm glad you got a couple of slices. One for you and Millie Kay?" she asked, taking the lid off.

"Yes." I wondered if Patty was just being nice since she'd not mentioned Mama's fate. "Do you not know?"

"Of course I know." Carefully she slid two pieces of Bundt cake in a to-go container without the insides oozing out. "You're talking about your mama, right?"

"Yeah. I guess everyone knows." It wasn't too different from Normal—the gossip, that was.

"I wasn't going to say anything. You learn really fast around here to keep your mouth shut. From what I also heard from Nate—" She drew her lips together, and her brows formed a V like she was battling within herself to even tell me what she'd heard.

"Go on," I encouraged her.

"It's nothing. Really. You take the Bundt on to your mama." She gave a quick shake to her head and took a third slice of Bundt cake out with the spatula. She fit it into my to-go box too. "On the house." She closed the box and handed it over the counter to me.

"What were you going to say about Nate?" I asked in a hushed whisper.

"Anything you can tell me would be greatly appreciated. I'm trying to help Mama, and I'm actually on my way now to meet Diffy Delk."

"Diffy will find out, so I guess—" She paused. "I can't lose my job." It was like she was warning me not to say anything if she did tell me.

"I'm a journalist. I never reveal my sources." It was an oath I did live by when it came to reporting, but right now my mama stood accused of killing Sally Westin, and my only concern was to get her out of Chief Strickland's custody.

"Nate said Tricia had stopped by to see Palmer."

"When?" I asked.

"This morning. He got a call from Palmer saying you stopped by the Groove and Go." Her eyes were shifty, like she was trying not to let everyone here in the diner know what she was telling me.

"So I was right." I gasped.

"What?" Patty questioned.

I gave Patty the once-over. I knew she was in her twenties, around my age, and honestly, the only other person I'd really gotten to know my age was Cherise. She was out of town with her job as a flight attendant, so I'd yet to be able to knock ideas around with her.

"You can tell me. I won't say a word. Trust me. I grew up around here, and I hate how everyone talks. I never ever tell anyone anything." She offered a smile. "It might be nice having a girlfriend around." Her big smile was so inviting. "Patty Hamilton."

"Well, Patty Hamilton, I was just thinking the same thing about you." I leaned in on my elbows. "Why don't you meet me at the jiggle joint later this afternoon. I need to go see Darren about the lighthouse he purchased."

"I get off around five. Is that good?" She shrugged, agreeing to go as my sidekick. That way Darren wouldn't be able to sweet-talk me, and she'd keep me on task to get the answers I needed from him, and that's all.

"Perfect." I picked up the box with the three slices of pie. "Thanks so much. Mama will love it."

"Your mom is precious. I had a lot of fun with her last night." She used the cleaning rag and wiped down the spot where I was sitting even though I'd not gotten any food there. "She's exactly the little spark we need around here."

"Don't tell her that, or she just might not ever leave." I almost told Patty about my parents' crazy idea to divorce after all these years but decided we might be able to bond over that later tonight. "I've got to go. Date with Diffy Delk."

"He's your guy." She waved me off into the crowd, where people just so happened to be muttering my name under their breath as I was weaving my way through to the diner's front door.

Certainly stopping by Freedom Diner hadn't been on my list of things to do, but there was a reason for the sign, and that was what brought me in there, which made Tricia Lustig move up on my list of suspects even further. When I dropped by the bank next to Diffy's office to get the money from my savings account, my mind still didn't drop the questions fluttering around.

The big question I had was maybe going to be best answered by Nate Lustig himself. Why didn't he have a relationship with Tricia? Sure, he got the family spring, but why cut her out completely? Why give Palmer full decision-making power over it?

And I took those questions to Diffy Delk. Little did I realize Diffy was the owner of Dave the Rooster. Dave was sitting on a platform in the corner of Diffy's office.

"I've met Dave but not you." Just when I thought my day couldn't get any more strange.

"Dave is the most popular person other than the mayor." He snickered and looked back at the rooster. "He is really good at security and running people off. Most people are just scared of roosters. One coming at you really can keep you in line."

"Yes. I met him when I got into town. Rhett Strickland left out the part he was actually owned by someone." It wouldn't have been unusual for a rooster to be running all over my hometown, so when I met Dave, it didn't seem so strange.

"Do you have an opinion on my questions?" I went back to the questions I'd told him I'd wondered about with the Lustig family.

"Mmhmmm." He sat behind a much-too-big oak desk with the same exact suit he had on in his photo on the website.

Online I couldn't really tell the fabric, but in person it was all polyester.

His hairline was also much deeper in person, but if he was as good as his motto and what Patty said, his strange and very dated appearance was overlooked.

"I can't speak to why the Lustig family does anything. Strange people." His statement was what we southerners would call "calling the kettle black" since Diffy was odd himself. "But I can tell you that Millie Kay isn't the only citizen in Holiday Junction with mothballs. I bet if you went over to the Holiday Village and pull back some of the closet doors, you're going to find all sorts of mothballs."

He waved his hand in front of his nose as if he were pushing an odor away when he referred to the smell of mothballs.

"Holiday Village?" I asked.

"The home of the near death." He jerked his head back. "It's a little further out of town past the airport."

"I've not ventured that far." I made a mental note to check the place out online. Maybe someone I'd come in contact with or someone who knew Sally worked there or had a family member there. It was worth checking out.

"Unless you've got a foot in the grave plus four toes of the other foot, don't go." His lips duck billed. "Anyways, I've been pondering your mother's case. I went by to see her this morning after I got your call, and let's just say she's not doing so well." He moved his eyes past my face down to the envelope in my hand.

"Oh." I set the money on his desk and slid it across. "Here's the money."

He picked it up and opened the flap, running his finger along the one-hundred-dollar bills before he opened the top drawer of his desk, where he put the envelope.

"Really, I'm not concerned with the Lustigs. I'm concerned with Millie Kay." He picked up the phone and punched in a few numbers. "Please send her in."

He hung up the phone. The bookcase behind his desk opened to expose a secret room or something. I leaned really far to the right to see around him, but all I could see was Mama walking through.

"Mama!" I jumped up and ran to her, throwing my arms around her. "Are you okay?" I asked as I pushed her out to arm's length to get a good look before I curled her right back into my arms. "I called Daddy, and well, let's just say we won't discuss that anymore."

I wouldn't discuss it with her anymore, but once this all got cleared up, Daddy sure would be hearing from me.

It also just dawned on me how Diffy had already gotten Mama out and was waiting on me to give him the money.

"What if I didn't bring the money? Were you going to hold her hostage?" I let go of Mama and questioned just what type of attorney he was.

"Nah. I'd just have given her back to Matthew." At least he was honest.

CHAPTER SEVENTEEN

"I don't know about him, Mama." Once Mama and I left Diffy's office, we decided to walk down to Holiday Park and sit in one of the amphitheater rows while we ate our cake, with our fingers, something Mama would've never let me do, but I guessed her getting out of jail was an exception to her southern manner rule.

"He seems just fine. Maybe a little crooked, but that's what it's going to take in this town for someone out of town to win." Mama shoved the small triangle end of the Bundt cake in her mouth. "No wonder Sally wanted my pie. This is delicious."

"Speaking of Sally." I'd yet to ask Mama why she was at the spring, but the time had come. "I've decided that I'm going to do everything I can and use all the resources to find other suspects and motives to clear you off that list."

"Why don't you let Diffy do that?" Mama wondered.

There was some noise up on the stage of the amphitheater, and the sign posted said the actual show wasn't until Sunday, Mother's Day.

"He's going to be busy defending you. Let him do that job." I wasn't sure if she knew the role of a lawyer since I'd never recalled her ever having to use one, but then again, I never recalled her and Daddy having any troubles either. "I need you to be straight with me. I need to know exactly what you did after I left the inn last night."

"You mean what I did after you snuck out to go play kissy-face with Darren?" At least Mama's tone didn't seem to hold any sort of dislike about Darren, like it had before he gave her a lie in her alibi.

"I've never kissed Darren Strickland in my life," I protested even though it wasn't important at this moment.

"My my, you certainly are huffy about it." Mama knocked her shoulder into me with a smile.

"How do you do it?" I looked over at her. "How are you in such a good mood after you've been accused of killing someone?"

"I know I didn't kill no one, and I believe the truth will come out. I've got the best person on the case." She seemed pretty confident.

I wasn't feeling it.

"I've not really looked into Diffy Delk, but from the one person who said he was good and by the way his website looks, I guess he's the best." I had to give him the benefit of the doubt. I had no choice. We had no other options.

"I'm not talking about the polyester king." Mama's witty humor was rarely seen by me, though I'd heard from many people when I was growing up how I should be a little more relaxed like Mama.

Mama had never been relaxed when I was a kid.

"I'm talking about you, Violet Rhinehammer." She nudged me again. A look of confidence washed over me when she looked at me with a smile. "What? You look surprised."

"I never ever thought you even looked at me like from anything other than my mama." I stuffed my feelings down by taking another big bite of pie.

"I guess I don't do a great job of showing it. I admit I was too busy trying to raise you up properly and give you the best. Make you proud of yourself." She cleared her throat. "So now what do we do?"

"First I want to go to the hospital and see if Sally's husband is working. I highly doubt it, but at least I can ask him about Sally and her sister. I really want to talk to the sister." I knew if I could get to her and find out what her arrangements were with Sally about getting some of the spring water, then I could possibly learn of Sally's action. Making a good timeline for her would also help with Mama's timeline.

"Did anyone see you leave the inn?" I wondered.

"Of course. I talked to Kristine. She's the one who pointed out your work bag on the floor. She said she was taking Mayor Paisley for another walk, and that's when she saw you walking down the street." Mama's lips pulled together. "I thought you might be going to see Rhett, so I gave it a while and decided to take a walk myself. It wasn't until several minutes later and me playing with my phone did I get the directions to Lustig Spring. That's when I decided it was such a pretty night that I'd walk there."

"You got there and then what?" I asked.

"That's when I called Rhett to see if you were there. My feet were aching because I didn't have on sensible shoes, and that's when he told me you weren't with him. He said he'd stop by the office and see if you were there." Mama made it clear why Rhett had been there and why he had been upset seeing me with Darren. "He said he'd grab you and come get me. That's when I told him to bring me a few empty jugs if he had any."

"You'd not seen Sally at this point?" I asked.

"No." She held up a finger and licked the raspberry filling off of it. "I did see a few jugs on the ground and thought to myself I might fill those up and leave the ones Rhett was going to bring me. I walked around the spring structure to see if I really did have to open the little door or if there was something behind it, like a pump or valve. That's when I noticed her feet, then her legs, before my eyes registered her entire body." Mama's voice cracked a few times as she told me how she found Sally's body. "I called you, and as soon as I hung up the phone was when Rhett showed up. I told him I called you, and he waited there with me. Told me he'd bring us back, but apparently you were with a different Strickland."

"I ran into Darren by chance." I didn't want her to think I was dating around. "I had a late-night meeting, and when I left, I took the seaside walk home. It's wide open and safe."

"Is this what you're telling me in order for me to feel better about where you went so late? Because you can stop yourself right there. You are an adult. I am an adult, and if we've learned anything here today, it's how we can communicate as adults and possibly more than just mother and daughter." She put her hand on my leg. "I think of you as my friend, and we can talk openly."

"And you're not going to judge me, try to give me advice, or butt into anything I want to do while you're here?" I asked.

"Criss-cross applesauce." She lifted her pinky and crossed her heart with it before she dangled it in front of me to pinky swear. Something we did when I was a little girl.

"Fine." I couldn't help but smile from the memory and gesture we'd not done in a very long time. "When I moved here, I discovered by accident the real Merry Maker. Unfortunately they are not able to do it anymore." I made sure I kept Vern's identity under wraps. There was no need at this point to let the cat out of the bag since he was no longer the Merry Maker. "The person asked me to meet with them and discuss the possibility of me being the Merry Maker, and I was pulled into the spell of the sales pitch."

Mama giggled.

"I was enticed by being able to be the person, and not only that but do some sort of post in the paper about the Merry Maker, keeping it confidential as though I had the main source." I thought it was a clever idea for Vern to sell me on, and I still liked the idea.

"You are the source, so it's perfect," Mama proclaimed before she finished off the last bite of the pie.

"I was walking down near the sea when I ran into Darren. He was on his way home and walked with me." I left out the part how he insisted he walk with me and how he didn't like me walking alone at night.

It felt like an intimate detail I wanted to keep for myself. Something I'd never felt with any man before, and it was comforting, even if it was just a line.

"That's when I discovered he owns the lighthouse." My comment made Mama jerk back with interest on her face. "Yep. He lives there, and I got a tour. So when you called, I was sitting up on top of it. Me and my Merry Maker sign."

"He knows you're the Merry Maker?"

"Yep. And he has a moped. When you called, I grabbed the sign, and off we went to find you." I had to laugh at the situation since it all sounded so silly how it had gone down. "When we showed up to the spring, he must've put the sign down, and from there Curtis assumed Sally had put it there."

"When you come to think of it and by Sally's actions about the spring and her accessibility to it, she'd do something like make the last hurrah for Mother's Day as the Merry Maker there, just to get at Nate and Palmer." Mama was kinda good at this sleuthing stuff.

"Looky there, you don't need me to help you." I looked out at the Leading Ladies starting to take the stage, and when a couple of strums of a guitar caught my attention, I noticed Patrick Strickland was off to the side, looking at what seemed like sheet music being held by Tricia Lustig. "But who killed her?"

"You are looking at that woman, and by the sound of your voice, you think she might have something to do with it." Mama and I were now both staring. "Who is she?" Mama asked.

"That's Tricia Lustig. Nate Lustig's sister and the owner of the Groove and Go dance studio near our new house." I looked at Mama and lifted my brows. "Before I came to the house this morning, I made a quick pit stop there because I'd heard from a few sources she was a little troubled with her brother's decision about not letting the public have access to the spring any longer. I asked her about the fountain-of-youth idea Palmer had, to gauge her reaction."

"I'm guessing she was cool as a cucumber but boiling inside?" Mama wondered.

"Let's say she didn't know anything about it and ran down to the Freedom Diner to say something to Nate after I left to go meet you at the house." I didn't reveal how Patty told me about it. "And this afternoon I'm going to meet my source to get a little more history about this spring and the Lustig family."

"This all sounds so official. You really should start a crime podcast. You'd get a million followers after one show." Mama's enthusiasm exuded from her, overshadowing the fact she was still the lead suspect in Sally's murder.

"I don't have time. I barely have time to write something online every day for the *Junction Journal*." I moved my gaze as soon as Tricia looked over at us. "While I was doing my research, I'd come across how springs aren't really owned by someone and how they thread through various properties. From the looks of a free online database, the Lustig Spring almost starts around the seaside, and if I'm reading it correctly, near the lighthouse."

"Are you saying Darren Strickland might want access to the spring and he could've possibly killed Sally in order for the Lustigs to not get a deal with their notion of fountain of youth?" Mama made an observation I'd not thought of.

"No, but I guess there could be a possibility that someone with land that part of the spring runs through could. But not Darren." I refused to believe it. "He's not that complicated."

"You never know." Mama shrugged and picked up the empty to-go container from the Freedom Diner. "Look there!" Mama pointed to the Leading Ladies.

They were all trying to do some sort of choreographed dance. It was a little entertaining, and you could see how some of them had great coordination and some didn't.

Tricia Lustig was trying her hardest to dance a tap routine while they sang behind her and did the simple steps she'd been trying to teach them.

"Mama, didn't you belong to the Daniel Boone Cloggers?" I put my arm around her and watched her pick up a piece of the pie.

"Mmhmm." She nodded. Her toe was tapping to Patrick's guitar.

"Did you bring your clogging shoes to Holiday Junction?" I asked.

"I did. I brought everything." Her shoulders were now swaying to the music. It wouldn't take too much for me to coax Mama.

"It's time to dust off those shoes. You're going to join the Leading Ladies." I knew I had to get in front of Tricia Lustig, and Mama was going to have to pull her load in getting her name cleared.

No better way than Mama bringing a little southern clogging to Holiday Junction.

CHAPTER EIGHTEEN

It didn't take too much persuasion to talk Marge and Louise into taking responsibility for Mama as the newest Leading Lady. They knew I was using Mama to get her integrated into the world of the Lustigs, specifically Tricia. If anyone could get Tricia to spill some gossip, which might or might not be what I needed to prove she either did kill Sally or knew something about someone who did, Mama was my informant.

She would use the old southern saying about catching flies with honey instead of trying to catch them with vinegar. Good thing Mama was full of sweet sass. Mama's specialty was making you feel so warm and fuzzy until she walked away leaving you wondering if she'd just given you a compliment or an insult.

With Mama safe in the Leading Ladies' hands, I headed back across Holiday Park with the top of the hospital in my sight, which was next to the police station and near Diffy Delk's office.

Since Holiday Park was a skip and a hop from the hospital, it didn't take me long to get there. If I thought the airport was small, the hospital was even smaller.

"Excuse me," I asked the person in scrubs sitting outside of the hospital, his face to the sun. "Can you tell me where the pharmacy is located?"

"Basement," he said and went back to basking in the sun, something I wished I was doing instead of trying to figure out why someone would want to kill Sally other than the intense desire to have spring water.

There was only one set of elevators I had noticed when I entered the entrance through the double sliding doors. It was down the hallway and on the right. There was one thing for sure, the smell of rubbing alcohol and old tile floor was no different than the hospital back home.

It was one of those smells you never forget. Kinda like the smell of live Christmas firs. There were so many signs posted in the hall recognizing mothers who worked as hospital employees. It was nice to see, and I couldn't help but sneak a look at a couple of the photos along the way to the elevators.

When I finally made it to the basement, I saw that the pharmacy was located to the right from the elevator doors, which made it pretty easy for patients or family members to find if they needed a prescription filled.

There was a woman standing behind the long panel of glass. She must've heard the elevator door, because she was looking at me as soon as I got off. A warm smile was on her face.

"Can I help you?" she asked me after she slid the small glass window open underneath the sign that read Drop Off.

"I'm looking for Dr. Westin." I did a quick look behind her. The tall wooden rows of white shelves made it difficult to see if anyone other than her was there.

"I'm sorry. He only came in for a few minutes." Her brows furrowed. "His wife died, and he might be taking a leave of absence."

"Yes. I heard." I frowned. "But he came in?"

"Yes. He had to get the nursing home medications over there. I told him I'd do it, but he insisted." She pinched her lips down. "I guess he was going to check on his sister-in-law. Poor guy. He's been battling Sally for years for her to stop drinking the water from the Lustig Spring and give her the medication. But Sally wouldn't listen to him. I'd hear them arguing and fussing. He'd accuse her of killing Hanna, and she'd accuse him of killing everyone he filled a prescription for."

"Hanna," I said the name so I wouldn't forget.

"Yes. Hanna Rain. That's Sally's sister." The pharmacy tech frowned. "It's sad. If the Lustig Spring gets this whole fountain-of-youth thing I hear

Palmer Lustig is trying to do, then it'll put us out of business. People won't want to take medication anymore. At least not this kind."

"Out of business? Doesn't the hospital own and operate the pharmacy?" I asked.

"Oh no. This is all Raymond's. His life's work. He just rents the space. Don't get me wrong, the hospital takes its chunk, but still it's Raymond's. Like all of Holiday Junction, our shops aren't normal." She snickered.

"The autoimmune disease." I didn't mean to let my thoughts slip. "If Hanna can't drink the spring water because it might be poisoned, then they will give her the medication now that Sally is dead."

My head started to put together the puzzle pieces of a reason Raymond would want to kill his wife. *Your mama killed my dreams, Violet. Now it's my time.* Daddy was trying to communicate with me, and I didn't listen to him. That was something I was going to have to reconcile with at a later time.

I still couldn't get the echo of his words out of my head as I wondered if this was something men went through as they got older. Sacrificed for the women they loved while trying to do their passion, then only to wake up one day and realize the women had taken that passion away. This whole concept of men having a midlife crisis suddenly seemed real. And would give Raymond a great motive to have killed his wife.

"Yes. So sad because Sally really did take care of her every single day." The pharmacy tech shook her head. "But I can help you. Do you have a prescription to drop off or pick up?"

"Thanks!" I took the opportunity of someone getting off the elevator to jump back in and not give the woman any information she could relay to Raymond Westin that I didn't want to tell him myself.

When I walked back out of the hospital, the man was still sitting outside.

"I hate to bother you again," I interrupted his little nap. "I'm sure you're on your lunch break."

"What gave it away?" he asked sarcastically.

"Yes. Well, can I ask you where the nursing home is located?" He answered my question by lifting his finger in the air and pointing across the way to another building. "Goodness. It's like everything is right here."

"Yep. That's why they call this Central Square. Everything you possibly need for daily life in the Village is here, like government and medical." The man sighed but never once opened his eyes.

"Thanks again." I was learning so much about my new town. I had barely taken time off the past couple of months to even explore it.

It was a shame too. Holiday Junction was unlike any place I'd ever been, and the slow-paced life with all the gorgeous landscape and scenery was one I needed to take the time to enjoy. Before I let the thoughts of my next actions pop into my head where they would take up a lot of space, I knew I needed to add a section to the *Junction Journal* where I could feature something about Holiday Junction.

The nursing home was going to be my first feature.

The streets were beginning to fill up with people heading to Holiday Park to enjoy the Mother's Day Festival booths and local shops that had set up for the day. It was definitely something I wanted to check out, if not for my own personal reasons, for the paper.

The nursing home appeared to be a very long ranch-style building with several entrances along the front covered with an awning and places for people to sit and gather. It appeared to be in good shape, well landscaped with all sorts of colorful flowers.

Inside the door was a sign-in desk with a hand sanitizer station, along with a sign about how some residents have sensitive immune systems and even catching a simple cold puts them in grave danger.

From what I could see, there was a homey commons area with couches and chairs, along with wide hallways going in each direction. A few people were in wheelchairs as family members walked beside them.

"Can I help you?" the receptionist asked.

"Hi. I'm from the *Junction Journal*," I started to say.

"Are you here to take photos of the Mother's Day project?" She had so much glee in her voice, I just knew I couldn't take that away from her.

"Yes. Yes I am." I nodded and smiled, wondering if God was going to send me straight to hell after it was my time to go for all the lying I'd gotten good at.

But in my head, I could spin it as a way to use it for good. Solve Sally Westin's murder. I couldn't think of anything better to lie about.

"In fact, Hanna Rains in particular, since her sister and all—" I frowned and blinked a few times to try to get a little tear to pop up.

Nothing. Dry as an old bone.

"It's awful. Just awful." The receptionist pointed over to the common area where the tables were set up for the arts and craft project she must've been talking about. "They will bring all the residents out to make their projects, and there's a little show-type party in the kitchen with a magician with snacky things. So if you want to just wander around and take photos…" Her eyes searched my body as if she were looking for a camera.

"I use my phone nowadays. Just not as bulky, and it takes great photos." I took my phone out and wiggled it in the air.

"It has gotten so much easier, hasn't it?" She shrugged. "You can sign in right here." She laid a pen on top of the clipboard resting on her desk.

I filled out my name by putting "Junction Journal" in its place then wrote the time and date.

"Reason for visit would be 'feature in the journal,'" she told me as she watched me fill out the form.

"Do you have everyone who comes sign in?" I wondered.

"Yes. No one gets past me," she said with stern pride as she reached for the clipboard.

"Oh." I picked it up just in time. "I forgot to write my name. Silly me." I rolled my eyes. "I put 'Junction Journal.'"

With the clipboard a little tilted, I pretend to scribble my name, though I was scanning down the sign-in sheet to see who was here, specifically Raymond Westin.

He wasn't on there, but one name in particular caught my attention.

Tricia Lustig.

"Thank you." I handed the clipboard back to her and wondered why Tricia Lustig was here. Wasn't she at the amphitheater?

I checked the time on my phone and realized I'd taken much longer than I'd realized. Tricia would've had plenty of time to do what she needed to do with the Leading Ladies and head straight here.

"One more question." I turned back to the receptionist. "Is the Groove and Go putting on the show for the residents today?"

"No." She shook her head. "I told you it was a magician."

"You did. Got it." I turned and looked down the hall. *Where are you, Tricia? Where are you, Raymond?*

"Three B," the receptionist said as I was walking away.

"I'm sorry?" I was confused.

"You asked about Hanna. Hanna Rains." Her brows knitted. Now she was confused. "She lives in three B."

"Yes. Thank you!" I called and headed to the hallway with the numbers pointing in all sorts of directions to get the right way to go to Hanna's room.

For good measure I snapped a few photos along the way so if the receptionist was looking at me, she'd think I was simply doing my job and not playing some amateur sleuth like on TV.

When I finally wormed around the hallways to three B, I was happy to be greeted by an open door.

Walking past it first, I rubbernecked to see inside. I wasn't about to walk in if I saw Raymond in there. I did a second drive-by coming from the other direction, pretty confident no one was in there. Not even Hanna.

I slipped in and pulled the big door handle behind me. I wanted to make sure I could hear someone coming in if they did. The room was narrow with an adjustable bed with side rails. Next to the bed was a basic wooden nightstand with a pull-out drawer. There was a digital clock and a copy of the *Junction Journal* neatly folded next to the clock.

I looked down when my feet hit something and noticed it was a pair of slippers tucked underneath the bed.

I moved across the room and parted the heavy drapes on the windows to see the location of the room to the outside world. Hanna had a great view of the nursing home courtyard with a small flower garden in the center. Some people were out there sitting on the benches visiting.

Satisfied, I closed the curtains like they had been and moved to the bathroom. It was completely made for a wheelchair, with a large roll-in shower and a toilet with handicap bars, along with a pull cord to call for help.

There didn't seem to be anything out of the ordinary, and it was very clean. I walked back out into the room and noticed the television was encased in a wooden structure with a long and skinny floor-to-ceiling-style closet. I pulled the handle open, and there it was.

Jugs and jugs of water. A good conclusion was it was water from the Lustig Spring that Sally Westin had stolen and kept here for Hanna.

Suddenly my mind shifted from what my eyes were seeing to what my nose was smelling. My nosed twitched a few times while I sniffed out what I thought I was smelling.

Mothballs.

Frantically I moved a couple of the jugs as my eyes darted about in the closet until I found the little stinky buggers.

"Violet Rhinehammer?" I must've been so wrapped up in my thoughts I'd not realized someone had come in. "What on earth are you doing in here?"

Tricia Lustig and Raymond Westin stood inside of Hanna's door. Hanna Rains was sitting in a wheelchair.

CHAPTER NINETEEN

"I am here to do a story on the Mother's Day projects for the *Junction Journal*." I swallowed and tried to make my way past them after I'd put the jugs down where I'd found them, covering up the mothballs.

Raymond Westin took a step to block me from the doorway.

"I think it's safe to say we can all have a little chat." He didn't take his eyes off of me as Tricia pushed Hanna into the room. "Hanna, this is Violet. She's a new resident in Holiday Junction and works for the journal."

"I know you. At least I've heard of you. My sister Sally told me all about you and your mom." Hanna's hands were folded in her lap. She didn't appear to be the standard age for a nursing home.

"I'm guessing it's not too flattering." I turned to talk to her since Raymond wasn't allowing me to leave.

"Sally worked so hard to get me some spring water that she didn't care who she hurt if they got in the way, and from what I understand your mom, won the cake competition. So you must thank her for giving Sally the cake." Hanna grinned. "Sally said she told Matthew she was going to file assault charges if your mom didn't give her the raspberry bundt cake, but she was all talk."

I followed Hanna's eyes over to the adjustable table in the corner that was on wheels. There was the cake box from the cake walk, along with several small clear plastic cups used to dispense medication.

"It was our last piece of cake together. So thank you. I'll always cherish the memory." Hanna seemed to be really nice and likable. Too bad she was in the company of killers.

"Knock, knock." The door swung open, and a nurse's helper walked in. "Hanna, it's time for you to go down and do the Mother's Day project."

"Great!" I walked over to take the handles of the wheelchair from Tricia. "I'm Violet Rhinehammer from the *Junction Journal*, and I'm here to take photos for a piece in the journal. I'll take her."

"No. We will let the staff take her while we answer any of the questions you have for the journal." Tricia's voice came through her gritted-teeth smile. Her eyes didn't look happy.

The helper walked in.

"Great." She replaced Tricia.

"Don't forget I'm Violet Rhinehammer from the *Junction Journal* if anyone asks." I made sure she heard me say my name again in case Tricia and Raymond decided to get rid of me like they did Sally.

For a moment I felt a little relief when the door to the room was left open, before Tricia used the toe of her shoe to tap it, and it closed on its own.

"Why are you really here, Violet Rhinehammer from the *Junction Journal*?" Tricia crossed her arms. "I noticed you dumped your mom on the Leading Ladies, who I just so happen to be involved with, so you might's'well spill the beans."

"Fine." This was one of those moments I felt pretty confident I could scream my head off and someone would hear me. I'd not been in many of them, but I'd have guessed there were a lot of people around here who would hear me. Them having good mobility could be questioned. Then it hit me how most of them probably needed hearing assistance as well.

I was going to use caution on the side of them hearing me

"I went to the pharmacy to talk to you about your wife and what potential reason she might've been at the spring. I know she took the water for her sister, but I was going to ask you if you knew of anyone who would want to hurt her?" I shot a glare at Tricia. "Then," I stopped Tricia from saying something, "I talked to your tech, and she said you had all the accounts over here, and it dawned on me how you could've killed your wife because she was going to ruin your business by spouting off how her sister had gotten so much better with the spring water."

Tricia opened her mouth.

"I'm talking. You asked me to explain, and that's what I'm doing. Besides" —I gave her a long narrow-eyed stare—"I've not even started on you yet."

"*He insisted*, the pharmacy tech had told me why Raymond didn't want the tech to bring over the medication." I raised a brow as if that wasn't evidence enough. "Of course you insisted to bring over the medications. You two are in cahoots and both have a very good motive to have killed Sally Westin." I stomped and drew my shoulders back, very proud of the investigative work I'd done.

"Cahoots?" Tricia scoffed. "Cahoots and Clogging should be the headline of your next and last article at the *Junction Journal*. And when we tell the community about your unethical reasons to barge into a beloved village nursing home like you did, they will run you and your little mama out of town."

"With a sister like you who appears to be having an affair with the likes of him, you two killed Sally so it would look like the spring is deadly so your brother and his wife can't get rich off the spring, because you were cut out of owning any part of it." I jabbed my finger at her.

"You have one thing right." Raymond's chin lifted. "Tricia and I are in a relationship. Sally and I had been living apart for some time now, and no one knows but Tricia. But as for killing Sally, you're dead wrong. Yes. Sally did believe the spring water has healed her sister." He walked over to the closet where all those jugs of spring water sat. He pulled out a baggie full of syringes filled with liquid. "I come over here every time Sally brings a jug."

He popped the lid off one of the jugs.

"Plus you have the nursing home contract, and if everyone here finds out the Lustig Spring water has done wonders for Hanna, they won't need you anymore." I didn't let up, though I was about to ask what was in those syringes.

"See the little mark? Tricia and Sally were friends, and sometimes Tricia would give Sally jugs from the spring so Sally wouldn't trespass. Tricia marks the bottles so we know which ones are new." He put the syringe down into the jug and hit the plug, causing all the liquid to mix in with the spring water. "Now I take my pen and put a diagonal line with Tricia's to make an X."

He turned the jug around and showed me.

"This way I know I've put Hanna's medication in the water so she gets it. Sally believed it was the spring water and didn't want to give Hanna her medication. I couldn't let her slowly kill Hanna by making her drink the water which has zero healing properties, nor could I speak out about the spring. I'd not do that to the Lustigs." He gave the jug a good shake before he replaced it and started to inject the other jugs, repeatedly until he'd put the medication in them. "Not that I need to do it now with Sally gone. I have all legal power of attorney over Hanna, and she could start taking the pill form since Sally won't be here to stop her."

"You see, Raymond was saving Hanna's life, not trying to kill her or Sally." Tricia opened up her big mouth.

"What about you? Taking your best friend's husband? Not having any part of the spring water so you have to continue to give dance lessons at the Groove and Go? Huh?" I put my hand on my hip, for sure I'd gotten her on this one. "With Sally out of the way, you could have her husband and make the world think your brother and sister-in-law have poison in their spring so they don't make the spring water global with their fountain-of-youth idea."

"Have you seen Palmer?" Tricia cackled. "Do you think it's natural spring water that gave her the shiny forehead and big eyes along with those plumped-up lips? There's nothing natural on her, and trust me, there's plastic surgery records to prove it. She's always looking for ways to make money."

"I did notice her youthful appearance." My brows furrowed as I started to question my theory about these two. "She's telling the big cosmetic company her appearance is due to drinking the water from their spring?"

"Yes, Violet Rhinehammer, investigative reporter for the *Junction Journal*. And we were here last night helping out with the Mother's Day social. In fact, I ended up sleeping on the couch in Denver Shuman's room." Who on earth was she yammering on about? I gave her a look like, *who are you talking*

263

about? "Denver Shuman is a long-time donor to the Groove and Go. His daughter and granddaughters had taken lessons from me for years. He is ill and has dementia. When he gets upset, I can calm him down by talking to him and helping him relive old dance recital memories."

"Mr. Shuman is a very kind man. Unfortunately his personality had changed as his dementia had progressed." Raymond looked at Tricia and smiled. "That's just one nice thing she does for this community no one knows about."

"Another thing that has us bothered is how Sally was able to keep being the Merry Maker from anyone." Tricia must've seen the slight change in my eyes. Just hearing "Merry Maker" made me uncomfortable. "You know something." She took a couple of steps toward me away from the door, wagging her finger. "You know who the Merry Maker is, and it's not Sally. But you wanted to come here to confront Raymond just so you could be sure he didn't kill his wife."

"I have no idea what you are talking about." The verbal gymnastics started between us.

"Yes, you do." She moved her finger and pointed to herself. "I've got women's intuition too."

"I mean, I know there's someone who goes around being the Merry Maker since I've moved here, but I don't know—" I stopped and acted surprised. "Are you telling me Sally was the Merry Maker?"

"You aren't fooling me, Violet Rhinehammer." At least she left off my title this time. "You know who it is, and that is probably the killer." She pulled her phone out.

"What are you doing?" I asked.

"I'm calling Chief Strickland. You're not the only nosy person in this town." She let me past her. "I'd suggest you not leave town or cross the county line with any harebrained leads. I'm thinking the chief is going to want to see what you know."

"Don't you worry." I flipped around to face them. I wasn't about to let them bully me. "I'm going to go over there myself and tell Chief Strickland everything I've seen here today!"

CHAPTER TWENTY

"Now, now, Violet." Chief Strickland sat back in his chair with his hands folded across his stomach. He'd been silent the entire time while I'd told him what I'd encountered at the nursing home.

I tried not to seem so flustered after I noticed the Mother's Day Merry Maker sign we'd left at the Lustig Spring, which he'd taken into evidence.

"We don't go around telling people's personal problems, so if Tricia Lustig and Raymond Westin are friendly, that doesn't mean they killed anyone."

"You aren't listening to me." I grabbed a piece of the paper from the top of his pile and flipped it over. After clicking the ink pen, I laid it all out for him to see. "Sally had stopped giving Hanna the medication because she thought the spring water was healing her, when in reality, it was Raymond giving Hanna liquid medication in the spring water. That's how Sally believed it was healing Hanna."

Chief Strickland's brows furrowed, and his head tilted to the other side as he gave me a hard stare.

Frustrated, I continued, "This gives him a motive to have killed her. Don't you see?" I jabbed the paper with the pen for him to look at it. "Raymond has the entire nursing home account. That's a lot of cash and business. If word got around—and from what I know about Sally, it sure did get

265

around—then all the residents could've stopped needing him because they'd want to drink the spring water. Which would mean he'd lose the account."

Chief Strickland's brows finally rose to the top of his hairline after he realized what I was saying. He moved his hands from his belly to the top of his desk as he leaned forward to get a better look at the diagram.

"That's not the best part." I didn't want to leave this little piece out. "Hanna has mothballs in her closet. How easy would it be for Raymond to have used some of those mothballs in Sally's water? She drank it. Boom. Dead!" I smacked my hands together.

He jumped.

"Sorry. I get excited when I figure out murders. It's sorta a thing. Like Jay Mann." I shrugged confidently. "Not that I take pleasure in my talent, but I just have a way."

"What does Tricia Lustig have to do with this?" Was he really asking me this question?

"I've gone over this with you about how Tricia doesn't have any sort of ties with the family spring. Not only does she not get along with Palmer, who somehow has convinced Nate to give her authority over the spring but also turn it into some sort of money-making, false advertising…" My words trailed off as my mind flew in a new direction.

"What?" He sat straight up. "What are you thinking?"

"Nothing." I glanced up at the clock. "I'm thinking I've got to go. I've got an appointment."

Not that it was entirely a lie. I had told Patty I'd meet her at the jiggle joint, and if anyone knew anything about property, it was Rhett Strickland. Which made me wonder if Darren was just as knowledgeable.

I didn't know a whole lot about natural springs, but surely a landscaper would.

"Say." I turned before I left Chief Strickland's office. "Is there a good landscaper around here? Me and Mama bought a house over on Heart, and well—" I bit my lip. The lies were piling up. "We need a good landscaper."

"Lawn and Order Landscaping is the only one in Holiday Junction. Petey Puddles will give you a discount if you run an ad for him in the *Junction Journal*. That's what me and Louise did when we needed some lawn care. Then again, I bet you could use Reed. He's the handyman for all."

"Yeah. I thought about him. But he's pretty busy." Petey Puddles? I repeated in my head and tried not to laugh. His name was almost as bad as the name of his lawn care service. "Thanks!" I called and took a step outside his office door.

"Violet, one more thing." He stopped me right as I almost got away.

"Mmhmmm." I turned back around and pinched a grin.

"What's the deal with you and Darren?" His question knocked me for a loop. I'd much rather have answered questions about the murder and the suspects.

"Deal?" I expelled a nervous laugh. "There's no deal."

"There's a deal. I know what the boy looks like or how he looks at someone when he's got some vested time with them. You have had some vested time with him when I thought you were seeing my nephew Rhett."

"My goodness. Look at the time." I skirted on out of there in hopes he'd not find out I was heading straight over to the jiggle joint to, in fact, see his son.

There were so many things I had to do, and one of those was getting in touch with Vern McKenna to find out what I need to do for the Mother's Day Festival ending now that it appeared Sally Westin was the Merry Maker.

"I've been waiting for your call" was exactly how Vern answered my call. "You've managed to take a two-hundred-year-old tradition and practically ruin it within less than twenty-four hours of you being appointed the position."

There was no denying the anger in his tone, and how he pounced on the phone let me know he'd been waiting for me to call.

"Listen, I didn't mess anything up. It was Darren Strickland. He's the one who took the sign to the spring after Mama called to tell me about finding Sally. I know I wasn't even thinking about the sign when Chief Strickland showed up." By the time I'd gotten finished explaining to Vern what happened, I was walking past the fountain in Holiday Square so I could take the paved sidewalk down toward the seaside where I could meet Patty.

There were still some Mother's Day activities taking place in the park, and I couldn't resist using my cell phone to snap a few photos for the *Junc-*

tion Journal so I could have some sort of content to get on there. I'd really neglected my job, and I had to think about that too.

All of these issues were making me grumpy, so after I'd snapped a few shots of some kids making paper flowers for their moms, I headed toward the hot dog vendor.

Vern was silent. I was thinking this was a good sign. Because he'd been the Merry Maker for a while, I was sure he was coming up with a good solution.

"I guess we can make a new sign and put it up somewhere different," I suggested. "Vern?" I pulled the phone from my ear to make sure he was still on the line. The seconds were still ticking. "Vern?"

"Yeah." There was a bit more anger in the sigh than I had anticipated.

"Now what?" I asked as I held up my finger to the vendor for one hot dog in exchange for some cash. "Keep the change," I whispered.

"Did I hear you correctly when you said Darren Strickland somehow got ahold of the sign?"

"Oh." I bit down into the hot dog and kept the position while I closed my eyes after I'd realized what I'd done.

"You told Darren you're the Merry Maker, didn't you?" His words were fast and frenzied. "What am I going to do now? I've been married to Leni for," he hesitated, "too long, and she never knew I was the Merry Maker. If anyone should know, it should be my wife I've had forever, who I live with, share meals with, and lied to when I would have to go put the sign up during the wee hours of the night after she'd wake up. Do you know how many times Leni has accused me of cheating on her?"

"I'm sorry. It was by pure accident. Really." I would have tried to explain the whole situation, but then it would have sounded like me and Darren were on a date. I couldn't even begin to figure out how to make the situation any better. "Yeah. I guess I've taken a two-hundred-year-old tradition and kinda put us in a pickle, but all that doesn't matter. What matters is what am I going to do? The sign is being held for evidence in Chief Strickland's office, and then there's the matter of the spring. It's roped off, and I can guarantee Nate and Palmer aren't going to let the festival end there when they don't want anyone on their property, even if Chief Strickland is going to release the crime scene."

"Honestly, I have no idea what I was thinking." Vern wasn't listening to me. "I should've known some out-of-towner never would take the time, care, and love of the Merry Maker."

"I can do this," I protested and chomped more off the hot dog as my determination set in. "I know I can make this right. This will be a good thing."

"And just how do you plan on doing that, Violet Rhinehammer?" he asked sarcastically.

"I don't know, but I'm going to figure it out." Then it dawned on me. "Darren and I are going to be co-Merry Makers. That's it!"

"No. There's no co anything. Do you understand me?" Vern shouted at me.

"I think it's a great idea, and as the current Merry Maker, I'm making Darren a co-Merry Maker. I'll keep you posted." I hung up the phone and chowed down the rest of the hot dog in an attempt to eat the words that'd come out of my mouth and feelings in the pit of my stomach.

And boy, was I regretting my idea when I walked into the jiggle joint and my eyes locked with Darren.

I was in trouble. I knew it at the lighthouse. Being that close to him made my head swim and my heart hurt in ways it'd never done, and now that I'd made a mess of the Merry Maker gig, this was my only option.

"I thought you'd sworn yourself off of ever coming in here or just seeing me in general." His dimples slowly deepened as the smile crawled along his lips. His biceps bulged with each swipe of the rag he was using to dry the inside of the beer stein.

"We have to talk." I'd rushed over to the bar top and leaned over so only he could hear me.

"No 'thank you Darren for telling your dad me and my mama,'" he was talking in my accent or at least giving it a good go, "'was with you at the bar.'"

"Thank you, I've already found the killer, but we have bigger problems." I gestured between us. "Merry Maker," I mouthed.

"I have nothing to do with that." He shook his head and reached the beer stein up to place on the shelf with the others. "That's your gig. This is mine."

"It's totally your gig now. Thanks to you for bringing the sign to the spring where your dad told the world Sally Westin was the Merry Maker.

Which would be fine, but now the party? What about the party?" I questioned.

Darren didn't pay a bit of attention to me. He'd grabbed a beer glass and had pulled the handle of one of the many taps, tugging it toward him as he poured a glass.

"Nate and Palmer will not let the town hold the final Mother's Day Festival there." He slid the beer glass my way.

"Drink it. You could use the opportunity to be quiet and hear yourself." What, was he giving advice?

"So now you're giving people advice?" I let it slip out of my head. "Maybe you need to write an advice column for the paper."

Owen and Shawn's beady eyes were staring at me.

"What?" I asked them and picked up the beer, taking a nice, long swig. "I just might start day-drinking with you."

"Listen." Darren used the rag to wipe down the bar top, which wasn't unusual, but he did turn his back on Tooth Fairy and Easter Bunny. "I don't know what is going on in that head of yours, but I can't be the Merry Maker. You're going on this alone."

"No. You are, and you and I are going to figure out this little Mother's Day party together." I hid my lips behind the glass, just in case Tooth Fairy or the Easter Bunny could read lips.

"Just move it," Darren suggested like that was an option. "Move the party. Make a new sign."

"You make this two-hundred-year-old tradition sound so flippant. I can't do that. It's not how the Merry Maker works. If we move the party, then it looks like the Merry Maker killed Sally. And if we just keep it there, it looks like Sally is the Merry Maker, and the process of finding a new one begins in the secret world of Merry Making." I didn't make a lick of sense, but he got the drift.

The door opened, letting the only view of the outdoor world inside. The silhouette stood in the door outlined by the sunlight, but I knew that pose. I knew that body. As soon as the person took a step inside and the door closed behind, all eyes were on Millie Kay Rhinehammer.

This day was just not letting me do the things I needed to do.

"What on earth are you doing in here, Mama?" I jumped off the stool and headed over to her.

"I've come to get my afternoon cocktail before we go to the Leading Ladies' get-together tonight for supper." There were two things with Mama's sentence that I didn't like. One being Leading Ladies' get-together we—emphasis on the we—were going to go to, and the other supper.

"You mean you?" I asked. When she gave me the mama look, my body deflated. "Mama. I have too much on my plate today. I can't go. Time is precious right now, and now that I've found the killer—killers, you can go anywhere you want to alone."

"Killers?" Mama and Darren along with Shawn and Owen said in unison.

"You'll find out soon enough, but let's just say that I found mothballs in a very interesting place where Sheriff Strickland is going to look into," I confidently stated and drank the last of my beer.

"Then you should be free. Meet me in the golf cart at seven p.m." Mama tootled on past me. I watched her walk over to Owen and Shawn, where she took a seat. A beer was waiting for the person—they must've been expecting her. "Shall we talk business, gentleman?"

"Business?" I looked at Darren in disbelief. "What does that mean?" I asked.

"Who knows." He shrugged and picked up the glass. "Another one?"

"No. I'm here to meet Patty." I glanced around to see who came in and turned back around when I noticed it wasn't her.

"From the Freedom Diner?" Darren asked.

"Yeah. I want to pick her brain about the conversation Nate and Tricia had with Palmer about my stopping by. She couldn't talk at the diner, so we decided to meet here around five." It was almost five.

"Just ask Nate." Darren threw a finger gesture down to the far end of the bar.

"That's Nate?" I didn't even recognize him with his cap on his head. He was really keeping it down and was looking at something with a drink in his hand.

"Yep. Comes in every day after the lunch crowd to read. He gets one bourbon and coke and sips it while he reads his books." What Darren said struck me as funny. It was a jiggle joint with background music and stale air.

Who could enjoy a book in this environment?

"You go down there and listen to what type of business deal my mother is making with those two yahoos." I knew it wasn't the best compliment, but I didn't know these people that well, and certainly my mama didn't. They could be taking her for all she would be getting in a divorce settlement for all I knew.

"They're fine." Darren turned his attention back to the door. It was Patty this time.

She waved, smiled, and came right over.

"I'm a little early. The diner was slow because it's right before the supper crowd, and I wanted to leave before Nate showed up or he'd probably ask me to take a late shift. He's done this every night this week. Every single night I've closed, which means I'm there until two or three a.m." She sighed and sat down.

"Don't get too comfortable." Darren's head nodded toward the end of the bar. "Nate's down there reading his book."

"Crap." Patty swiveled her head away and walked to the left of me to sit down instead of the right where she was going to sit. "Did he see me?"

"He's not going to see anything until the timer goes off on his phone." Darren poured Patty a beer. "Your favorite."

"Thanks." She picked it up. "Tastes so good after a long week." Patty started to tell me about her day while I kept one eye on Darren. He'd dropped off another cocktail to Mama and said something to make her look at Nate.

She popped up off her stool with her drink in hand and forced her way into Nate's space, causing the poor man to look up from his book.

"You wouldn't believe the people who send back orders. The orders they had specifically ordered." Patty's voice was merely white noise.

Nate put his book on top of the bar, and he gave his full attention to whatever Mama had to say.

It wasn't long before Mama had come back with a big ole possum grin on her face with Nate walking next to her. He was laughing at something she'd said. They talked a few seconds more, and he was out the door.

"I really do need to find a new job, or Nate has to hire someone." Patty twisted around. "Did he just leave?"

"Yeah." I noticed this wasn't going to be a lucrative meeting like I'd thought. I guessed when I suggested to Patty I needed friends she was all in, which was good, but my head just wasn't in the chitchat game. Another time, sure, but not right now. "Did you overhear anything Tricia had said to Nate? Because I think she and Raymond Westin killed Sally."

Patty's jaw dropped.

"I'm going to need another one now, Darren!" she called out to him.

"Gotcha." Darren let her know she'd be next. The jiggle joint was getting filled up from what looked to be people coming in from after work.

"I never would've thought about it, but you do know those two." Patty wiggled her brows and clicked her tongue. "Everyone knows. Been happening for years. So it's gotten to be no big deal."

"I think it's horrible, but I did find mothballs in Hanna's room at the nursing home." I told the story as the look of unbelief continued to hit Patty's expression a few times.

"Violet, it's for you." Darren held the receiver of the old phone attached to the wall.

"Me?" I questioned him to make sure he was talking to me.

"Yep. You're the only Violet in here."

I got up off the stool and wondered who on earth had found me at the jiggle joint.

"Hello?" I asked after putting the phone up to my ear but keeping the receiver with the stale beer smell far away from my mouth.

"Tricia and Raymond check out." It was Chief Strickland.

"How did you know I was here?" I asked.

"I told you I know you and my son are hanging out. Wherever he is, you are." He cleared his throat. "Just don't tell my wife. She's been looking all over town for you."

"I'm not hanging out with your son. And they did do it." I gnawed on my lip, knowing I was going to have to now follow the other journalist hunch I had about calling Petey Puddles.

"They didn't. Everyone in that nursing home has mothballs. And just so you know, the time of death for Sally and the times we traced your mom's phone's GPS around that time, along with what little video footage we found of her sneaking to the spring, doesn't match. Which brings me pleasure in letting you know she's no longer a suspect, so please call off Diffy because he's driving us nuts here." This was the only bit of news Chief Strickland mentioned that I loved.

My eyes shifted from Patty to Darren as I made my way back around the bar to my stool.

"Looks like our snooping isn't finished. The two people I was certain who killed Sally," I paused to see their confirmations on their faces, "both have checked-out alibis."

CHAPTER TWENTY-ONE

"What was the chat with Nate about?" I asked Mama since we both left the jiggle joint at the same time, which was about the right time for us to make it back to the Jubilee Inn and change our clothes, fix our hair, and get all gussied up to play nice for the Leading Ladies now that Mama had taken a vested interest in joining them.

"We had a little chat. That was all. Nice man." Mama had driven the golf cart, making it so much nicer to hitch a ride instead of walk back. "Now that I'm cleared of those bogus charges for killing Sally, I think it's time we talked about our new house."

"Don't you think we need to talk about Daddy?" Their divorce was another issue I had in my head to help resolve. Ever since I'd talked to him, the conversation had rolled around and around in my head.

We southerners were good at thinkin' on something a little too long. It was like driving a car over it a million times, then backing the car over it to make sure we couldn't come up with a solution when there clearly wasn't one to be had. It was the whole "beat a dead horse" thing we liked to say. Only this situation made me really want to beat that dead horse all the ways to Sunday.

"Violet. There's nothing to talk about." Mama whipped the wheel, taking the curvy and now wooded terrain road back toward town. "Really what we need to talk about is this business between you, Rhett, and Darren. Now talk on the street."

"Talk on the street?" I interrupted her. "Mayor Paisley better watch out. It seems like you're the talk on the street, or talking to everyone on the street."

"Is that any way to talk to your Mama?" She pushed the pedal on the golf cart even further down. "You act like that because you know you need to talk all this out, and well, you don't have any good friends to talk to yet."

"Yes, I do. Mama, I've been here a few months, and I've made friends. Didn't you just see me with Patty? What about Cherise? And then there's Fern." So Fern was iffy at best—Mama didn't need to know that.

"Fern is trying to land the most eligible bachelor in town. Rhett Strickland. And you've got the opportunity to snag him. That's just the talk on the street." Mama gave me the once-over. "Violet, you are approaching thirty, and no matter where we live, there's a time frame for such milestones."

"Talk on the street." The idea of an advice column for the *Junction Journal* had tickled my mind over the last few months, and well, with Mama in town, I knew she'd hear all the gossip. She was one who took pride in being in all the social circles, and just her time here these last few days had proved she was way more social than I was.

"That means—" she started to tell me what it meant, as if I didn't know.

"I know what it means, but what if there was a section in the *Junction Journal* called 'Talk on the Street'?" I tossed her a look.

"Oh, Violet. I think it would be wonderful! More than the social section. It could be things sent in anonymously." Mama threw out some really great ideas.

"This is great." I wanted to pull out my phone to take notes in the note app, but I couldn't let go of the side handles of the golf cart in fear Mama was going to dump me out when she took a turn.

"When do I start?" Mama hit the horn on the wheel and waved as we passed a few ladies walking down the sidewalk.

"Good evening, Millie Kay!" They all said hello to Mama and sometimes called her by name.

"How do you know these people?" I dared ask.

"When you socialize and be friendly, not stuck up in some motel room then in a dilapidated house as an office all day, you get to know people, and I already have a great topic for Talk of the Town." Mama was itching to tell me.

"What's that?" I asked and couldn't help but look down Rhett's street when we passed it, though I couldn't see his house. It was too far down at the opposite end.

"Merry Maker."

"I'm listening." Trust me, if there was a solution to be had about my little problem, Mama could probably fix it.

"You know when you asked me what Nate and I were discussing at the jiggle joint?" She smiled. There was definitely something up her sleeve.

"I hope you weren't trying to hit on Nate. He's married." Not that I would think she would, but it was best to just put it out there in case it was up in that hard head of hers.

"Lordy, child. Heavens no." She snorted like it was the most impossible thing in the world. "He's going to host the Mother's Day Festival ending tomorrow at the spring. I told him how this tradition was so important to the community, and if he wanted to save his reputation with the spring not being poisoned, he needed to open it up to the community for just the festival, so if Palmer did try to sell the spring water as some sort of fountain of youth, it wouldn't be tainted by false accusations."

"Mama! This is amazing!" My hands flew to my mouth but quickly grabbed the handle when she took a sharp turn into a parking space in Holiday Park.

CHAPTER TWENTY-TWO

"Here." Mama grabbed her purse from the back of the golf cart. "You could use a little of this."

She took a tube of lipstick out of it and rolled it up.

"Pouty Pink. Just your color."

"I thought we were going to the Jubilee Hotel to get changed." I glanced down Main Street, where the motel was a stone's throw.

"We don't have time now that I'm undercover for Talk of the Town. Do you or don't you want this covered?" She had a point, or at least made me think she did.

I couldn't tell if she was using her mama southern voodoo on me. You know the guilt trip and even the sly way to say "bless your heart." Mmhmmm. Mama was the queen of it.

"Fine." I swiped some lipstick on, and luckily I could give my long blond hair a shake, giving it a natural wave as it fell down around my shoulders.

"What about some powder?" Mama took out an entire makeup bag.

"No." I pushed her hand away. "I'm fine."

The whiz of another golf cart pulled up next to us.

"Good evening." Fern Banks pinched a fake grin. Her eyes squinted, and she'd not shaken her long black hair. It was neatly pulled up in a very sophisticated bun. She had on a sleeveless tank hitting perfectly at the seam of her linen pants. "You must be Millie Kay."

"My goodness. If I didn't know the mayor was a dog, I'd think you were pretty important." Mama gushed.

"Mama, this is Fern Banks." I didn't really do the proper way of introductions, but the proper way and Holiday Junction way were two completely different acts.

"You're Fern Banks!" Mama snapped her mouth shut, but her eyes didn't stop fluttering about Fern. Taking her all in.

"I see you've heard of me." Fern fluttered her eyelashes.

"It wasn't in a good way," Mama muttered.

"Excuse me?" Fern's lashes flew up.

"It's all good." Mama smiled real big.

"I'll see you at the dinner. Or I guess y'all call it supper." Fern mocked us more ways than one.

Mama snarled and grunted a few times as Fern walked away before she turned, licked her hand, and started to pat down my hair.

"What are you doing?" I jerked to the left to miss another swipe of her spit.

"Your hair is standing forty ways to Sunday, and that's what you're competing with for the most eligible bachelor." Mama took a step back, giving me a hard look. "Maybe you do have time to go back and change."

"I'm not doing it." I sighed, rolled my eyes, and took off toward the amphitheater. "I'm hungry. And I have to get an article written about the Merry Maker Mother's Day Festival ending, plus possibly an article for the Talk of the Town."

In an evil sorta way, I put my hands together and drummed my fingers.

"Maybe there's going to be an anonymous comment about Fern Banks," Mama teased and took off, leaving me standing there with her sentence hanging in the air.

Gosh. I sure hoped Mama was teasing.

"Be sure you get some good photos for tomorrow's paper." Marge Strickland had rushed over to me. Louise was standing clear across the amphitheater talking to Tricia Lustig, and both of them looked at me before they quickly looked away.

"What do you reckon that's about?" Mama, too, had noticed.

"Tricia's all upset because Matthew had brought her and Raymond in the department for questioning, and he might've said it was Violet who accused them of killing Sally." Marge waved her thin long fingers in the air. "Tricia is always complaining, but if you ask me, it's high time someone called out their affair. We all see it. But no one ever wants to discuss it in public."

"Sweeping it under the rug." Mama's eyes squinted. "What on earth do you think she sees in him?"

I'd seen this move by Mama many times at the church socials when I was growing up. She was able to get deep dark family secrets, even guarded family recipes, out of people.

"Money. That man has the monopoly on medication around here. They don't have no option to get their prescriptions filled anywhere." Marge put a smile on her face and waved at Goldie Bennett when she walked by. "If anyone would know anything, it's her."

Marge shifted her look between us and Goldie.

"She hears all sorts of things on that trolley. Do you think she needs to drive the trolley? Heck no. We should have a holiday called Gossip. She'd definitely win the queen title over Fern Banks." Marge lifted a chin and smiled when someone called her name. "Excuse me."

"Did you ask her?" Mama wanted to know if Marge had cleared the Talk of the Town section.

"Yeah. It's fine." Goodness. Now I was telling my mama little white lies. It was like I was going down this spiral of deceit I couldn't get off of.

Not that I'd not told a few little white lies when I worked at my hometown paper, but it wasn't like Mama was all up in my business there either. She just promoted me.

This time, now, it was different. Her active role in my life and career was new, but I was confident Marge would be fine. At least I hoped so.

"Good. I'm going to scout out some information." Mama was content now she'd gotten Nate to host the party and wasn't really thinking about the murder, but Sally's death was still in the forefront of my mind.

I should've just left it all up to Chief Strickland and let go of Tricia and Raymond, but Tricia seemed to be trying to make herself look better since I'd shined a light on the affair.

While Mama went off in her direction, I decided to do the job I was paid to do and take photos, make notes, and get my head together for what was going to be a long night of working at the office.

I thought southern women had spectacular spreads, but The Leading Ladies were giving Mama and her friends back home a run for their money.

They had four large banquet-style tables lined with a white tablecloth with a place setting of China, along with sterling silverware and glass goblets filled to the top with water. There was a string-piece orchestra lightly playing background music from the stage of the amphitheater. With the mountain view behind us and the sun setting over the sea in front of us, the glow of happiness was on everyone's faces. Even Tricia's.

The floral arrangements were in glass vases with a budding yellow flower bouquet. The pop of color with the white was a gorgeous contrast. The entire tablescape made for a beautiful digital photograph, and I was sure it was going to be the one to feature the article.

The ladies chatted away, and when I saw Goldie Bennett alone, I wandered over her way just to see what she had to say. I swiped one champagne flute and a water from the small bar setup on my way over.

"I guess we are going to keep running into each other." I handed her the flute.

"Not drinking?" she asked. "I know you do. I clearly remember everyone talking about the new girl outdrinking Fern Banks at the St. Patrick's Day stein competition."

"That was a once-in-a-lifetime thing." I swigged the water. "Water for me. Besides, I'm covering this event for the *Junction Journal*."

"Aww. I see." She was really a nice lady. I liked Goldie. She had been the nicest to me since my life started here. I wasn't sure I'd be able to print anything she'd say, or at least not quote her by name.

"Remember when you mentioned how your husband wasn't a big fan of Tricia's?" I had to bring it up. Elvin, though highly unlikely, was still on my list of suspects. He did have some grumblings with Tricia Lustig.

"I'm following a lead into Sally's death, and I really wanted to know what you knew about her," I subtly kept a close eye on her body language.

"Don't get me started on Elvin and what he thinks about all that spring stuff. Yes. Everyone knows Tricia and Raymond are all lovey-dovey, even Sally. But Sally didn't care. She just wanted to make sure Hanna was taken care of. But that spring water isn't no fountain of youth. Heck, if they think that, then they can just tap right in on it down by the lighthouse." That was when it hit me that I'd yet to call Lawn and Order Landscaping because that was my question, and I hadn't asked Darren while I was at the jiggle joint because he was so busy.

"Lighthouse?" I asked. This time knowing what I'd found online was correct. "According to what I found online, I noticed there was a spring called Holiday Junction Spring."

"Yep. That's it. That's where the natural spring starts. But Palmer and Nate decided to call it Lustig Spring from their property." That was an interesting bit of news. "They even had the old stone concrete built to make it look old. That's the kinda work money can get you, which is why Elvin has a beef with Tricia."

"My searching was right. The spring does flow from the area near the lighthouse to the Lustig property." I was always leery to take things for truth on the internet.

"Haven't you seen people going down to the sea trying to get water?" she asked, prompting the memory of the people milling around the lighthouse that night and Darren covering it up as they were thirsty.

Why would he cover it up? Even if he wasn't deliberately doing it, he knew I was looking into this spring. And he was with me when we went to get Mama, and then he gave Mama an alibi.

What did Darren Strickland have to gain from not telling me? What was he hiding?

This looked like it might be the first Talk of the Town. If you were going to not only toy with me and my emotions—which even thinking about having emotions with him made my heart drop—there was no way I was going to let him mess with my mama.

"Violet, are you okay?" Goldie's eyes held a look of concern.

"Yeah." I shook my head, smiled, and took a sip of water which didn't even touch the sudden onset of dry mouth. "I'm fine. I was just thinking. That's all. When did you and Elvin hear about Sally?"

She rattled on about the grandkids, and I'd gotten so good at tuning her out on that topic, but then she said, "We were eating at the Freedom Diner that night. Palmer was there, and she left in a huff."

Did she? I snorted a puff of air out my nose as I wondered if somehow Palmer Lustig did kill Sally. Somehow Darren knew it. Had Darren confronted Palmer about using the spring to promote a fountain of youth? Did he want a kickback from the proceeds? How on earth did he really afford that prime piece of property on the beach?

Every time I went into the jiggle joint, it was literally five customers at the most. That included Owen and Shawn.

What about the Mother's Day Merry Maker sign? Why did he carry it to the spring and not leave it by his moped? Did he plant it?

"Violet, what's going on?" Mama had rushed over. "I saw you looked funny. What's wrong?"

"Nothing, Mama." I snapped out of it and offered her a smile. "I've got to get back to the office. I've got enough here for the article. It's still early, so I'll walk and be home pretty early."

"Are you sure?" she asked, a little apprehensive.

"Positive." I took one last look around before I took the path from Holiday Park back down to the seaside, where it opened just a little beyond the lighthouse.

I dragged my eyes across the beach and saw a couple of people near the spot where the Google map had told me the Holiday Junction Spring started. I hurried past the shops and didn't even look at the jiggle joint when I passed. I knew Darren wouldn't see me because there were no windows to look out, but I just couldn't bring myself to do it.

There was a feeling he'd played my feelings this entire time to see what I knew about the turn of events. If I had to guess, I'd say he and Palmer had never intended for Mama to happen upon Sally that night. Palmer had given her alibi to Chief Strickland, and I was Darren's alibi, though he'd lumped Mama in there.

Did he give Mama her alibi so it would make me stop snooping around if Mama was cleared? Of course his dad was going to believe him. Right?

The more I thought about it, the angrier I got and the harder I stomped as I made my way up to the cottage office, where it looked like Lawanda had left all her tools.

"Lawanda," I sighed when I noticed the door was cracked and she'd not shut or locked it. My mind was all aflutter about Darren and how I was going to spin the Talk of the Town article to out him but not necessarily point a finger, and word it as such so Mama couldn't be suggested to be the suspect again. But I needed some other information.

"Just what do Palmer and Darren have to gain by teaming up?" I asked myself and flipped on the light after I shut the door behind me.

"Excuse me?" Palmer was sitting in my chair at my desk. "Teaming up?"

"Palmer?" I was taken aback. I looked around to see if we were alone. "What are you doing here? And in the dark?"

"I was waiting on you, and I didn't want anyone to see the lights on or me here." She stood up and grabbed her water bottle.

I eyeballed it, wondering if it had the infamous Lustig Spring water in it.

"You can have your seat."

I didn't move. I stood there waiting for her next move, which was true to what she said. She sat down in the extra chair in the office.

"What was this business of me and Darren Strickland you were talking about?" she asked.

"I wonder if you two had anything to do with Sally's murder?" I had the urge to get this conversation on record, so I took my phone out. "I'm going to put my phone on 'do not disturb.' My mama might call a million times."

Boy, was this lying starting to come naturally.

I set the phone on top of my desk and waited for Palmer's reply.

"Why would Darren Strickland and I have any sort of business dealings?" she asked, taking a drink.

"I'm not sure how he owns the lighthouse, but I do know the spring starts near or on his property." I almost pulled it up on the map I'd found online, but didn't. I wanted her out of here as fast as I could, so I continued. "And you are trying to take the spring and bottle it as a fountain of youth when you don't technically own all of the spring. So you went to Darren to give him a deal. That's why he used me as an alibi that night."

Her body shifted. Her eyes lifted as the smile curled up on her lip.

"You and Darren?" she asked as though nothing I said sparked any other type of interest. "Fine. And how do you think I killed her? I have an alibi."

"And what is that?" I asked.

"I was at the diner."

"Yes. Someone told me they saw you there, but you left." I wasn't about to give up my source. Goldie Bennett.

"I left to get to the store to get some degreaser." She opened her purse and searched through then pulled out a receipt. "See? It's Mother's Day. Everyone in town knows we close on Mother's Day every year to finish getting ready for the inspector."

"Inspector?" I wasn't following.

"The health inspector. Since Nate is so tight, he refuses to keep anyone over their allotted part-time status so he doesn't have to pay health insurance." She stood up. "Do you have a bathroom?"

"Yes. Wait." I stopped her. "Doesn't he pay his waitresses overtime because he's short-staffed?"

"Are you kidding?" She scoffed. "Those girls are begging for work, but Nate is so tight. He never gives anyone overtime. That's why we have alibis the night of Sally's murder. We were cleaning the fryers because every year after Mother's Day the health department shows up, and if those fryers aren't spotless, they'll close us in no time. And I have no plans to do anything with the spring water. We just want people off our property."

"Down the hall." I haphazardly told her where the bathroom was through my state of confusion.

Patty had told me she'd been doing overtime at the diner, which made me wonder why Palmer was lying. She didn't know Patty had told me. Probably didn't know I was friends with Patty, so she came in here wanting to give me some sort of lie so I would stop nosing around.

Was I getting close? I looked out the window at the ocean's edge, where just a hint of the top of the sun would take a dip out of sight with the slightest of waves.

"What on earth are you doing here?" Patty walked in without me hearing. "I saw the light on and thought I'd bring up some coffee in case you were in here. Burning the midnight oil to get the paper out. Though it's not midnight." She set the coffee on the desk.

"You aren't going to believe this," I said in a hushed whisper and waved her over. "I think Darren and Palmer are somehow in on this whole spring thing."

"Why are you being quiet?" she asked.

"Palmer is here. Why would she come here?" I asked Patty. She looked stunned. "She told me her alibi was the diner and how she was the one who stayed late there to work and then clean everything, giving me some lame excuse how the health department comes to do their inspection. She even said Nate never pays overtime when I know you work overtime all the time."

"She's here to make you stop, I bet. You're getting closer, and it's making her uncomfortable." Patty looked over her shoulder. "She's here now?"

"Yes. In the bathroom." I heard a click coming from the hall, like the door was unlocking.

"Good thing I brought you some caffeine to rid you of that headache," Patty teased, picking up the coffee, and handed it to me again.

I set it back down.

"Patty. Hi. I didn't know you two knew each other." Palmer was shocked.

"I bet you didn't," I muttered and picked up the coffee. "Patty brought me some fresh coffee from the diner when she saw the light on. Wasn't that nice of her?"

"Where on earth did you get that cup?" Palmer walked over and took it from me before I could even get a drink. "This had to have been from five years ago." Palmer really had delighted in seeing it. "This was the first logo I designed for the diner when we got married. He retired it five years ago after some big shot told us we needed to rebrand. We don't use them anymore."

"You can drink it if you want. I don't want any coffee." I shrugged.

Patty's face stilled.

"We were just talking about Darren." Palmer wasn't holding back. "Every time I think of him, I can't help but to think of how he bought your family's lighthouse. Nate and I had spent a lot of time getting all that storage out of there."

"Storage?" My eyes shifted between Patty and Palmer.

"Yes. Nate needed storage for things like these cups. It was so close to the diner and the lighthouse wasn't a working lighthouse, so Nate paid Patty's family a storage fee." Palmer laughed. "That's where you must've gotten that cup. Not from the diner."

"I bought it about five years ago." That's what Darren told me. *"We haven't used those cups in five years."* Palmer said five years.

"I didn't know your family owned the lighthouse property." I wondered why Patty hadn't even mentioned it. "You knew I was looking into Sally's murder and the spring and how it starts around the lighthouse."

That's when it all clicked.

"Patty," I gasped. "What did you do?" I jumped up and ran over to knock the cup of coffee out of Palmer's hand, sending the hot, scolding drink all over Patty.

Patty screamed out in pain as she dropped to the ground holding her hands to her face.

"Violet! Are you crazy?" Palmer yelled, rushing over to Patty's side.

I didn't have time to answer.

I grabbed my phone and dialed 9-1-1.

"This is Violet Rhinehammer, and I need the sheriff to get to the *Junction Journal* offices immediately. I have Sally Westin's killer in custody! Hurry!"

CHAPTER TWENTY-THREE

Merry Maker Message
Happy Mother's Day Festival, or should I say Happy Caught a Murder Day.

As the town Merry Maker, I'm delighted to let you know the Mother's Day Festival will end exactly where I planned it.

The Lustig Spring.

Bring your mother and enjoy the last day of festivities. After all, there's no better time to hear all the gossip swirling around Holiday Junction.

If you've not heard, the newest citizen of Holiday Junction, Violet Rhinehammer, along with our very own Palmer Lustig, caught Sally Westin's killer, Patty Hamilton.

It's not confirmed, but it's rumored Patty didn't want anyone profiting off her family land that was sold on the steps of the Holiday Junction courthouse five years ago due to back taxes owed, and with the boost in economy here, all our taxes are going up.

From what I understand, Patty wasn't about to let anyone make money off the water spring since it started on her family's property and by rights wasn't the Lustigs' to do so, but in the end, Palmer Lustig's rumored idea to sell the water as a fountain of youth was just a rumor.

Speaking of five years ago. Has anyone questioned how Darren Strickland was able to pay for a prime piece of real estate? Can only make you wonder just how sneaky those Stricklands can be. Think about it. Rhett Strickland owns half of the property in town. Darren only owns the strip club that never has more than four or five people in there. Then there's Marge and Louise, who just sold this paper to Millie Kay Rhinehammer, or else the Rhinehammers might not have let me run my article anonymously. What about Chief Strickland? We've had three murders this year, and still nothing is being done to keep our streets safe. Nothing but raising our taxes.

I wonder if you should bring these tax issues up to the mayor. From what I hear, Mayor Paisley has gained an extra three pounds from all the Mother's Day visitors in town taking her treats to bribe her for photo opportunities. Bribes. That's a funny word, isn't it?

I'm off to scout where the next big festival finale will take place. As the owners of the Junction Journal would say, "If you ain't got nothin' nice to say, come sit by me."

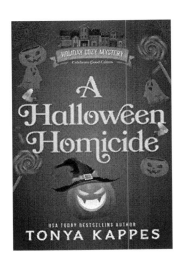

Keep reading for a sneak peek of the next book in the series. Halloween Homicide is now available to purchase on Amazon.

Book Club Discussion Questions
Mother's Day Murder

Question #1:

Violet is settling into her new town of Holiday Junction. As the reporter for the Junction Journal, she sees several people in town, and is still learning who they are, let alone their names. When the trolley driver, Goldie reminds Violet she was her seatmate from the airplane. Violet cringes. She has a flashback to the dreadful flight, the murder, and the reason she is now stuck in Holiday Junction.

Would you have changed directions to avoid a conversation? Or maybe acted as if you were busy doing something?

Question #2:

Holiday Junction goes all for every holiday. The next one they are celebrating is Mother's Day. As the reporter, covering all the activities, this meant Violet was unable to fly home for Mother's Day. As a result, Violet had been screening her calls to avoid talking to her Mama. When her phone rang, thinking it was Vern, she answered her phone, only to realize it was her Mama. Saved by the knock on the door, she hung with her and opened the door to find Mama right in front of her, and talking about divorcing her Daddy.

I would have loved to see the look on Violet's face. What were your thoughts?

Question #3:

Rhett convinces Violet to take her mom to the park and spend some time with her. She was thinking she'd only be there for a couple days. Until Rhett informed her there were no flights out until the following Monday.

How did you think this new turn of events would affect Violet?

Question #4:

It seems like Millie Kay is going to keep Violet on her toes. Milly Kay had no problem heading into the "jiggle joint" to get drinks. While she is chatting with two of the regulars, Violet is getting information from Darren about Lustig Spring. Violet's interest was piqued when Goldie mentioned the Spring and the family. The more Darren talked about it the more determined Violet was to check it out. Lustig Spring was known to have healing properties. People come to fill up their jugs full of the "healing tonic."

There are several hot springs all around the US. People do think that many of them have healing effects. Have you been to one? What did you think? Would you go to one?

Question #5:

Violet's mom is like a kid in a candy store. So many things to see and do in Holiday Junction. As they get to the park, Millie Kay sees a cake walk game and wants to join in. This game was like musical chairs. Music played and when it stopped you grabbed a chair, until only one remained. That person was the winner of a cake. Mama wanted to win a raspberry bundt cake.

Have you ever participated in a cake walk? What kind of cake would you like to win?

Question #6:

When the last chair was open, Millie Kay and another contestant, Sally Westin. When the music ended, Millie Kay gave Sally a push sending her to the ground. When the Chief of Police arrived, he saw video footage which clearly showed Millie Kay pushing Sally off the chair. The choice was to give Sally the cake, or Sally would press charges.

Violet had never seen this side of Millie Kay, the competitive side. Do you consider yourself competitive? If so, what are you most competitive about?

Question #7:

As part of the Mother's Day festivities, the Freedom Diner is offering a cooking class. There are so many places now that will offer classes. My cooking class was in school.

Have you ever taken a cooking class? If you have, tell us about it. If not, is it something that would interest you?

Question #8:

Violet is dead set on investigating the springs, even though Nate Lustig didn't want her to. There seemed to be a little bit of controversy as to who really wanted Lustig Spring available to outsiders.

What were thoughts at this point? Was there really are story there? Is it something you would pursue if you were a reporter?

Question #9:

Violet get's Millie Kay settled for the night at the Inn and takes off to meet up with Vern about the Merry Maker. Even though she was telling herself she couldn't do it, she ends up being the Merry Maker. On her way to deliver the Mother's Day basket, Darren appears on the path. As they begin walking, Darren invites her to the lighthouse, which he owns for a beer and she goes. While they are there, Millie Kay calls asking her to come to the Spring. Sally Westin is dead.

There were several things going on at this point. Darren, the spring, Millie Kay and a dead body. What were your thoughts at this point?

Question #10

THE ENDING!!!!!

Without telling us who the killer was, that would be a spoiler but, did you figure this one out, or was it a complete surprise?

Question #11

We are coming to the end of our discussion. Any thoughts or questions? Was there a favorite scene in the book to share? Remember, no spoilers please.

HALLOWEEN HOMICIDE

A HOLIDAY COZY MYSTERY BOOK 3

Then the dummy fell out face forward, a knife sticking out of its back.

"Is that blood?" I asked when I noticed something that looked like real blood dripping from the knife.

"That's an added extra. And so real." Hazelynn couldn't contain the excited squeak in her voice.

"I didn't do that." Hershal's voice cracked. I smiled at the effect because it looked so real.

"You got us. This is pretty real looking." Darren patted Hershal on the back.

"It was supposed to be a jack-in-the-box clown." Hershal couldn't take his eyes off the dummy. "You know, for a good scream."

Hershal wasn't joking. The realization this wasn't what was supposed to happen on the ghost walk sank in.

"I think it is real." I took a step closer to see the knife sticking out of the man's back. "And that sure does look like real blood." With a grave look on my face, I stared at Darren. "Call your dad."

Darren stepped away, and I could hear him, though his voice sounded muffled. I couldn't focus on what he was saying to his dad, Chief Matthew Strickland, and process if this was a crime scene.

"Hershal, what is going on here?" Hazelynn's voice had gone from calm to hysterical. "What is happening?"

"I don't know, Hazelynn," Hershal said, his words coming out statically. "You tell me." He pulled off his top hat, and sweat beaded on his forehead. "You're the one who put the jack-in-the-box in there a little bit ago. It was your idea."

I put them out of my head and inspected the man more closely.

Streams of blood forked off down the man's side and pooled in the grass. I bent down to get a look at the blood then carefully reached to check his pulse.

"What are you doing?" Mama gasped, reaching for me when I put my fingers on the man's wrist.

"Making sure he's dead." My gaze slid past my shoulders, setting the mood for what was surely going to be a hexed night ahead.

TONYA KAPPES
WEEKLY NEWSLETTER

Want a behind-the-scenes journey of me as a writer?
The ups and downs, new deals, book sales, giveaways and more? I share it all!

As a special thank you for joining, you'll get an exclusive copy of my cross-over short story, *A CHARMING BLEND.* Go to Tonyakappes.com and click on subscribe in the upper right corner to join.

CHAPTER ONE

Boo! *All you ghosts and goblins get ready for a month full of fun, since Halloweenie is set to open this weekend. Don't miss the Lighthouse Glow kickoff on Friday night followed by a party by the sea to kick off Halloweenie. It looks like the Merry Maker hasn't set a place for the final Halloweenie night of celebration, but we do know the weather has turned in our favor. The last few weeks have been rainy, but the forecast for the next week is unseasonably cool but dry.*

Grab your pillowcase and look for hauntingly delicious treats. They will be served at events like pumpkin painting, pumpkin carving, the parents' night out, the haunted hayride, the haunted ghost walk, and the Great Jack-O'-Lantern Blaze. These events, vendors, and games will all be at Holiday Park.

Be sure to hit the events calendar at the top of the page to download your Halloweenie schedule. You won't want to miss out on this ghostly good time.

Who will take home this year's top prize at the costume contest? Emily's Treasures has a new stock of disguises for every age. Be sure to let her know you saw it in the Junction Journal and get ten percent off your total purchase.

This article wasn't the best I'd ever written, and I knew it. It was the best article that would go out, though, since my heart wasn't into this month-long celebration of Halloween, my least favorite holiday.

Before I could publish the article for tomorrow's online version of *Junc-*

tion Journal, at which I was currently the only editor and journalist, I needed to go to the library and find some archived photos of last year's festival.

I looked out at the sea from the window of the *Junction Journal* building and watched as the waves curled over one another before they spread out along the beach. By their appearance and the shining sun, it would appear to be a gorgeous day for a good ocean swim, but that wasn't the case. The water, like the temperature, was cold. From what I'd gathered during this, my first time in Holiday Junction for the fall season, this was normal for the time of the year.

I loved a good chilly autumn night, and I thought of sitting on the beach in front of some sort of campfire while wrapped up in a blanket. That was much more appealing than sitting on the beach this Friday night with hundreds of people who were so excited to see Darren Strickland kick off the month-long chain of haunted events. He did that by changing the lighthouse bulb to orange.

From what I'd heard around town, tourists would be invading our little village, which was truly a paradise, except for this month.

Holiday Junction was a cozy village nestled in between the sea and mountains. It was literally the best of both worlds if you liked to escape into the woods or listen to the ocean. Holiday Junction had celebrated every single holiday since it became a town. Tourists came from all over the world to visit during the current holiday. No holiday was too big or too small.

There was absolutely no way that I, the newest citizen, was going to tell anyone my major dislike for October thirty-first. I feared being flogged by the village folks, who celebrated anything that could be celebrated.

For two very good reasons, I'd kept a forced smile on my face this entire month: it was Halloween season, which I had to write on, and I was the Merry Maker.

Now, my mama, Millie Kay Rhinehammer, was a whole different story. She loved Halloween, and since she, too, lived in Holiday Junction, she was already planning the decorations for our new house, just in time for us to move in this week.

My mama would tell you how cute I was when she dressed me up all those years, and she would follow up with how I begged to eat each piece of candy along the trick-or-treat route. She was right. I did love me some candy—not so much the itchy, scary costumes, wigs, and loads of fake makeup on my face.

Thinking about Friday's event, which would involve sitting in the dark with the sound of the ocean in front of us and the shrieks of the animals in the woods behind us, chilled me to the bone and took me right out of my thoughts.

I clicked open my email to procrastinate and noticed an email headed "Ghost Walk," which had been sitting in my inbox for a good part of three weeks. I hadn't opened or responded to it, but now the time to at least look at it was upon me.

It appeared to be from the Holiday Junction Planning Committee, which was the mother of all the committees in Holiday Junction. They had a committee for every holiday, but this one was the main one, and everyone wanted a seat at the table there.

Including Mama.

The email started out very formally with "Dear Ms. Rhinehammer." I continued to read it.

The Holiday Junction Planning Committee is excited about this year's Ghost Walk. The walk will take place nightly, starting at the fountain in Holiday Park with tales of Holiday Junction's ghostly past. This walk will take the south path along the wooded trail leading down to the ocean and end at the steps of the lighthouse. We are excited to offer you an exclusive private walk with our hosts, Hershal and Hazelynn Hudson, owners of Brewing Beans, the sponsor of the walk. We are requesting a write-up in the Junction Journal *to help promote the walk and raise money for the Holiday Junction Planning Committee.*

Sincerely,

Peter Hill, President

I closed the email, intending to claim I'd never gotten it or say it went to my spam folder. "No thank you, Mr. President."

I groaned.

Ghost Walk.

Since when did Holiday Junction become a ghost town? In all the research I'd done about the small town, I'd never come across any stories of it being haunted. Trust me, it would've caught my eye.

"Something real." I glanced at the office phone when it rang. *"Junction Journal*, Violet Rhinehammer speaking."

"Good morning, Violet." I recognized Hershal Hudson's deep voice. Every morning, I stopped by Brewing Beans to grab a hot cup of black coffee before I boarded the trolley to ride to the office. "I see you've read the email about the Ghost Walk. I was beginning to think you didn't like Halloween."

I growled to myself, realizing they had that email notification turned on that alerted you when someone opened an email you'd sent.

"It's something all the tourists expect when they come to visit for Halloween," Hershal Hudson said. "And we are thrilled you're here because you've covered all the holidays so much better than they have been in the past. Since we are close to opening night, I have time tonight to take you on the walk."

"Tonight?" I flipped the notebook in front of me with a deliberate whip of my wrist to make it sound like I was checking my calendar. "I can't tonight. Other obligations for the festival."

Surely that would satisfy him.

Wrong.

"What about tomorrow night or the next night? Heck, any night this week before Friday is a good time for Hazelynn and me." He wasn't going to stop.

"You know, I do have this afternoon open." The thought of a ghost walk in the daylight didn't seem so… scary.

"Afternoon?" he asked. "Who has ever done a ghost walk in the afternoon?"

"We will if you'd like me to write up an article about it for tomorrow's paper." I knew the faster I could get it in the paper, the more open he'd be to whatever time I was available. Seeing how I wasn't a big fan of ghosts and darkness, daylight was when I was open.

"We will see you around lunchtime at the fountain. Gotta go. Busy crowd this morning. Everyone is wanting a coffee with Hazelynn's famous Halloween latte art." The line went dead.

"Coffee art?" I shook my head thinking about all the people walking around downtown Holiday Junction with a cup of coffee that had a ghost, pumpkin, or spiderweb design floating on top. I clicked back on the email to reread what exactly I'd just gotten myself into.

The bell over the office door jingled.

"I'm in here!" I hollered out of the office into the hall.

"Why can't you just stay home?" Mama walked in, wearing a black sweater with big orange spiders on it and a pair of orange capri jeans. She also sported dangling spider earrings and an enamel spider bracelet. "I told you I don't want to be bothered right now. Can't you give me some peace?"

"I can't even look at you with that on," I whispered and put my hand over my eyes.

"Noah, I won't hear of it. You stay in Normal until the holidays are over. Then we can talk." Mama was talking to my daddy.

"Mama, talk to him." I tried to encourage her to hear him out. He'd been driving me crazy since Mama showed up on my doorstep with a few suitcases containing her most valuable possessions.

She'd brought news that she and Daddy were getting divorced after all those years of marriage. I couldn't turn her away, and when he started to call me, I couldn't turn him away either.

"Don't you quit your job." Mama's lips puckered, and the lines deepened around them as she threatened him. "Do you hear me, Noah? Don't you dare quit your job. No, sir." She continued to fuss.

I got up from my desk to leave the office, where Mama had planted herself in a chair while arguing with Daddy on the phone, and walked down the hall to where the small kitchen had recently been remodeled.

The office was basically an old, dilapidated sea cottage owned by Rhett Strickland. Since his family owned the *Junction Journal* and pretty much most of Holiday Junction, I'd talked them into converting the old cottage into the office, where I could come and work anytime.

The office was in their home, if that told you anything about the flailing paper that barely had a heartbeat when I'd moved here. My idea turned out to be somewhat good. The numbers of people checking the paper online for the daily updates had gone up, and so had the sales of the paper version we printed once a week.

As long as the profit margin's trajectory went up, I felt I had some job security. Plus, I'd added the weekly column from the Merry Maker. Marge and Louise, the *Junction Journal* owners, were beyond pleased I'd scored such an exclusive. Little did they know I was the Merry Maker.

"Of all times for your father to call," Mama said, a hint of annoyance in her southern drawl as it projected down the hall. "I told him I'd call him after Halloween." The tone of her voice held so much glee that I wondered if she was taking some enjoyment in her little cat-and-mouse game.

"Mama." I addressed her when she walked into the kitchen. She looked like the holiday display for the Emily's Treasures clothing boutique. "Are you playing with Daddy?"

"Playing?" Mama pressed her lips together. She gave me one hard stare before she shimmied over to the coffeepot and filled up one of my mugs. "I don't know what you are talking about, Violet. Your daddy won't give me my space like I told him to."

"If you don't call several states away from him space, I'm not sure how you define it, Mama." It was rare for me to talk to her like that, and I'd had it up to here with them both dragging me into their web.

"That's not for your pretty little head to worry with." Mama shrugged and passed by me. "Now, what is this about a ghost walk?"

"How did you know about it?" I asked and followed her down with a mug of freshened up coffee.

"I read it on your computer while your daddy was saying something about holiday season and whatever. He just has to look in the attic and find the boxes with the holiday written on them to find any decorations." She rambled on about whatever it was she and Daddy had been fussing over. "Anyways, aren't you excited about the ghost walk?"

"That's the problem," I groaned and sat down at the desk, where the invitation to the ghost walk was staring me in the face. Taunting me.

"It'll be fun. And…" She moseyed over, leaned in really close as if someone was around to hear, and whispered, "We can figure out where the holiday will end because you're the you-know-what."

"Shhh." My finger flew up to my mouth.

"What?" She took a couple of steps back. "It's not like anyone is here, and no one would ever suspect you're the Merry Maker."

Not by choice but by chance and obligation I'd been named the Merry Maker. The responsibility and feeling should have gone with the suggested name, but at the moment, I wasn't feeling too merry. Halloween made me feel quite the opposite, which boosted my gumption to sneak out of the Jubilee Inn at night, tiptoe through the streets, and try to find my way through the woods to Vern McKenna's shed. There, he painted up a large piece of wood in the shape of and with the face of a big jolly jack-o'-lantern.

"We can't talk about that." I refused to tell Mama anything about the Merry Maker, even though she'd found out I was the secret jolly cheer spreader by accident.

I'd come to the village by emergency airplane landing and never left. Mama came to town because I was here. That was when she dropped the bomb about her and my dad getting divorced then decided she was staying here with me. When she'd gotten herself into a little pickle the night I'd picked up the painted sign, I'd had to come to her rescue, and she'd put two and two together.

One problem. She and I weren't alone. Darren Strickland, my boss's son and the local sheriff's son, was also with me. Though he didn't want any part of the Merry Maker position and had to wonder how the two-hundred-year-old tradition had been passed to someone who'd lived in the town for only a few months, he was now my fellow Merry Maker.

There weren't clear rules about the Merry Maker. The only rules were these: no one could know, and there had to be a person-sized sign in the shape of the holiday planted in the area where the Merry Maker wanted the holiday's last hurrah to take place. No one had ever known if co-Merry Makers existed, but I decided on that rule when Darren caused Mama to find out about my secret identity.

Playing the part had been fun up until Halloween, which brought me right back to where we were now.

Hours away from a private screening of the ghost walk. I was already feeling faint.

"Oh look! It's Darren." Mama hurried out of the office and back to the front door. "I'm so glad you're here," Mama said to Darren. "You've got to talk some sense into her," I heard her tell him before they turned to walk into the office.

"I can't help it if I can't stand Halloween." I tried not to stare too much at Darren. We'd had a few of what I called "moments" since I'd moved here, and those were outside of the co-Merry Maker gig I forced him to take part in.

It was almost difficult for me to avoid getting lost in his dimples when he flashed his charming smile, or in the dark eyes against his olive skin. Something about a dark-haired man sent my heart into orbit.

Regardless, no matter how good the man looked, I still wasn't going to let him talk me into liking Halloween.

"How on earth do you not like Halloween? You can dress up and be anyone you want for the night. No one would even know it's you." He had a point. "It makes it easy to be the Merry Maker."

"Co." I gestured between Darren and Mama. "And if memory serves me right, it's your turn to figure out where the end of the holiday party will be."

"I had a thought," Mama chimed in. "What about somewhere on the ghost walk?"

"That's a perfect idea." Darren smacked his hands together and rubbed them against each other vigorously. He had a very contagious grin. His dark eyes and brows danced with joy at my uneasiness.

"Wait. Have you two forgotten I don't like Halloween, including ghost walks?" My cheeks puffed out and filled with frustrated air, which I let seep out of my mouth in one long, steady, nerve-racking stream. "Why on earth would I want the holiday to end where there could be potential ghosts we'd have to deal with for the entire evening?"

"Fine." Darren looked out the window and at the sea. He wore a long-sleeved plaid shirt rolled up at the cuffs; a pair of baggy, wrinkled khakis; and a pair of tennis shoes. "What if I call Hershal and Hazelynn and tell them I'm going to come with you and Millie Kay on behalf of my mom? You know, part of the journal to make sure she'd agree to such a piece."

"Deal." Mama wasn't going to pass up any sort of possible new adventures. "This is going to be fun."

Mama's numerous Halloween baubles on her armful of bracelets jingled together as she rubbed her own hands together.

She leaned in a little closer. Out of the side of her mouth, she whispered, "He's got that new-car smell." I jerked around and gave her the side-eye.

In her oh-so-Southern way, she was letting me know Darren seemed to be available, and it was exciting when you smelled that new-car scent. Everyone knew what that smell was, and it was an exciting one.

"I'm sorry. I didn't hear you. What did you say?" Darren asked Mama.

"She said let's go." I stood there looking at my mama, who I didn't recognize, and Darren, who I recognized all too well.

CHAPTER TWO

The trolley had routes all over Holiday Junction, and Darren had suggested taking it, even though Mama wanted to drive her golf cart. Word around town was to keep an eye out for Millie Kay Rhinehammer and her golf cart.

"I'm not risking my life," he whispered to me in rushed words so Mama couldn't hear him after he'd made up some sort of excuse about needing to make sure the mechanics of the trolley were working.

I guessed Mama fell for it.

"How's the mechanics been working today?" Mama asked Goldie Bennett as soon as she got on and stuck her nickels into the slot to pay for her ride.

"Mechanics?" Goldie drew back with a snarl. "What in the world are you talking about?"

"Millie." Darren put his finger up to his mouth. "You can't say it out loud or the other passengers will get scared and think something is wrong." He slipped his money into the slot, getting the go-ahead from Goldie.

"Something is wrong." Mama's eyes grew big. "The mechanics."

"I assure you the mechanics are fine for where we are going, Mama." I sucked in a deep breath, and my cheeks puffed out when I exhaled. "How's Joey, Chance, and Lizzy?" I asked Goldie about her grandchildren.

"Ya know." She looked at me from underneath the visor with its clear orange bill. It complemented her jack-o'-lantern earrings, matching necklace, multiple jiggly bracelets, and the pumpkin sweatshirt she was wearing.

I was one hundred percent positive Goldie had gotten all her attire from Emily's Treasures too.

"Them kiddos keep me and Elvin young. If it isn't one sport after the other, and now Lizzy has started a new dance session at the Groove and Go. But they are excited about the pumpkin painting and the costume party. Which reminds me—when are you going to get the calendar of events posted on the *Junction Journal* website?"

Goldie was so proud of her grandchildren, as she should have been. Of course, I asked her every time I saw her, so I already knew their schedule probably better than she did, but my southern manners inspired me to ask. Plus, Mama was with me, and I'd get the subtle pinch from her if I didn't show the manners she'd taught me growing up.

Even though I was a grown-up, Mama would tell me that I wasn't too big to be mothered.

"We are on our way now to do the ghost walk, so I'll make sure Violet gets that calendar up today." Mama had even started to answer for me.

Darren snickered. I didn't find it too amusing.

"I love your pumpkins." Mama sat on the trolley bench right behind Goldie. "Where'd you get them?"

"Emily's Treasures has a whole table full of Halloween jewelry. If you want some for Thanksgiving and Christmas, you'll have to act fast when she puts them out because people gobble those up within minutes of Emily opening her doors." Goldie knew all the ins and outs of everyone and their business in this town.

If I needed to know something or check out a fact for the paper, I knew I had to ride the trolley.

"Have you driven through the village and seen all the fun for Halloweenie?" Goldie asked Mama.

"Have I?" Mama asked sarcastically. "I've even gotten decorations for the new house me and Violet bought over on Heart Way."

"You mean the one on the corner?" Goldie turned the trolley up the road going away from the sea, which took us the long way around Holiday Junction. "The one with the little building in the backyard?"

"Yep. That's the one. The little building is Violet's apartment." Mama and I had put a contract on the home a few months ago but were just now able to take it over per the contract.

We'd been living in a motel room at the Jubilee Inn that suited us just fine.

"Violet don't like Halloween, but it's part of her job to go on these ghost walks." I had no idea why Mama felt the need to tell everyone my business.

"But whatcha gonna do? It comes with the job. Nora and I were just talking about the pumpkin-carving contest at the library. Right, Nora?" Goldie called out to the woman sitting next to me.

"That's right. Not unless you decide to join the Holiday Junction Planning Committee." Nora LaBelle was someone I'd seen at the library a couple of times when I'd gone in there for research, but no one ever formally introduced me to her. "At least that's what they told me when I complained about them hosting the contest in the library." She stuck her tongue out. "What if guts get all over my books?"

She had a point.

Nora was probably a smidgen older than me, maybe not yet thirty but close. The purple long-sleeved knit shirt she wore made her blue eyes sparkle. Or maybe that was because of the friendly smile on her face.

"I'm Violet. I've seen you a few times at the library." I turned slightly to say hello.

"Yeah. I've seen you in there a few times, and of course we have people coming in the library all the time wanting to read the newspaper. I tell them to subscribe online. I love how you do a daily update plus the section where you list the events of each festival." Clearly, she'd been online to see the *Junction Journal's* new format.

I elbowed Darren.

"Did you hear that?" I asked him. "You can tell your mama people come in daily to read the *Junction Journal* online. Nora said she liked it too."

Marge and Louise Strickland owned the *Junction Journal*. Louise was Darren's mama, so hearing Nora's compliment from him would make her take notice. If I told her, she'd just think I was making sure they would continue to pay to keep the journal online.

It was hard to get the older generation to go online for their news when all they really wanted to do was sit at a table with a cup of coffee, possibly dunking a cookie in the liquid, while reading a physical newspaper.

I understood that as a journalist and still loved the paper version. That was why I still had the Printing Press, owned by Clara and Garnett Ness, print a weekly run.

"How does one get on the planning committee?" Mama's interest was piqued.

Goldie, Mama, and Nora talked about the committee while I turned around and looked out the open trolley's windows.

Goldie had turned down Main Street at the far end, where the houses stood like grand pieces of art. They were old brick homes, each with a couple of acres. The buildings were majestic and screamed wealth. The gates keeping out the riffraff like me were a telltale sign that rich people lived in those houses.

Darren's family numbered among those rich people.

Some of the houses had fodder shocks on each side of their gates, gathered at the center with a festive bow, while others included hay bales with all sorts of pumpkins and gourds as decorations.

We passed Darren's parents' compound, where a few other family members occupied a couple of houses on the property.

They had a large display of six ghosts in a circle holding hands around a fake flaming cauldron, as if they were telling a ghost story. I shivered and quickly turned away only to see we were passing the cemetery.

Even that place had a pumpkin with a carved scary face stuck right down on the pointer of an entrance's fencepost.

One after the other, the houses' front lawns were already decorated for the frightful month. They ranged from single ghosts and goblins to simple fall decorations like hay bales, which were more my speed.

"Are you ready for the big kickoff?" Nora asked Darren.

"I'll be putting the bulbs in tonight and testing them out over the next few days. I can't let the village down." He smiled.

"You like this crazy holiday, don't you?" I asked him.

I never pegged Darren to be sentimental about anything, much less how putting orange bulbs in the lighthouse beacon would affect him.

"Holiday Park!" Goldie screamed as she brought the trolley to a stop then opened the door. The seat beneath her groaned as she turned around to make sure we all were getting up.

"Saved by the ghost walk," Darren teased, since he didn't have to answer my question now.

"I'll see you later this afternoon," I told Nora when I got to my feet. "I need to stop by and look at the archived photos from previous Halloweens."

"Sure. I'll get them pulled up for you." Nora seemed excited to have something to do.

Mama and Darren had gotten off the trolley and waited for me on the sidewalk in front of Holiday Park.

Main Street dead-ended into Holiday Park. The park was magnificent. In its center was a huge lake. You could take a swan-shaped paddle boat out on it as well as fish or just sit on one of the many benches around it.

Holiday Park also had a fountain about twelve feet in diameter and a two-foot-deep pool with four ceramic swans spouting water from their mouths. The top of the fountain was a large ceramic water can, ever so slightly tipped over with water pouring out of it.

Furthermore, the park had an amphitheater where the Village Players, the local acting troupe, loved to put on plays when the weather permitted. Mama had joined the Leading Ladies, a small but mighty group of women who worked with the Village Players and also hosted their own events like afternoon teas, community yard sales, and much more.

"It looks like everyone is getting ready for the big month ahead." Darren had a little too much excitement in his voice. He looked at me with a sly grin as he tried to poke the bear, but I wouldn't let him.

"Yes." I smacked my hands together. "Let's get this awesome ghost walk over. Shall we?" I pointed at the fountain, where I could see Hershal standing in costume. Hazelynn next to him.

She had one of the cardboard drink carriers in her hands.

"Welcome to a hair-raising encounter with the spirited side of Holiday Junction." Hershal stood behind Hazelynn as she gave Mama, Darren, and me one of her coffee concoctions.

Hershal was in a top hat, black coattails, and a bow tie with ghosts on it. He had a cane and a gaslight lantern he held up to his eyes.

I thought it was for effect, as was the deeper tone in his already deep voice. His eyes shifted before they settled on the most excited member of our party of three.

Mama.

"Tonight, um, today, we will be visited by unresolved affairs throughout Holiday Junction." Hershal jerked up. Mama squealed in delight and clapped her hands together. "Which are many."

Hazelynn wasn't in costume yet, though she did have one of those plastic black spider rings on her pointer finger.

"Now we are going to open it up with something like that," Hazelynn said directly to me. "What do you think?"

"Me?" I put a hand up to my chest.

"Yes. We want your opinion so you can write up a good review for the walk so everyone will participate." Hazelynn's thick brows knitted, and her lips pressed together. "Remember, we asked you to do an article, so we invited you so you could write it up properly."

"Yes. I was thinking I"—I gestured to Mama and Darren—"we were going to get the full ghost walk, but I'm fine with you just telling me a couple of stories right here before it gets dark, and we can call it good."

"No way." Mama stomped a foot. "Violet, you've said it yourself. In order to write a good piece, you have to feel it in the depths of your soul. Put yourself into the situation."

"Just like you did on the airplane ride that brought you to Holiday Junction." Darren snickered. I shot him a look. He grinned, lifting his hands up and backing away.

"Mama, that's different. That's real stories," I muttered on the other side of my smile through gritted teeth.

"I beg your pardon. These are real stories." Hershal's facial muscles went slack. "As real as you feel them in your soul."

At the sounds of a horse braying and hooves on the ground, I jumped out of the way just in time. A horse trotted past, bearing someone dressed as the Headless Horseman. A shiver crawled along my spine as the horseman's shoulders shifted sideways, as though he was looking at me, even though, of course, I couldn't see the eyes.

"You should see your face." Darren burst out laughing and gave Hershal a whack on the biceps with the back of his hand. "Good one."

"That was just by chance. We didn't have anyone dress up and do it, but it was a good one." Hershal's face lit up in delight. "Even in the bright sunshine, you seem too nervous."

"Funny." My voice was flat, and I looked at both of them with a narrow-eyed stare. "Let's just get this over with."

"Oh, honey. Mama is right here if you get scared." She put her hand out. She might've been teasing when she said she was by my side, but I felt a sense of comfort with her there. I wasn't so sure Darren, Hershal, or Hazelynn would be as comforting.

Hershal spoke in his scary, deep voice while we walked around the fountain. He pointed in the air at nothing as he spoke of the ghost wisping by. Hazelynn would jump, hold her heart, and gasp for effect.

"Of course, there's not a ghost, but in the dark, people won't know." Hazelynn snickered.

To keep my mind off the stories Hershal was telling, I pretended to take notes on my phone. In reality, I was checking social media and looking at the *Junction Journal* website dashboard for the updated stats in case I ran into Marge and Louise at the park.

So many people were setting up their vendor tents.

"Violet," Mama gasped, grabbing me around my elbow.

"What?" I jerked up from my phone.

"We have to go to Bubbly Boutique." She pointed at the tent across from us. There was a chalkboard sign in front of the vendor.

"You'll have to go another time," Hazelynn said under her breath just as Mama was about to take off.

"That's right, Mama." I grabbed the hem of her sweater so she couldn't get any farther away. "You said you were going to be right by my side on this ghost walk, remember?"

We passed the caramel popcorn stand. A mix of salt and sweetness floated underneath my nose. I took a big whiff, which lifted a grin to my face. I was definitely going to get a big bag when I came back to enjoy the festival on my terms.

"No, I mean she'll have to go to the physical Bubbly Boutique shop because Peter Hill revoked her vendor's license this morning," Hazelynn said in a hushed tone and glanced at Hershal.

He'd been telling his ghost tales to a very interested Darren, allowing Mama, Hazelynn, and me to hang back a little. Good for me because I didn't care to listen, though I would still write a nice article.

There was nothing to dislike about the ghost walk. It was family friendly, and everyone was around, so it didn't seem so scary. Granted, that could be because the ghost walk was in daylight, but all the lights on the vendor tents would provide enough light at night to make it an activity for all ages.

"I know you two don't know me well. And I'm not one to gossip," Hazelynn said, establishing that right off. She walked around a bale of hay. Someone was sticking a family of scarecrows there and setting pumpkins, gourds, and mums at the base.

I pinched my lips together to avoid smiling.

"But Peter Hill and Nettie got into somewhat of an argument." Hazelynn's brows rose, and her forehead wrinkled like a little bulldog's. "I'm being kind when I say 'somewhat' because there was some name-calling, and some of those names weren't very nice. Peter don't give two squashes what someone calls him, but when Nettie hollered out that she wasn't going to vote him in for reelection, that got Peter's pumpkin rolling."

"Is reelection this year?" I questioned.

"It sure is." Her facial features squashed together. "Remember, you're in Holiday Junction. We do things a little differently around here."

"You'd think candidates would want to put an ad in the paper." I was always trying to come up with different ways to get a little extra money going to the *Junction Journal* instead of relying on the subscriptions.

"Something you could talk to Peter about." Mama twisted her head around. "Hazelynn, which one is he?"

Mama tossed her empty coffee cup in the next garbage can we passed. Even the garbage can couldn't just be a garbage can. It was painted orange, like a pumpkin, with black triangle eyes, an upside-down triangle nose, and a toothy smile.

All these things I made sure to note on my phone app so I could write about the festival's special little details.

"I haven't seen him since he and Nettie got into the fight. He darted off toward the lighthouse." She fluttered her hands in the air. "Something about the lighthouse. But Nettie did come in this morning very early, much earlier than normal for a cup of coffee, and..." She drew her lips in. The lines between her eyes creased, as did the ones on her forehead. "Nettie was in the same clothes as yesterday. She never wears the same thing twice."

"What is it about the Bubbly Boutique?" I quickly typed the shop's name and Nettie's in the notes. It was something I'd explore later when I wrote the article on the upcoming election.

I knew nothing about this matter, so when Hazelynn mentioned it, I knew it was an article I could dig my teeth into, making this little ghost-walk adventure worth all the anxiety and fear I'd had around it.

All the tension fell off me as we talked about the election. I didn't even realize we'd started down the path toward the lighthouse until Mama mentioned the carriage lights.

"Isn't that adorable?" Mama pointed at the large plastic pumpkins that fit over the carriage lights perfectly.

"Yes. At night, when it's dark, the lights make the pumpkins glow, so it's a lot spookier then." Hazelynn was proud of the lights, and by rights, she should have been. They were cute.

She and Hershal didn't skimp on the decorations along the walk either.

"Nettie loves New Year's and everything about it." Hazelynn continued to talk with her hands. She waved and flailed them in perfect time with her words. "You know the whole new beginning, fresh start, yada yada."

"I love a good fresh start." Mama nodded and pointed out the wall with the witch hanging off it, the backside to us as though the witch had flown straight into the wall. "That's why I'm here."

"Mama, not now." I didn't feel like hearing about her and Daddy. Did she listen to me? Well, no.

"I'm getting divorced." It rolled off her tongue like she'd been practicing saying it for years. "When my Violet moved here for her fresh start, I knew I could too."

"Mine wasn't a fresh start," I reminded her. "I moved here because I didn't have a job after I couldn't leave here."

"You make a perfect addition to Holiday Junction." Hazelynn continued to point things out on the path so I could make note of them. This one was a rubber rat that was about the size of a dog.

This kind of scariness was about my speed. I was feeling pretty good about the ghost walk until the clap of the horse's hooves echoed behind us.

The horse let out a bray and reared up on its back legs while the Headless Horseman lifted his sword in the air, with a fake and bloody head stuck to the point. Then he darted off toward the lighthouse.

"He's a good one." Mama clapped in delight.

Hershal and Darren turned around, both amused by the actor on the horse. Darren gave me a subtle wink. I gulped. Mama squeaked a little, obviously having seen Darren's gesture.

"I think he's scary." The goose bumps curled up my arm from the horse's hooves clapping off in the distance. "Let's talk about the boutique," I whispered because Hershal had gone back to telling another story I had no interest in hearing.

Hazelynn gave me the one-finger gesture to hold on so Hershal didn't get wind we weren't listening.

"Welcome to the spooky graveyard." When he said "graveyard," it was enough to raise the hairs on my neck. "We have the Ghost of Halloween Past." He lifted the lantern in one hand and tapped the freestanding vampire-style wooden coffin with the cane.

The spooky graveyard consisted mainly of cutout Styrofoam tombstones with different epitaphs written on them. Some of them were funny and pun based.

When we got to another freestanding vampire-style wooden coffin, Hershal stopped.

"Here lies Halloween Future." The tone of his voice dove three octaves deeper. "I want you to see what's in store for Holiday Junction."

He gave the front of the coffin three hard taps with the cane.

"This is going to be sooo good." Mama bounced on her toes in anticipation.

"It looks so much scarier at night. Hershal has a really good shifty spooky-eye effect along with that voice." Hazelynn's shoulders lifted to her ears in delight.

"It's supposed to open on the third one." Hershal turned a couple shades of red. He gave it another good college try. "Here lies Halloween Future." The tone of his voice wasn't only deeper but louder. Much louder. "I want you to see what's in store for Holiday Junction."

This time, the harder knocks of the cane did the trick. The door slowly opened, and I would have to say it was a good effect.

Then the dummy fell out face forward, a knife sticking out of its back.

"Is that blood?" I asked when I noticed something that looked like real blood dripping from the knife.

"That's an added extra. And so real." Hazelynn couldn't contain the excited squeak in her voice.

"I didn't do that." Hershal's voice cracked. I smiled at the effect because it looked so real.

"You got us. This is pretty real looking." Darren patted Hershal on the back.

"It was supposed to be a jack-in-the-box clown." Hershal couldn't take his eyes off the dummy. "You know, for a good scream."

Hershal wasn't joking. The realization this wasn't what was supposed to happen on the ghost walk sank in.

"I think it is real." I took a step closer to see the knife sticking out of the man's back. "And that sure does look like real blood." With a grave look on my face, I stared at Darren. "Call your dad."

Darren stepped away, and I could hear him, though his voice sounded muffled. I couldn't focus on what he was saying to his dad, Chief Matthew Strickland, and process if this was a crime scene.

"Hershal, what is going on here?" Hazelynn's voice had gone from calm to hysterical. "What is happening?"

"I don't know, Hazelynn," Hershal said, his words coming out statically. "You tell me." He pulled off his top hat, and sweat beaded on his forehead. "You're the one who put the jack-in-the-box in there a little bit ago. It was your idea."

I put them out of my head and inspected the man more closely.

Streams of blood forked off down the man's side and pooled in the grass.

I bent down to get a look at the blood then carefully reached to check his pulse.

"What are you doing?" Mama gasped, reaching for me when I put my fingers on the man's wrist.

"Making sure he's dead." My gaze slid past my shoulders, setting the mood for what was surely going to be a hexed night ahead.

CHAPTER THREE

E very single crunch of a fallen leaf made the five of us jump, even though we were standing there with Chief Strickland and a couple of deputies.

Chief Strickland had not yet done anything with the body other than rope off the entire path from Holiday Park to the beach. He made Mama, Darren, Hershal, Hazelynn, and me sit down on the concrete pathway about twenty feet from what I was calling a crime scene.

"We do not know if it's a crime scene." Chief Strickland insisted we wait until Curtis Robinson, the coroner, showed up.

"Clearly he didn't reach behind his own back with a knife and jab it in far enough to kill himself, Matthew." Mama called him by his first name, which I'd not really done yet.

"I hate to inform you, as I have your daughter"—he slid a glance at me then gave Darren a hard stare—"but we do things differently here in Holiday Junction. Not like where you come from." He sucked in a deep breath and muttered under his freshly grown beard and mustache, new to his look. "Wherever it is you come from."

"Pardon me?" Mama moved her head and tilted her chin up just enough that she appeared to have an air about herself.

"Just stay right there." His annoyed tone wasn't unnoticed, but it did make Mama smile.

"I think I got his goat." Mama nudged me and wiggled her brows. "Who do you think it is?" she asked Hershal.

"I don't know." He held his top hat to his chest and leaned over to talk to me. "You aren't going to put this in your review, are you?"

"Are you kidding?" Mama spoke with pride. "This is what my Violet would call a front-page story."

"I wouldn't say it was front page." I tried to be nice and sugarcoat it, but Mama was having none of that.

"Why, yes it will be." Mama acted as though she had a say in the matter. "This will bring sales up quicker than a jackrabbit."

"I didn't say I wasn't going to make it a front-page story." My words put a worried expression on Hershal's face. "But I'll be sure to put the review of the ghost walk right after it."

"Are you going to leave out the part about the cemetery find?" Hazelynn lifted her hand, held it close to her body, and pointed at the body like no one knew what she was asking me.

"I can leave out a lot of the details." I nodded.

"None of that matters." Mama stood up and brushed herself off. "What we need to do is come up with why this happened so we can have Hallowee-nie. This could cause things to go south real fast."

She arched her back a few times before curling her body to each side in a good stretch. The sight must've been appealing to all of us because we all stood up, too, but the only stretching I did was craning my neck to see the source of the squeaking that came from the direction of Holiday Park.

All of us stared down the concrete path. We all held our breath and let out collective sighs of relief when Curtis and another person from the coroner's office came pushing the church cart down the path.

"That doesn't add to the scene," Mama said sarcastically as the eerie wheels cried with each turn. "You need to oil up them wheels," she told Curtis as he passed by.

He paid her no attention, but Hershal and Hazelynn snickered.

Mama and the Hudsons started to talk about the various reasons someone would do such a thing to someone, which I did want to know, but

I was more interested in what Chief Strickland and Curtis were saying, so I tuned them out.

"What do you think?" After I overheard Chief Strickland ask Curtis this question, I gnawed on my lips and turned my body slightly away from the officer.

Darren gave a little head gesture to make sure I was listening.

"There's no wounds to his chest or cuts to his arms or hands." Curtis was bent over the body, shielding any view of the victim's face.

"He didn't put up a fight." Curtis was able to tell all of that from just observing the body lying there. "Didn't see it coming, perhaps?" Curtis made it sound like whoever stabbed Peter had snuck up on him.

"Time of death?" Chief asked.

"About eight to twelve hours ago. Just by the way the blood coagulated around the wound." He wasn't giving a true time of death, just the initial estimate and covering himself if we were wrong. "Here's his wallet and ID. I guess you should probably pay Vickie a visit."

Hazelynn let out an audible cry.

"What?" I asked.

"Did he say Vickie?" Her eyes filled with tears. "That's Peter Hill's wife. Is that Peter Hill?" Frantically, her hands moved in front of her before her fingers pointed in the body's direction.

Her hands were shaking so much, the legs on the plastic spider ring looked like they were moving.

CHAPTER FOUR

"You honestly amaze me." Darren didn't seem to mean it in a good sort of way at all. "You loathe anything Halloween yet thrive on murders," he whispered so his dad, who was walking over, didn't hear us.

"I love a good story, and murder, well"—I snorted—"you can't top that."

"You two." Chief Strickland pointed at me and then at Darren before he moved his fingers a little farther down to point. "Over there."

Mama looked at me. I looked at her and shrugged.

"What's going on with his face?" I couldn't help but ask Darren on our way over to his dad.

"The beard and mustache are what he calls his winter wear," Darren whispered out of the corner of his mouth. "He says it's like a woman who changes out her wardrobe seasonally. He lets his facial hair grow during the winter months."

Okay. If we were in a much different situation, I would've laughed at this, but the mood was not one in which snickering was appropriate.

"I shouldn't be surprised that you are here," Chief Strickland said to me. "But now you?" He gave Darren a hard look.

"I, we, um," Darren began, but his dad put his hand up.

"Chief Strickland—" I was going to tell him all about it, but he stopped me too.

"It doesn't look like you are going anywhere anytime soon. And my wife said so, too, so you can call me Matthew from now on," he said. "Tell me why you, Millie Kay, and you are here? I understand why the Hudsons would be here, but why you?"

"First off, let me tell you that Halloween is not my favorite holiday." From the reaction my words inspired in Matthew, you'd think I'd run over to Peter Hill's body, pulled out the knife from his back, and stabbed the chief himself. "I'm sorry it's not, so I've been avoiding the Hudsons' calls and emails asking me to come to the ghost walk so I could write it up in the paper." I looked at Darren. "No thanks to him and Mama, they talked me into coming here today, during daylight hours, to do the ghost walk, and they would come with me for moral support."

Matthew looked at his son.

"That is true," Darren confirmed.

"We took the trolley straight here and met the Hudsons by the fountain in Holiday Park. They told ghost stories along the way and then talked about Nettie." My face jerked wide awake with my eyes popping open and my jaw dropping. I snapped my fingers then shook my pointer finger at no one in particular. "Nettie. Bubbly Boutique."

"What are you talking about?" Matthew's body froze.

"Hazelynn told Mama and me about Nettie's boutique." I wasn't being clear. "When we started down the path, Mama noticed Bubbly Boutique's vendor booth. Nettie was packing things up. Hazelynn told us Nettie and Peter Hill got into a fight after he told her she wasn't complying with the Holiday Junction Planning Committee rules. That was when she told him she wasn't voting for him. He was then seen going to the path to the lighthouse."

"Nettie made it clear she wasn't happy with his decision." Darren was getting the hang of this sleuthing stuff. "Peter left to go check on my house, and Nettie was mad. She followed him, and when no one was looking, not even Peter, she stabbed him."

"But could she pick him up and put him in the coffin?" I asked Darren.

"Whoa with the accusations." Matthew stopped us. "Hazelynn heard the argument?" He'd taken out his little notepad and pen so he could jot down what we were saying.

"I can't remember if she heard it or overheard it. Either way"—I wagged my finger in the air—"they had a fight. He stopped her from selling her items, which would probably make her a pretty penny. Not only would he make her look like a fool, he also would hurt her bottom line."

"Those are two very good reasons to kill someone." Darren was glowing with excitement, which only fueled me even more to find out who murdered Peter Hill, even if it wasn't Nettie.

"Okay, you two. That's enough. I never even said the body was Peter Hill." Matthew's lips pressed together.

"We heard you tell Curtis you were going to have to call Vickie, so it wasn't hard to put two and two together." I lifted two fingers in the air and rotated my wrist back and forth.

"I'm not going to have Nettie's reputation ruined over some hearsay, but I will go see her to make sure she didn't do it." His body stiffened, but he never confirmed it was Peter Hill. Nor did he deny it. "Did either of you see anyone walk down the path while you were doing the ghost walk?"

We both shook our heads.

"Hear anything?" he asked us.

We shook our heads again.

"We were standing here, and Hershal was telling us about the cemetery then gave it a good hard knock. That was when Peter fell out."

"I never said it was Peter Hill," he insisted right as Curtis was pushing the gurney past us with the body bag on top.

"I'm taking Peter down to the morgue. Are you going to call Vickie?" Curtis asked Matthew.

"You didn't say it was Peter, but he did," I pointed out, but it didn't land so well on Matthew. His cheeks puffed out before he blew out some air.

"I'll go see her," he finally confirmed to Curtis.

I gave Curtis a friendly smile when he looked at me and started to push the cart past us and up the path.

"Don't forget about oiling those wheels," I heard Mama call out to him when he passed her and the Hudsons.

"If you remember anything, let me know. For right now, this is between us until I can get the rest of the statements and go see Vickie. It's not right for her to hear about Peter or read about him online." Matthew really wasn't talking to Darren. He'd directed his next moves toward me. "This is not a homicide."

"Yet," I muttered loudly enough for him to hear me. "Fine," I groaned. "What time can I expect a statement? Part of the job, and you benefit from it."

"Are we talking the amateur sleuthing job, the *Junction Journal* job, or the Me—" Darren was about to let it slip that I was the Merry Maker before I gave him a good elbow punch to his gut.

"I need to be at any sort of press conference if you're going to be giving one," I said.

"I'll do the press conference tomorrow morning in front of the fountain. It will give me time to go see Vickie, get Curtis's initial report, and figure out the status of Halloweenie with the Holiday Junction Planning Committee." Matthew had his plan in place, and now I needed to get mine figured out. "You two don't mention this to anyone. I'm going to interview the Hudsons and Millie Kay, so you can go."

Matthew cleared his throat and took a few steps toward the Hudsons and Mama. "Millie Kay?" He waved her over.

"You go on back to the office." Mama quirked an eyebrow. It was her way of letting me know she was ready to get going on this case.

"What on earth have I turned her into?" I jokingly asked Darren. He replied with a snort.

When we walked past the open coffin, I wondered where the jack-in-the-box Hershal had mentioned had gone.

"Hershal." I got his attention when I approached. "You said you had Hazelynn put a jack-in-the-box in the coffin."

"He did. I did," Hazelynn confirmed. "I don't see it anywhere either."

"That means whoever killed Peter must have taken out the jack-in-the-box." There were so many reasons we needed to find this piece of decoration. "Whoever killed Peter has it or had it. We need to find it."

"Keep your eyes open," Darren told the eager couple. "Call me if you see anything."

We left the Hudsons and Mama behind with Matthew.

"Let's take the path to the lighthouse," I told Darren. "Keep your eyes peeled for anything out of the ordinary."

Slowly we took the path and tried to distinguish what was a decoration from the Hudsons' ghost walk and what wasn't, making it very difficult to see anything that the potential killer would have left behind.

"You take that side of the path, and I'll take this side." I studied the grass and muddy spots, since it'd been raining on and off the past few weeks, and the normal dirt along the path was still wet. When we got to the sandy part of the dunes just before the beach, the sand was in clumps, but the fresh horse hoofprints weren't.

"The Headless Horseman," I blurted out. "We forgot about the Headless Horseman."

It didn't surprise me to realize Darren and I had both forgotten to mention it to Matthew. When you had a traumatic experience, such as finding a dead body, it wasn't unusual to block certain things from your mind for a little bit.

Those little details would come back, but it might take years.

"I think we need to go tell him." Darren started to turn around, and I stopped him.

"It can wait. He's got a lot to do, and if we can figure out who the Horseman was, we can possibly go there, find the jack-in-the-box, and then tell your dad." I didn't want to confront a killer. I just wanted the story for the front page of tomorrow's *Junction Journal*.

I took my cell phone out and started to snap photos of the horse's hoofprints.

"Who around here has a horse?" I asked.

"I don't know, but I do know the Headless Horseman hasn't been to Halloweenie in a few years. Like a lot of years." Darren made my thoughts swirl so fast I couldn't keep up with all of them.

"Why now?" I started to sputter the thoughts as they came so I wouldn't lose them. "Why Peter? Why eight to twelve hours ago? When was the fight between Nettie and Peter?"

"All good questions that we aren't going to solve until we check them out." Darren and I walked down the path.

"Yeah. You're right, but where do we start?" I stepped off the concrete path and onto the sand.

329

"I think we should start by eating something. I'm starving, and I can't think." Darren smiled. "What about the Freedom Diner?"

"Sounds delicious." Suddenly, my stomach growled. "After that, we need to go see Vern McKenna."

"We?" Darren waved his hand no. "That is all you. Besides, I've got to go to work."

"The jiggle joint?" I snorted. "Work?"

"Everyone around here thinks my bar isn't a legit business and my job. I'm tired of it." Darren released a theatrical groan. "Yes. We might have a couple of dancers, and yes, we serve only alcohol, but people love it, and I love it."

"Fine, but you got me into this Merry Maker mess, and you are going to be the co-Merry Maker." Though Darren had protested many times about my decision for him to join me as the co-Merry Maker over the past few months, I'd never given in. "That means you and I have to go see Vern together."

"I already told you that I don't want to be co-anything. Nothing." His hands gestured a clean slate in the air. I could tell by the sand whipping up from the backs of the heels of his tennis shoes that he was stomping.

"Too bad. You're helping. And you almost said 'Merry Maker' back there with your dad. You can't do that." It was a shame I, the new citizen, was able to keep the two-hundred-year-old secret better than the man who grew up in Holiday Junction.

"You're not letting me out of this, are you?" He stopped walking and faced me as soon as we got to the street where all the seaside shops, including his bar and the diner, were located.

"Not a chance." I gave a good shrug and walked past him toward the diner in silence until we got there.

A cemetery scene with grey tombstones, a few ghosts, and a tree with empty branches was painted on the front windows of the diner. Orange and black flags hung along the diner's roof, flickering from the natural ocean breeze.

"Hey, you two," Palmer Lustig said to us from far across the diner. She was cleaning off a spot at the counter. "Got two right here!" she hollered, pointing at the far end of the bar.

330

Palmer and her husband, Nate, owned the diner and famous Lustig Spring, a natural running spring on their property. People came from far and wide to get a drink or even fill up a jug from their spring.

Just lately, they'd opened the spring to anyone who wanted to enjoy it.

I nodded and glanced back at Darren for his approval. We weaved our way around the café tables. The diner had good food that ranged from grilled meats to the fried stuff. Plus Nate made the best desserts.

I was from the South, and it was virtually impossible to find anything here that compared.

Until I tried Nate's amazing pies. Each dessert was as delicious as the other.

Naturally, I looked at all the plated pies in the glass rotating pie case when we walked by. My mouth watered. The pumpkin pie looked nice and thick.

"Did you hear about the body someone found at Fountain Park?" Palmer had not been privy to the knowledge that we'd found Peter's body.

I pulled out the menu from between the scarecrow salt and pepper shakers without making eye contact with her.

"Hold on, you two." She plucked the menus from our hands, forcing us to look at her. "You," she gasped, moving her finger between us. "You two found the body, didn't you?" Her narrowed eyes were framed by the stray strands of her fallen salt-and-pepper hair from the messy bun atop her head. Ghost earrings dangled from her earlobes.

She tucked her hands into her apron pockets. Bright orange pumpkins with green vines were embroidered on each one.

"I'd like a BLT." Darren didn't need to look at the menu to know what he wanted. "With fries."

"Make it two," I said to make it easier.

"Dish." She leaned her hip on the edge of the counter. "I want all the details." She curled her arms. "First, who is it?"

Out of the corner of my eye, I could see Darren staring at me. He'd turned his body slightly and put his elbow on top of the counter, scratching his chin.

"Yeah, Violet." Darren snickered. "Tell her."

"No, Darren. You." I picked at the paper napkin and rolled a piece I'd torn off into a ball the size of a BB. "Your dad is the chief."

"Got me on that one." He laughed. "Oh, and a Coke," he said, adding to his order.

"I'll have one of the cinnamon spice coffees I saw y'all advertise in the *Junction Journal*."

"I'm going to get your drinks, and then you're going to tell me everything," Palmer warned. She shoved off the counter to go get our drinks.

"What is up?" Darren leaned back. His shoe landed on my stool's footrest. "I thought you didn't like Halloween."

"I don't," I confirmed and looked away from his dark eyes. They seemed to always pull me in. Right now, I needed to get some food, see Vern McKenna, and get on with finding out as much information as I could about Peter Hill.

"Then what's up with all the seasonal drinks? One from Brewing Beans and now here." He used his shoe to rotate my chair around.

He was sorely mistaken about my love for fall.

"I said I don't like Halloween, but I love fall." I pushed my chair around with my hand on the counter and looked at the Halloween garland hanging down from the ceiling and around the diner.

"You are something else." He smiled. "Did you know Nate caters all the Holiday Junction Planning Committee meetings?"

"How do you know?" I asked, knowing exactly what he was getting at.

"You do remember how he comes to the bar every day." He drummed his fingers on the counter. "He also comes to the bar after he drops off all the box dinners the committee orders. Says he needs a drink after being there because they all bicker. About everything."

"Bickering, huh?" My curiosity dinged, which made my little mind run through all sorts of reasons someone would want to murder the committee's president.

Peter Hill.

Someone from the kitchen yelled for Palmer, and a huge crash followed. All the customers started to clap before a cackle of laughter fell across the café.

"There go the BLTs!" Palmer screamed from the back before she emerged again from the kitchen. "Nate isn't here today, and he left me in charge of the kitchen. Bad idea. But your food will be up in a minute."

Someone else yelled for her.

She tapped the counter.

"I'll be back. I want to hear about this body." She hurried off, back into the kitchen.

It wasn't too long before they got our BLTs and fries out to us. We must've been starving because we didn't talk while we scarfed down our food.

"Do you think Palmer is right about the riffraff?" My mind turned from the possibility of a disgruntled committee member having done the deed to someone random.

"We won't know until you hurry up and eat your pie so I can walk you to Vern's. I have to work."

"You're the owner." I forked a piece of the pumpkin pie and slid the edge of it across the whipped cream. My eyes closed as the savory and sweetness hit my taste buds all at once. *Delightful.* I sighed happily.

"I'm also the bartender, the opener, the closer, and the cleaner, not to mention the businessman who won't have a business because Owen and Shawn will take full advantage of being in charge while I come down to the office to see you." He pulled the sleeve of his plaid shirt up to look at his watch. "Which was about two hours ago."

"Fine." I stuck the last bite of pie in my mouth and stood up. Darren had laid down enough money for the bill and tip before I could even get my debit card out. "You don't need to pay for me."

"I asked you to eat. I'm paying." His tone held zero room for negotiation, and he'd already walked off, which told me not to argue about it.

"I'll catch up with you two later!" Palmer yelled across the diner as we left.

"She's not going to stop, is she?" I asked Darren since he grew up here and knew the Lustigs well.

"Not a chance." Darren held the door for me. "After you." He gestured me the opposite way of his bar. We'd take the side street away from the ocean and toward the woods, where we'd find Vern's shed.

"Honestly, you can go to the bar." I knew it was getting later and later in the day. The sun was starting to set, and I didn't need to see that beautiful sunset with Darren.

"No. I told you I was making sure you were safe. Especially now that there's a killer who could've stabbed Peter, run down to the beach, and started on the very path we are walking right now." The likelihood of that event happening was unlikely.

A shadow of fear passed over me, darkening my features as the very thought played out in my head.

"If you go, that means you're for sure the co-Merry Maker." The little cat-and-mouse game had become a teasing exchange between us.

He wrapped his arm around me as we walked along the sidewalk, causing my feet to fumble one over the other. If not for his strong hold on me, I might've fallen and broken an ankle.

"You know I won't leave you in a lurch." He gave me a couple of quick pulls into his chest.

The door of Bubbly Boutique swung open, barely missing Darren.

"I'm so sorry!" The familiar-looking woman's black hair was pulled back into a neat bun atop her head, and large black sunglasses hid her eyes. She was tall, thin, and striking in her black jumpsuit that left little to the imagination. "My, my. Look what we have here." She pulled off the sunglasses and threw a tight smile.

"Fern." She was the last person I expected to see today.

"This is interesting." The corners of her eyes drew up, as did her lips. "Are you two an item? Or did you get a new job?"

"Fern, don't start." Darren grabbed my hand and dragged me a little before my body stiffened. He tugged. I dug my heels in. "Don't waste your time, Violet."

"I'm guessing you're an item by the looks of the way he took your hand and protected you from little ol' me." The pumpkin-shaped diamond ring on her finger sparkled as she dramatically placed a flat palm on her chest and let out a dramatic sigh.

"It was good to see you, Fern."

Mama's voice popped into my head. *If you can't say nothing nice, come sit by me.*

I started to laugh so hard Darren began to snort.

"Are you two drunk?" Fern stuck her long, lanky leg out to the side with her hands planted on her hips. "I don't have time for this. I've got to help Mom get ready for our own Halloweenie festival."

The sudden softening of her features caused me to stop laughing immediately, but I couldn't help give one more little snort.

"What?" I asked and should've just walked like Darren was dragging me to do.

"I really love you two together. I mean, Darren is a catch." She talked like he wasn't even there. "Any Strickland is." She rubbed her thumb, pointer, and middle fingers together in the money gesture. "And I'd love to help you update your wardrobe. You know. Fit in a little more around here."

"What's wrong with my clothes?" I looked down at my jeans and blue-and-white-striped sweater. Sure, I could've stood to run a brush through my long blond hair, but give me a break. I just found a dead body.

"I think you should add a little bling to it for the holiday." Even her tone changed.

"Did you say something about Bubbly Boutique being shut down at the Halloweenie festival?" Darren asked, giving up on dragging me down the street.

"Darren," Fern said, her upbeat tone taking a dramatic shift, "I can't believe you'd think…" She let the sentence dangle.

"Think you'd do anything to make sure the Bubbly Boutique took the limelight from the entire festival? You bet, sweetie." His brows winged.

"Do you know Nettie?" I wasn't going to count out what she was proposing. I'd had enough skin in this journalist game to be able to sniff out the "if I scratch your back, you'll scratch mine" game.

"Know her?" She looked down at me with arrogant eyes. "She's my mother."

CHAPTER FIVE

"Next time there's a crime in Holiday Junction, remind me that you'd make a deal with the devil to solve it." Darren stomped down the path toward Vern's shed. "Fern is the devil."

"And her mother could be Peter's killer." Did I already have to remind him? "If I need to deal with a little bit of Fern to get some information from Nettie, I'm going to do it."

We'd walked down the neighborhood street and gotten deep into the woods. The sun was penetrating the naked part of the forest, making it much easier for us to see the clear path to Vern's shed. Technically, it was a well-traveled way from the sea to the other side of the woods to the more rural area of Holiday Junction.

There were some subdivisions and some houses with a few acres. Vern's wife, Leni, was a seamstress with a small sewing shop.

The twigs snapped under our feet, and the damp smell of wet wood was a far cry from the pumpkin, sugar, and fried-food aromas at the Freedom Diner. Both clusters of scents reminded me of the fall. The thought of the cozy weather coming up chased away the sadness of the day's events for just a moment as Vern's shed came into sight.

It was a secret shed where Vern and Reed, the village handyman, had made all the huge wooden signs for the Merry Maker over the years.

The smell of paint seeped from the shed, reminding me of when I figured out Vern was the Merry Maker after I'd moved here during the St. Patrick's Day holiday. It was a mix of happiness, sadness, and fear all rolled up into one.

"I was wondering when you two were going to get here. I've been finishing up the Halloweenie Merry Maker sign." Vern was sitting outside the shed on the wooden bench I was sure he or Reed had made.

"We are late because we needed to eat. Since Peter Hill knocked us out of any free festival food on our ghost walk." Darren was itching to tell someone about the murder. If anyone could keep a secret, it was Vern.

"Leni called and just told me she'd gotten a call from Palmer Lustig about Peter. Murder, she said." Vern looked off into the woods. "I reckon they'd had enough of him down at the Holiday Junction Planning Committee, and finally someone knocked him off." He shrugged. "Could've been the mayor, though. Meaning the Mayor's owner."

He stood up and brushed his hands up and down his arms if the thought chilled him. There was the incident with Peter getting bitten by Mayor Paisley but I doubt Kristine would kill anyone. Thought I didn't know her that well.

"I don't know if I'm coming down with something or the chill got me to know someone killed Peter." Vern's voice held a sadness. "Come on in. I've got the Halloweenie Merry Maker cutout all ready."

We followed him into his shed, which was probably the only building in Holiday Junction that wasn't decorated for Halloween.

"Maybe I can stay in here until Halloween is over." My joke fell flat. I could tell by the pinched look on Vern's face.

"Hold on to your skeleton." Darren's joke did make Vern laugh. "Miss Merry Maker isn't a fan of Halloween."

"Not a fan?" Vern's shock made me wonder why Darren couldn't keep my distaste for the haunting season between us.

"But she loves a good murder." Darren shrugged. "Go figure."

"Go figure nothing. It's just the whole spookiness of it all, and now that we found Peter Hill murdered on the ghost walk—well, that's just too close for comfort." I shivered.

The lights of the shed flickered.

"You found Peter?" Vern asked in a commanding voice. "Leni forgot to mention that."

"And you weren't supposed to mention it." Darren gave me a stern look. "Vern, Dad will die if the town finds out we found him. He's trying to get all the facts straight before he gives a press conference tomorrow at the fountain."

"He needs to talk to the mayor and those people on the committee," Vern said. My ears perked to take in whatever he was talking about. "I'll keep my lips sealed."

"Don't keep them sealed on my account," I blurted out. Vern and Darren looked at me. "I mean right now. If you know a reason why Chief Strickland, um, Matthew, should take a closer look at someone, we can tell him."

Obviously, I was on a hunting mission so I could explore for the new article circulating in my head. I'd never name someone a suspect or even a person of interest, but I could use information and facts to find out why someone might have wanted to kill Peter.

"And Mayor Paisley is a dog." Did I have to remind him how they'd elected a dog as the village mayor? All the decisions for the village were made by the chamber of commerce.

Each holiday had their own committee, and if the committee needed something special like a permit, they had to go through the chamber of commerce.

"And she didn't like Peter. Bit him several times. Kristine never did anything about it, even after Peter filed a complaint with the chamber." Vern walked over to his workstation. He motioned for Darren to come over, and they picked up the piece of plywood Vern had turned into the Halloweenie Merry Maker sign.

"I don't know Kristine and Hubert Whitlock well, but I hardly think Kristine could've killed Peter." My eyes adjusted to the dark lighting, and I could clearly see the ghost cutout.

It wasn't just a ghost. It was a ghost that had its tail waving, as though it was floating. It also had arms ending in hands that held a very surprised jack-o'-lantern.

"The ghost did a sweep past the pumpkin and picked him up. That's the look on the pumpkin's face." Vern grinned but then stilled. "Back to your observation of the Whitlocks. They are nice people. They do a lot of good for the village, but they, too, have been burnt by the Holiday Junction Planning Committee, of which Peter Hill was the president."

I noticed a subtle shift in his demeanor.

"What?" I asked and sat up a little taller.

"Right over here," Vern instructed Darren, and they walked the ghost over near the door. "I guess Carol Dunn is finally going to get her shot at the title."

"Title?" I was having a hard time following what conversation we were in. It felt like we were playing a game of Halloween Tag. Who could we tag that had the most motive?

"Yeah. Carol Dunn will automatically go in the president's position now that Peter is dead." Vern had a similar situation happen to him with the Hibernian Society. "She's been trying to beat Peter for a long time but never has."

"She has enough motive to have killed him for the position?" I wanted details. A lot of them.

"Between her and the Whitlocks, yeah." Vern nodded with confidence.

"I don't know Carol Dunn, but I do know Kristine, and unless there's a good reason, then I'm not going to even think she could do such a thing." I just couldn't put the theory in my head.

"Like I said, the Holiday Junction Planning Committee does every single event in the village and that means tourism. When a tourist comes to the village, they have to have a place to stay." Vern leaned his back end on his workstation and crossed his legs at his ankles. "How did you know about the Jubilee Inn? Did you see it on a poster at the airport? Did you see any sort of advertisement for the inn? Any whatsoever?"

"No. Rhett Strickland took me there."

"Have you ever heard of a dog being elected mayor?" Tilting his head back, he peered at my face.

"No." His questioning had to be reaching a point.

Then he knocked me for a loop.

"Peter Hill is the"—Vern cleared his throat—"was the president of the Holiday Junction Planning Committee. They are the ones who would decide on whether the mayor was a human or an animal. He's been pushing for the village to have a real mayor, and that vote was coming this spring. The Whitlocks would not only lose the extra income they got from Mayor Paisley's appearances, but they'd also have to start paying taxes on their building and business."

"Surely they make enough to cover those things if something happened." I wasn't a business owner, but I'd seen many people come and go from the Jubilee Inn since I'd lived there.

"You'd think, but the Holiday Junction Holiday Committee also takes out all the ads in the paper, your paper."

"Let me guess." The puzzle pieces clicked together. "Those are run by the Holiday Junction Planning Committee. And I've never seen one by the Jubilee Inn come through the system. Which means Peter Hill was trying to run them out of business."

"That gives them a motive to kill." Darren's eyes were as cold as the words that left his mouth.

"Another thing about Peter." Vern walked us to the door, where Darren picked up the Halloweenie Merry Maker sign. "He couldn't stand that he didn't know the identity of the Merry Maker."

"Really?" I scoffed.

"Yeah. Said if the Holiday Junction Planning Committee was to approve all festival functions, they needed to approve all the Merry Maker sites." Vern named just a few possible suspects.

"I'm going to need a list of Merry Makers from the last"—I threw a shoulder—"um, two hundred years."

"Impossible." Vern snickered. "I can only name a few, and even they're sworn to secrecy as Merry Makers. No one knows you're the Merry Maker but me and this guy." He referred to Darren.

And Mama, I thought and gave Darren a hard look so he'd keep his mouth shut.

The mischief in his eyes danced, tickling my insides and forcing me to look away.

"What if Peter was going to do something about the Merry Maker as president, and one of the retired Merry Makers found out, and they were the one who killed him?" I threw it out there.

"Sorry. No can do." Vern tugged his lips together. His phone chirped, and he looked down at it. His eyes scanned whatever notification he'd gotten. His finger slowly scrolled down. Whatever he was reading put a wry grin on his face.

As if he suddenly realized we were there, he looked away from the phone. "But the library keeps all the minutes of every single Holiday Junction Planning Committee meeting from as far back as who knows when. I bet you can use the bulldog reporter in you to find something in there." He shrugged. "Or you can go to the emergency meeting Carol Dunn has just sent out to the committee in an email."

"What?" Emergency meeting? "She didn't waste any time."

"Like I said, I wouldn't doubt it if she did have a hand in what happened to Peter. She's been waiting for this for a long time." Vern tapped his phone and then held it out for Darren and me to see. "Interim President," he snickered.

"Thank you for yet another amazing sign." I was very grateful he'd continued to make the signs for the Merry Maker since I didn't have a artists bone in my body to make the signs on my own.

"I'm sure you'll get it where it needs to go without anyone seeing." His statement made me see what Darren had to say, since I'd not thought about it.

My mind was elsewhere.

On Peter Hill, Kristine Whitlock, and Carol Dunn to be exact.

Darren assured Vern he had a plan. I had no clue what it was but let him worry about it. I'd follow along for fear if I did question him, he'd drop the sign and break our agreement to be co-Merry Makers, and there I'd be. High and dry.

"Are you two coming to the costume contest sponsored by the Hibernian Society?" Vern asked with pride, since he was in his first term as the society's president.

"Of course we are. Violet wouldn't miss her first Halloweenie costume contest." Darren rocked back on the heels of his tennis shoes and hoisted the large ghost up to carry it out of the shed. "I mean, she competed in the beer stein contest during the St. Patrick's Day festival with Rhett. She has to make it, even if she has to go to the costume contest with me."

Vern grinned and shook his head.

"You two boys have always had that Strickland competitive side, ever since you could talk." What Vern said really caught my ear.

Rhett and Darren were cousins, and yet so many people around town talked about the two men as if they were enemies. I'd yet to figure it out, and neither of them had mentioned anything to me.

Give me time. That was all I needed to get down to the bottom of it.

"If we hurry, we can see it." Darren took off into the woods not using the path we'd taken but one he seemed to be forging on his own. He used the sign in his hands as if it were a small picture frame and not a life-size wood cutout of a ghost.

"What's the rush?" I asked, not sure if he'd heard me since he was way ahead of me.

The sun had fallen past the treetops so much it was hard to see through even the empty tree branches where the trees were shedding their leaves.

The sound of waves lapping up to shore guided me to where the woods and the sand met. Just beyond the lighthouse.

I scanned the beach area in search of Darren. Instead, the ghostly cutout was already sticking out of the sand near the path leading up to Holiday Fountain. The path where Peter Hill was murdered.

Darren appeared from behind the ghost and dusted off his hands. My shoes slipped and sank into the dry sand before I finally took them off so I could hasten over to Darren to protest the ghost before anyone noticed it.

"Now you know why this is a perfect spot to place the Merry Maker ghost." Darren knew the possibility of a murder would be very hard for me to turn down when it came to all the write-ups and sales of *the Junction Journal*. "You can't beat these fall sunsets."

"Fall sunsets?" I turned my eyes to the ocean, where the orange and yellow glow of the sun skittered across the top of the glass sea. The waves moved and glistened.

"Yeah. Think of it. The final Halloweenie party here on the beach." It was like he'd already planned it in his head. "This." He took his hands, placed them on my shoulders, and turned my body to where my head was already in position. "Nothing can beat a glorious night of fright but an amazing Holiday Junction sunset."

His hands caressed down my arms. A satisfied sigh escaped his lips before his hands landed around my waist in an almost embrace.

He said something, but I had no idea what it was. My neck caught his hot breath. My phone rang, taking me out of the moment.

"I… um…" I took a step away from his embrace, reached around, and took my phone from my back pocket. "It could be my mama."

The screen lit up.

"It's my dad."

CHAPTER SIX

"Don't forget the new carpet is being laid today. And finish the lighting in the house. I told Rhett you'd be over there to pay his guy the money." Mama had already started, and it wasn't even six in the morning.

Fortunately, she was in the bathroom getting ready for the day and didn't see my eyes roll. Mama was more than capable of paying the man. She only wanted me around Rhett not just because she'd settled on him being the big love of my life but also to see for herself if the two of us had some sort of chemistry.

"Did you forget about Peter Hill, Mama?" I called and threw the comforter off me. I tried to remind myself that my living situation with Mama in the one-room suite at the Jubilee Inn was temporary, and one day I'd be so grateful for this time spent together. I had really started looking forward to the day I would be able to wake up without hearing Mama barking all sorts of orders and plans for me.

"Of course I didn't. We've got to get to the emergency meeting today too." She popped her head out of the bathroom and looked at me as she swiped her lipstick over her lips. "That means no hem-hawing today. You need to get up, fix your hair, put on some makeup, and use that sweet southern accent to get information out of these people."

"How did you know about the emergency meeting?" I shouldn't have even asked. Mama always had a way of getting information out of people.

"While you were off doing the you-know-what"—Mama referred to my secret job as the Merry Maker by stringing three words together—"I was having some sweet tea downstairs with Kristine and Hubert. They were talking about it, since Hubert is running for a position on the board of the planning committee this fall."

She walked out of the bathroom, dressed head to toe in orange—down to her shoes. She had on a pair of mummy earrings, an embroidered mummy on her orange sweater, and even little mummies all over her slip-on shoes.

"Mama, you're starting to have theme days with your clothes." I sighed.

"Whatever it takes to show them I'm part of this community now. Embracing their holidays with glee so I can get on a committee." She bent down, looked into the dressing table mirror, and dug her fingertips into the roots of her hair. She gave it a little tease before moving her fingers down to the corner of her lips and swiping off any lipstick that'd gone outside of the lip liner.

Mama stood up and tugged on the hem of the sweater, rotating back and forth. Then she stepped back to get a full profile look until she was satisfied that she was ready to make her mummy appearance.

"Don't get me wrong." She walked over to her side of the bed and pulled out the drawer of the bedside table, where she hunted around until she picked out the appropriate jewelry. She slipped on a couple of different bangle bracelets and a few rings, and her wedding ring wasn't one of them.

I didn't tell her Daddy had called and left me a message. I'd not even listened to the message and knew I'd have to do that when she wasn't around.

"I love the Leading Ladies, but it just doesn't give me fulfillment like I thought it was going to. They are nice ladies." She grabbed her purse and flung it over her shoulder. "But they gossip and carry on about things I don't know."

"Mama, you love to gossip." I got up and walked into the bathroom.

"Yes, I do, and that's why I have to get on a committee—so I know who they are gossiping about." Her comment made me snicker. I should've known even Mama had a reason to join a committee. "I'll see you at the new house around noon!"

I heard the door shut.

Instead of trying to go back to bed for another hour, I'd decided to get up and get ready. The one person I knew I could question about Peter Hill at this hour would definitely be up.

Kristine Whitlock. Vern had made it sound like Kristine or Hubert could be a suspect in Peter's case, but I knew that couldn't be. They were the nicest couple and really took me by the hand when I moved here. They'd been so kind to Mama, and they owned the mayor, who really should be the suspect in question, but she was a Boston terrier. Somehow, I was fairly certain she didn't stab Peter.

Eventually, I'd gotten ready and looked around the room to make sure I'd gathered all the things I needed for my day at the office—and anything else, thanks to the press conference Matthew was supposed to have this morning. I'd also have to go to the library to check out the archives of the committee meetings and meet Rhett before noon and Mama at the new house. That left little time to do anything.

I was really looking forward to having my own space again. That meant I could have my own little home office, so if I did happen to go home for lunch, I could still keep an eye on the paper from home or even the news. As it was here and now with Mama's things all over, I had to make sure I had everything I needed for the day, and most of my work stuff did stay at the office.

As I hoisted my work bag up on my shoulder, I noticed the black sweater lying on top of Mama's suitcase. I schlepped the bag back to the floor, walked over, and picked up the sweater. It was not as gaudy as the other sweaters Mama had purchased for the holiday. This one was more slimming with a little puff to the shoulders and a small orange sequined pumpkin where a pocket would be. The pumpkin was no bigger than the palm of my hand. The sweater was something I could wear and be part of the community, as Mama would say.

The Jubilee Inn had taken on a skeleton theme for the festive Halloween holiday. They'd decorated the stairs of the inn with black cobwebs entwined with little neon spiders. At the base of the steps was a black tree decorated with little skeletons, skeleton keys, and a few eyeballs. Plastic pumpkins of various sizes, some black and some orange, sat around the floor.

The skeleton standing next to the complimentary coffee station wore a red beret and a festive, happy smile on its bony face, and its hand rested on top of one of the industrial coffeemakers. The lampshade sitting on the table was covered with a lacey black scarf and cage with a fake crow perched inside.

Kristine had really played up the inn-related aspect of the decorations. She had piled antique-style luggage items on top of one another for decorative effect but added a rubber white rat with a long skinny tail, which was just spooky enough to make the luggage not so cute.

"Look at you." Kristine eyeballed the sweater right off. "Are we starting to rub off on you or did Millie Kay hold you down like a little baby and put that on you?"

"You've gotten to know Mama really well over the last few months," I joked and flipped over the ceramic mug to pour some coffee.

"Are you staying this morning?" Kristine gave me another strange look, since I always hit her up for a to-go cup that would hold me over until I got to Brewing Beans. "I guess it is a little early." She looked at her watch.

Paisley's tapping nails against the hardwood floor alerted us to her impending arrival before she darted around the corner and danced around us.

"Good morning." Kristine's voice happily greeted the mayor. "Time to go potty." Paisley obviously knew that word because she bolted toward the inn's entrance. "Do you want to go with us?"

"You know?" I smiled. "I do." I glanced around, and Kristine must've known I was looking for a to-go cup. She pointed at the cabinet door next to my leg. After I opened it up, I said, "Thank you. Do you want one?"

"Nah. I've had my fair share of coffee this morning with all the gossip swirling around." She waited for me while I poured the coffee.

"Peter Hill?" I asked because I knew by now word had gotten around about his murder, and Kristine was someone I wanted to question.

"Yes. Can you believe it?" she asked with sadness in her tone. She frowned, which struck me as odd.

She opened the inn's front door, and Paisley bolted out.

"I'm not sure if you'd heard that it was Mama, Darren Strickland, and I who actually were with Hershal and Hazelynn when Peter toppled out of the coffin." I stopped where she was still holding the door to see how she reacted.

"Oh no." She drew a hand to her mouth. "I'd not heard that. The only thing I knew was they'd found him in Holiday Park, and now they have a meeting today to discuss what needs to be done about Halloweenie."

I wasn't sure how to bring up my knowledge of Paisley biting Peter because then I'd have to tell her I'd gone to see Vern or possibly let slip why I had seen him. I always had to keep the secret that I was the Merry Maker, which was hard to do.

"Have they ever canceled Halloweenie?" I asked.

"Years ago. I'm talking something like fifteen years ago." She didn't elaborate, but it didn't matter.

We walked down the steps of the inn, and I was careful not to trip over the pumpkins she'd placed on each stair. I glanced back and smiled when I saw the front. She'd put the same lacey black cobwebs across the front door and a happy skeleton in a chair, sitting there as if he were greeting everyone who was about to enter.

"I'm so sad for Vicki. They've been married a long time." Kristine let Paisley pick the direction for her morning sniff walk.

We took a left away from the park and headed in the direction of Brewing Beans, which was great for me, since I wanted to talk to the Hudsons before I really got my day started.

"You said he fell out of a coffin?" Kristine and I kept up with Paisley as she darted from object to object.

"The Hudsons asked me to do a review on the ghost walk so people would participate, and when Hershal tapped the fake coffin with his cane, a jack-in-the-box was supposed to pop out, but it was Peter Hill instead." I took a drink and waited for Kristine to say something, but she didn't. "You know I'll be looking into it even though Matthew asked me not to."

"Matthew? First-name basis now?" She glowed with anticipation. "You and Darren going public?"

"Public?" I played her question off with a laugh. "What are you talking about?"

"Fine." She slowly walked next to me with her eyes on Paisley. "If you don't want to admit it, you don't have to."

"Matthew told me to call him Matthew." I put my active imagination at ease. "It's difficult too."

We passed by all the pots filled with colorful mums along the sidewalk and in front of shops. Each shop throughout the downtown area had incorporated a cobweb theme, with one continuous web and spiders of all different sizes. The shops had different displays at their entrances and were all very festive, not so scary.

"Anyways, you know this will be a great story for the *Junction Journal*, and somehow I have to keep the ghost walk out of it." I'd yet to figure out an angle for the story in which Peter had fallen out of the coffin but did not include the ghost walk trail. "The Hudsons were devastated."

"I can only imagine. They've been talking about bringing the ghost walk back after all this time." Kristine was talking, but I kept trying to figure out how to bring up Mayor Paisley and her past with the victim.

So I just said it.

"I heard Mayor Paisley and Peter Hill had their own kinda issues." Kristine stopped walking as soon as I said it.

"I guess they did. I think animals know when someone isn't the most kindhearted person, and I'm guessing you have heard Peter Hill could be difficult." Kristine's head slightly shook as her lips turned down. "He has held a grudge against me and the Jubilee Inn ever since she bit him."

"Why would she bite him?" I asked, and we started to walk again.

"He came into the inn a few years back and wanted me to have Paisley resign as the mayor so the committee could vote for an actual mayor, who would be him, since he was the committee president." She gulped. "Used to be the committee president. Anyways, he marched into the office, and Paisley was napping. I was upstairs with a guest, and she bit him."

An audible sigh escaped her.

"I wasn't about to do that. An animal has been the mayor of Holiday Junction since the village was established, and I'm not about to change history." She whistled when Paisley disappeared. Paisley came running back. "He made it his mission to try to run the inn out of business. As president, he had the committee vote to use any extra money for the holiday's advertising. I'm sure I don't have to tell you, since you put the paper together. It didn't stop there."

The sun had completely popped over the buildings, chasing away the morning dew. The day was going to be really nice, with temperatures in the mid-sixties and plenty of sunshine. It would be what I'd call a perfect fall day if it weren't for Peter Hill's murder.

That little detail left a chill in the air no amount of warm sunshine could drive away.

"He made sure if there was something they could advertise to the local businesses, then we were out." She grinned. "I found a way to work around it, and it drove him nuts."

"Yeah? What's that?"

"You know the photo sessions we do with Mayor Paisley on the outside of the inn?" She looked at me. Right after I nodded, she continued, "I can use those to advertise her because she's a major reason people come to town. They all want to get a photo with the mayor. I own the mayor, and we live at the Jubilee Inn, so I make these meet and greets in front of the inn. It's the best advertising, and I can write it off my taxes."

"You are so smart. I bet that really made him mad." From what people had mentioned over the last twenty or so hours about Peter, I knew he'd not been the nicest person, but he certainly didn't deserve to die.

"He was so mad and tried so hard to fight it, but Diffy Delk assured him it was on the up-and-up." Diffy Delk was a local attorney. "He does the same with Dave."

Dave was the local rooster. He was known to keep law and order better than any security guard or police officer.

"It was the best revenge for what he'd been trying to do to Hubert and me." Kristine clicked her tongue for Paisley to come back. She did. "Chief Strickland came by last night while you were out and your mama was having some tea."

"He did?" I wondered why Mama didn't say anything.

"Oh yeah. He wanted to make sure I wasn't near Fountain Park between the hours Curtis had placed Peter's death. Of course I wasn't. Paisley and I had just finished a haunted meet and greet on the front porch for Meet the Mayor at Moonlight. It's very popular with the tourists."

Ding, ding.

The trolley came rumbling down Main Street.

Goldie Bennett brought the trolley to a stop and slid open the door.

"You getting on?" she asked me.

"We have to get back to the inn." Kristine picked Paisley up and cradled her in her arms.

"I'll see you later. Thanks for the coffee." I held up the cup before I got on the trolley. "Can you take me to the library?" I asked.

"Next stop!" Goldie hollered into the empty trolley and slammed the door shut. "Holiday Junction Library!"

CHAPTER SEVEN

"What are you going to the library for this early in the morning?" Goldie was about as subtle as a fart. She glanced in the rearview mirror at me. I could see her eyes, even though her orange visor was pulled down tight over her brows.

"I'm going to go through the Holiday Junction Planning Committee meeting minutes to see if I can find anyone who would have a motive to kill Peter Hill." My frankness opened a can of worms.

"There are plenty of people, and I'm sure you're going to see, if Nora recorded it, him and Carol Dunn squabbling." Again, someone else named Carol Dunn as an individual with a very clear motive. "From what I understand, he continued to keep her silent, even moved the vice president's chair clear to the other side of the table and not next to the president's chair."

The trolley passed the shops and the Jubilee Inn before Goldie hung a right to take the road that went around Fountain Park, where most of the official buildings in the village were located. These were places like the bank, lawyers' offices, government buildings, the nursing home, the pharmacy, the library, and the police station.

They were located on the mountain terrain side of town, which was literally a five-to-ten-minute walk from anywhere in Holiday Junction.

"Nora keeps the minutes for the committee, but she can tell you all about it. I doubt anyone will be in there this early but her." The trolley abruptly stopped. "Library!" Goldie hollered as if anyone else were on the trolley. She took her job seriously.

"While you're in there, give the poor girl tips on how to get a date. She's single, and she's a good catch." Goldie frowned. "Do you need me to swing back by any certain time to pick you up?"

"I'll call you if I do." I stepped off the trolley, and Goldie threw it in gear and took off to her next stop. I waved goodbye.

The Holiday Junction Public Library was like every other library I'd seen. Full of shelves with books, a children's area, and a reference area. It wasn't the largest library, but it also wasn't the smallest. However, it was definitely the quietest.

"Nora?" I called from the front when I didn't hear anything. No movement—nothing.

"Coming!" There was a faint yell from the back before she emerged with a box in her hands. "Hi, Violet." She had a big grin on her face. "What on earth are you doing here this morning?"

She sat the box on the reference desk, opened it, and took out a Halloween decoration. It was a black cat wearing a witch's hat sitting on top of a stack of books. She wiped some dust off the decoration before she was satisfied and sat it next to the box. Then she dug back in to take out another decoration.

"I was told the Holiday Junction Planning Committee kept their meeting archives here, and I wanted to get a look at them before the emergency meeting today." I didn't specifically say because I wanted to look into why someone might want to kill Peter Hill, but with how she looked at me, I knew she knew without me even saying.

"Sure. I know exactly where they are. I've been the secretary for about five years now." She set the decorations aside and had me follow her to the far-right corner of the library.

"Secretary. That means you did more than take minutes." I was happy to hear this.

"Yeah. When I started to work here five years ago, Peter had asked if they could use the conference room for their meetings. They'd been using the Jubilee Inn's hospitality room." She shrugged like she'd not known what had happened between Peter and Kristine about the whole mayor thing.

I didn't say anything. A good journalist kept all her secrets to herself. But I would definitely ask Kristine about that little bit of information she'd left out.

"Of course they could use it. It's the library. Free to everyone." She pointed at some old ledger and then at the computer. "I've got a lot of free time, so I've spent a lot of my off hours putting it all on the computer. Do you have a library card?"

"No." I shook my head.

"You could access them online if you did." She clasped her hands. "I'll go get you signed up for one. That way you can hop on whenever you like."

"Thanks, Nora." I sat down at the computer.

"Great. I'll be back with your card." She left me there with the computer and the ledgers.

Figuring the computer would be more up to date or at least from this century, not to mention from Peter's term, I started there. The function was pretty much what I was used to for any sort of town council meeting or committee meeting. The basic call to meeting in which the committee members were listed and their presence or absence noted, a few house-keeping things, and discussion of the posted agenda along with concerns from the public.

Nora had everything timed down to the minute and who said what. She'd even used perfect punctuation, including quotation marks for the members' dialogue.

I moved the mouse to the custom date field and selected a few years back. I was most interested in seeing when Carol Dunn had joined, and I continued to click the dates until I noticed that underneath the label of Vice President was Carol's name.

"Voilà." I clicked on the year, which was five years ago. Then I hit the print button. The printer next to the computer started to spit out a lot of printed pages. I realized I'd not selected a page range on the print settings. I wanted just the one page with the date on it so I could ask the Holiday Junction Planning Committee about that time.

"You find something?" Nora asked, breaking the silence of the empty library.

"I was trying to find out when Carol Dunn started on the committee." I didn't want to bother Nora when I could easily find that on my own. If I had a question, I would definitely ask her.

I heard the squeaky wheels of her book cart before I saw her walking behind it on her way back toward me.

"That was about six years ago." Nora was off a year.

"Five." I corrected her but should've known better because she came back to set me straight.

"Nope. She was on the committee as a voting member without a title for a year. Then she stepped up to the vice president role when the person in the position had stepped down." She stopped the cart and bent over to look at the screen. "That was when she and Peter started to get into little..." She stopped talking and looked at me with big wide-open eyes. "You don't think Carol killed Peter?" her brows knitted. "You do," she gasped, flinging her hand up to cover her mouth.

"I didn't say that. I'm only checking a few leads." I didn't want to alarm anyone, but Nora looked alarmed. "If you have any reason to believe she didn't have motive, I'd love to know."

Now was a perfect opportunity for Nora to tell me anything she knew about the committee and the dynamics among the members.

She pulled out the chair next to me where the other desk and computer were located. Her shoulders slumped. Heavy sighs escaped her, and she looked down at her hands folded between her knees.

"I guess I never really thought about it. They don't get along. Didn't." Her voice trailed off, and her head shot up. "But I don't think Carol could've done something like that, even though he did shoot down every single idea she had."

"He did?" I knew it would take some time to go through the minutes to find anything that alluded to that.

"Yes, but in his defense, he did have to look out for the good of the village." She gulped. "Though Carol did have some great ideas." She laid her hand on her chest. "At least, I thought they were good, but what do I know?"

My theory didn't sit well with Nora. Her eyes darted around like she was trying to find something in her mind before she looked back at me, gnawing on her lips like she didn't want something to come out.

"Nora." I had to use a calm voice if I was going to get anything out of her. I pushed a piece of my blond hair behind my ear and put my hands on my thighs, leaning a little closer to her. "If you know something, you can tell me, and I'll check it out, or you can anonymously turn in a tip. I'm not saying Peter Hill was the best guy in the world, but think about his wife. Any family members. They need peace, and that's why I do what I do."

"When you put it that way, it doesn't sound like I'm snitching, and I'm not," she assured me, shaking her head. "Everyone on the committee will tell you that Peter was mean to Carol. He wasn't really the nicest man at all. He interrupted the meeting, and it was hard for me to keep minutes because he didn't want to stay on the agenda. Carol would ask what good an agenda was if we didn't stick to it. Then after that, she told him she was going to run against him, and I thought he was going to go nuts."

Nora licked her lips then sucked in the bottom one.

"What is it, Nora?" I needed to know.

"After Carol filed the necessary paperwork to run in the next election, Peter got wind of it. I'm not sure who, but someone told him, and he started to hold secret meetings here in the library." She frowned. "I knew I should've told someone, but he's the highest-ranking office holder in Holiday Junction."

"Did you take notes?" I asked, wondering if she meant a real meeting.

"Oh no. This wasn't any sort of planned meeting. It was strange, really." She sat back. Her shoulders fell from her ears.

"How so?" I wondered. I wanted to take advantage of her more relaxed state by continuing to ask her questions.

"Peter Hill never came to the library other than for the one meeting a month. He didn't even bother helping me set up the room or asking if he could donate to the library. Past presidents did do that. But not Peter. He seemed to be too busy or always in a rush. When he started to come, and a few other committee members joined him, I knew they were trying not to be seen by the public." She shifted, turned around, and pointed at the far corner of the library. "They would stand over there and whisper."

"Did you ever overhear anything he was saying to them?" I asked.

"Don't judge me, but I did try once or twice." She gave a slight smile. "I wasn't very good at it, and they heard me both times. They would move to a different bookshelf and continue talking because I made it look like I was straightening the shelves where they had been talking. But I did overhear Peter say things like Carol was out to get him and how she was a woman and could get the rest of the women in Holiday Junction to vote for her."

"Do you know what Carol was upset about with Peter to run against him?" I asked.

"Sure. There are countless things. He never let her talk at the meetings. I made sure I put that in the meeting notes, and he'd never know because he never read them after I put them together," she said. "He was supposed to sign off on them, and he did, but he just signed them. Never looked at them. I could've written in there the committee had overturned his elected position, and he'd never know. He'd have signed off on it and then been outed. I didn't."

"Hmm." I took in everything she told me because it sure did look as though Carol had a major motive.

"I thought they'd all put it behind him since Peter and Sawyer were talking," she mentioned in passing as though it didn't matter, but to my trained ear, it all mattered.

"When did you see them talking?" I asked.

"Here." The creases between her eyes deepened as if she said something wrong. "Back there."

"You mean Sawyer was in one of the private meetings Peter held here?" I wanted to make sure I was following her when I noticed her demeanor had changed. "I know you don't want to get involved, but it would be a great help to the investigation."

She nodded. It was all I needed to see to confirm the meeting.

"Do you remember anything else that would make Carol so mad that she'd want him dead? Urgently?" Something must have sent her over the edge, and I needed to know if it was enough for her to be a suspect.

"The ghost walk." Her words shook me to my core, and her face flushed white. "Oh my gosh. Peter was found on the ghost walk, wasn't he?"

"She called an emergency meeting for today, didn't she?" I asked.

"Yes. I mean she would be taking over the position." Nora swallowed hard. "That would make it easy for her to step into the president role without having to do the election."

Her eyes bolted open. Carol's motive had sunk in for her.

My phone chirped.

"Excuse me." I wasn't sure what I was supposed to say, but I knew I wanted to keep some specific details for the article. I looked at my phone and saw the text message was from Darren.

No "good morning." No "how are you doing after finding a dead body?" Even a "did you sleep well?" would've been nice.

Nope. He just said there was a press conference in ten minutes at the Holiday Fountain.

"I've got to go." I jumped up, plucked the printed pages from the printer, stuck them in my bag, and continued to gather up my things. "You mentioned I could get on the archives online with a library membership."

"Yes. Are you leaving now?" she asked.

"Chief Strickland is holding a press conference in a few minutes, and I don't want to be late." I pointed up front. "Can you get me that card?"

"It's up at the desk waiting for you." She stayed put in the chair. "You know, Carol isn't the only one who had a beef with Peter Hill. Nettie Banks did too. She was the vice president who stepped down when Carol took her place."

"You mean Bubbly Boutique's Nettie Banks?" I asked.

"Yeah. Peter canceled the beauty pageant for Halloweenie, and she was so mad because she wanted Fern to get the title. Something about if you get so many beauty pageant titles in a year, you get to go to national pageants. Those are the ones that give scholarships to winners to go to college and stuff." Nora was full of information. Now I knew exactly where I needed to come if I had a question.

For now, those questions would have to wait.

"What time is the emergency meeting?" I asked on my way out of the library.

"Noon!" she yelled.

CHAPTER EIGHT

Outside the library, the day had turned grey. It fit the mood that blanketed Holiday Junction. Death lingered in the air, and I didn't mean because of the frightful Halloween decorations, though they were very fitting for the Halloween season.

Darren was waiting for me near the fountain and gave me a very slight wave when our eyes caught. The vendors were putting their finishing touches on their tents before the big festival opening tomorrow. They'd all have some sort of dangling lights that either glowed orange or were shaped like pumpkins, witches' brooms, or even scary cats. Those things didn't scare me. They were actually cute. The things like dead people falling out in front of me were what kept the creepy holiday from sitting too well with me.

The smell of roasted pumpkin seeds and heavy salt came from the large cast-iron pot in one of the vendor's booths and made my mouth water. When I passed, I couldn't help lingering for a second to see what else they had to offer. I'd not eaten anything all morning, and my stomach was letting me know.

That or it was just because I loved all the foods this time of the season.

Popcorn bubbled over in the popcorn machine, and I stood there for a moment too long watching the owner scoop out the freshly salted corn into a plastic bag before they drizzled caramel over the top and sealed it with a twisty tie.

"Violet! Come on!" Darren yelled for me. "It's starting!"

Putting the treats in the back of my mind but not forgetting about going back to buy some for the office today, I picked up my step and made a beeline for Darren. More and more people were gathering in front of the fountain, making it hard to get a good view of the setting up of the press conference.

"You aren't going to believe what I just found out." I rattled off all the information Nora had told me while some people put out three chairs on each side of the podium. A woman walked up and sat in the first chair to the podium's right. She was dressed in a pair of khaki riding pants, knee-high boots, and a long burnt-orange knitted sweater. "I think Carol Dunn is a more likely suspect than Nettie Banks. You didn't even tell me Nettie was the vice president before Carol."

"How was I to know?" Darren asked.

"And I didn't sleep a wink. Thank you for asking." I noted and glanced around to see if anyone I knew was there. "The emergency meeting is going to be at the library at noon. I have a problem."

"Only one?" Darren joked. His eyes twinkled when he smiled at me, as though he wanted a reaction.

"Yes. One." I dug down into my bag to get my little tape recorder so I could make an audio recording of the press conference. "I have to be at my house at noon. So you're going to have to go to the planning committee meeting at noon at the library."

"I can't do that." Darren acted as though I'd just asked him to cut off a limb. "Violet, I'm sorry, but I can't just gallivant all over town doing what you need me to do. I have a job. A business to run, if you've not realized it."

"A bar? That's a job? You get two customers in there." I didn't need to remind him of the Easter Bunny and Tooth Fairy drunks who probably stayed the night there, and I never asked or wanted to know about them.

"I get way more than two customers. It's my job. It's what I have decided to do for a living, and I've got to live. That means you're going to have to find someone else to go." Not that it wasn't the end of the world if he didn't go.

At least Nora would be there and taking better minutes than I could if I was physically present. It was the one part of Darren's observation of me that set my alarm off.

"You're right. I'm sorry. I had a silly moment thinking we were going to solve this together. Kinda like the Merry Maker." I leaned into him and whispered the last part.

"That is over after this holiday." He gave me a hard nod. "I mean it. No more. I'm out."

"We'll see." I sighed. I was happy to hear the microphone squeak on and see Matthew appear at the podium.

He flicked it with his finger a couple of times to make sure it was turned on before he leaned over it.

"Testing, one, two, three," he said and jerked away when it echoed too loudly. Someone came over and fixed it, and he repeated his test, this time sounding so much better.

The crowd's chatter came to an abrupt halt, and all eyes were on Matthew.

"My name is Matthew Strickland." He looked around the crowd. Several reporters stood at the front with their hands sticking up in the air. A microphone jutted toward the podium with their station logo on the sides. "I'm the chief of police in Holiday Junction. Yesterday afternoon, Peter Hill, the local Holiday Junction Planning Committee president, was found on the path between the Holiday Junction Park and the ocean. Curtis Robinson, our coroner, has ruled Mr. Hill's death a homicide. We will not be reporting any details about the murder except that he was stabbed one time in the back."

The news reporters groaned with disappointment.

"Settle down. I know you wanted more information than this, but Peter has been a long-time citizen and friend to the community. He's spent a great deal of his life serving to better Holiday Junction and raise his family here. We are sad for Vickie and their grown children and want to respect their privacy at this time. By the same token, we are here today to ask for any sort of video footage or photos you might've taken at all yesterday either at Holiday Park or the sea near the lighthouse. Even if you think it's nothing. The slightest photo or blip in a photo can give us so many details. Something that seems insignificant to you could be what breaks this case wide open."

He talked about where the public could forward their photos and videos before he introduced the next speaker.

"I would like to invite Carol Dunn up. She will be the interim president until the election this fall. She will be able to give you some insight on the festival and where we stand with the activities moving forward." Matthew glanced over his shoulder at the lady I'd seen earlier.

"Is she wearing horse-riding pants?" I asked.

"Who?" he asked.

I pointed at the woman who was sitting in the chair next to Carol Dunn and Chief Strickland.

"Millard Ramsey. She owns the wild stallion farm." Darren had failed to mention that to me.

"Wild stallion as in horses?" I asked under my breath so as not to disturb everyone around me who was listening.

"Yes. Tourists love to ride horses on the beach." Darren crossed his arms and twisted back to listen. "Until Peter Hill made a motion to stop the rides because of beach erosion or something like that. But I believe the committee tabled it until the next meeting, but from what I heard at the bar when some committee members came by for a drink, they were seriously considering voting for Peter Hill's idea."

"So was she the Headless Horseman?" I asked, though the time frame Curtis Robinson had given for Peter's murder wasn't when we saw the Headless Horseman.

"Her son is the Horseman, but no one is supposed to know." Darren's eyes narrowed. "Her son," he repeated.

"Yep. And if someone disrespected your mom in public, you'd take up for her, wouldn't you." My statement hit home. I watched as it landed hard on him. "Which makes me wonder if her son is a potential suspect."

"Our list is growing by the second." Darren lifted his chin in the air and looked around the crowd.

"Our list? Now you want to help." I snorted.

"Like you said, I know people around here." He tugged the strap of my bag on my shoulder. "Let's get out of here and go to your office so we can make a clear plan."

"Sounds good to me." I didn't need to stand around and listen to Carol Dunn express her grief for someone she didn't give two hoots about. They would be empty words, and right now, I didn't have time for anything other than substance, which also meant food.

"Where are you going?" Darren asked when I didn't follow him toward the path to the lighthouse. One, because the last time we were there, we found Peter, and I just didn't want to do that today. And two, I wanted some popcorn from the vendor.

"I'm going to go back to the office because your father"—I emphasized "your"—"didn't say anything we didn't already know. Now I've wasted time I could have used to get real answers from people who had good motive to kill Peter Hill."

"Do I need to remind you how it's not our place to find the killer?" Darren had yet to get the hang of things. Or at least of how I did things or even how my mind worked.

And it was my duty to take the time to tell him while he followed me down the path and across the seaside shops. He lingered in front of his bar for a moment before picking up his pace again to catch back up with me, at which point I educated him on just how I liked things.

"That means…" I unlocked the door of the office cottage and shut the screen behind us, leaving the main door open because the fall breeze whipping off the ocean felt so good and refreshing as it floated through the cottage. I stood there enjoying the fresh air while Darren stopped just inside to let me finish what I'd been saying. "I take my job as a reporter very seriously. When there's a murder, I don't even think about your father and his job or duties to Holiday Junction. I am thinking about the article and the information that needs to get out to the public. That means that I'm doing my job and making your mom happy."

I passed by him and noticed the crown molding for the second office that'd been lying in the hallway had been moved.

The cottage was owned by Rhett Strickland, Darren's cousin, and I'd been able to get him to lease the run-down cottage to his aunts and move the *Junction Journal* from their home to here. I had to ask him to do some major repairs.

I imagined that in its heyday, the home was gorgeous not only on the inside but from the seaside looking up past the dunes. The clapboard siding had been replaced, as had the shutters in the two-bedroom home. It was small but perfect for what the *Junction Journal* needed.

Plus, the view was spectacular and helped me come up with all sorts of stories, features, and articles for the paper. The view also helped me think of creative ways to work on cases such as Peter Hill's, which meant there was no time to dillydally.

"We have Carol Dunn, Nettie Banks, and a whole slew of documents we can go through to see who else might've had some motive." I walked toward the office but had my head turned back to Darren. "I think we can make—" I started to say when I walked into the office and found Louise and Marge Strickland waiting for me.

Marge Strickland sat in my chair with her legs crossed. Her bobbed silver hair hit perfectly at her cheekbones and framed her petite face and pointy nose. Her orange lipstick matched her orange fingernails. She wore a brown shawl, khaki pants, and brown saddle loafers. She was the more elegant of the two Strickland women.

I'd expect no different since she was a Strickland by blood and not by marriage like Louise, Darren's mother, and Matthew's wife.

"Mom." Darren pushed past me, hurried over to his mother, and kissed her on the cheek. "And Marge."

He moved around the desk to greet her just the same as he did his mom.

"Darren, shouldn't you be at work?" Louise's perfectly shaped brows rose, not a wrinkle on her forehead. She had a much different style than her sister-in-law.

Louise wore a deep green caftan dress that flowed well past her feet. The trim of the dress had little pumpkins along the edges, and the sleeves had a long ruffle down each side.

Her style was amazing. I would've loved to grow old as gracefully as she appeared to be doing.

"I was walking Violet back to the office from the press conference." He talked to them while I searched my head to see if I'd mentioned the Merry Maker.

"Be sure you come for dinner tonight." Louise made it clear she needed to talk to me and that Darren was to go to work.

Darren waffled back and forth between his mom and me before he finally said, "I'll talk to you later."

"Yeah. See ya." I sighed and turned back to Marge and Louise. "Good morning." I greeted them as if we were starting over. "I've got some good leads on the Peter Hill article I'm working on."

"That's why we are here." Marge stood up and gestured for me to sit. She moved in front of my desk and paced between the two windows that looked out over the dunes and down to the sea. The sheer long, flowing curtains on each side of the open windows danced in the wind that passed through.

"We are very pleased with the numbers not only for subscriptions to the physical paper, but the online paper is starting to get up into a million views a week," she continued.

She turned toward me and clasped her hands in front of her, a smile on her face.

"That's great!" I squealed in delight. "I'm so glad. Did you look into the insights and what was getting the most views?"

"The online paper has a great read-through rate. The ads seem to be helping, too, but now that Peter Hill is no longer in charge of ads for the Holiday Junction Planning Committee, I fear the ads will go down." Louise sat up on the edge of the chair and put her hand on top of the desk.

"I told you, Louise, that we would worry about that." By the tone of Marge's voice, I sensed there was an issue.

"You might as well tell me now what you're trying not to tell me because I can see there's clearly a concern with Peter no longer alive." My eyes narrowed as I watched the sisters-in-law give each other a subtle look. "You two had something with him about the advertising, didn't you?"

"Holiday Junction is a small town, and it's all about who you know." Louise was the first to admit I was right in my observation. "Favors aren't unusual around here."

"Favors are one thing, but when you have arguments with people, it's another." Marge's hands moved from the clasped position to folded and guarded, and a scowl formed along her face. "That was what Louise did when Matthew was up for reelection. She made a deal with Peter Hill."

"What kind of deal?" My eyes shifted between the two, waiting to see who was going to talk first.

"I only made the deal for the life of the *Junction Journal*." Louise suddenly made it very clear that the *Junction Journal* had been living off ad spend from the ads Peter Hill was taking out. He used the extra funds from the planning committee for that. Kristine had told me that was exactly why she never advertised in the newspaper.

"And when Carol Dunn's husband, Sawyer, wanted to put an ad in the paper, we weren't able to do it because Peter Hill didn't like Sawyer. Carol was the vice president of the committee, but we were strongly advised by Peter Hill to not take their money." Marge told the story about how Peter Hill had made sure the advertising took care of his friends and family but didn't care about the others as long as his favors were done. Matthew Strickland would have all the votes to stay in office.

Though it wasn't truly illegal, it surely wasn't on the up-and-up, which made the Strickland sisters look a little guilty or even as if they'd had a motive to kill Peter themselves.

"You two could be seen as having a motive to have killed him." I could tell by their nonreaction they'd already thought of that.

"We have an alibi. We were at the Leading Ladies all morning, and we were at home all night before that. And it's my understanding the murder occurred in the wee hours of the morning." Louise had given me more information than her husband at his press conference. "And neither of us go out before noon."

"Noon?" I jerked up to look at the clock on the wall and noticed Mama's golf cart parked in front of the cottage and her striding up the front walk with her purse dangling off her arm. "I was supposed to go meet my mom and the contractor at the house."

Marge and Louise looked out the window and saw Mama.

"Violet, you aren't going to believe what I heard about the Stricklands and the *Junction Journal*!" Mama hollered as soon as she bolted through the screen door. "I just met with my contractor, Sawyer Dunn." Mama continued to talk from the hallway as she hung her pocketbook on the coat-tree next to the door.

"Mama, in here!" I yelled, hoping to get her to stop talking.

That didn't happen. She kept yammering on and on about the Dunns.

"He said the Strickland sisters are in big trouble with the paper now that Peter Hill is dead."

"Mama!" I yelled again with a tight smile on my face to try to cover up the embarrassment. "Mama!"

"They only let people advertise who will keep them in power. Whoo-wee, my palms are itching." She stopped shy of the door, scratching her palm. "That means I'm gonna get some money." She finally walked in. "Why didn't you tell me you had company?"

"I tried to, but you kept on talking," I said flatly.

"Don't you roll your eyes at me in that tone of voice." Mama walked past the office door. "I'm gonna put on a pot of coffee. You ladies staying?"

It was one of those times Mama didn't really care if they would be around to have a cup of coffee but wanted to get past the uncomfortable situation she'd put us all in.

"I'm sorry about that." I picked up my bag off the floor and stood up. "I'll clear out my things and be gone in a few."

"What are you doing?" Louise put her hand out.

"I'm sure you don't want me working for you or the paper now that this little bit of information could be exposed, and clearly it's out there." I couldn't with a clear conscience write about the murder of Peter Hill and his influence on the community without also showing the dealings he had in the community, the *Junction Journal* being one of them.

"No way. That was why we came here." Marge glared at Louise. "To help clean up Louise's mess. We had a file from the trial, but it appears to be missing."

Trial? I wondered what she was talking but Louise wasn't about to let Marge accuse her of being messy.

"My mess? Don't look at me like that. I didn't get rid of the file." Louise jerked around in the chair and looked at Marge. "You liked the perks of being the chief's sister just as much as I liked the perks of being his wife. It's part of the gig."

"So I have a job?" I wanted to confirm that before I started thinking about how I could spin the details of their little advertising-budget scheme with Peter Hill.

"Yes." Both made peace for the moment to agree on me staying.

"I can print an article where we can talk about how the *Junction Journal* had in the past done what other newspapers have done and endorsed a candidate running for election." As I told them my idea, the stress and tension fell off their faces and bodies.

"What about Millie Kay?" Marge asked, eyeballing me.

They'd obviously been privy to Mama's idea of hearsay, overhearing, and all things gossip.

"I've got an idea." Louise stood up and excused herself, leaving Marge and me to wonder what she was up to. "I was just coming to see you about that coffee," Louise said, the sweetness dripping off her.

Little did she realize that Mama could smell a sweet talker from miles away. But good on Mama—she played right along.

"Here," I heard Mama say, "you take this one, and I'll get another one."

"First, why don't you follow me?" The sound of Louise's shoes and Mama's shuffle came back down the hall toward the office, but instead of coming into my office, they went into the other room across the hall.

The second office.

"Marge and I were talking about the office and how we were going to use this as a joint office. We are here because Violet has not only doubled the subscriptions but tripled them." Louise made it sound good but the fact the subscriptions had tripled wasn't that big of a deal, since we'd started with only around fifty subscribers when I'd taken over. "And we think she needs a full-time secretary more than us here looking over her shoulder."

"Do you mean an assistant?" Mama corrected her as she played along. "You're right. Violet could use a full-time assistant with all the perks."

Before too long, Mama had a better job and perks than I had as my new assistant.

"I told you I was going to get some money." Mama held up her red palm, which she'd been scratching. "Isn't this going to be great?" Mama asked between her closed-toothed smile, waving her red palm at Marge and

Louise as they walked down the sidewalk of the office. "We are going to be working together."

"Yeah. Great," I grumbled because I truly had no say in what Marge and Louise did with the newspaper. I had no sort of ownership, no sort of hiring privileges, and certainly no say in Mama's new position.

"Which means we need to get on down to Dunn Contractors and pick out those light fixtures for your house." Mama was stretching the term "house" to mean the garage apartment I was going to live in behind the house she'd purchased from Rhett Strickland. "He said that his wife would be there to help if he wasn't."

"His wife?" Now Mama had my attention.

"Mm-hmm. Carol Dunn." Mama grinned, knowing Carol Dunn was at the top of my suspect list.

"Only if we take the trolley." I wasn't about to get in that golf cart with her.

CHAPTER NINE

"Did you talk to Nora about dating?" Goldie Bennett started in as soon as I sat down.

"You were going to give dating advice?" Mama looked so shocked. "I mean, we have strict commandments when it comes to dating." She sat straight as a stick with her ankles crossed. "It was how I got your daddy."

Did she forget that she'd also left my daddy?

"First off, Nora needs to know that she's got to dress a little better. Impressing the mama and daddy of her suitor is important. Which means she needs to be chivalrous and state right off the bat she needs to be treated like royalty." As Mama gave Goldie her dating commandments, I was starting to see why I was single. "Which circles right back around to how she looks. Nora is a pretty girl, but it looks like it takes her less than five minutes to get ready. Now that just won't do. It takes me five minutes to put on my second coat of lipstick."

I sighed and stared out the trolley's windows. The smell of the sea had long passed as the trolley made its way to the countryside of Holiday Junction. Freshly rolled hay wafted through the windows and reminded me of taking hayrides at the local pumpkin patch when I was a child. Those memories included Mama and Daddy, reminding me I'd yet to call him back. I needed to.

"Not that I see Nora doing this, but she certainly doesn't need to chase any men, flirt with every one of them, or cross the line of a hoochie mama." Goldie snorted out loud, just encouraging Mama to continue. "She needs to master dating. If he likes to boat, hike, or just read, she needs to be able to do all of those activities and seem like she enjoys them. Ain't that right, Violet?"

"Mm-hmm." I just agreed, though I was still thinking about Carol Dunn and how to approach the subject of Peter Hill.

"Now, I don't know if Nora has any exes, but she's going to run into them in this small village if she does. She needs to know how to handle those situations. And don't get me started on how she needs to expect a big wedding. Full wedding regalia portrait and all. China registry and at least nine or ten bridesmaids." Mama had done married off poor Nora. "Don't get me going on her fingernails. Poor girl chews them down to the nubbins. But most important of all, she's gonna have to realize she's gonna always play second fiddle to the spouse's parents. That's why Violet hasn't found the right man yet. Right, Violet?"

"Whatever you say, Mama." I found Mama's commandments on dating similar to directions southerners gave. *You know, go yonder and turn by the big flagpole. Once you turn there, you'll go about 'nother mile or two until you see that big rock on the side of the road. Once you're past that, you'll see a gravel road to the right. Take that road and you'll be there.*

Only southerners understood one another, and by the way Goldie Bennett was looking at Mama when we'd made it back to downtown Holiday Junction, Mama had entertained her.

"She's a fun one, your mama." Goldie didn't have to tell me that when I got off the trolley.

"After this I thought we'd go to the jiggle joint to get a celebratory drink for my new job." Mama stood on the sidewalk in front of Brewing Beans and pointed at the alley next to it. "Let's go."

"Behind there?" I peeked down the small space, and a chill crawled up my leg.

"That's where Dunn Contractors is located." Mama led the way behind Brewing Beans, where we walked up a flight of metal stairs to a door with

Dunn Contractors lettered on it in vinyl. "Knock, knock," Mama said, announcing her entrance as she opened the door.

The office space was wide open with three desks. All three of them faced the door, and the view from the windows was breathtaking.

You could take in the ocean as far as it went. The lighthouse stood tall. Even though it was sunny out, I could see the lights atop Darren's home rolling around and a flicker of orange from where he'd changed the bulbs for Halloweenie.

My breath caught and my heart jumped when I caught sight of the small outside deck of the lighthouse. Darren and I had sat there for a long time one night.

"Hi do," Mama said to someone I recognized as Carol Dunn from the online searching I'd done at the library. "I'm Millie Kay Rhinehammer, assistant to the editor in chief of the *Junction Journal*." She pointed at me. "My daughter, Violet. And we are here to talk to you about a motive to have killed Peter Hill and to pick out some lights for Violet's apartment."

"Excuse me?" Carol Dunn's look of horror was worse than Peter Hill's look of death.

"Let me talk." I moved past Mama with my hand outstretched. "I'm Violet Rhinehammer, and your husband, Sawyer, just met my mama over at her new house on Heart Way."

Carol shook my hand but with a little reluctancy.

"Sawyer told me about that project." She pulled her hand away and stuck them both in the front pockets of her long-sleeved black romper. There was a subtle hint of the Halloweenie spirit on the chest pocket, where she'd stuck a pin that read Happy Halloween. Other than that, she didn't seem to be too much in the holiday spirit for someone who slid right into the role she'd been trying to secure, based on what I understood of the last few years.

President of Holiday Junction Planning Committee.

"While we do need to pick out some lights for my apartment, I'm also wanting to talk to you about Peter Hill. I'd love to get your side of the relationship between the two of you." I was going to dance around the fact that Peter had shot down every single idea Carol had brought to the committee, but maybe Mama's tactic was just better.

"Here goes nothing." I shrugged and looked at Mama, who gave a wide smile. Then I turned back to Carol. "You see, all the research I've done for the article going in the *Junction Journal* points at an unhealthy working environment between you and Peter. The two of you never saw eye to eye on a project."

"Eye to eye?" She cackled. "You mean he never laid an eye on what I had proposed?"

"Exactly. I understand by reading the minutes taken at the meetings, he shot down anything you had to offer. Also, I was told you were planning on running against him in the next election for the president role."

"Something you don't have to do if he's dead." Mama's head swiveled as she pointed that out with a little more vigor than necessary. "Just admit you are a tiny bit happy you get to sample the job before they haul you off to jail."

"Mama." I gasped and swung my head toward her. "Here." I dug down into the pocket of my bag and pulled out my credit card. "I want to get outfits to wear throughout the event. You know the kind you have with the cute pumpkins and stuff." I knew I was going to regret sending her there. "Why don't you go over to Emily's Treasures and check out what they've got?"

"You're joking, right?" Mama was more surprised at me asking her to go get me an outfit than I was.

"Does it look like I'm joking? You've bought my clothes plenty of times." She did, but I never wore them.

"I'll be right back in a jiffy." She snatched the credit card from my fingers. Then she shook it at me. "I know exactly what I want to get. I told Emily the other day—'Emily,' I said"—Mama loved to retell her conversations—"'my daughter, Violet Rhinehammer. You know, the editor of the *Junction Journal*.'"

Carol shifted her weight to the side and took her hands out of her pockets. She crossed her arms over her chest and tilted her head. Her lips pressed together.

"Of course she knew you, but I said, 'My Violet would look so good in this outfit.'" Mama smiled so big. "Well, I'd love to stay to see how all this turns out, but I better get going if I want to get that outfit before someone else grabs it right up."

Carol and I stood there in silence until we heard the last of Mama's footsteps on the metal stairs.

"I'm sorry. Mama gets a little ahead of herself." I needed to apologize for Mama. Something I was getting really good at since she'd moved to Holiday Junction.

"I get it. I look guilty. I admit it, but I would never kill someone over a committee job. I only want to do what's best for Holiday Junction, which means if the tourists come, the shops want to expand, grow, and hire Sawyer to do the work. It's an equal opportunity for everyone." When Carol put it that way, she didn't seem so scary or deadly or even a killer.

"Not even if you got upset all those times he shot down any sort of idea or new projects you'd try to propose at any of the meetings?" I watched her body language.

All reporters had to learn to do that if they were going to be good at their job. There were so many times I'd been interviewing someone, and they'd shrug off a question, but the slightest wiggle of the shoe, straightening of the shoulders, or even twitch of the lip told me they were avoiding something. That was when a good reporter continued to pepper them with questions in hopes they'd break.

But Carol didn't. She was as cool as a cucumber.

I wasn't that threatening either.

"You don't hold any sort of grudge or malice toward him for not letting Dunn Contractors run ads in the journal?" I tried to be as direct as Mama to see if Carol would confess. "I mean, if I couldn't run an ad because the man I was on a committee with had some sort of vendetta against me because he bought up all the ad space, I'd be fairly upset. Upset enough that over time I'd want it to stop, and the only way for it to stop would be to get rid of the one making it happen."

"Look, Violet." Carol shook her head and motioned for me to sit down as she took a seat behind one of the three desks. "Am I a saint? No. But am I a killer? Absolutely not. I knew he was doing those things, so we got smarter. We started to go door to door with flyers for Dunn Contractors. My husband went to each shop and put business cards at the counter. He even leased some space from Rhett Strickland to erect our own billboards. I'm lucky I'm not dead because Peter went crazy and tried to get the committee to vote down the billboards when we had plenty of billboards here, only they weren't from Dunn. I decided to run so I could work my way up the committee and eventually run for the presidential role. If I can get rid of the ad scheme he was running, though it was hard to prove it, since he was hiding behind the funding from the committee, I know I can effectively continue to use the ad spend money by including all the shops and business regardless of my personal feelings about the owners."

She made so much sense that I was clearly going down the wrong path to point at her as the suspect.

"It will bring tourism and keep up all our profits. What benefits one should benefit the others. That's how I'm trying to make sure our tourism doesn't slow down like it has in the past few years from Peter's lack of good advertising," she finished.

"Can you tell me why Peter had such a hard time with you and Sawyer?" I asked.

"Sure. Years ago, there was a murder during the Halloweenie festival. Peter Hill and a few others gave witness statements about who they saw commit the murder. There was no way the man put behind bars did it. He worked for us, and at the time of the murder, he was at our house, sleeping off a bender."

"A bender? You mean drunk?" I had to know for sure what type of substance this man used.

"Alcohol." She frowned. "He was a good kid. He didn't hurt anyone. Even if they said he was robbing them. He had no reason to rob them. We paid him nicely. Don't get me wrong, Jay has a temper, but I don't think he killed Peter's father."

"Peter's father?" I asked. She confirmed with a solid nod. "Can you give me his name?"

"Jay Renner." She sighed.

"Why would Peter hold something like Jay Renner's arrest against you?" It wasn't adding up to a good reason. I just couldn't believe Jay would go to jail on Peter Hill's statement alone.

"We've been fighting for Jay's release all these years." She gnawed on her lip. "The problem is with all of this happening right now, it's probably not a coincidence Peter was killed." She hesitated. "Normally I wouldn't talk about this and certainly not to a reporter, but if there's the possibility someone thinks Sawyer or I did it, then I need to tell my story."

"I'm willing to print it." I pulled out my notebook from my bag and crossed my legs to use my top thigh as a desk so I could write. "Can I also record this conversation?"

"Yes." Carol waited for me to get all set up before she started. "Do you want me to start from the beginning?"

"Yes. Please." I opened the voice memo tool on my phone and scooted it across the desk so it was closer to her.

"Jay Renner was a young man who ran away from somewhere north and showed up in Holiday Junction. He was hanging around the downtown area, and when Sawyer noticed him, he offered him a job. After he took the job, we knew he could afford food but couldn't afford to pay rent or even rent a room at the Jubilee Inn. We opened the top of Sawyer's workshop over the garage as a place for Jay to stay." She smiled as if it were a fond memory. "I'd never seen someone get so excited over an old military cot and a space heater."

She waved her hands up as if she were trying to get back to her story.

"Jay did odd jobs around the house after getting home from a full day on a contracted job. After we'd gotten to know Jay fairly well, Sawyer and I had finally convinced him to reach out to his family just so they had peace knowing he wasn't dead, even though by the time we'd gotten him to do it he was already an adult." She opened the top drawer of the desk and pulled out a photo frame. "That's him between Sawyer and me."

The man in the photo stood taller than Carol or Sawyer. He wore a soiled white tee and a pair of khaki pants, the hems of the latter haphazardly tucked into the tongues of his work boots. His hair was a little long and scraggly from what appeared to be a long day's work.

The smile on his face was bright and moved your eyes past the observation that his clothes weren't tidy, but neither were Sawyer's.

"Anyways, Peter's father, Alan, was the president of the committee at the time, and there were some issues with Halloweenie that year. I wasn't sure what, but Alan had been down at the square. He was a gruff man, and if you don't think Peter got along with anyone, he got it honest." She sat back and sighed. "Someone heard some yelling while everyone was down setting up their vendor tents and getting ready for the weeklong celebration. That was when Peter and Sawyer took off, when they heard the screaming. Someone had run from the scene with a Dunn Contractors jacket on. There was only one person who owned that jacket."

"Jay Renner," I stated.

"Yes. We'd gotten him the jacket because he loved to work out in the cold. He said the fresh air did him good, and I couldn't let him get cold." She frowned. "Since he worked for the company and we were growing at the time, I thought it would be neat for him to be sort of a walking billboard. He loved it."

"Which brings me back to the questions…" I leaned forward and put my hands and notebook on the desk. "Why would Jay have killed Alan, and why would you and Sawyer not think it was him if he was seen running away with the jacket on?"

"Alan and Peter were trying to take over everything dealing with tourism at the time. Alan was the president, and Peter had been elected vice president. Everything was done in their favor, not the good of the community. Even business sanctions and taxes had to be approved. If it didn't benefit the Hills, then it didn't benefit Holiday Junction." As she told the story, I remembered that a few months ago, when I started to take over the failing paper, the Stricklands had mentioned how tourism had slowed down over time.

Carol's story made complete sense of that now.

"That was when I decided to run against Alan for president that year. When Alan was killed and Peter was put in the position automatically, Peter started to point fingers at Jay and give all sorts of statements about him hanging around different places. Here and there, snooping. Taking notes. All sorts of accusations that just so happened to be around property owned by the Hills." She picked up the frame and looked at it again. There was slight movement on the edges of her lips. "The theory in court was we'd taken Jay in and now the Hills were doing everything they could to make life hard for us, and that meant him as well. If Jay got rid of Alan, things would get better."

"Was he taking notes?" Carol looked up, a little bafflement on her face.

"Is that what you got out of this? An innocent man is sitting in jail because a powerful person in the community swore in court it was him." She leaned back, looked away, and rolled her eyes.

"No. I'm saying if there were some documentations, like Jay writing things down in a notebook like Peter had testified, then maybe you have evidence he wasn't writing anything down. I don't know." I shook my head. "In my line of work, anything and nothing are potential leads. Clues to help."

My mind shifted back to the little argument Louise and Marge had in my office when Marge accused Louise of losing a file for the trial. Was this the trial? I put the assumption in the back of my head so I could concentrate on what Carol was saying.

"Jay is an artist. He's very good at drawing. He would sit for hours with his notebook and sketch," she said.

"Do you still have those?" I would love to see them to find if they had any clues about Jay and what he was doing around the Hills' property as Peter Hill had claimed.

"Yes. We have them in a box in the apartment garage." She blinked a few times. "He's been in jail for over ten years. What good is that going to do now?"

"The real question is why would someone kill Peter Hill?" I said.

"Jay is up for parole. They couldn't get him on full murder charges because there was no other evidence than Peter's testimony. Peter was scheduled to go to the parole hearing to give a statement." Carol gulped. "Oh no. It does look like I'm a suspect."

"With you being the vice president—now the president—and Jay up for parole, the only thing stopping you from having both was Peter Hill and his testimony." I knew I had to go back to the office to get some information on this murder case concerning Jay Renner.

"I didn't do it. I was at home with Sawyer."

"I hate to play devil's advocate, but wouldn't Sawyer be your alibi even if you weren't with him?" I had to ask.

"Probably, but we have cameras on our property. If someone comes and goes, we have it recorded. I can prove I didn't leave all night until the next day, and from what I understand, Peter had been dead at least eight hours before he was found." The phone on her desk rang. "I'm sorry. I have to get back to work, but if you want to swing by the house, I'm more than happy to let you see Jay's notebooks."

She answered the phone and at the same time scribbled her address on a sticky note, which she handed to me.

My phone rang, so I waved goodbye to Carol, whispering that I'd call her later and held the sticky note up in the air so she knew what I was talking about.

"I'm coming, Mama," I said when I answered the phone, since she'd be calling about right now to let me know she'd scored me the perfect outfit.

"It's your daddy." My father's voice caught me off guard.

"Daddy. I'm so sorry. I was expecting..." I pulled my lips together and tugged on the door handle behind me to make sure the door was shut.

I stood on the little platform of the steps and took in the view. There was no better time to stand still so Mama could stay in her happy place of shopping for me while I talked to Daddy.

"I know you're busy, pretty girl." Daddy called me by the name he always used for me. It was always pretty girl this, pretty girl that. My daddy was my biggest cheerleader even when I wasn't so pretty on the inside.

"Not too busy for you, Daddy." My heart ached from the tone in his voice. He was always such a strong man in appearance and tone. "Are you getting the house ready for Halloween? I know there's all those boxes up in the attic that are labeled. Mama did a good job of making sure every holiday decoration was tidy, neat, and put away perfectly so you didn't have to hunt and peek come time next year."

"I can't even think about the next few months of holidays without your mama here." Concern laced Daddy's voice. "How is Millie Kay? Is she all right, pretty girl?"

"You know Mama. She makes the tea sweeter even if it tastes bitter." I sighed as I tried to think of something to say. "Daddy, why did Mama come out here? I mean, she's welcome anytime and so are you, but why all this talk of a divorce?"

Of course I'd talked to my father over the course of the time Mama had been here, but I had never approached the subject of divorce in hopes Mama would eventually come to her senses, which she clearly had not. It was time to find out exactly what was going on.

"You don't need to bother your pretty little head with all this." Daddy always tried to shield me from everything, not just things that went on at home, so to say I was shocked when Mama showed up talking of divorce was an understatement. "I just need to talk to her—if she'd just talk to me."

"If I knew what was wrong, I could talk to her and find out what was going on." I encouraged him to open up to me.

"She said there's no spark. You were the spark, and you jetted off, leaving us with no spark." Daddy had just told me exactly what I'd feared.

I glanced down to the bottom of the stairs, where Mama had turned up with an armful of bags.

"Daddy, I can't talk right now, but I will call you back." I hung up the phone and threw it in my bag. "I'm coming down."

"You're done already?" Mama looked up. She flung her hand up to her brows, covering the glare of the sun so she could see me. A bag nearly knocked her in the head.

"Yes, and we've got a lot to find out. I'm glad you're my assistant because you're gonna be busy," I told her when I greeted her at the bottom of the stairs.

Having Mama scour the internet for everything she could find out about Jay Renner was the perfect job to keep her busy while I figured out what to do about her and Daddy—and knowing that I dulled the spark in their life.

A heavy burden for a daughter they encouraged to shine.

With mama all set up at the office, though she wasn't doing a bit of work, more importantly investigative work, she was going through the shopping bags. When I left her to head down to the jiggle joint, she was talking to herself about how she liked each item she'd bought.

"Can you believe that?" I picked up my empty glass and rattled the ice against it, signaling Darren for another vodka and soda.

"Honey." Owen sighed and looked at Shawn, the other full-time bar customer. "Sometimes these things happen."

"You're not a parent yet, but when you make your whole world about your kids and not your marriage, the kids leave, and you look at your spouse, not recognizing who you married." Shawn wasn't too bad on giving me the truth about what probably happened to my parents.

"But we were the perfect family." I tipped the glass back and sucked a piece of ice into my mouth.

"You were, are, but they aren't the perfect couple." Owen didn't have to be so bold.

I glared at him.

"Darren!" I hollered over the thumping music the dancer on stage had chosen as her accompaniment. "I need a refill."

"No, you don't." Darren moseyed down the back side of the bar. He grabbed my empty glass, whipped the towel from his shoulder, and wiped off the wet ring the glass had made on the counter. "You need to get back to work."

"I left my new assistant at the office to look up some stuff while I came here to take a much-needed break." I pointed at the glass. "Fill 'er up."

When Owen picked up the full beer bottle in front of him, Darren shot a look at him as if he could read Owen's mind. "Nope," Darren said. "You give her that bottle and you'll never see me serve you another one. Ever."

Slowly, Owen pulled his hand away from the beer.

"Sorry, kiddo," Owen said out of the side of his mouth. "Looks like you're on your own on this one."

The sun bolted through the door of the jiggle joint, giving off the only real light besides the many neon signs hanging up behind the bar and the dim spotlight on the dancer.

A dark silhouette covered up some of the sunshine before another person hid the rest. It wasn't until they both walked in that I noticed it was Fern Banks and another woman.

I slumped down on the stool and slightly turned toward Shawn and Owen so she didn't see me.

"Too late." Darren tapped the bar with his fingertips. "Ladies, welcome!"

I slightly turned my chin to glance over my shoulder, and Fern was still standing at the front of the bar with the woman next to her and the door closed.

She blinked a few times before she squinted and pointed at me. The music was too loud for me to hear what she was saying, but I could see she was clearly coming my way.

"Go figure. I knew you were a drinker, even though you claimed you never drank when you beat me at the stein competition on St. Patrick's Day." Fern wore a body-hugging white dress that was decorated like a ghost, its face and mouth painted on. The hem was scalloped like a waving ghost. "This is my mom, Nettie."

"What?" I asked and put an ear toward her.

"This is my mom, Nettie Banks!" Fern screamed.

"Nice to meet you!" I yelled over the music. Then I smiled and wiggled my shoulders to the music.

"We need you." Fern was talking, but I couldn't hear her.

I tucked my hair behind my ear closer to them so I could hear.

"I can't hear you," I mouthed because there was no sense in trying to really talk.

The music ended just as Fern opened her mouth.

"Matthew Strickland has named my mother a suspect in Peter Hill's murder, and we need you to help us!" she screamed in the dead silence of the bar and glared at Darren.

CHAPTER TEN

After Fern Banks came into the jiggle joint, wielding her sword of words against not just Chief Matthew Strickland, who had hauled Nettie down to the station for questioning, but the entire Strickland family, it took about two drinks to calm her down.

The facts were the facts, and Nettie was someone who'd had a public argument with Peter. That little bit of information alone made her look suspicious, as did the fact that Peter had put a little dent in her income. Money was a huge motive for murder.

I wasn't saying she did it, but I wasn't saying she didn't. She clearly had motive and no alibi, which didn't put her in the best place to be marked off the suspect list.

With some coaxing and assurance, because I had to deal with my own family issues and didn't have time to listen to Fern and Nettie ramble on about the Stricklands, I told them I'd stop by Bubbly Boutique tomorrow and see what I could find.

Clearly, I needed to do some more digging around about the case. Now that it looked as though Carol Dunn didn't do it, I had to know all about this murder that'd taken place ten years ago.

Fern wasn't happy that my plan required waiting until tomorrow. Nettie was the more reasonable one, though she had some deep-rooted fears in her eyes when she reluctantly agreed to meet me in the morning. First thing. As soon as the store opened. That was the agreement.

Of course Daddy wasn't letting up. At some point I was going to have to address this whole divorce idea the two of them had. That included more text messages from Mama and Daddy. Daddy sent more of the sad sorta texts, including photos of an uncarved pumpkin sitting on the fireplace. Clearly not what we'd been used too.

There wasn't even a string of the light-up candy corn garland Mama used to string across the mantel year after year. It was just a sad, lonely orange pumpkin, and even that was lopsided. Something else Mama would-n't've done.

But Mama's texts—man, oh, man, they had a different tone than Daddy's. She was sending me photos of the small courtyard of the house on Heart Way, where she'd strung up new lights of both the garland and twinkly white Christmas-style types. She also had several carved and uncarved pumpkins of various sizes were stacked on top of one another. Some sat on the bale of hay beside the fodder shock, and the scarecrow stuck next to it.

Mama also sent a photo of the long patio table she'd bought, which looked like it was set for supper. I didn't doubt that it was, even though Mama always kept her table set as if she were expecting company. And that was her excuse. She said that you always needed to be prepared for visitors, since most of the time they came calling around suppertime.

She was a true southern hostess, and that included celebrating every single holiday and decorating for it to the hilt. Mama fit right in with Holiday Junction but left poor Daddy out in the cold.

Mama had told me to come to the house instead of the inn because she'd started to move more and more boxes into the house. The inspector had given her a temporary move-in occupancy until the lights were completed in my apartment.

Good news for me because that meant Mama could sleep at her new house and I could have the bed at the Jubilee Inn all to myself tonight.

Flowerworks, the local florist, was still open, and it dawned on me when I passed by the tablescape display in the window that Mama didn't have a centerpiece on the patio table.

Bringing her one would be a nice gesture, and she'd love it. Also, I couldn't resist taking in all the gorgeous arrangements I could see sitting on the tables in Flowerworks.

Like most of the shops in Holiday Junction, Flowerworks was a punny take on "fireworks. The Fourth of July was another huge occasion for Holiday Junction. Even the shop's logo was adorable—a stick of dynamite that shot bright and colorful flowers and had the Flowerworks name imprinted on the side.

The large yellow sunflowers in the three mason jars nestled in a long wooden tray with handles on each end caught my eye. Immediately, I walked over to the display, which was arranged on a wooden farmhouse table with four place settings sitting on wicker plate chargers. My mama would've done that to her table.

"Hi there." The woman greeted me with a smile. "You're the new reporter in town." She pointed at me.

Didn't her mama tell her it wasn't nice to point at someone? I didn't say it out loud and realized that was something Mama would've said. My goodness. It was time Mama moved into her own place.

"I am." I stuck my hand out, very professional. "Violet Rhinehammer."

"Betsy Carmichael." There was an instant likability about her. "Nice to meet you. What can I help you with? Something about Peter Hill?"

I blinked a few times. Did people see me as just the reporter and not part of the community? If that was the case, I knew it wasn't good.

"I'm sorry." She put a hand to her chest. "I just assumed you were here because you helped with the other cases, and I will just stop talking now."

"Actually, I'm here to pick up something for my mama's new place on Heart Way. And this caught my eye right away." I reached out and touched the sunflowers. "They're real." I was surprised because they were so perfect.

"Everything we design is real and alive except some of the embellishments like the pumpkins and ribbons. If you were to purchase this, I'd love to jazz it up a little with some of the orange ribbon with the gold trim. We just got it in this afternoon, and I've been so busy fulfilling orders for the Hills that I wasn't able to get any designs made with it." She didn't bother waiting for me to agree or disagree. She hurried off and said, "I'll be right back."

I liked her. She seemed open to talking about Peter Hill and owned a shop, so she might have been affected by the advertising scheme in which Peter seemed to be involved.

"I saw these when I was opening the ribbon box and just have to throw a few of those in there too." She held up a couple of little plastic pumpkins. "The sunflowers will last about seven days at their peak, and Millie Kay is more than welcome to come in and get a new boutique to refresh the look. Or..." She grinned. "Not that I want to upsell you, but Millie Kay seems to decorate a lot with flowers."

By the way she was talking about Mama and calling her by name, I knew they'd been introduced.

"You know her already." My eyes grew, and I grinned and shook my head, wondering if that was a good thing or a bad one.

"She's always in here buying flowers for everyone," Betsy said and sighed. "Always thinking of others."

"Mm-hmm. That's Mama."

Thinking of others, my hiney. When Mama brought flowers to someone, unless she was sending them to a funeral, she was hunting for something.

"I had to stop Millie Kay from buying up all my flowers during Mother's Day week. She was in here every day." Betsy's words jogged my memory.

"I forgot about that." I laughed. "If you didn't know, she's been living with me at the Jubilee Inn until her house is ready, and the week of Mother's Day, she had that place looking like she'd started her own florist's shop."

"She does have an eye for decorating, and I offered her a job, but she said you were her full-time job." Betsy snickered. "Her house must be ready if you're in here wanting to purchase the tablescape."

Betsy picked up the arrangement and took it to the workstation in the back corner of the shop. All the tools needed to decorate, design, cut, and wrap hung on hooks attached to the wall beneath the open shelves, where vases in all sorts of colors, sizes, shapes, and designs sat.

"Today, the inspector gave her temporary occupancy, and she's already taken full advantage of it by fixing supper." I lollygagged as I made my way back to talk to her, taking in all the different types of boutiques and arrangements Betsy had in the shop.

"Then we must zhuzh it up for her." Betsy pulled a long piece of the sparkly orange ribbon out at arm's length before she cut it. She weaved it in, out, and around all the mason jars, fluffing the edges up as she went along. Then she took another long piece and did the same to the other side of the tray to fill in its gaps. "I'm guessing she's planning on staying if she's bought a home."

I wasn't sure if Betsy was asking or just making small talk, but I knew it was a good way for me to ask her about her time here in Holiday Junction.

"She does." I left out the part about her wanting to divorce my dad. "I'm going to be living in the garage she's had made into an apartment-type dwelling, but it's more of a house, and I'm going to be paying rent."

Something in me felt the need to tell her I wasn't a freeloader on Mama.

"You mentioned something about Peter Hill and how you'd been busy making flowers for him." I gave her a quick glance out of the corner of my eye to see if she had a reaction. When nothing was visible, I continued, "Have they made funeral arrangements yet?"

"No. Curtis hasn't released his body yet, but everyone is getting in their orders because I can get really backed up." She stepped back from the arrangement and tilted her head a few times before she dug her hands back in, fluffing, moving, and rearranging the elements until she repeated the activity.

"Did you know Peter Hill well?" I asked.

"I know Vickie." She picked at the edges of the ribbon and made them wavy. "She comes in a lot. She's a member of the Red, White, and Bloom club." She pulled her hands out of the flowers and took a brochure from the acrylic holder sitting on one of the shelves behind her. "Which was what I was going to say about Millie Kay. It's an awards program where you pay two hundred dollars a year and can come in here to pick out a fresh bouquet each week. When you spend money, you also get rewards to upgrade your weekly bouquet. There's also the holiday discount that goes with each holiday or special occasion." She said out of the side of her mouth like it was a secret, "If you've not realized it yet, every holiday around Holiday Junction is a special occasion."

Something caught her attention, and she glanced up and waved.

I looked back to the front of the shop to see who she was waving at and saw it was Kristine and Paisley. They had to be on their nightly walk.

We waved to one another too.

"You're going to miss the Jubilee Inn." Betsy threw herself back into the tablescape.

"Oh yes, I am. She's been amazing since I moved here and very welcoming." I sighed and knew I would miss my daily conversations and check-ins with Kristine—not that I couldn't stop by there to chat, but it was different when you practically lived with someone other than your mama.

"Not that you didn't know." Betsy shifted her eyes and gave me a quick glance before she moved them back to the arrangement. "But Peter Hill sure did make it hard for people around here to advertise in the *Junction Journal*. Today, I went to the emergency meeting, and Carol Dunn made a promise to fix the bylaw stating the extra money was going to be used for everyone. That's promising."

"I couldn't go to the meeting, but I think I can get the minutes from Nora. I heard some rumblings about Peter and how he was creative with the ad spend money." I didn't say anything about what I'd really heard because it wasn't good for my journalist reputation to be a gossip.

"I don't deal with the ads much. That's up to Marge and Louise, but after someone mentioned it to me, I totally went down that rabbit hole." I picked up the piece of ribbon Betsy had clipped off and curled it around my finger. "Not that most of those shop owners didn't have motive. Money is one of the number-one reasons people get murdered, but it's this whole Jay Renner deal that's got me curious."

"Jay Renner." Betsy jerked up. "I forgot all about that."

"It was ten years ago." I refreshed her memory, hoping she'd have something to say.

"It doesn't seem like that long ago. I'd heard they brought the ghost walk back."

"The ghost walk? You mean Hershal's over at the Brewing Beans?" I asked to verify.

"That was when Jay killed Peter's dad." She moved one of the pumpkins to the side of the middle mason jar and then moved it back to where she'd plucked it from.

"Did you know Jay?" I asked.

"Everyone knew him. He was a kid when he got to town, which was when the Dunns took him in. He was an adult by the time the trial took place, so that was how he got convicted." She stepped back again to get another look at her handiwork. "It was all circumstantial evidence, and I swear Carol Dunn ran for vice president just to keep a reminder to Peter about Jay. Peter was awful to the Dunns after that."

She looked up. A curious thought appeared to have crossed her mind. Her mouth opened as though she was going to say something, then she closed it.

"What?" I asked.

"If I recall correctly, after Jay Renner went to prison, Peter started to buy up all the advertising." Betsy picked up the tray and rotated it around before she set it back down. Satisfied with her work and the additions she'd made to it, she started to pick up all the stray pieces and extras she didn't use on the workstation. "After the advertisers who had somehow bothered Peter or the Hills in general started to realize what he'd done by snatching up all the spots, they started to boycott the paper, and that only left Marge and Louise in a bind."

"How so?" I asked and remembered Carol Dunn mentioned they had cameras to verify she was home and that footage would be easy for Chief Strickland to obtain.

"I didn't want to subscribe to the paper after what he'd done to Kristine and Hubert. And the rest of the shops who were left out of his little scheme felt the same." She picked up one of those sales pads and wrote out my ticket. She ripped off the top copy and handed it to me. "We might be small businesses, but we are mighty in numbers. The decline and death of the newspaper was inevitable until you showed up. You're breathing new life into it, and with Peter gone, maybe we will start advertising again."

"I'd love to have you in there," I said. Even though it wasn't my department to get ads, Marge and Louise had told me to keep up the good work. This was good work. "Why don't we start now? I can give you a ten percent discount on a quarter-page ad in the physical paper next week along with a write-up featuring Mama's tablescape, and I can also give you a side bar on the online ad."

"And I'll give you fifty percent off a Red, White, and Bloom subscription for just making my day." Betsy took the receipt back and finagled it back to where she'd torn it so she could write up the subscription.

"Put another one on there for Mama too." I winked.

CHAPTER ELEVEN

Mama was listening to some Barry Manilow in the small courtyard of the new house on Heart Way when I got there.

"You didn't," she gushed and took the tablescape. "I've been looking for something to go on my table."

"I noticed in the photos you sent me that you didn't have anything, and what is a Millie Kay table without a gorgeous arrangement?" I said.

She took it from me, hurried it over, and put it right in the middle of the patio table, where it looked better than I'd pictured it.

"And you can go each week to swap out flowers because I've given you a subscription to Flowerworks's Red, White, and Bloom." I took the brochure out of my bag and handed it to her. "My housewarming gift to you."

"Oh, Violet." Mama squealed with glee. "Thank you, honey."

She stood there looking at me with tears in her eyes.

"It's just flowers," I reminded her. "If I'd known you were going to cry, I wouldn't've brought them."

"It's not that. It's just that your daddy and I talked about this moment when you were a little girl. He'd complain about all those clothes I'd buy you and how I'd take you down to Cute-icles to get your hair all done up by Helen Pyle before all your beauty pageants, because it was costly. And I told him one day it'd pay off and you'd be doing things for me."

"I always do things for you. I love doing things for you." I hugged her.

"I mean doing things without there being a takeaway." Mama confused me. "Like this. You did this on your own with your own money without any sort of holiday or reason. Just because I moved into this silly old house." She wiped the tears off her cheek.

"I love you, and I want you to be happy." I meant that even if I didn't understand what she and Daddy were doing, but I was willing to see both sides and love them both equally. But I understood what she was saying.

In no uncertain terms, she was saying I'd grown up. This seemed to be a defining moment in our relationship from mother raising a daughter to a mother-and-daughter friendship.

We gave each other one last hug. Then we pulled away and looked at how ideal the piece I'd picked out was as the finishing touch she needed to make the perfect autumn outdoor space.

I was about to tell Mama that we needed to look into Millard Ramsey and her son, the Headless Horseman, because she had a motive to kill Peter. He was going to get rid of her horseback-riding tourist attraction. Then there was the whole aspect of Nettie Banks being named a suspect—and the matter of the beauty pageant. I was still having a hard time wrapping my head around Jay Renner and how he killed Peter's dad on the last ghost walk.

Now with Mama working at the paper, I could give her some things to look up or even go to see Nora at the library to get the meeting notes from when Peter had brought up Millard Ramsey.

"I can't be looking like I've been crying when company gets here." She rushed over and picked up a spoon from the set table and looked at herself.

"Company?" I figured she'd had the table set like she'd always done.

"Mm-hmm." A mischievous smile curled up on the edges of her face. "I think they are here now."

Marge, Louise, Kristine, Darren, and Carol Dunn all walked around the corner of the house and let themselves in through the gate.

"Mama? What did you do?" I asked.

"Got all the suspects in one place. We are gonna solve this thing right here and right now." There were no limits to what mama could do.

CHAPTER TWELVE

Mama always did say to go to the source. I just didn't figure she'd bring all the sources to me. I couldn't discuss all the things I needed to with her in this mixed company. Everyone here still had motive, but I'd pretty much eliminated them from the suspect list.

"When Millie Kay called," Marge said across the table from me. Next to her sat Carol Dunn. Mama squeezed in a third on that side with Kristine next to Carol. She paused as though she were choosing her words.

I took a moment to look around where Mama had placed everyone around the table. Make no mistake, everyone had a place to be where they were sitting. Only mama knew why she put them there.

Next to me was Darren, and I was sure Mama had strategically placed him there. Mama sat at the head of the table to my left, and Louise was at the opposite head of the table to my right. Again, the seating was planned out of respect for her being my possible love interest's mama. I can guarantee that was Mama's thinking process.

"Louise and I were a little skeptical. Then we got to thinking about what might happen if we did an exposé with the people who did have motive." Marge planted her elbows on the table and folded her hands together. She looked down the table at Louise. "We could help Matthew's investigation by spurring things along and not dillydallying on these two."

Kristine and Carol both shifted uncomfortably when Marge pointed them out.

The cricket song in the yard took over the silence that'd fallen over the table.

"Millie Kay." Leave it to the man in the group, who probably felt so uncomfortable with the silence that he had to talk. Not us women. We were waiting to see who was going to crack first. "You've really outdone yourself with this house."

"Thank you." She pointed out the small concrete patio, where she'd put a rattan sofa and chair with those big fluffy cushions and pillows in front of the stone fireplace, which she'd insisted Sawyer Dunn create out of large stones. "Carol's husband spent a lot of time pouring the patio and building the stone fireplace exactly how I wanted it, which brings me back to a reason Carol and Sawyer would want Peter dead. I mean, if it weren't for me and all the work I had Dunn Contractors do, he said they'd be scraping by."

"He didn't mean that literally." Carol scoffed a nervous laugh and reached for the bowl of southern green beans.

Mama had put all the vegetables in big bowls. Family style, she called it.

"Honey, pass that on to Marge," Mama instructed. "We will just pass this way."

Mama was teaching them southern table manners, only they didn't know it. It was like the way southern women used the famous "bless your heart," and when you were slapped with it, you didn't realize until later it wasn't quite the compliment you thought it was at the time. Mama did that with a lot of things.

And I could guarantee the next time I went to supper at the Stricklands' home, we'd be passing the beans just like Mama was showing them.

"Then how did he mean it?" Mama circled back around to Carol. "From what I understand, these two"—Mama had no problem pointing at Marge and Louise—"let him have the monopoly on advertisements in their newspaper."

"Now I wouldn't say he *had* the monopoly." Louise cleared her throat and took the plate of cornbread from Darren.

"What did you call it, then?" Kristine found her voice. "He didn't give

Jubilee Inn a spot from the committee advertising budget, and when I called
—" She sucked in a deep breath, leaned her elbows on the table, and started
to say something before Mama gestured for her to take her elbows off the
table. Kristine moved them and leaned in on her forearms. Mama nodded
with approval. "I correct myself. I didn't call. I walked down to your house
and asked you with cash in my hand to take out an ad, and you said the
Holiday Junction Planning Committee had bought up all the advertising for
the year. Then the next year, I did the same thing, and you said the same
thing."

"Your dog was the one who bit him. Maybe that was your first attempt to
kill him." Marge's words began to heat up the conversation even more. "If I
recall, Peter had gotten a staph infection."

"He must have already had the infection dormant in his body. Besides, he
shouldn't've broke into the office of the Jubilee Inn, where the mayor was
resting." Kristine looked around the table. "Mayor Paisley takes her naps
seriously."

Kristine intended it to be a joke that lightened the mood, but no one
thought it was funny.

"Honestly," Kristine said with a sigh, putting her hands in her lap, "do
you think I killed Peter?" She glanced around and found everyone had
answered yes by either nodding or speaking. "Seriously? Peter was a jerk,
and he did monopolize the newspaper ads, but was it illegal? No. In the
committee bylaws, it states they can use the extra funds to promote tourism.
He used it to promote his friends, and I came up with a clever way to
promote the inn by hosting the photo shoots. They did become wildly
popular, and as you know"—she pointed at me—"the lines for a photo with
Mayor Paisley wrap around the inn, and they are the most popular events
during the festivals."

"That's true. I've seen it several times because it's hard to leave the inn
when there's a photo event." I backed her up.

"And even if I could advertise," Kristine said, throwing Marge a shoulder
and twisting in her chair, "I'm not sure I'd waste my money. Nothing is
better than the mayor. And Paisley is so cute."

"What about Peter having you pay for his medical bills for the staph?"
Marge shifted herself toward Kristine.

"I offered to pay for them. He didn't ask me to or even bring it up. I did it because it was the right thing to do." Kristine scoffed. "Not that you'd know what the right thing is or you'd never take a deal with the devil, who was Peter." She jutted her finger to Marge. "If anyone had motive to kill him, it was you and her. Only because Violet single-handedly saved your newspaper over the last few months, and you knew if you didn't go along with Peter's ad scheme, Violet was going to realize it. There's no way she'd support that. I think she's made that pretty clear here tonight."

"I didn't say—" I tried to interject, but Kristine kept going.

"If Violet's not happy, she leaves, and then you go back to the same old rag as before. But me, I'm throwing my hat behind Carol being the new president and voting for her in the fall to stop what's been happening. And if you've not heard, Hubert is going to run for a board position."

"I'm going to be updating the bylaws." Carol nodded.

"I want to clarify I didn't kill him, and I've already told Sheriff Strickland. Not that all of you need to know my alibi." Kristine crossed her arms, shutting down her part of the conversation.

The tension lay over the table and was louder than any chatter darting back and forth.

"And I really love how you've got this eating area with the twinkly lights. It gives it a nice cozy feel." Darren tried desperately to get them off the subject of Peter Hill.

I kicked him underneath the table.

"Ouch," he said and threw me a hard look.

"Thank you, Darren." Mama always made sure to be polite, but she went right back to why she'd asked us all here and began her line of questioning. "I believe that's the same issue with the Dunns. So it looks like all y'all had motive to kill Peter Hill."

"I think we agree on that." Carol wiped her mouth with her napkin and set it on top of the table next to her plate.

Mama pointed at the napkin and shook her head, so Carol slowly slipped her napkin into her lap.

"Now that we've established the reason for motive is money." All the ladies opened their mouths like baby birds when she mentioned money, and Mama lifted her hand to silence them. "The *Junction Journal* needed the money to run the paper. The newspaper to have the backing of the committee is also a very big deal. And to have someone like Peter Hill endorse Matthew for re-election is a perk."

Louise crossed her legs.

"And it looks like you've put up more lights because I see some more poles out there by the garage apartment." Darren cleared his throat. Something about his discomfort was cute.

"Yes. It'll be so romantic." Mama winked and shimmied her shoulders. "Back to the issue at hand." Mama gave an uncomfortable sigh that made it clear to Darren he was to stop interrupting.

I knew he'd gotten the message when he shook his head and focused on eating the piece of cornbread. I hoped he was stuffing his mouth to stop talking because that would make Mama encourage me not to date him.

"Carol and Kristine, as small business owners and two women who have clearly done good for the well-being of Holiday Junction"—Mama pointed at Carol—"you want to see tourism grow, and Violet here found all the minutes of the meetings where Peter shut down any discussion of topics you wanted to put on the docket." She moved her finger to Kristine. "Of course, you being the owner of the mayor and having to do those awful photo shoots to make ends meet is downright disgraceful. Not to mention Mayor Paisley using Peter as a squeaky toy." Mama wagged her finger. "My Violet can tell you being in the limelight is hard. But you two know that because you snatched her right up, but shame on you for not telling her who really pays her salary."

"What?" I leaned forward and looked at Mama.

"Peter Hill pays the paper's employees with his little ad scheme. Violet," Mama said, pronouncing my name shamefully, "you're smarter and a better investigative reporter than that. With all the guaranteed ad spend the planning committee gives to Peter at the helm, do you think our new president is going to approve that budget?" Mama sat back and laughed. "I don't think so. After all these years of being left out." She rested each elbow on the arms of the chair and folded her hands in the air in front of her. She stared down the table at Carol and then shifted to Louise. "Really, why I brought you here wasn't because we really had to know who killed Peter. How are we going to come to an agreement between the Holiday Junction

Planning Committee and *Junction Journal* on how to pay their two best employees?"

Mama unclasped her fingers and pointed between her and me.

"I'm out." Darren pushed back from the table. "Thank you, Millie Kay, for the yummy food and colorful discussion, but I have always sat at the table with the Stricklands, and all they do is discuss business. I am an adult now and don't have to listen to this." He stood up and looked down at me. "This is why I don't do a lot with my family."

He answered a question I'd asked him many times before when I'd heard Darren referred to as the black sheep of the family.

"I'm going too." I wiped my mouth with my napkin and laid it on my plate, which was the southern way to say you were finished eating. "Thanks, Mama. I'll leave it up to y'all to discuss the way we get paid."

I gave Mama a kiss on the cheek and left in a rush so no one could stop Darren and me.

Darren and I walked out of the backyard, not a word between us. I wasn't sure if I should apologize for Mama's behavior or if I should just leave it. Clearly, Mama wasn't going anywhere, and people around here would have to get used to her bluntness, though she could have a little more couth to herself. She'd tell me she was using couth by getting to the bottom of the matter.

"Well?" Darren called out to me when I started walking down the side-walk so I could walk back to the Jubilee Inn.

"What?" I saw him holding up an extra helmet for his moped.

"Are you coming with me or not?" He shook the helmet.

"I guess." I haphazardly shrugged like it was no big deal. It was a big deal, though, because some sort of battle was going on between my two biggest bodily organs, my brain and my heart. My heart was battling for my legs to walk, but my brain warned them of danger.

As soon as I took the helmet from him, I swear my brain might've cursed at my heart.

"Here." He got annoyed with me fiddling with the strap and pushed my hands away. He stood a couple of inches from me, staring into my eyes as he buckled the strap underneath my chin with ease. "How's that? Too tight?"

"No," I said in a whisper as my breath caught. "No," I stated louder. "It feels good. Good." I shook my head.

"Great." He got on the moped, and I snickered. "What?" He leaned back a little to look at me from the sides of his eyes as I got on behind him.

"It's funny a grown man drives a moped. That's all." I curled my arms around him.

"Only so I can have the ladies hold me." He snickered and patted my hands before he rotated the handle to make the moped move forward.

He drove down Heart Way and up to Main Street, passing the Jubilee Inn.

"Where are you going?" I asked, seeing the little bit of sun moving down past the shops, about to set as we drove past them. "To see the sunset?"

My mind replayed the sunset he'd shown me the other night. I forced myself to stick it in the back of my head. I felt like a teenager back in the Daniel Boone National Park who'd just climbed out of her window to go meet a boy. That was a feeling you never forgot.

"I don't know. Any place you want to go?" He shrugged and slowed down, allowing us to hear each other.

"Do you know Sawyer Dunn?" I knew we'd just gotten his wife's alibi, but we didn't get his. "I was told he and Peter were in the library having a secret conversation."

"We are going to go see Sawyer Dunn." The whiz of the moped engine shifted up, and then my thoughts moved into a totally different direction. "He owes me a favor."

CHAPTER THIRTEEN

"For someone who wants to be on the Holiday Junction Planning Committee, Carol sure doesn't have the Halloween vibe going." I got off Darren's moped, glanced around the front yard, and looked up at the front of the Dunn house.

"Not everyone loves every holiday, remember?" Darren reached out to take the helmet from me and hung it off the rack on the back.

"Oh, really? Around here?" I joked and laid my hand on my chest. "I thought it was just me."

I really had started to like the lighthearted banter Darren and I seemed to fall into when we were around each other.

"What kind of favor does he owe you?" I asked.

"Let's just say it's a favor and leave it at that." Darren wasn't going to give up his secret. Since I was a great journalist, I knew I could figure it out if I tried hard enough.

The moon hung in the dark sky among the multitudes of twinkling stars. It reminded me of home, where there were no big-city lights to hinder the true beauty of a pitch-black night sky. The view was something to behold.

"Breathtaking, right?" Darren noticed I'd stopped to look around us. "The one thing we have in Holiday Junction is a gorgeous setting all the time."

"Yeah. It's beautiful here. You should see where I'm from." I rambled on and on about the Daniel Boone National Forest back in my hometown in Kentucky. "And the hikes are amazing too. Plus, there's all these amazing caves." I followed him up on the porch. He knocked on the door. "You can even take a boat ride in one cave."

"I can't wait to see it." Darren's response stopped me in my tracks. He smiled as he knocked again. "Don't worry. I'm not asking you to take me."

"I, um, I didn't say I wouldn't take you." I gulped back the sudden strange feelings I was having.

"Your face did." The door swung open right on time, so I didn't have to say anything about my face. I was generally great at covering my feelings.

What was it about Darren that made me let down my guard?

"Darren." Sawyer looked past Darren's shoulder. He greeted me with a nod and smile. "Hi there." He popped the storm door open. "Come on in. Carol isn't here right now. She's gone to a dinner party or something."

He turned and walked back into the house.

Darren held the storm door and gestured for me to go ahead of him, like a good gentleman would do. It didn't make me feel right because I didn't know the Dunns and he did, so I pointed for him to go.

"Probably something about fundraising or something. You know Carol." We landed in the kitchen, where it looked as if he were doing some work for his contractor company at the bar. A drink was on the counter too. "Sit down."

Darren pulled out a stool and then another—one for him and one for me. I climbed up on the high stool and sat down, looking around for any sort of Halloween decoration. There was nary a pumpkin to be seen.

"What can I get you to drink?" He glanced at Darren and me.

"I'll have what you're drinking. Looks good." Darren noticed the small glass that held one large round ice cube.

"Bourbon straight up." Sawyer turned around to the small bar on the kitchen counter. He pulled a small glass from the cabinet and popped the bourbon's cork. "What about you?" He turned over his shoulder as if he were searching for something.

"Violet Rhinehammer." By the way he asked me what I wanted to drink, I knew he was trying to follow it up with my name. "I'm Violet."

"Yeah. I thought I recognized the name." He nodded and grinned.

"The *Junction Journal*." I sat back and watched him pour the brown liquid from the bottle with ease.

"Nope. Millie Kay." He picked up the glass, turned back around, and placed it on the island in front of Darren.

"That's right." I laughed. "I should've known. I'm sorry."

"No." Sawyer waved me off. "What would you like to drink? Margarita, beer, wine?" He rattled off a few other drinks and cocktails.

"Water is fine." I didn't even want that but took the cold bottle he'd retrieved from the refrigerator with a grateful smile.

"Your mother is one of a kind." He didn't have to tell Darren or me that. "She's been real fun to work with. In fact, Carol told me what she said today about the lights when she came in and then snuck in the comment about why Carol would have killed Peter Hill."

A wry grin crossed his lips. He picked up his glass and held it up to toast Darren.

"She did what?" Darren leaned back on the stool and looked at me. "You didn't tell me that."

"I hadn't gotten to talk to you much." I reminded him that it'd all happened today and not much time had passed between us leaving Mama's little impromptu get-together and now. "You know Mama. She gets right to the issue. Which is why we are here." I nudged Darren.

"Yeah?" Sawyer laid the drink on the island, never taking his hand from around it. He looked at Darren. "Do you think she killed Peter Hill?" He snickered and took a drink. "Or do you think I killed Peter Hill?"

"Neither. But I do think it has something to do with Alan Hill." Immediately, I recognized Darren was beating around the bush about Jay Renner.

"How's that?" Sawyer was going to make us work for it. He glanced down at his drink, not looking at us.

"There hasn't been a ghost walk on Halloweenie since Alan Hill was murdered. From what I understand, Jay was convicted of the murder, but you and the Hills disagreed. Every time Jay is up for a parole hearing, Peter Hill goes to make sure he doesn't get out." I snorted. "Because we all know Jay was sent away on circumstantial evidence."

"Small town. People want to get justice or feel like they've locked up someone so they can feel safe again." Sawyer nodded and lifted his glass to me before he took a drink. "They didn't even give him a fair chance."

His lips drew apart as the bourbon slid down his throat.

"Ahh," he sighed. "But it also doesn't mean we killed Peter Hill just because there's a parole hearing coming up."

With his hand gripped around the glass, he uncurled his pointer finger and gestured it toward me.

"You be sure you write that too." He smiled. "Because that's why you're here, right?" He wagged the one finger between Darren and me. "You work for his mom. You want the scoop, but you"—he stopped wagging his finger and pointed it at Darren—"you want to make daddy mad, so you're helping her."

"Not true at all. In fact, Violet is a great investigator, and she's helped Dad on a couple of cases. She wants to make sure Carol isn't named one of Dad's suspects."

"That and the fact we have a witness who said you and Peter Hill had met privately a few days before he was murdered." Suddenly I felt like Mama—saying whatever words came to my mind without giving them a second thought, which you could get away with at Mama's age but not in your twenties.

"You're right. The conversation Peter and I had before his death was something that would change Jay's life and people of this town." Sawyer gnawed on the inside of his cheek and stared at us intently for a few seconds before he turned around and retrieved the bourbon bottle. "Peter had a memory of the night his father was murdered. He saw Jay down at the jiggle joint." He slowly poured the bourbon in the glass, and the thick, creamy liquid seeped over the ice cube. He looked up from underneath his brows and focused on Darren. "Peter got up and left Jay there. He took the ghost walk trail from the seashore to the park, not figuring he'd run into anyone, since it was way past everyone's bedtime. The ghost walk would've been closed much earlier, so he didn't want people to see him drunk."

That must've been the part of the reason Sawyer owed Darren a favor, but what was Sawyer really referring to? I leaned in a little more.

"Then he saw someone running away with Jay's jacket on. The cops came, and he told them it was Jay with the jacket on. He was so drunk he'd forgotten he'd left Jay at the jiggle joint a few minutes earlier, and there wasn't enough time. Jay couldn't run up through the woods near the jiggle joint, down Main Street, through Holiday Park, and down the trail to kill Alan Hill."

Sawyer shook his head.

"No one wanted to hear that little timeline. Darren didn't want to get involved until a few years ago after he got a conscience about him."

"That's not true. I wasn't sure what had happened. When I left the bar, I left the two of them there with the other employees. I saw someone run the opposite direction when I was up on the lighthouse having my last drink of the night. I saw the jacket, too, and figured it was Jay until I found out later Jay had actually slept on the couch at the bar. Needed to sleep off the drinks." Darren tried to tell his side.

"The police searched all over Holiday Junction for him and went door to door. That was when they saw him at the bar."

"Not necessarily true. They didn't find him at the bar because the bar was closed. My employees at the time didn't know he was in there sleeping in my office. They didn't check my office when they closed the bar because I wasn't there and figured I'd locked it up." Darren swirled his glass around. The ice cube rattled against the sides. "I got to the bar the next day, and there he was. I called the police because I knew they were looking for him."

"How did Darren help again?" It seemed to me he'd turned Jay in, not helped him.

"It wasn't until a few years ago when Darren had grown up and realized Jay probably hadn't run past the lighthouse the opposite way after Alan was murdered because Jay was at the bar, passed out. The employees who work at the bar in the summer are generally kids who want to work at the beach for a summer job. They come and go. Seasonal help." Sawyer glanced at Darren for confirmation.

"I get a lot of that, but you didn't come to the bar much over the summer, so you would think most of the young college students were tourists or something." Darren clarified because of the confused look on my face. "I'd not grown up. I just started to follow the newspaper, listen to what my mom and aunt were saying. Plus, my dad. He wasn't the chief then but was on the force. He, too, agreed there wasn't much real evidence to hold Jay on the murder."

"Darren came to me, and we've been looking at the case ever since." Sawyer opened one of the drawers on the island and pulled out some papers. "We scoured all the paper clipping and filings."

"We didn't. Nora helped," Darren corrected him. "The library has it all. Better than the courthouse."

"The meeting Peter and I had was all the information I'd collected. He agreed he might've gotten it wrong, so he was expected to change his statement at the upcoming parole hearing." Sawyer's bit of news was something huge to chew on.

"You mean to tell me Peter Hill was going to tell the parole board that he has changed his testimony and is now not sure at all who killed his father?" I had to make this very clear. "This would turn the case upside down and could give Jay immediate release."

"Right." Sawyer tapped the top of the file. "And this also means someone Peter told didn't want Jay to go free."

"The killer," I said. A chill hit the room.

"The killer." Sawyer nodded, his eyes ghostly and hollow.

"And it wouldn't be Carol." I knew she definitely wasn't a suspect.

"Which reminds me why we are here," Darren said. He downed the last bit of his drink. "Can you give us a copy of your security footage from the entire night until Carol left for work the next day? We want to make sure Dad doesn't try to pin it on her."

"Too late. He already came by to get it." Sawyer glanced between us. "He cleared her."

"Did you tell him about you and Peter meeting?" I asked.

"No. I kept it to myself for fear I'd be next." A look of fright crossed his face for a moment before he cleared his throat. "Ahem." He sat up straighter as though he'd realized his body language had shifted. "Not that I'm scared of anyone, but until Matthew gets some good leads, then I'll come forward. I don't want to hinder the case, you know."

"Yeah. Thanks for the drink." Darren got up from the stool and looked at me. "Ready to go?"

"One more thing." I got down and asked about something I needed to know. "Whatever happened to Jay's jacket?"

"We never found the jacket." The words I didn't want to hear came out of his mouth.

"I know you said Carol has been taken off the suspect list, but how did she feel about Peter's change of testimony?" I had to know because she was planning on running against him in the next election.

"Carol didn't want Peter to go to the hearing because it would hurt her chances of beating him in the election. People around here took it hard when Alan was murdered. Unlike today, murders back then were years, if not decades, apart." Sawyer started to walk us to the door. "She wanted us to collect all the evidence we could and start to leak it over the weeks leading up to the election so people could see how Peter didn't tell the truth." He stopped shy of the front door. "I know that makes Carol look bad, but again, small town, small politics. Do things now that might not be on the up-and-up and apologize later. That's the motto around here."

I planted a fake smile on my face and gave him a good southern thank-you.

Darren was fine to drive the moped. He wasn't drunk or even the slightest bit tipsy. The buzz of the moped in my ear, mixed with all the stuff and story Sawyer told me, played like a movie, and before I realized it, Darren was parking at the base of the lighthouse.

"Why didn't you take me to the Jubilee Inn?" I asked.

"Because I know from your silence you've been muddling over what you just heard and need to process it by talking it through." He turned the moped off and made sure the kickstand was solidly on the ground before he got off. Then he took my hand and helped me to the ground.

Electricity pulsed in my fingertips and hit my heart, causing me to suddenly inhale. I coughed to cover it up.

"You think you know me so well, don't you, Darren Strickland?" I asked him.

"Am I wrong?" The moon shined down on him, illuminating his smirk.

"Whatever." I pulled the straps off from under my chin and handed him the helmet. "I guess we can talk about it. But now I want to know who doesn't want Jay out of prison."

"The killer. The real killer."

"Name?" I asked, making sure he knew I wanted a name, not just the obvious.

"And that's what we need to find out." He opened the door of the lighthouse, and we took the few stairs up to his living quarters.

Immediately he headed to the refrigerator and took out two bottles of beer. I looked around the circular room and decided to sit on the built-in half-moon couch that overlooked the side facing the ocean.

I curled my leg up under me, twisted my body to the back, and laid my elbows out to rest my chin on my crossed-over hands.

"It's so pretty." The sound of the waves penetrated the walls, and the spotlight of the moon waved in and over the dark sea. "Every time is better than the last."

Darren had called the 1800s lighthouse a real-life kaleidoscope once, and ever since, I saw it from his eyes.

"Here." He handed me the beer bottle.

"Is it true what he said?" I didn't want to repeat what Sawyer had said about why Darren was hanging out with me. It hurt too much. I didn't want to be anyone's pawn, but I also had to face it—I certainly didn't want that to be the only reason for Darren's attention.

"It's all true. Jay couldn't've done it." He sat down next to me and slipped off his shoes.

"No, I mean the part where you're only hanging around me to make your dad mad." There was this heavy blanket of silence between us, making it hard for me to breathe. "My gosh." I got up and walked across the round room to the kitchen, where I set the beer on the counter. "I'm leaving."

"What? Why?" Darren hurried across the room. He took big strides and blocked the door. "Why, Violet?"

"Why?" I laughed and turned back around. "I didn't realize I was some sort of pawn in your silly little family game, Darren. Your dad obviously doesn't like the fact I'm a reporter, and he must take that up with your mom. I can handle that. But you." I pointed at him from across the room, where I'd finally stopped at the window overlooking the ocean. "I never figured this" —I gestured between us—"was because you wanted to use me to hurt your family."

"That's not true." He stalked over, his eyes roaming over me.

"What? Are you trying to win me over from Rhett? I'm the prize in this silly little game? I don't play games."

"Violet," he said with a laugh. He ran his hand through his hair, and I was eerily aware of his closeness. "You play games with everyone in this town to get the next big scoop. Do you think I don't know that you are searching for the one big story to get you out of here? That's why you don't want to get too involved as the Merry Maker. That's why you don't want your mother to live here or join any of the women's groups. If anyone is using anyone, it's you. You're using me to get information."

"You are so full of yourself, Darren Strickland, that it makes me sick. I— I. Ugh." I fisted my hands and jutted them to my side. "My mama warned me about guys like you! You've got more moves than a Slinky!"

I pushed past him and then quickly turned on the balls of my feet.

"Yep. She was right. You've got that new-car smell." I stalked off to the door.

Not quick enough. He bolted past me and stood between the outside world and me.

Suddenly, the moonlight filtered through the dark lighthouse, catching the twinkle in his eyes.

"Violet Rhinehammer, I do believe you're falling for me." He grinned. I stood there speechless. "That's good." He leaned forward and lowered his voice. "I've fallen for you too."

He slid his arm around my waist, pulled me to him, and gave me a kiss like I'd never had before.

I was a goner.

Smitten.

CHAPTER FOURTEEN

"Did you have fun last night?" Mama came into the office with a mug of coffee in each hand. She set one of them down on my desk.

"Last night?" I picked up the coffee mug and held it in front of my face so she didn't see how red it was.

"I didn't even hear you come in. It must've been well after midnight." Mama sat down in the chair and eyeballed me over the rim of her mug as she took a drink. "I'm guessing you were doing last-minute"—she lowered the mug and whispered—"Merry Maker stuff, since today is the first day of the Halloweenie Festival."

"I have to admit I was surprised you were at the inn when I got back." I had to change the subject.

There was no way I was going to tell Mama about the many kisses between Darren and me, which were why I'd gotten home around one in the morning. Much too late for me.

"Then I knew you were thinking about it because when I got up, you'd already left to come to work. But I knew you'd come home because I had to pick up your clothes off the floor and your work bag was gone," she trilled.

"Aren't you the regular Miss Marple?" My right brow twitched up. I took another drink of coffee. "I am excited about the festival but not as the you-know-what. And stop saying it out loud," I warned her. "You never know who will come through the doors."

I glanced out the office window, hoping Darren was waltzing up the walkway. He wasn't.

The sky glowed a faint pink as the sun was about to start trickling up over the office and then settling high in the sky for a bright fall day for the big festival.

"I have to get the morning edition out with all the activities for the event page. Thank you for the coffee." I took one more drink before I turned my attention back to the online morning edition of the *Junction Journal*.

"Hurry up." She got up. "We need to get over to Bubbly Boutique. Fern already called me about you talking to her and her mama. And we can pick up our Halloween costumes while we are there for tonight's costume party."

"I forgot all about that." I sighed. My thoughts immediately went to couple costumes and how fun it would be for Darren and me to go as something together. But we weren't a couple.

At least, I told myself that, since we'd not even committed to each other. It was just a kiss—or a few. That was all.

The phone rang, causing Mama to rush off.

"Happy Halloweenie," I heard Mama call out in her excited voice. "This is the *Junction Journal*, Millie Kay speaking." There were several mm-hmms and yeses on Mama's end before I heard her say, "Let me get her. Hold on."

Mama appeared at my office door.

"Hershal is on the phone." She put her hand in the pocket of her dress, which had ghosts on the fabric. "He wants to talk to you about what you're going to write about the ghost walk."

"I'll talk to him." I picked up the phone. "Good morning, Hershal. Happy Halloweenie." I hoped my happy tone would somewhat mitigate his worries. "I was just working on the online edition for this morning. I'm excited to talk about the ghost walk."

"That means you won't be mentioning the…" His sentence dangled.

"I don't think it's part of the walk, is it?" It was my way of not mentioning the unmentionable but also letting him know.

"Violet. You are a gem to this community. Kristine told us that, and she's right." He paused. "Do you know what you're going to say?"

"I'll let you read it for yourself. I hope you have a wonderful day." After he attempted one more time to get it out of me, we said our goodbyes. In reality, I had no idea what I was even going to write, since it was next on my list.

Really, it'd been first on the list, but Darren was first in my heart, and clearly, the kiss had been tattooed in my mind, making it hard to concentrate on anything.

"You've got this." I nodded at the screen and hunkered down to get the online paper ready to go out before everyone got up for the day.

The clock read 6:30 a.m. Our time of highest internet traffic was between seven and nine. The festival didn't get kicked off until noon at Holiday Park with Kristine and Mayor Paisley as the masters of ceremony.

"Thank you to the Merry Maker for picking this year's final Halloweenie send-off." I plopped in a photo of the sign Vern had made, which Darren had hammered down into the sandy spot next to the path on the seashore side. "We will be having a fun Halloweenie beach bonfire not only to mark the very end of the warmer beach nights but to come together as a community during the thankful holiday season coming up."

It was my way of giving a little nod to Thanksgiving.

"And send." I hit the return key to make the online paper go live.

I picked up my phone and opened the messaging app so I could send Fern a text.

Me: Good morning, Fern. Sorry to be so early, but I thought I could come by the shop before your mom opens. I'd like to talk to her without anyone around.

Fern: We are going there now. We are opening an hour early thanks to the great response we got from the flyers we put around town about the Halloween costume sale.

Me: Maybe we can get you an ad going in the paper too.

Fern: Are we becoming friendly, Violet?

Me: We will see... see you in a little bit.

I snorted and put down my phone.

"Mama," I called across the hall to her office. "Are you ready to go to the Bubbly Boutique? I just texted Fern, and she said they were on their way there. They are opening early because of a sale, and I wanted to talk to her before they open."

"Violet." Mama walked in and smiled. "The paper is wonderful. I love how you put in all the little scary puns with the ghost walk. Ghostly good time." Her eyes grew as big as the grin on her face. "Haunting fun." Her shoulder shimmied. "They are going to love it."

"Get your purse." I clicked my computer off, threw my phone into my bag, and picked it up. Then I met Mama at the door. "Did you drive the golf cart?"

"Are you going to let me drive us?" she asked.

"I sure am." I put my arm around her as we walked down the sidewalk and the little sandy path to what was once the driveway of the old cottage house.

It wasn't much of a driveway. There were small diamond pavers on top of the sand with dune grass growing in the crack. Perfect for Mama's little golf cart.

The Bubbly Boutique was located on Main Street with the other boutiques. Mama hadn't yet discovered it because she always had her eyes set on Emily's Treasures, which was way more than just clothing. The Bubbly Boutique had more upscale clothes and things I'd never wear except on special occasions like New Year's Eve, a wedding, possibly a funeral, or maybe a romantic dinner.

The last idea got me all giggly.

"What?" Mama glanced at me and put the golf cart in reverse. "You just thought of something that made you happy."

"Daddy called." I was bound and determined not to let Mama know about the kisses. Bringing up Daddy would certainly not let her read my facial features. "He misses you, and he hasn't decorated a single thing. Weeks before now, you'd have all the fall decorations out. Why on earth do you want a divorce?"

"I told you that after you left, we had nothing in common. It was like we sat there searching for things to talk about." Mama pushed the pedal down, zooming away from the ocean.

As soon as we headed down Main Street, the sky took on a much different look. The baby blues, pinks, and oranges collided where the very tip-top of the sun started to wink over the mountains. Soon I'd be able to remove my sweatshirt, since the sunshine would take the dew off the roofs and blades of grass.

Sprinkles of yellow and orange and a splash of red painted the leaves of the trees for what would probably be the last week before they dropped to the ground and left the trees bare until the springtime budding.

"What did he say?" It was the first time Mama appeared to be interested. I mean really interested.

"He said it wasn't the same and he missed you. He was even crying." Though he'd never admit it, I could tell by his voice. It wasn't the strong voice I used to talk to on the phone before Mama had lost her mind.

"He was?" Mama's brows dipped for a moment. Just a moment, giving me a little glimpse of hope. "He didn't cry when I was there. They don't know what they got until it's gone. Just like that song."

"Don't you think it means he now sees it and can be more appreciative?" It was a Hail Mary for me that she didn't dare try to catch.

"A little too late." She gripped the wheel as a big sigh caused her shoulders to move up around her ears and then fall back into position. "Now. What costumes are we going to wear to the costume party?"

"I'm not sure." I reached down into my bag and looked at my phone to see if there was a text from Darren. Not that I was invested in him too much, I told myself, but it would be fun to go as something with him. "I'm sure we'll find something."

I lifted my fingers to my lips. I swear I could still feel the tingle.

Nothing.

Mama parked the golf cart in front of Bubbly Boutique. "Everything okay?" she asked. "You got awful quiet after you checked your phone."

"I'm good. You know I'm always wondering about the views and readership of the paper. Now that Peter Hill has died, I can't help but hope people like Nettie, Kristine, and the Dunns will be able to advertise in there." It was a lie, but maybe how I felt about the kiss was a lie to myself.

It was a simple kiss, and Darren probably didn't mean anything by it. Just a kiss. Not a marriage proposal. Or even a let's-do-it-again type event. If it was, he'd have already called or texted or something. Right?

All the scenarios popped into my head as I sat there and flat-out lied to my mama's face.

"Just a lot to digest over the last twenty-four hours." Now that wasn't a lie, and it did make me feel a little better.

"Twenty-four hours?" Mama scoffed and got out of the golf cart to meet me on the sidewalk. "You mean forty-eight hours."

"Let's go in here and see how we can help Nettie." When I tugged on the shop door, it was locked.

Mama and I put our hands over our eyes as we plastered our faces against the shop window to see inside. I gave it a hard knock. Then I noticed Fern had walked across the back of the shop to get our attention.

"Sorry. We keep it locked until we open because it never fails that someone will come in before we open." Fern greeted us and looked both ways before she let us inside. She locked the door behind us. "I know we haven't been the best to each other." Fern drew her shoulders back and then down as she stood tall in front of me. "But I'm hoping we can put that behind us."

"I don't think it was my Violet who didn't put her best foot forward when it came to you," Mama said, jumping to my defense.

"It's fine, Mama." I put a hand on her forearm to stop her from going any further. It was best to just agree and accept the way Fern saw things instead of trying to get my point of view across. "I agree. Let's move forward."

"Mom!" Fern called to the back of the shop. "Violet and Millie Kay are here!"

While we waited for Nettie to emerge from the back room, Mama and I looked around at the costumes.

"Are you going to the costume party tonight?" Fern asked.

"We are." I ran my hand down a few of the costumes and slid back a hanger here and there to see what the disguise was.

"What about this one?" Mama stood at another rack of costumes and help a gangster-looking outfit.

"Nah. Why don't we go as some sort of sleuths?" I found the idea to be kinda funny and fitting.

"I have a perfect one!" Fern's excitement was contagious.

Mama and I hurried over to the rack where Fern dug through the hangers to find the one she thought we'd like.

"A tree?" Mama's enthusiasm waned when Fern pulled out a dead tree trunk with a hole for the face.

"And this." In her other hand, she held up a costume looking more like Sherlock Holmes's outfit. "One of you can be the detective or investigator while the other is the tree."

Fern laughed with a huge smile.

"I don't get it." Mama's face pinched like she'd just eaten a very sour dill pickle.

"The investigator can stand behind the tree and look around with the magnifying glass in her hand like you're snooping." Fern role-played.

"That's hilarious!" I clapped my hands. "Mama, that's hilarious."

"Mmm." Mama's nose curled. "I'm not so sure. I was thinking more along the lines of something more sophisticated."

"That's the beauty of this." Fern shook both hands, dangling the costumes in front of us. "No one would ever think you'd come to a costume party dressed like this."

"And there is a contest," I reminded Mama.

"Fine. But I'm not the tree." Mama insisted and took the Sherlock outfit.

"I'm sorry!" Nettie rushed out the door from behind the counter. "I was trying to get all the things done for Fern for the shop just in case Matthew Strickland hauled me off to jail."

Mama had found the dressing room.

"Hazelynn told me about the public argument you had with Peter. He didn't allow you to have a vendor tent at Holiday Park during Halloweenie thanks to some sort of broken rule." I got to the point. "And I don't need to know any of those particulars. I also know you were left out of the advertising scheme, though it technically wasn't a scheme but more of a morality issue."

If any of the shop owners Peter had decided not to use the advertising dollars for had tried to call it a scheme or sue him, I knew it wouldn't have held up in court. He didn't really break a rule. He just didn't include everyone, and from the minutes I'd read during the night, he made sure it was on record each time a shop owner asked if there was somehow an oversight.

"I guess what the chief is going on about is the argument. What will get you off the hook is the alibi." I watched Nettie shift uncomfortably.

"That's the problem. Once he made me leave the park, I had to haul all the stuff back here. It was late afternoon when it was all completed. I worked on a plan on how to get customers here during the festival. By the time I got it planned out, it was way up into the wee hours of the night, so I slept here." She sighed. "The only person who saw me the next morning was Hazelynn when I went to get a coffee at Brewing Beans."

"She did mention how you were there really early. Earlier than normal and in the same clothes." I hated to tell her what Hazelynn had told me because I was sure this was where Matthew had gotten his information. "I'll need you to find a way to prove you weren't there or anywhere near the park."

"How?" she asked and shook her head.

"I don't know. Did you get on social media? Did you make a call? What about the GPS on your phone?" I questioned.

"Mom!" Fern squealed. "I have you on my GPS. I wonder if someone can look at my phone and somehow see your information."

"That doesn't necessarily mean she didn't have her phone with her, but it's worth a shot." I didn't really see much of a solution to helping her with an alibi. "Other than that, I'm just hoping to find the killer or that Matthew finds the killer. Do you know Millard Ramsey?"

"Yes. We know pretty much everyone here." Fern answered for them both.

"Right before Peter was found, the Headless Horseman teased us before racing the horse down the path. Can you think of any reason Millard's son would want to have killed Peter?"

The color fell from their faces.

"Tito Ramsey, Millard's son, is best friends with Jay Renner."

Fern's words sent chills up my spine.

CHAPTER FIFTEEN

I couldn't get on with my day until I went to check out Millard Ramsey's horseback-riding tourist attraction at the Hippity-Hoppity Ranch.

Mama had been too busy in the dressing room to even hear most of the conversation I'd had with Nettie and Fern, so it was easy to drop her off and tell her to go back over the meeting minutes to see if she could research anything else involving Peter Hill.

One problem with getting to Hippity-Hoppity Ranch was that I had to walk down the seaside sidewalk, past the jiggle joint, and even farther past the lighthouse, doubling my chances of running into or at least seeing Darren.

Without hesitation, I power walked like I was on fire past both of Darren's hot spots with my head down. That was probably the fastest I'd walked in years.

The ranch was on the beach and had what looked to be about five acres with a barn built in the back. There was an open stable in an enclosed fence area, where I noticed some movement. As I made my way up there, I started to imagine how I wanted the conversation to go.

In my mind, it was made easy, and if Tito did do it, he'd come clean and beg for forgiveness while I made the 911 call to the police station, and that would be it.

Did it go that way? Never.

"I hope you aren't here to ride." The woman glanced up. Her brown hair appeared to be one length and pulled back at the nape of her neck in a small ponytail. She wore a plaid long-sleeved shirt and bootcut light-blue jeans, the tips of her cowboy boots sticking out from the hems. "You look a little too fancied up."

She shoved the pitchfork in the ground and leaned on it. The woman pushed back the stray strands of hair from around her face with the back of her gloved hand.

I looked down at the outfit I'd thrown on from Mama's stash of Halloween garb and laughed.

"No." I shook my head and took out a business card I'd had from my previous job, which reminded me that I needed to order a new one. This one was fine, since it had my name and phone number on it. "I'm Violet Rhinehammer from the *Junction Journal*. I'm posting the daily events for Halloweenie, and I understand your son is the Headless Horseman."

"Oh, that." She let go of the pitchfork, pulled off the gloves, and took my card. She looked at it. "He does that for fun. I used to do it when they paid me. Not so much anymore."

"I was there when he did it a couple of days ago for a sneak peek of the ghost walk." By the look on her face and the hard stance she took, she knew why I was really there.

Out of the corner of my eye, I saw someone's head pop up from the stall next to us, but I didn't act like I saw it when the person disappeared as quick as they'd come up.

"You're here to ask about Peter Hill, aren't you?" She gave a slight shift of her eyes toward the other stall. So subtle, she didn't know I'd noticed her little movement. "You're not here to do an article on the Headless Horsemen. I'm going to have to ask you to leave."

"Don't you want to see justice prevail?" I asked, digging my shoes in the sand. "If your son had something to do with Peter Hill because he was Jay Renner's best friend, I would think he'd want to know he hurt a man who was actually going to Jay's parole hearing to tell what he remembered about that night his father was killed. Jay couldn't've killed Alan."

"He was going to what?" Tito popped up in the next stall. He, too, had a pitchfork in his hand. Those tools were for mucking the stalls, but they sure did look like deadly weapons to me.

"Do you mind putting those down and coming over here so we can talk?" I made the suggestion, feeling much better when they both did exactly as I had asked.

"Why don't you come on in the barn where my office is located? I just started some coffee because Tito and I like to get warm by the small potbelly and sip on some coffee during the cooler months." Millard was inviting, and I agreed.

Am I walking toward my death? I thought with each step of the way as the silence wrapped its arms around me. The closer I got to the barn, the cooler the temperature seemed to get, and the cold settled deep into my bones.

The barn was not really a barn for animals but more like what we'd call a pole barn in Kentucky. It was an erected building that stood like a barn, but the inside had all the luxuries of an office or even a home. They'd been built as such where I was from.

In this case, it held the offices for Hippity-Hoppity Ranch, and the logo was as cute as the name. It was a horse wearing a straw hat with bunny ears on it.

The barn was a true working office. Other people in there and in different spaces saw us come in, which assured that if I did go missing, there were many people in here that would notice I was gone.

"Did you think we were going to come in here and kill you?" Millard snorted once we walked to the back of the barn, where there was a potbelly stove with a kettle on top. The smell of coffee was much more pleasant than the horse dung from the stalls. "I could see your face relax."

"You never know." I took the mug she handed me and looked inside. "Cowboy coffee."

"I like you. You know your coffee, and I love your accent. I heard you were from the South." She picked up the kettle and poured the hot water into the mug, where it mixed with the grounds to make the perfect-tasting coffee.

"Thank you. I do know a few things about coffee and the South. Not much about horses, so I think it's really cool what you do here." Tito made his own coffee, and he sat down in one of the many rocking chairs, which was a strange decoration for an office, but whatever.

"What was it you were saying about Peter Hill and the parole board?" Tito took a vested interest.

"I was saying whoever killed Peter probably knew he was going to the parole board to reverse his previous statements after some of his memories of the night his father was murdered had surfaced." Not really what I was going to say, but at least it was a more positive spin than accusing Tito of killing Peter to avenge his best friend.

"He remembered." Tito let out a big sigh of relief. "So when is Jay getting out?"

"He isn't. Peter didn't get to the parole board hearing. It's coming up." I watched Tito's face change expressions. "I'm sorry, but I do have to ask if you killed Peter Hill that morning after I'd seen you on the path?"

"No," he stated with certainty. "I can't believe you'd even ask me that. I knew they were bringing back the ghost walk, so I put on the costume in hopes they'd see me and ask us to participate again. That's it. Boy, that backfired."

"It's a case of being in the wrong place at the wrong time." Millard looked at her son with love. "No one is accusing. She's a reporter. It's what they do to get information from people."

I let her comment wash right over me.

"Have you thought about the idea that someone wanted Jay to stay in jail and knew Peter was going to change his statement?" Tito asked before he jumped up and took off, leaving me a good question I'd not considered. Millard politely told me to have a good day before she darted after her son.

Tito's question might have sent me down the rabbit hole if I'd not glanced around on my way out of the barn. In the corner of the office with Tito Ramsey's name on the door sat what clearly looked like a jack-in-the-box.

I pulled my phone out of my pocket and walked out the barn door. No messages from Darren. I hit my contact list, and on my way back to the office, I dialed Chief Matthew Strickland.

"Don't ask me yet. I'll come down and give a statement tomorrow." That was exactly how I started my phone conversation when he answered. "But the jack-in-the-box Peter Hill's body replaced from the ghost walk coffin is sitting in the corner office of Tito Ramsey, the Headless Horseman and best friend to Jay Renner."

It was enough for Matthew to thank me and tell me, "Good job."

CHAPTER SIXTEEN

The rumbles about Tito Ramsey wrapped around the gossip mill like the vine around a pumpkin's stem. Everyone had heard that Holiday Junction Police had gotten a warrant to search Hippity-Hoppity Ranch, where they found the jack-in-the-box and the Headless Horseman outfit. Both had Tito's fingerprints on them, making them sufficient evidence for the police to hold Tito for questioning.

Even though Halloweenie was in full swing, it was when the news broke that Matthew had formally charged Tito that the holiday excitement really got going.

I'd been able to publish updates on the case all afternoon until it was time to go back to the inn, where I'd meet Mama so we could get ready for the costume party and go together. Especially now that she was Sherlock Holmes and I was the tree she'd stand behind all night. She'd peek around me through her magnifying glass as if she were peeping.

The lack of communication from Darren told me everything I needed to know. Whatever attraction I thought I had for him was just my imagination.

The party tent had been erected at Holiday Park. It wasn't at all scary like I thought. Twinkly lights dangled from not only the tent but from the trees, as did hanging solar-powered chandeliers. All the carriage lights throughout the park were turned on, and their bases had twinkling lights curled around them. Too bad this wasn't what every holiday looked like.

I stood there in my tree stump costume and looked at all the fun costumes going in and out from underneath that tent. There were hot dogs, spiders, a Spider-Man, bat wings, prisoners, colorful tutus, skeletons, popcorn, athletes, and a banana along with the typical clown and animal get-ups. The ages ranged from babies to elderly people in wheelchairs.

The crowd was large, and I was sure that was because everyone was relieved the police had someone in custody.

"Tonight, we will be visited by unresolved affairs throughout Holiday Junction," Hershal said, his voice booming deeply as he stood in full costume next to the fountain where he had a crowd of about twenty in front of him.

I smiled. Hazelynn stood next to him and noticed Mama and me. She gave a slight wave. Mama jumped behind me and looked around with the magnifying glass up to her eye. Hazelynn gave us a thumbs-up.

Someone with a clipboard, a full beard, and a huge clock dangling from his neck gave us a once-over before writing something down on the clipboard.

"That must be the judge." Mama adjusted the Sherlock Holmes hat and really started to dance back and forth behind me, peeking out from both sides. "We are a sleuthing duo," she told the man. He nodded and stayed there, watching Mama continue to woo him with her sneaky techniques while I stood still.

Finally, he walked off and headed to another partygoer.

"We should've curled twinkly lights around you like the trees here in the park." Mama's eyes were hidden by the cap. "Let's go do that."

"No, Mama." I wasn't about to walk around with twinkly lights on me. "He already judged us and moved on."

"I want to win that prize." She stomped, on the verge of a hissy fit, when Darren walked up. "What on earth are you supposed to be?"

"Darren Strickland. I think I make a good one." He smiled, shifting his eyes to me. "Tree trunk." He nodded.

"Not just any tree trunk," Mama said, saving me from cussing him out. "I'm hiding behind her and sleuthing for clues." Mama's voice took on a mysterious tone.

"Good one." He nodded but kept his eyes on me. The band at the amphitheater started to play, giving Mama the itch to dance.

"I see some of the Leading Ladies," Mama pointed out. "Come over there when you two are done with whatever business got Violet so worked up today."

"Mama." I gasped.

"You think you can keep whatever is bothering you a secret from me, but you can't. Violet Jean Rhinehammer, I know you better than you know yourself." Mama waved the magnifying glass at me and took off toward the amphitheater, leaving me alone with Darren.

"I've been bothering you today?" Darren's snarky tone made the question sound like a compliment.

"I'm fine." I wasn't about to give him any reason to think otherwise, even though Mama had pointed it out. "She's lost her mind. I never even mentioned you today."

"I can see you're bothered." Darren winked.

"I'm bothered you think you're too good to be in a costume." I put my hand on my tree-trunk hip.

"I'm the judge of the costume party, so they told me not to come in costume. The bar is sponsoring the prize." He pointed at the vendor booth where Owen and Shawn stood behind beer taps, pouring the beer into plastic cups. "My own mama wouldn't let me take out an ad."

"Hmm." I was going to say something smart-alecky but jerked up. "You are the judge?"

"Yes." He slowly nodded. "Why? What's the look?"

"We need to find the man in the long beard, clock, and clip board." I suddenly wondered who that was and why he'd taken a long time to watch Mama and me. "I think we have the wrong killer. Why else would Tito display the jack-in-the-box? If he was the killer, surely to goodness, he must have hidden it.

At this point I was rambling to myself and sorting out all the details in my head.

It was like Darren could read my mind. Immediately, we parted, one going one way and one going the other. Darren headed to the amphitheater while I ran into the large crowd underneath the tent where the food was currently being served.

I weaved in and out, darting around a dog, banana, hot dog, and witch, until I finally saw the man with the beard, clock, and clipboard.

All of a sudden, the lights went out in the tent, leaving everyone in the dark for a moment. Several screams and cries followed.

The lights came right back on.

"Don't worry! The plug was accidentally pulled out of the circuit," I overheard someone yell out before a shrill scream stopped everyone right where they were.

"Help! Help!" The voice I recognized was Carol Dunn's. "You! Get him! He stabbed my husband!"

I ran toward the yelling as fast as I could.

"Call an ambulance! Call an ambulance!" she shrieked, panic in her voice.

When I got through the crowd, Carol was crouched down on the ground. Someone dressed as Snoopy had tackled the man with the clock around his neck and held him against the ground while Sawyer Dunn was lying in a pool of blood.

"It was him!" Carol's eyes blazed with anger and uncertainty as she held Sawyer's hand.

I reached down and ripped off the man's beard just as Matthew Strickland ran up.

"Dad?" I asked when I recognized the face.

CHAPTER SEVENTEEN

To say Mama and I spent all night at the jail in shock and despair was an understatement. We not only looked like fools in our tree and detective costumes, but we looked like fools to the community who had embraced and loved us now that my dad was in custody for the attempted murder of Sawyer Dunn.

"He didn't do it. No way did your father do it." Mama was going to rub the skin right off her hands if she didn't stop rubbing on them. "Did you even know your father was in town?"

"No." My mind had so many thoughts it was hard to say even a single word.

"What on earth, Violet Jean?" Mama had called me by my two names twice tonight, both times with worry. That was the only time she called me by my two names.

"Do you think he did it?" she asked again.

"I don't know, Mama." I wasn't sure, and I certainly wasn't going to sit there and tell her the details of what I'd seen or about Daddy holding the knife.

"My dad said it's going to be a while, so you two should probably go back to the inn and get some sleep. Come back tomorrow around visiting hours or if you have a lawyer." I saw Darren's mouth moving, but all I heard was "blah, blah, blah."

And something about a lawyer.

With a little coaxing, I got Mama to leave the jail. We both decided to walk to the house on Heart Way instead of going to the inn. Even though there wasn't any real furniture in the house, we could at least sit on the outdoor furniture with her fireplace going to keep us warm. We weren't going to sleep.

"Who are you calling at this hour?" Mama questioned me, breaking the silence in the dead of night.

"Diffy Delk." He was the only lawyer I knew who had any dealings in Holiday Junction. "He didn't answer." I held onto my phone because it was too hard to try to get to my jeans pocket with the tree trunk on.

But the tree trunk was keeping me warm. The temperature had dropped to at least fifty degrees, and Mama was already dressed in a long trench coat.

"Did you know he was the judge of the costume contest?" Mama asked so innocently. "I wonder if we were going to win?"

"Mama, he wasn't the judge. He was only pretending to be. Darren was the judge. That was why he wasn't dressed up."

"Oh," she whispered.

For the rest of the walk, we were silent. As soon as we hit the backyard, she started talking and didn't stop until the sun came up.

She told me there was no way Daddy did this and that she was on a mission to get to the office and research everything and everyone associated with Peter Hill, but as she talked, I got to thinking about what Tito had said to me.

"Mama, do you think we are on the wrong trail?" I asked and looked up over the house as the sun started to peek over the mountain.

"What?" The early morning sunrise illuminated Mama's face. Her mascara had dripped down her cheeks, and the lines around her eyes had gotten deeper as the worry lay on her like makeup, thick and heavy.

"Maybe someone knew Peter was going to retract his testimony against Jay Renner and they didn't want Jay Renner to come out of jail."

"Violet, who on earth would do that?" Mama asked.

"The real killer." My jaw dropped. "I didn't see it last night because I was so upset about Daddy."

I stood up to get my blood going. The tree-trunk costume now lay across the back of one of the chairs at the table with the gorgeous Flowerworks tablescape.

"Peter and Sawyer met the other day before Peter was murdered. Peter told him he was going to retract his statement after he'd had a memory and that there was no way Jay could have been at the scene of his father's murder." I gulped. "I think whoever really killed Alan Hill knew Peter was going to go before the parole board and try to get Jay a new trial, so they killed him to keep him silent. Then they found out Sawyer knew and took the opportunity to use the costume party to kill Sawyer."

"You go figure that out, and I'm going to go to the jail." She rubbed the makeup from her face, and the determined look I'd seen her wear before shined. "Give me Diffy's number. I'm calling him to meet me at the jail right now or I'm going to his house."

"I'm going to go to the library to get information on Jay Renner's trial and see what there is on Jay." I followed Mama into the house, where she'd had her boxes from Kentucky delivered. A few pieces of clothing items were in there, so we could at least change.

After we got dressed and walked out of the house, we stood on the end of Heart Way.

"Keep me posted about what Diffy has to say." I hugged her and went off to the library, determined to get some good information and new leads because now this was personal.

CHAPTER EIGHTEEN

Never in a million years did I think I'd see Carol Dunn standing in the library, and never in a million years did I ever think my father would be in jail for the attempted murder of Carol Dunn's husband.

"I'm surprised you're showing your face around here." She glowered at me. Nora stood beside her fidgeting uncomfortably with the pumpkin carving tool in her hands. "Luckily, your father didn't critically injure Sawyer, so he's not dead."

"I'm sorry, Carol. I just don't think my dad did this." I had no idea why I let the words roll out of my mouth. "I'm sorry about what happened to Sawyer. There's no reason for my father to have done such a thing."

"Before he stabbed him, he was talking to us about the town and asked about the paper. That was when Sawyer told him about your mom's house and you. Sawyer really talked up your mom, and if someone didn't know better, they'd think Sawyer had a thing for your mom, so I'm sure your father thought that and got jealous." Carol would have told a very believable story if it hadn't been about my dad, making it completely unbelievable to me.

"Did he lunge at him? What was said before he did it?" I pleaded with her to know.

"I have no idea. The lights went out, and when they flickered back on, your father was standing over him. Then he bent down and plucked the knife out of Sawyer's side."

"Wait." A little bit of hope bubbled up in me. "You mean you didn't see him do it?"

"No. I told you the lights went out." Carol glared.

"Then there's a possibility he didn't do it," Nora squeaked out. Carol shot her a look. Nora put her fingers in her mouth.

"Yes!" I agreed wholeheartedly and nodded. "That's why I'm here. Think about it." I put my hands out for her to listen to my reasoning, though she had great cause not to give me the time. She stayed put, so I continued. "Peter had confided in Sawyer he was going to retract his testimony, which at best meant Jay Renner could get a new trial, be found not guilty, and get out." I watched Carol digest that information. "What if the real killer found out and not only killed Peter to stop him but also got into a costume and stabbed Sawyer, hoping he'd die with the information Peter gave him?"

The doors of the library opened, and someone came in pulling a wagon behind them that was filled with pumpkins.

"Excuse me," Nora said. "I've got the pumpkin-carving contest to set up." She patted my arm and gave me a sympathetic smile.

"I'm sure my daddy is here to win back my mama." I blinked a few times. "And your theory about him being jealous would be possible if it weren't my dad. There have been so many times men have flirted with Mama and Daddy has been so proud. Please," I begged. "I'm just asking for a little more time to find something or someone close to Jay's past other than Tito."

"I have no idea who it would be." She crossed her arms. "Jay was with us all the time." She looked at Nora. "Right, Nora?"

"I guess." Nora shrugged.

"On occasion he went out but mainly to the jiggle joint," Carol finished.

"And that was where he was the night of Alan's murder. Sawyer told me you never recovered the special jacket of Jay's. If we could find that or who would've had the opportunity to take it…" I sucked in a deep breath.

"Fine. I'll give you some time only because Sawyer really does like your mom and working at her new house, but that's it. If Chief Strickland comes back and names your dad as Sawyer's attacker, we will go for the full punishment possible."

That was all I needed to hear before I left her to finish doing her part as the interim president to set up the pumpkin-carving contest. I headed back to the computer, where I needed to pull up everything on Jay Renner and his trial.

That included his social media, his contacts, and any sort of newspaper articles about him.

"Do you need anything before it gets busy?" Nora came up and stood next to me.

"No. I've been here for an hour now, and I did find some photos from the courtroom."

I used the mouse to bring up the photos and magnify them.

"I can see everyone we know." I pointed at the photo on the screen. "Peter, Vickie, Carol, Peter, Kristine, and..." I hit the plus sign again to enlarge the photo. "Is that you?"

"Mm-hmm," she agreed in her quiet way.

"When I pulled up the police report and the description of Jay, there were some scratches on his arms, but it wasn't Alan's DNA found under them." I clicked between the tabs to show her, looking for any insight she might have. "Alan didn't have any scratch marks. So who did Jay get into a fight with? Whose DNA is on his arm?"

I looked up and around, realizing not a single person was in the library.

"I thought there was a pumpkin-carving contest?" I asked Nora and saw the tables set up in the front of the library. Each place was set with a pumpkin and a pumpkin-carving kit.

"It's not until noon," she said, her voice cracking.

"Are you sure you're okay?" I asked.

"It's fine." Nora fiddled with the pumpkin-carving tools. "I have some old articles in the office about the trial if you want to see them. I'm not sure what they will tell you, but maybe something will spark an idea or clue."

"Yeah."

"And I know Peter and Sawyer were going to go to his parole hearing to tell them they remembered a key detail that might get him out of jail," she said behind her as I followed her to the office. She picked her fingers on the way.

Then I noticed Nora was visibly shaken. "Are you okay?" I asked.

"I'm fine." She opened the office door, and we went inside. "I think the file is here." She opened a file cabinet and dug through the files. "There's a lot of photos of the trial from the Stricklands."

"Carol made it sound like you were around Jay Renner." I gestured to the door. "In the lobby, she said Jay was only around them, then she asked you for confirmation." I took the file and started to flip through the photos.

There were sticky notes in Louise Strickland's handwriting that I recognized.

Something clicked, bringing me out of my confused thoughts. I turned to see Nora standing at the door. Her hand was on the door lock, which I could see wasn't fully clicked.

"Nora?" I looked at her. Her attitude had changed. Her gaze shifted past me and landed at the file on the desk.

I turned back and picked up a photo from the courtroom, the same photo I'd seen with her in the room.

"Nora. Did you know Jay Renner?" There was more to this than I knew, and she apparently thought I knew something, since she'd locked the door so no one would come in to disturb us. I looked at the photo of the much younger version of her and saw her fingernails were long. Much longer. Like longer enough for a good cat-scratching fight. "Did you scratch Jay Renner?"

"You don't know him." Her nose flared. Her throat moved up and down as she swallowed back the tears pooling in her eyes. "Yes. I knew him. I met him at the Dunn home. I was a kid just like him. The Dunns took in everyone who needed a home. A job. I cleaned Sawyer's houses after he finished working on them. I met Jay through them, and yeah, we kinda became a couple. He was abusive."

She threw a chin.

"If you look in the photo, I've got a black eye. He did that." She gulped. "I knew I had to get him out of my life. He told me there was no way he was going to leave me alone. He said I couldn't break up with him. He slapped me around. I knew if he killed or appeared to have killed an important citizen, then he'd be put to death. I took his jacket that everyone knew he wore, and I waited for Alan Hill to approve the ghost walk that year. When he walked down the path, I jumped out, stabbed him, and left him there to die."

She took a couple of steps forward and opened another file cabinet. While she patted around the inside, keeping her eyes on me, I slowly shifted my gaze to make my plan to run around her and see which way would be best to get a clear shot at the door.

I calculated the time it would take to run to the door, fully unlock it, and hightail it out of the library. My phone was out next to the computer I'd left my bag beside, so it was useless to even think of calling someone. Not that Nora was going to let me. I noticed the knife she'd pulled from the drawer.

The dark stain along the blade was no doubt the years-old blood of Alan Hill.

"I'd been volunteering here at the library and hid the knife here. You wouldn't believe how many books out there on the shelves never get touched." She smiled at her cleverness. "I never figured I'd have to kill someone in the library. And I was beginning to like you. Your daddy," she said, mocking my accent. "He came in here looking around, and I told him about the costume contest, even gave him a costume."

I knew the library had so much more than books, and that included costumes, art pieces, and many more unusual things.

According to the wall clock, it was almost noon. Surely some people were starting to come into the library for the carving contest.

"So you knew Peter was going to recant his testimony and make Jay leave jail!" I yelled, hoping someone would hear me.

Nora tried to keep her quiet composure, but the edges of her hair were shaking. Her jaw was clenched.

I continued to hammer her.

"You overheard them in the library talking, and you knew you didn't want Jay out of jail so you could stay safe." I continued to raise my voice.

"He sent me letters all these years," she spat. "I have them hidden in the encyclopedia under *J* for Jay. No one ever uses encyclopedias anymore."

"His letters, did they say he was coming home? To you?" I asked. "Did you tell Carol what he did to you?"

"He said he knew it was me and when he got out, he was going to make me pay." Her voice held so much hate that I could tell she was almost out of her mind and not fully aware of what was truly happening here. "I never told anyone we dated."

"I can't let him get out. He needs to be behind bars for hurting me." She wielded the knife in front of her. "And I can't let you ruin what I've got here."

"You have nothing but lies built upon more lies. What are you going to do? Wait until Sawyer gets out of the hospital and when he goes to Jay's parole hearing to tell them what Peter said, kill off everyone who knows?" I asked. "You'll never make it that far."

The door handle jiggled, and the half-locked door popped open.

"Excuse me." A lady and her child were standing at the door. Her eyes shifted to the knife, and she pulled her child to her, face away from the scene. "We are here for the pumpkin-carving contest."

"Excuse me!" I heard Mama's voice.

"In here, Mama!" I screamed.

Mama appeared at the door behind the lady and her child, Chief Matthew Strickland next to her.

"Yes. We are having the pumpkin-carving contest. Right this way." Mama glanced over at the scene, making it clear everything was going to be taken care of now that she and Matthew were here.

CHAPTER NINETEEN

M erry Maker Message
    It looks like another Halloweenie has come and gone. No doubt without its murders... er, glitches. We always hold on to the hope for a smoother event during next year's haunting holiday.

Ghosts from the past were revealed. The ghost of the present needed to come into the light to be exposed, making Holiday Junction once again a safe tourist town.

Now we look ahead to the next holiday we celebrate in Holiday Junction. The season of giving, being thankful, and renewal is upon us.

As the Merry Maker, I feel it's my duty to let you know some secrets are kept hidden even better than my identity. If anyone should reveal these secrets, during a holiday where everyone comes together and chatter begins.

So keep your ears peeled for not only what is going on with our newest citizens but where the next party will end.

Keep reading for a sneak peek of the next book in the series. New Year Nuisance is now available to purchase on Amazon or read for FREE in Kindle Unlimited.

Chapter One of Book Four
New Year Nuisance

"Don't even get me started on your replacement." Mae West wore a pair of black skintight leggings with a lime-green wool sweater and her fancy New York booties. I'd noticed those right off when she rolled into my hometown of Normal, Kentucky, a few years ago before I'd moved to Holiday Junction.

I mean literally rolled into town in a camper van.

She'd not stopped talking since walking off the airplane at the Holiday Junction airport, which was about the size of her camper van.

"Mae, this is Rhett Strickland." I barely got the words out between her breaths before a huge smile curled up on her face.

She abruptly stopped, flung a strand of her curly honey-blond hair behind her shoulder, and threw her arms around him.

"Rhett!" From her voice, she clearly thought he was someone he wasn't. "Nice to meet you. Any friend of Violet's is a friend of mine."

"Welcome to Holiday Junction." He peeled himself off Mae. His brows rose, and he looked at me with a half-cocked smile. "Are all the people from Kentucky this friendly? Because Violet sure wasn't this friendly the day I met her right in this very spot."

He grabbed the handle of Mae's luggage and jerked it to full extension so he could roll it behind him.

"I guess Violet'll have to bring you home for a visit." Mae wiggled her brows.

"Oh no." I cackled out loud and pinched off a piece of the bagel I'd gotten from the airport's small café while I'd waited for Mae's plane to land. "We aren't an item. Heck no."

A weird nervous laugh I'd not recognized came out of me.

"You said Strickland." Mae started to say something that didn't need to be said before I grabbed her by the elbow, jerking her to me.

"I'm so glad you called after the Christmas you had." I had to change the subject of my love life when I didn't even know what my love life was all about. "Let's get you in the car."

Rhett was a catch. Don't get me wrong. And we'd had a little spark between us. I'm talking tiny. Just a flicker, really. After there'd been too much going on in my new life to even think about lighting that wick, it was quickly put out.

On the other hand, his cousin, Darren, didn't seem like my type, and even though I wasn't on the prowl, he seemed to be around.... everywhere.

Over Halloween, we'd shared a kiss, but it'd never gone any further than that. By the way he'd slid me into his arms that night, I thought for sure I'd have a date to the New Year's Eve celebration, the famous Sparkle Ball, but he was like a cricket.

Silent during the day but loud at night.

Calling him "loud" was giving him too much credit. It was the bar he owned that was loud at night. The jiggle joint.

At least that was what I called it, even though the name on the solid door read BAR.

I didn't think I had to say much more than that it was... a jiggle joint. Truly, there was a lot more drinking, throwing darts, and rowdy chatter than jiggling going on.

I had to walk past the bar every night on my way home from my office at the *Junction Journal*, the local newspaper of which I was the editor in chief, photographer, journalist, and, well, all the things.

"Rhett is the security guard here at the airport," I told her.

We followed Rhett into the one-room terminal before he stopped shy of the one TSA agent and Dave.

Mae's eyes grew big when she saw Dave.

"Okay. You have no business talking about the strange animals we have back home." Mae laughed.

I bet she couldn't wait to tell people back home about him.

"He was the local rooster who was part of the security team. Dave was better than any sniffing security dog out there." Rhett was confident in telling Mae about Dave and a few of his rooster-sniffing stories. "And we have a dog for mayor."

"That I do know." Mae pointed at the jar on the podium where Dave and the TSA agent were perched. "What's that?"

"Those are worms—treats." Rhett picked up the jar. Dave clucked to life and stood tall like a soldier.

"I've seen it all." Mae turned to me and wagged a finger. "Don't you ever make fun of Normal again."

I smiled. Being around Mae brought a sense of familiarity that made me long for the comforts of home. Though I couldn't get back to Kentucky anytime soon, I was going to soak up all the joy it brought my soul to see her and gab about all the friends we knew.

Rhett unscrewed the lid off the jar and held it out for Mae, who took a dehydrated piece of worm.

"Just give it to him," Rhett instructed her and pretended to hold a piece for reference.

"Thanks, Dave." Mae threw her head back and laughed with her mouth wide open. "We might be hillbillies in Kentucky, but this town is strange," she whispered between us.

"When I saw Violet come in this morning to greet you, I was thinking she was sneaking off to some big interview. You know, I met her the day her plane made the emergency landing." Rhett continued to walk us through the one-room airport toward the door. "She certainly didn't like my uncle then and can barely be in the same room with him now."

"You're the police chief's nephew. Not son." Mae snapped her finger, and the emerald ring she wore flickered as the light inside the airport caught it.

"Mae," I gasped and grabbed her hand to look at the engagement ring Hank Sharp had given her. "I love it."

I did love it but was a little shocked it was an emerald.

"I keep forgetting you've been gone since I got engaged." She curled her hand in and pulled it to her chest as though she didn't want me to see it or talk about it. "Speaking of rings, you aren't going to believe what I'm about to tell you."

"I can't wait." I was giggly with excitement to have Mae here, even if it was only for a few days and most of those would be taken up by writing the coverage of the New Year festivities for the *Junction Journal*.

Holiday Junction was a small town, just like my hometown. And true to its name, they celebrated every single holiday. But the big ones—you know, Easter, Thanksgiving, Fourth of July, Christmas—now those celebrations were over-the-top.

The Sparkle Ball was this year's theme for the New Year's Eve celebration.

When Mae called to wish me a merry Christmas, I had mentioned the big Sparkle Ball and how the *Junction Journal* was sponsoring it. Within seconds, she invited herself, and here she was, a couple of days away from the turn of the new year.

Trust me when I say I was surprised. It wasn't like Mae and I were best friends in Normal. Honestly, quite the opposite. We'd fought tooth and nail, butted heads, to be truthful. Never in a million years did I ever think I'd be celebrating the turn of a new year with Mae West.

"This is far as I go, ladies." Rhett stopped shy of the double sliding doors leading to the outside world. "Duty calls. The next plane should be arriving, um"—Rhett joked and checked his phone—"two days from now."

Holiday Junction had very few flights in and out, but there was a much bigger airport an hour or so away. If anyone needed a flight, they could drive there.

"It was nice to meet you, Rhett." Mae had really put on the Southern charm, a far cry from when I'd met her years ago, when she showed a hard exterior. "I sure hope to see you at the fancy Sparkle Ball."

"You sure will." Rhett said his goodbyes.

It was nice to see this side of her, and it made me happy she was here. We'd never had any sort of sleepover or true get-together just as friends. More times than not, we met during my interviewing days as a reporter for Channel Two news, my daily talk show, or for the *Normal Gazette*.

"I have to admit I was a little nervous when you told me you were coming out," I said and walked out of the airport. "Are you okay?" I asked, pointing at the trolley stop sign.

"Yeah. You know." Mae wiggled her finger in the air. "Wedding stuff plus Mary Elizabeth and, well, the whole Sharp family saga."

She left the word hanging and looked out into the distance.

"That's gorgeous." She pointed at the snow-covered landscape where the mountains rose in the distance. A few of the peaks were hidden behind a veil of white, as if reaching up to touch the sky.

"And this crisp air." She sucked in a deep breath.

"It is amazing here." I took in the trees, which were coated in a layer of frost. The branches were heavy with snow, and the ground was a blanket of white. The snow crunched underfoot as we walked into the glass enclosure to wait for the next ride into town.

"It really is pretty here." She looked at me, and her eyes dipped.

There was more to Mae's visit than just a visit, but I'd give her space, and in her own time, she'd tell me. I had to ask about the word she'd let dangle before she'd noticed the landscape.

"Saga?" I asked and saw Goldie Bennett was at the helm of the trolley. The shimmery red-sequined shirt looked like Goldie was starting her own personal New Year's party.

Ding, ding. The clanking trolley bell clapped as it approached. Goldie slammed the brakes on and pushed the lever that swung the door open.

"Welcome to Holiday Junction, Mae!" Goldie blew on the dazzling, shiny gold-and-silver fringe blowout on one of those cone-shaped cardboard New Year's Eve hats with fuzz all over the edges. "We are so excited you're here. Climb on in."

"Okay." Mae's eyes lit up. When she took a step up, she glanced back at me. "And I thought this was going to be a boring week."

"Nope. Normal, Kentucky, has nothing on Holiday Junction." My body shivered as the goose bumps crawled along my skin.

New Year Nuisance is now available to purchase or in Kindle Unlimited.

Book Club Discussion Questions
A Halloween Homicide

Join us as we discuss A Halloween Homicide. The 3rd book in the Holiday Cozy Mystery Series.

Question #1:

Boo! All you ghosts and goblins get ready for a month full of fun, since Halloweenie is set to open this weekend. Grab your pillowcase and look for hauntingly delicious treats. They will be served at events like pumpkin painting, pumpkin carving, the parents' night out, the haunted hayride, the haunted ghost walk, and the Great Jack O'Lantern Blaze. These events, vendors, and games will all be at Holiday Park.

Are you like violet and dislike the holiday or Millie Kay who goes all out?

Question #2:

As the reporter, covering all the activities, this means Violet has to experience and write about the events. As a result, Violet had been avoiding the Ghost Walk as it's just too scary of a thought. Darren Strickland and Millie Kay decide to go with her.

Halloween time can be spooky...

Which would you prefer:

Ghost walk or Haunted corn maze?

Question #3:

While riding the trolley to get to the ghost walk, Goldie brings up the pumpkin carving contest being held at the library. Librarian Nora is none too pleased about it but unless you're on the Holiday Junction Planning Committee there's not much you can do about it.

Have you ever been on a committee either during the holidays or some other time?

Question #4:

"Welcome to the spooky graveyard." When he said "graveyard," it was enough to raise the hairs on my neck. "We have the Ghost of Halloween Past." He lifted the lantern in one hand and tapped 3 times on the free-standing vampire-style wooden coffin with the cane.

The dummy fell out face forward, a knife sticking out of its back. "Is that blood?"

The realization this wasn't what was supposed to happen on the ghost walk sank in. "I think it is real." I took a step closer to see the knife sticking out of the man's back. "And that sure does look like real blood." With a grave look on my face, I stared at Darren. "Call your dad."

What were your thoughts at that moment on who the dead guy was?

Question #5:

"Are you two coming to the costume contest sponsored by the Hibernian Society?" Vern asked with pride, since he was in his first term as the society's president. "Of course we are. Violet wouldn't miss her first Halloweenie costume contest."

Do you like to dress up for Halloween?

Show us your costume if they have one to share...

Question #6:

With respect to Violet's love life are you team Rhett (like Millie Kay) or team Darren?

Question #7

THE ENDING!!!!!

Without telling us who the killer was, that would be a spoiler but, did you figure this one out, or was it a complete surprise?

Question #8

We are coming to the end of our discussion. Any thoughts or questions? Was there a favorite scene in the book to share? Remember, no spoilers please.

If you enjoyed reading this book as much as I enjoyed writing it then be sure to return to the Amazon page and leave a review.

Go to Tonyakappes.com for a full reading order of my novels and while there join my newsletter. You can also find links to Facebook, Instagram and Goodreads.

Join like-minded readers like YOU in the Cozy Krew Facebook Group for dream casting, fan theories, and live Q & A's. It's like a BIG GIANT BOOK CLUB! But if you want to have your own book club, be sure you let me know! I love to send goodies.

Also By Tonya Kappes

A Camper and Criminals Cozy Mystery
BEACHES, BUNGALOWS, & BURGLARIES
DESERTS, DRIVERS, & DERELICTS
FORESTS, FISHING, & FORGERY
CHRISTMAS, CRIMINALS, & CAMPERS
MOTORHOMES, MAPS, & MURDER
CANYONS, CARAVANS, & CADAVERS
HITCHES, HIDEOUTS, & HOMICIDE
ASSAILANTS, ASPHALT, & ALIBIS
VALLEYS, VEHICLES & VICTIMS
SUNSETS, SABBATICAL, & SCANDAL
TENTS, TRAILS, & TURMOIL
KICKBACKS, KAYAKS, & KIDNAPPING
GEAR, GRILLS, & GUNS
EGGNOG, EXTORTION, & EVERGREENS
ROPES, RIDDLES, & ROBBERIES
PADDLERS, PROMISES, & POISON
INSECTS, IVY, & INVESTIGATIONS
OUTDOORS, OARS, & OATHS
WILDLIFE, WARRANTS, & WEAPONS
BLOSSOMS, BARBEQUE, & BLACKMAIL
LANTERNS, LAKES, & LARCENY
JACKETS, JACK-O-LANTERN, & JUSTICE
SANTA, SUNRISES, & SUSPICIONS
VISTAS, VICES, & VALENTINES
ADVENTURE, ABDUCTION, & ARREST
RANGERS, RV'S, & REVENGE
CAMPFIRES, COURAGE, & CONVICTS
TRAPPING, TURKEYS, & THANKSGIVING
GIFTS, GLAMPING, & GLOCKS
ZONING, ZEALOTS, & ZIPLINES
HAMMOCKS, HANDGUNS, & HEARSAY

447

Kenni Lowry Mystery Series
FIXIN' TO DIE
SOUTHERN FRIED
AX TO GRIND
SIX FEET UNDER
DEAD AS A DOORNAIL
TANGLED UP IN TINSEL
DIGGIN' UP DIRT
BLOWIN' UP A MURDER

Killer Coffee Mystery Series
SCENE OF THE GRIND
MOCHA AND MURDER
FRESHLY GROUND MURDER
COLD BLOODED BREW
DECAFFEINATED SCANDAL
A KILLER LATTE
HOLIDAY ROAST MORTEM
DEAD TO THE LAST DROP
A CHARMING BLEND NOVELLA (CROSSOVER WITH MAGICAL
CURES MYSTERY)
FROTHY FOUL PLAY
SPOONFUL OF MURDER
BARISTA BUMP-OFF
CAPPUCCINO CRIMINAL

Holiday Cozy Mystery
FOUR LEAF FELONY
MOTHER'S DAY MURDER
A HALLOWEEN HOMICIDE
NEW YEAR NUISANCE
CHOCOLATE BUNNY BETRAYAL
APRIL FOOL'S ALIBI
FATHER'S DAY MURDER
THANKSGIVING TREACHERY

A GHOSTLY UNDERTAKING

A GHOSTLY GRAVE

A GHOSTLY DEMISE

A GHOSTLY MURDER

A GHOSTLY REUNION

A GHOSTLY MORTALITY

A GHOSTLY SECRET

A GHOSTLY SUSPECT

A Southern Cake Baker Series
(WRITTEN UNDER MAYEE BELL)
CAKE AND PUNISHMENT
BATTER OFF DEAD

Spies and Spells Mystery Series
SPIES AND SPELLS
BETTING OFF DEAD
GET WITCH or DIE TRYING

A Laurel London Mystery Series
CHECKERED CRIME
CHECKERED PAST
CHECKERED THIEF

A Divorced Diva Beading Mystery Series
A BEAD OF DOUBT SHORT STORY
STRUNG OUT TO DIE
CRIMPED TO DEATH

Olivia Davis Paranormal Mystery Series
SPLITSVILLE.COM
COLOR ME LOVE (novella)
COLOR ME A CRIME

About Tonya

Tonya has written over 100 novels, all of which have graced numerous bestseller lists, including the USA Today. Best known for stories charged with emotion and humor and filled with flawed characters, her novels have garnered reader praise and glowing critical reviews. She lives with her husband and a very spoiled rescue cat named Ro. Tonya grew up in the small southern Kentucky town of Nicholasville. Now that her four boys are grown men, Tonya writes full-time in her camper she calls her SHAMPER (she-camper).

Learn more about her be sure to check out her website tonyakappes.com. Find her on Facebook, Twitter, BookBub, and Instagram

Sign up to receive her newsletter, where you'll get free books, exclusive bonus content, and news of her releases and sales.

If you liked this book, please take a few minutes to leave a review now! Authors (Tonya included) really appreciate this, and it helps draw more readers to books they might like. Thanks!

Cover artist: Mariah Sinclair: The Cover Vault

Made in the USA
Middletown, DE
28 August 2024

59930559R00254